WHERE THE TRUTH LIES

Also available by Katherine Greene

The Lake of Lost Girls

The Woods Are Waiting

WHERE THE TRUTH LIES

A NOVEL

KATHERINE GREENE

NEW YORK

Books should be disposed of and recycled according to local requirements. All paper materials used are FSC compliant.

Published in the United States by Crooked Lane Books, an imprint of The Quick Brown Fox & Company LLC.

Crooked Lane Books and its logo are trademarks of The Quick Brown Fox & Company LLC.

Library of Congress Catalog-in-Publication data available upon request.

ISBN (hardcover): 979-8-89242-487-5
ISBN (paperback): 979-8-89242-488-2
ISBN (ebook): 979-8-89242-489-9

Cover design by Lauren Harms

Printed in the United States.

www.crookedlanebooks.com

Crooked Lane Books
34 West 27th St., 10th Floor
New York, NY 10001

First Edition: April 2026

The authorized representative in the EU for product safety and compliance is eucomply OÜPärnu mnt 139b-14, 11317 Tallinn, Estonia, hello@eucompliancepartner.com, +33757690241

10 9 8 7 6 5 4 3 2 1

"Be a voice not an echo."

—Albert Einstein

NOTE FROM THE AUTHORS

THIS STORY WAS a hard one to write for many reasons. But mostly because it addresses the very serious themes of domestic and gender based violence, coercive control, toxic masculinity and sexual assault.

We wanted readers to be aware that these topics are present in this book and while it was important for us to depict these issues in a realistic way, we are aware it can be triggering for some, so reader discretion is advised.

To victims and survivors, we see you and know that you are not alone.

We have included a list of resources for those experiencing or have experienced violence at the end of this book.

KG

PROLOGUE

Jenn

The Past

July 12—Fifteen Years Ago

THE ROAD WAS dusty. So dusty that every time a car drove past, dirt flew into my mouth. Grit crunched as I ground my teeth in frustration.

It was too hot. I had never been able to cope with the southern heat. Maybe it was the humidity. The way that simply breathing felt like taking a gallon of water into my lungs. Perhaps that was appropriate. The longer I stayed here, the more it felt like I was drowning.

I needed to get out of town. I definitely had the feeling I had overstayed my welcome.

Particularly after everything that had happened. This wasn't a place where I could settle. That had been made abundantly clear. There was nothing here I could lay claim to as *mine.*

Leaving was my only option. And the sooner the better.

Though, not having a car had me relying on my thumb. Some would think it was a stupid decision.

"You're too young!"

"It's dangerous!"

But there was no one around to keep me safe anymore.

The road was pretty busy, but still no one stopped for the eighteen-year-old woman hitchhiking with a massive book bag weighing her down.

It held all of my earthly possessions. Everything that mattered fit into the canvas sack. I couldn't think about how depressing that was. Otherwise, I'd have to drop to my knees and sob.

I had nowhere to be. No real destination in mind.

In the beginning, that was the appeal. That's how I ended up here. But now, it felt like the *not knowing* was the worst possible outcome. I had wanted to make a plan this time, to be smarter, more logical. But after everything I knew, I needed to *get out.*

Before the choice was taken from me entirely.

Minutes passed. Or maybe hours. I couldn't be sure. Even though the sun had started to set, the air still felt sticky. My steps became sluggish, sweat dripping down my face, soaking the collar of my T-shirt. I slid the heavy gold ring along the chain around my neck, the weight of it imprinting on my skin. Maybe I should take it off. It's not like it meant anything now.

My thoughts became dark, miserable things. Swirling with equal parts regret and longing that felt heavier than my book bag.

I should never have come here.

Beep!

Startled, I looked over my shoulder and froze like a deer in headlights.

The beat-up white Honda Civic came to a stop beside me, and the driver rolled down their window. The young man driving gave me a shy grin that was tinged with something harder to read.

"Need a ride?"

I hesitated. I was still angry and upset with him, but I wanted to believe that maybe I had reacted too harshly. The truth was, I was leaving anyway, and I didn't want the memory of him to be tarnished forever. I'd been avoiding him all week, and I was tired of it. I needed to remember how he was in the beginning. Then maybe I wouldn't hate myself so much for trusting him.

"Sure," I said with a tired shrug, knowing I should have thought twice before accepting. Yet, I still felt longing flapping wildly against my ribcage. I headed to the passenger-side door and hopped into the seat, the sensation still strange, having only been given a ride once before.

I glanced behind me as he put the car in drive and wished I could jump out again.

My eyes widened at the sight of the self-righteous grin taunting me from the back seat.

"You," I snarled, the single word an accusation and a gasp of horror.

I turned back to the driver—the man I briefly loved with my whole heart. I had no idea they knew each other. How was that possible? I should have known that the worst kind of birds really did flock together.

I wanted to tell him to let me out. That I couldn't be in this car a moment longer. That I was scared.

No.

I was *petrified.*

There were so many people to fear. So many who wished me harm. But the most horrible of them were in this car.

Soon we were cruising at speed and my pleas died on my tongue. I should have screamed. I should have thrown myself from the moving vehicle. But I didn't. Maybe I really was a coward.

We were heading out of town. I slowly turned back around, though I knew better than to turn my back on a predator.

"I guess you're leaving." His eyes narrowed, his mouth set firm. "Were you planning to go without even saying goodbye? How could you do that to me? Haven't you seen my messages?" He sounded angry. I knew I should take notice of that.

I glanced at his now familiar face. He wasn't conventionally handsome, but he had been kind to me when I felt lost and alone.

And in the short time I had known him, he came to be important to me.

After everything I had learned, I knew we could never be together. And it was made clear to me that I needed to sever the tie between us completely.

"I couldn't. You know why," I said softly, looking out the window, trees whizzing by. I felt uncomfortable having this conversation in this car. I should shut it down. I didn't want to reveal too much. Especially when I could feel eyes on me from the backseat. The pronounced silence as they listened to every word.

"Jenn, I'm sorry it turned out like this. I only wanted you to hear me out. Let me tell my side of the story—"

"Is there really another side that matters?" I asked, surprised by the bite in my tone. Where did that backbone come from? I stiffened at the snickering behind me.

"Of course it matters!" he shouted. I watched the tick in his jaw as he clenched his teeth. He took a slow breath in an effort to calm himself down. "What I wanted to tell you is I don't care about all that. I want to come with you. Like we talked about."

God, how I wished I could say yes, but I knew I couldn't. What he had done was unforgivable.

"I'm sorry, but . . . this is for the best," I said.

His hand came down on the steering wheel. Hard.

The flash of anger wasn't unexpected, yet it startled me all the same. This time my own rage unfurled and opened its formidable jaws. No, it didn't have to be like this . . . if it weren't for him. If he had done things differently then maybe he could come with me. Leave this town and start new somewhere else. Together.

I looked at him. Really looked at him. This man who, for a brief time, I trusted. Who was he really?

A liar.

Or something worse?

Because I saw the real him he kept carefully tucked away and only let out when control was lost.

His eyes kept flicking toward me. He was afraid. Or angry. Maybe both.

"I'm sorry . . ."

My voice seemed to infuriate him.

"It didn't have to be like this, Jenn," he said again. Lower this time. Like a growl. I heard the mocking snicker behind me again and knew it was too late.

Things had gone too far, and I was an idiot to think I could undo the damage that had already been done.

Let me out!

The words were a violent scream inside me.

Let me out!

But they died on my lips, held back by my insidious hope.

I wished I could murder that hope. Kill it before it ruined me.

He kept driving.

And for the first time since meeting him, I dreaded where he was taking me.

CHAPTER

1

Lucinda

The Present

The knock at the door was like gunfire, disrupting the tense, too quiet night. Rhett and I stood there in the kitchen, facing each other. Sweat beaded his brow. My heart beat so hard and fast I thought it would come flying out of my chest.

Neither of us moved. A terror-fueled standoff.

They knocked again. Even louder this time.

"They'll wake up McKenzie," I hissed, watching my husband's face contort from blank neutrality to bone-chilling fear.

I stared at him—this man I had been married to for so long, and saw, not the mild-mannered, quietly handsome boy of our youth, but the weak and inadequate, middle-aged man he had become. He wouldn't meet my eyes.

"Rhett, you need to go with them. Remember, my dad said he will have a lawyer meet you at the station," I instructed, my phone in my hand, the screen now black.

Only moments before, we had received the phone call that had changed everything.

A warning that there was no choice but to heed.

* * *

"Rhett," Dad said my husband's name with absolute authority, "someone's come forward linking you to Jennifer Moore."

At the sound of the woman's name, everything inside me went cold. My limbs felt like lead. "What?" I demanded, though everyone ignored me.

"There's been some credible eyewitness testimony as well as some physical evidence that's come to light." My father cleared his throat, then an oddly awkward pause that was nearly deafening through the phone before he decided to drop the final grim piece of news. "Rhett, they're coming to your house. This evening."

"What?" I said again, louder this time. "What are you talking about? Jenn . . . she . . ." I cleared my throat. "That was fifteen years ago," I said. "Who cares about all that now?"

Rhett was quiet and I made a motion for him to speak, but his face bore a familiar blankness. He wouldn't meet my eyes and instead stared down at the phone as if it would swallow him whole.

The déjà vu was hard to stomach.

"It doesn't matter how long ago it was, Lucinda, they have evidence linking Rhett to that girl's murder, an eyewitness, too, and Chuck has sent two of his deputies to your house. They're on their way right now to take him in for questioning." He halted again, but only for a moment. "From the sounds of it, they could arrest him."

"Arrest him? Don't be ridiculous," I scoffed, surprised, as everyone else would be, that Charles Young, my father's longtime friend and Fern River chief of police, would send his deputies to my *house and take my husband down to the police station to question him about a crime that should have been forgotten years ago.*

"Lucinda, this is serious," my mother's anxious voice cut in. "Where's McKenzie?" Her first thought was always for my daughter. First and foremost.

"Asleep, of course. But I've got it all under control—"

"Clearly, you don't!" My father barked, shutting me up. I turned again to Rhett, glaring at him. Why wouldn't he speak? I

needed him to say something. For once, I wished he'd be the one comforting me.

"So what should we do?" I asked, knowing my father always had the answers.

"Rhett, you need to go with Chuck's men. Don't say anything, no matter how many questions they ask or how they try to butter you up. I'll have Glynn Walker meet you at the station. I've already called him," Dad instructed.

"You didn't have to do that, sir," Rhett finally said. He sounded so small. Inconsequential.

"You're my daughter's husband. I'll get this taken care of, just like I did before," Dad said, his impatience obvious. "Lucinda, you need to stay at the house. You can't have McKenzie waking up and being scared. You're her mother, your place is in your home. I'm going to head down to the station and see what I can find out, but you need to prepare yourself."

"Why is this coming up now, after all this time? Are they really taking it seriously?" Jennifer Moore had been dead for over a decade. It had become a cold case. A forgotten case. My father had said there was a link between my affable, mild-mannered husband and a murdered girl that people had long stopped caring about. A wheel had been set in motion and once it was out in the open, she would be the only thing people would be talking about.

The thing about Fern River is people took rumors as seriously as the gospel. Evidence and *an eyewitness meant Rhett would be tarred and feathered before lunch time..*

We had purposefully left this all in the past. We had to. For our family's sake.

For my sake.

But the thing about secrets is that they never stayed hidden. They bided their time until making their way into the light again.

I needed to be careful because I couldn't go back to that place I was mired in fifteen years ago. Once this hit the gossip mill, I'd have to deal with the looks and the whispers all over again. I hadn't handled it well before, so things would have to be different this time. Because I wouldn't become that woman again. Out of control and sloppy. I had buried her down deep, and she was meant to stay there.

Covered in dirt next to a dead girl.

* * *

My dad was the family fixer. Not just for me and my sister, but for our entire extended family. He had clawed up from the depths of poverty to now be well-connected all over the state. He was the goddamn Don Corleone of Fern River, Kentucky, woven into the fabric of the town like bourbon and bluegrass.

"I could have found my own attorney," Rhett began, his voice sounding tight.

"You're my husband, Rhett, of course he found someone for you. What would people say if Cliff Herbaugh didn't help out his son-in-law? Everyone knows my dad does whatever he can for his family."

"Except I'm not family. Not blood anyway." Rhett's eyes narrowed as he attempted to rehash an argument we'd had a hundred times before.

I took a deep breath and gave him what I hoped was a reassuring smile. "Just follow Dad's advice, and we'll be fine. This isn't our first rodeo."

Rhett nodded and swallowed. "Right."

"No one will believe for a moment you're involved with any of that." There was a catch in my voice as I spoke the bald-faced lie. "The people of this town know you, Rhett. They know me. They know our family. Good people don't commit murder. You teach their kids math, for Christ's sake!" I started biting my nails in a nervous gesture I hadn't done since I was a kid. Rhett's knowing eyes observed my tell.

I dropped my hands to my sides, curling them into fists.

"Except they believed it once before, don't forget. This town was all too quick to suspect me, even if they never said it to my face." Before I could say anything, he continued, not letting me go through the hassle of disputing the obvious fact. "Anyway, I don't know what evidence there is. It was over a decade ago. Anything tying me to Jenn should be long gone." I hated how his voice faltered as he spoke her name.

It was always the same. The hitch in breathing, the naked longing.

The way he hurled the name at me, seeking ultimate damage.

He knew what he was doing when he said it—each and every time.

Many people would take him at his word. Such was the man he presented to the world. Trustworthy. Honest. Dependable. He had worked hard to polish the image he now exuded.

But I knew him better than he knew himself.

There had been so many lies between us, I wasn't sure he even knew what the truth was anymore.

"Dad will get to the bottom of this. Maybe someone has a grudge against you or something. I'm sure it's nothing." I waved it away as if we were talking about small-town gossip. My confidence had gotten me far in life, and I relied on it now to sell a story I wasn't exactly buying.

The knocking on the door came again. Harder this time.

"Mr. Rhett Clark, this is the Fern River Police. You need to open the door immediately."

Each knock on the door was like a nail in our marriage's coffin, and a door being pushed open to a past I had forced myself not to think about.

Rhett gripped his head in his hands, closing his eyes. I watched as his whole body began to sag and he let out a keening moan that was more akin to grief than fear.

I felt the girl I used to be clawing her way up from the abyss. The girl whose heart had been chipped away only to be replaced with rage and violence.

It was so easy to lose rational thought when your whole life was on the line.

But my father had raised me well. And I would rise to the challenge now just as I had done before.

"Don't you dare go out there acting defeated," I told him with a forced smile. "You're *my* husband. Because of that, *you're* also a Herbaugh. And we don't roll over and play 'possum. Remember, everyone is watching."

"Right. Of course." He still wouldn't quite look at me, as if he wasn't listening to a word I was saying. He had the expression of a man preparing for the firing squad, and I felt myself soften. Ever so slightly.

The love I had for this man was there, quietly waiting below the surface. Drifting along in the ebb and flow of our mistakes and secrets. All the years of forced normalcy had worked hard to dull the intense affection I once held for him.

But it was still there.

Which is what made all this so much harder.

There were still flashes of the loving, quiet man I had fallen for. The man who had put my needs before his each and every time. The man who put me first.

Until he didn't.

Until I was replaced and then spent the next fifteen years trying to maneuver my way back into position, despising how the effort eroded away at my pride.

I grabbed his hands, squeezing hard enough to make him wince. "You are Rhett Clark, and I am Lucinda Herbaugh. We are good people. Everyone knows that." I wasn't sure my words reassured him.

"Everyone knows that," my husband parroted as blue flashing lights danced through the windows, casting shadows across our faces.

I pulled the curtain back to see the police cruiser parked in front of our house. "Oh god, I'm surprised Gloria from across the street doesn't have her face plastered to our window."

I gave him a not-so-gentle shove. "Answer the door, Rhett."

I watched him swallow thickly, giving me a curt nod.

I followed him down the hallway. I could see the shadows of two people on the other side of the door glass.

His hand stilled on the doorknob as he turned back to me. "I should've known we'd end up back here, Lucinda. Because I'll always love—" He stopped suddenly, as if his thoughts were severed at the source. Of course he waited until the worst possible moment to say this. He had no shame sometimes.

Then his eyes darkened ever so slightly. Just a hint of malevolence as if seeing something in me he didn't like.

"We've never talked about what happened that night because you didn't want to, and I guess I didn't either. But now, I think that was a mistake." He looked at me and waited for a single heartbeat. Then another. I noticed the way his hands shook. "We said we wouldn't keep secrets from each other again. And I haven't—" He caught himself before vocalizing his dishonesty. His hesitation said more than any words ever could. "But you . . ."

He never got the chance to finish what he was about to say.

The third knock at the door was accompanied by a deep voice.

"Mr. Clark, this is Fern River Police, we need you to open the door. I won't ask again."

"Rhett . . ." His name drifted off into nothing. I didn't know what else to say. So we stood there in those last few seconds—him scared and desperate, me filled with grief for everything we were about to lose, and a simmering rage that could easily consume me if I let it.

Who were these two people we had become?

I barely recognized them.

At one time we were an unstoppable team.

Now, we weren't sure how much to trust one another. Or if we could afford not to.

Finally, Rhett opened the door.

The officer, Deputy George Anderson, stepped over the threshold without waiting for permission. The man, only a few years older than me, had attended my childhood birthday parties and sat beside me in Sunday school every week until we turned thirteen. We were anything but strangers. And yet, the way he was looking at Rhett and me, you would think we were.

"We need you to come down to the station with us." George put his hand on the handcuffs dangling from his belt. Was he going to walk Rhett out in cuffs?

"Come on George, is all this necessary?" I asked. "Can't we chat here? I'll go get us all some coffee." I cast a nervous glance to the street, finding our neighbors already congregated outside their homes, drawn to the flashing lights like a beacon.

George ignored me. His eyes rested on my husband with a steely determination.

I wasn't their target.

I wasn't their prey.

"Rhett Clark, we need you to answer some questions about the murder of Jennifer Moore."

CHAPTER

2

Rhett

The Past

May—Fifteen Years Ago

THE SICKLY SWEET scent of freshly baked pastry and Lucy's mother's overly strong perfume hung in the air as we sat around the cake-laden table in Crème Dulce Bakery. The name made me want to laugh at its efforts to be chic and cosmopolitan. It was small, but stylishly decorated and seemed out of place, with its overpriced baked goods and high tea menu. After all, Fern River was a small town with not much else but a Dollar General, a two-screen movie theater, a bowling alley, and a diner that served the best home fries and derby pie I'd ever eaten.

I wasn't sure who had insisted on the five-tiered cake, but it was a perfect symbol of how out of control the wedding was becoming. Most of the people on the guest list I had never even met. I'd wanted something small and intimate, but it didn't matter. Lucy and her mother had taken over the wedding preparations with the tenacity of a couple of generals preparing for battle. My mom said this was normal, though, and to let Lucy have her moment to shine, so I'd taken a step back.

"How are we feeling about this one?" The bakery owner, whom Mabel had introduced as Leslie Franklin, asked with a tight smile. She'd brought over more cake samples for us to try, and seemed to be growing just as frustrated as I was with the lack of decision-making. "Obviously we'd decorate it with the right color scheme, maybe add some real flowers to match the bridal bouquet."

Leslie was a sweet-faced, gray-haired woman that my future mother-in-law seemed to know very well. Then again, she knew everyone—*and* their business. You couldn't take a shit without Mabel Herbaugh knowing about it two minutes later.

It was simultaneously fascinating and terrifying.

Mrs. Mabel Jean Herbaugh was beloved by most people in Fern River. Even if she did command that affection with an iron fist coated in southern gentility.

Mabel pushed the small plate away and scrunched her upturned nose. "Not really what we're looking for. We were hoping for something with a bit more 'wow' factor. Isn't that right, Lucinda?"

Lucy put her fork down and nodded. "I agree, don't you, Rhett?"

My opinion was completely redundant, yet still required, if only for them to shut it down in unified dismissal.

"Yeah, sure," I agreed uncomfortably.

I was a nineteen-year-old boy—cake was cake to me, no matter how they tried to sell it.

Mabel looked satisfied as both Lucy and I fell in line. She dabbed the side of her mouth with her napkin before speaking again. "I'm sure you must have something absolutely perfect. You're the best baker in town, Leslie." Mabel smiled at her friend, who preened at the compliment. Mabel's ability to make people feel good, while manipulating them to do exactly as she wanted, was quite the skill set. I couldn't help but be impressed as Leslie headed back to the kitchen again.

I inwardly sighed–*never* outwardly. "Is Bailey coming?" I asked, wondering where my future sister-in-law was. I couldn't imagine the fifteen-year-old missing out on an opportunity to eat as much cake as she wanted.

"Bailey?" Mabel scoffed absently. "No, she has volleyball practice and her math tutor afterward. Besides, too much cake isn't good for children . . . or wives-to-be." She raised an eyebrow as Lucy took another bite of cake.

"You know, I could help Bailey with math. If she's struggling or whatever. I'm really good with numbers."

"Bless you, Rhett," Mabel patted my hand, "but we've hired a great math tutor. I think he will know what's best for Bailey."

"Right," I muttered, sinking back into my seat.

Since my proposal almost a year ago, it had felt like I was on a circus ride I couldn't get off. Our wedding was looming like an ominous black cloud.

And everyone in this goddamn town seemed to have an opinion about my relationship. And my future.

It shouldn't have come as a surprise to me—the heavy burden of their gazes and sour-faced judgments. It was something I had come to accept over the years from the people of Fern River.

It was a small town filled with small-minded people who didn't like change—or outsiders. Despite having lived here for over ten years, I still wasn't really accepted as one of them. I had learned the hard way it was best to fall in line.

Lucy squeezed my hand under the table and gave me a forced smile. I looked at my fiancée and admired the sight of her. Her cheeks were flushed from the heat. Long strands of hair had come loose from her braid. She was traditionally beautiful with almost white blond hair, blue eyes, and a slim yet toned body. She really had it all. I, on the other hand, often felt like the beast to her beauty. The nerd to her homecoming queen.

It's not that I was bad looking. Enough girls had told me I was cute over the years, but we were on two different levels. We were as mismatched as two people could possibly be, yet somehow, against all odds, we made it work. Though, perhaps, that had more to do with Lucy's firm resolve than our undying love.

Lucy's family was well respected. Particularly her father, Mr. Clifford Herbaugh, who was the circuit court judge for the fifty-eighth district. He had built a name for himself, having come from nothing, to now be a man of power and influence. And her mother, the formidable Mabel Jean, was a former Miss Fern River Fair, which was a big deal in these parts. She would be the first to laughingly tell you her beauty pageant days were far behind her, yet her daughter had followed diligently in her footsteps. The professional photographs lining the hallway of their magnificent home were a testament to their glory days.

The people of Fern River valued beauty and strength above all else. And the Herbaughs had both in spades. So, of course, they were at the top of the social hierarchy. Her family existed in a privileged position bought and paid for by Mr. Herbaugh's role in the community. Because of this, they operated within a different stratosphere from everyone else. They wanted it, they got it. And I was lucky enough to reap the benefits because Lucy loved me.

Fern River was what people quaintly called a "one-horse town." It was tiny but with an affable charm that many around here seemed to love. It was an old town on the edge of the Cumberland Plateau, and dated back to 1780. While it tried to shake itself off and join the modern age, its old-time morals held true. People were still very conservative and a little too interested in what was going on with their neighbors, all in the name of "community." Maybe it was the way with all small towns, but in Fern River it felt particularly overbearing.

I wasn't a native. I was an implant, which Lucy loved to tease me about. And because of that, my affection was harder won. I didn't have the roots like the Herbaughs. My family was made of different stuff.

The Clarks weren't Kentucky born and bred. We came from Northern Virginia—the suburbs as Mabel stated, with a note of derision that she could never quite hide. My dad left Mom and me when I was little, and we hadn't heard from him since. After that, things were tough, so needing a fresh start, Mom moved us to Kentucky, where we had no connections and could start over. She had to work two jobs to keep a roof over our heads, and I was looking forward to the day when I could help out more.

Lucy took a small bite of the new cake sample and then immediately cut another small piece. "Oh my gosh, try this one!"

She pressed it to my lips before I had a chance to agree. I dutifully swallowed the vanilla, lemon, and ginger cake as my fiancée eagerly awaited my thoughts as if I were deliberating over world peace.

I nodded appreciatively. "Delicious."

Lucy took the comment seriously. "Though . . ." she took another bite of the overly frosted cake, "I bet the coconut and praline from earlier would be good too."

Mabel made a sound in the back of her throat and covered it with a cough. "Yes, the coconut is lovely. Maybe we can order it for your birthday," she suggested before turning back to Leslie. "I think for the wedding we need something more traditional, so we'll order the fruitcake with bourbon cream."

I wondered what this entire cake-tasting session had really been about, because Mabel had clearly known what she would order from the get-go.

I would have loved for my own mother to be a part of the preparations, but unfortunately, working two jobs left her with little time for much else.

Lucy's face fell, but she nodded as she fell in line with her mother's expectations. She picked up her fork again to take another bite, but her mother stopped her with a gentle pat on her arm.

"Not too much," her mother advised softly, wiping a smudge of frosting from her daughter's chin. "I'm not sure another dress fitting is in the wedding budget." She said it offhandedly, almost as if she were joking, but the point was made.

I saw the flash of hurt as Lucy lowered her fork. If Mabel noticed, she didn't let on.

I placed a hand on top of Lucy's. "One more small bite won't hurt—"

"Spoken like a man who never has to worry about his weight," her mother interrupted with a tight laugh.

"Mom's right, Rhett." Lucy shoved the plate away decisively.

"Moms usually are," Mabel remarked primly before taking a large bite of her own cake. Clearly those arbitrary rules about calories didn't apply to her.

* * *

"Well, that's another job on the list completed," Mabel said with an air of accomplishment.

The three of us stood together on the sidewalk outside the bakery. Mabel waved and called out greetings to most of the people that walked by. Everyone had a smile for the judge's wife.

"Okay, you two, I have to get to the Chamber meeting. I'm assuming I'll see you both this evening for dinner?" We nodded in unison. "Wonderful. Your father will be working until five, so we'll serve drinks at six."

While dinners at the Herbaughs' weren't expected, the routine of it had slotted into our lives easily. It was a little scary how quickly our days morphed into a pattern that was more or less molded by her parents. But it was done in such a seemingly well-meaning way, I couldn't voice any objection to it.

"Sounds good, Mom," Lucy responded as if by rote.

"See you two this evening," Mabel said with a final smile before crossing the street to join a woman who had stopped to wait for her. I recognized Dot Crabil, Mabel's friend who ran a coffee shop next to the courthouse.

Lucy and I silently watched her leave. I reached for Lucy's hand and gave it a gentle squeeze.

"I think she's finally starting to like me," I joked dryly.

"Definitely," Lucy replied with a small laugh. "Her niceness is almost ninety percent genuine now. The other ten percent will come soon enough." She winked at me and I felt the knot in my stomach loosen a bit.

I brought her hand to my lips, kissing the back of it. We had been together for only a few years, but I knew we were meant to be together as soon as we met. It wasn't the heart-stopping type of love you read about in books or see in the movies. It was different from that, but that didn't make it any less potent. She had been in my life longer than she had been out of it.

People thought we were crazy for getting married so young. We weren't even a year out of high school. But they didn't understand what Lucy brought to my life.

And what she could very easily take away if she decided to.

"Let's go get ice cream," I suggested, happy to be on our own for a little while.

When it was just Lucy and me, it was natural. We fit together well, and it was that ease I was signing up for when we'd agreed to marry.

Lucy shook her head. "I can't. Like Mom said, I should watch what I'm eating. Imagine the embarrassment of having my dress altered." She winced, and I knew her mom's words had cut deep. She checked her watch. "Crap, I need to get to my step class anyway. It starts in thirty minutes, and I need to change first. I'll meet you at my parents' tonight, okay?"

"Drinks at six," I remarked drolly.

"Drinks at six," she repeated but without any of the sarcasm.

I watched her walk down the street, wondering what to do with the rest of my day.

I thought about heading back to campus. I was a freshman at Salt River College in Jessop County, only a twenty-minute drive from Fern River. I didn't live in the dorms, instead choosing to save money and stay at home with my mom, commuting in every day. It made the whole college experience a little different from what I expected, but I was mostly enjoying it.

I had a bunch of studying to do for my final exams, but with all the wedding preparations, my focus wasn't where it should be. I had to be careful not to dip below a 3.5 GPA, or I'd lose my scholarship. But the thought of being stuck inside studying for something I didn't really care about was choking, and I felt smothered from the pressure.

Lucy's father and I had spoken at length about my future when Lucy and I had started dating. He had been the one to suggest I go into pre-law and then, after graduation, transfer to a law school of Judge Herbaugh's choice.

We talked about me getting my law license and helping him set up a private practice right here in Fern River once his term on the bench was finished. We'd be partners—well, not at first, but eventually.

Herbaugh and Clark, Attorneys at Law. I had to admit, it had a nice ring to it.

And it was a solid plan. One I had, at the time, agreed to. After all, having someone set it all out for me felt like the easiest solution. And if it meant that Lucy and I wouldn't have to scrimp and save like my mom and I had to, then I'd do my part.

But as reality kicked in, I had come to realize I couldn't make myself enjoy my classes on tax law or employment and labor law. It was all a grind, and I was finding that I detested every moment of it.

I walked down the street to Scoops Delight, the food truck that housed the town's ice cream stand, and ordered myself a mint chocolate chip ice cream from the pretty, young, blue-eyed girl manning the counter. She handed me the dripping cone, and I sat on one of the wooden benches outside to eat it. The fountain in the middle of town was on full blast. Kids ran through the jets, letting out delighted screams as the cold water doused them in the unseasonably warm weather.

The town was buzzing with activity on that spring day. It seemed everyone I knew was out and about, and I waved to at least half a dozen people. It was a safe town. People felt comfortable letting their children run around in the streets without hawkish supervision. The low crime rate was its greatest appeal.

Except for Jagged Point.

The scenic overlook was thirteen miles outside of town, and I had spent a lot of time there since I was old enough to leave the house on my own. Families hiked there. Teens partied there. But every single person remembered that it was also the place where hikers sometimes went missing. And a few decades ago, two bodies were discovered by the cliffs, their deaths never solved.

But today, I tried to see the positives of the town I called home. I laughed as a cute blond girl grabbed a boy of a similar age and dragged him into the jets with her. He looked to be only fourteen, but he was entering that difficult phase where he wasn't quite a man, but he also wasn't a boy anymore. It was a tricky time for anyone, but especially boys. Where the desire to have fun all the time ran in direct opposition to wanting to become a man that others looked up to and respected. I remembered the feeling well. Even though I never had my own father around to guide me, I had enough male friends to help me understand what was expected of me. And once I had Lucy on my arm, with her father backing my every move, I'd be well respected too.

Respect came in many forms, and I would take mine however I could get it.

I thought about blowing the rest of the day off and heading to Jagged Point for a run so I could let off some steam and be alone. Because at times it felt like I couldn't breathe.

All Lucy had ever talked about was having the house and the kids and the white picket fence like her parents expected of her. And with the plan her father had laid out for both of us, that was the life we would have.

It could be so simple.

All of it.

It's what she wanted.

It's what everyone wanted.

But was it what *I* wanted?

The ice cream had dripped onto my pants and I rubbed at the mess in irritation. Grumbling, I stood up and headed to the counter to grab some napkins, wiping furiously at the stain.

"I hate it when that happens," a feminine voice spoke from behind me. I turned to look, but didn't recognize her, which wasn't necessarily surprising—Fern River may be a small town, but we did have the occasional tourist passing through.

She was attractive and seemed about my age, with a long mane of red hair that trailed down her back in knotted waves. Her skin was tanned and her cheeks flushed pink. She didn't seem to be wearing any makeup, her skin dewy and natural—unlike Lucy, who never went anywhere without her face made up.

She was small in stature, which was all the more noticeable given that she carried a large bag on her back that dwarfed her tiny frame. The seams bulged as if the zipper was going to split open at any moment.

"Mint chocolate chip?" she asked with a smile.

I nodded, my mouth seemingly unable to form any actual words.

"That's one of my favorites," the girl commented. As we stood there in companionable silence, she tucked her hair behind one ear. I noticed she wore three silver bangles that jangled when she moved.

"Have you ever tried pistachio, though? My mom used to make her own. I swear you'll be like 'mint chocolate chip who?' once you try it." She laughed, and I found myself laughing with her.

"Pistachio, huh? Not sure I'm into nuts," I quipped, feeling stupid as soon as I said it. I felt the heat rise in my cheeks, and I was thankful it was a warm day so I could excuse it.

She raised an eyebrow. "Not into nuts. Duly noted."

Our eyes met, her full lips quirking slightly, and then we both laughed again.

"Not that there's anything wrong with nuts—"

"Quit while you're ahead, buddy." She chuckled, putting her hand on my arm. Our eyes met again, and this time I had to look away.

"You made a real mess of your pants there," she said, gesturing to the stained fabric.

"Yeah, I think they're ruined." I sighed. Lucy would be embarrassed if she could see it. And it didn't bear thinking about what her mother would say.

"No sense crying over melted ice cream. I say it's a good excuse to buy some new clothes." She grinned and inclined her head to the ice cream counter, "And another cone."

"You know," I said, throwing the soggy napkin in the trash, "I think you're right." I glanced up at the menu board before giving my new acquaintance a genuine grin. "And I think I'll try—" I clicked my fingers as I tried to recall the flavor she had suggested.

"Pistachio," she filled in for me, "though I thought you weren't into nuts."

"God, just shoot me now." I groaned good-naturedly and we shared another smile.

"It's cool. Sometimes some nuts are good for the soul," she teased and I groaned again.

"I don't think I'll live this one down," I joked.

She shook her head, a strand of her auburn hair falling in her face. "Never." She looped an arm through mine, as if we'd known each other for years, and pulled me toward the counter. "Come on, new friend, let's get you some nutty ice cream."

As I waited to place my order, I wondered if Lucy would like pistachio. If it was something we could share together later.

But then I remembered that she was allergic to nuts and so couldn't even try it.

I placed a new order for the pistachio cone and at the last minute, ordered a second one.

I turned around and handed the woman the ice cream. "I, umm . . . I got you one too. I hope that was okay."

"Thank you, that's so kind."

"I thought it only fair since it was your recommendation." I took a bite. Then another. Then another.

"Wow, this stuff is amazing."

"I know, right!" she exclaimed, finishing her own cone with large enough bites to equal mine. Ice cream dribbled down her chin, and without thinking I wiped at it with a napkin, my fingers brushing her skin in the process.

Her eyes widened slightly and I realized my presumption. "Oh, sorry, it's just you had something there. I shouldn't have, sorry . . ."

"It's okay." She said it softly and without censure. Her ease made me relax instantly.

She tilted her head back, closing her eyes briefly. The hollow of her throat was exposed, and I could see a gold chain draped around her neck that disappeared below the collar of the loose blouse she was wearing.

"I'm Jenn, by the way," she announced and held out her hand, her bracelets catching the sunlight.

"Rhett," I replied, taking her hand and giving it a quick shake with humorous solemnity. I became embarrassingly aware of how sticky my hand still was.

"Nice to meet you, Rhett." Her smile was really what set her apart. It was dazzling. She cast a quick look around. "So, any idea where a gal can lay her head for a couple of weeks? There doesn't seem to be any hotels for miles."

"Oh, well, there's the Millwood Guesthouse over there. Ms. Stanley runs it, she's really nice." I indicated the two-story colonial building with an American flag fluttering in the breeze out front.

"Is it pricey? I don't have a lot of cash on hand," Jenn said, furrowing her brow slightly.

"Nothing's pricey in Fern River," I scoffed. "And it's still the off season for another few weeks, so I'm sure you'll find it affordable."

"Oh, that's good. I'll check it out then." She repositioned her book bag on her shoulders. It honestly looked like it weighed more than she did.

"So you're here for a couple weeks, then?"

"Or longer." She shrugged. "We'll see."

A moment of silence passed between us, her lightheartedness disappearing until she seemed to shake herself out of whatever black mood had momentarily taken over. She looked back at me, her face brightening again.

"Anyway, thanks for the ice cream, Rhett. I hope to see you around."

"Yeah, me too." I started to turn away but then in a moment of spontaneity, I pulled out my cell phone. "Hey, maybe I could get your number and give you a tour around town sometime?"

She hesitated before smiling. "Okay, sure, it'll be nice to have a friend here." She pulled out her phone, and I couldn't help but laugh when I saw it was an old Nokia.

"Wow, I haven't seen one of those since 2001."

"Well, sorry, Mr. Fancy Pants, we can't all afford swanky phones like that." She gestured toward my Blackberry, and now it was my turn to flush red.

The phone had been a gift from Lucy for my birthday. Right along with putting me on her family plan so I didn't have to worry about monthly bills. I laughed uncomfortably.

She put her hand on my arm, her expression kind. "I'm only kidding." She rattled off the numbers and I tapped the digits into my keypad, before sending her a simple 'hi' so she had mine. Jenn smiled and saved my information.

"Okay, well, I better go and see if I can get a room at that B&B. It's been nice talking to you, Rhett." She gave me a small wave, then turned and walked across the street toward the Millwood Guesthouse.

I watched her until she was out of sight, a smile on my face as I watched her hips sashay as she moved.

The taste of pistachio ice cream lingered on my lips as I turned away, and I felt a lightness in my chest as I realized my usual growing panic had quieted to a dull throb.

Throwing my napkin in the trashcan I bumped into someone. I looked up and saw Alison Schaffer, Lucy's co-worker and the on-and-off-again girlfriend of my friend, Caleb. She was pretty enough, with long brown hair and legs for miles, but if I was being honest, I thought Caleb could do better. She had a jealous streak and could be incredibly possessive, which was a total turn-off.

"Hey, Alison." My cheeks grew hot like I had been caught doing something I shouldn't. I wasn't sure why I was so paranoid.

"Hey, Rhett," she replied with an overly eager smile. I had never quite warmed to her, for some reason. "Where's Lucy today?"

"An exercise class, I think," I said with a shrug.

"I saw you coming out of Crème Dulce Bakery earlier. Whatcha doin' there?"

Alison was always noticing things that had nothing to do with her. She was a shit stirrer and a gossip. The kind of girl that made sure she had her nose in everything.

I shoved my hands in my pockets. "Cake tasting," I replied brusquely, wanting to get away. Alison kind of creeped me out, though I never could put a finger on why. "Well, I better get going. Say hi to Caleb for me."

"Of course, no problem." She put her hand on my arm as I turned to walk away, her fingers cold on my skin. "It's always so nice to see you. We should spend more time together, don't ya think?" I noticed the way she seemed to catalog every detail, and I didn't want to think about what she saw when she looked at me.

I had to resist the urge to shudder as I left.

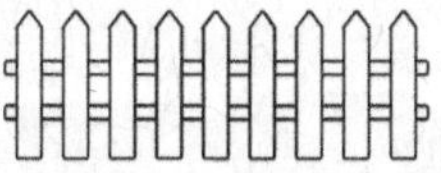

Message

Hi, this is Rhett. It was great meeting you yesterday. Hope it's okay that I'm messaging you. :-)

Options **Back**

CHAPTER

3

Lucy

The Past

July 15—Fifteen Years Ago

THE TOWN WAS talking of nothing else but the death of Jennifer Moore.

Just thinking her name made me want to throw up.

But equally it filled me with an anger I was afraid I wouldn't be able to control. I wanted to hit things. Break things.

She had come into our lives, and because of her everything had nearly been ruined. And now, even dead, she was still there, like a specter, throwing darkness over my life.

But I made sure to put on my Sephora lipstick every morning and smile so hard my teeth could break. All the while imagining the ways I wanted to blow things up—starting with Alison Schaffer and her pseudo concern.

"I talked to her a little bit at Jeremy's field party the other weekend. Right before—" She looked at me, realizing the faux pas she'd made by mentioning that night. "Um, anyway, she was a little, um . . . how to put this nicely . . ." Alison paused to pick up the toddler who was trying to pull herself up onto the table. "No, Cora, that's not safe," she cooed before turning back to me. "What was I saying?"

"You were talking about J—" I struggled to say her name. I cleared my throat. "Jenn."

"Oh, right." Alison bounced the cute little baby on her hip while maneuvering a bottle into the child's mouth. "All she talked about was Rhett this and Rhett that. It kinda pissed me off actually. I wanted to strangle her myself." She grimaced slightly. "Sorry, that was probably in bad taste."

"A little," I replied, sounding strained. It was more than bad taste to make jokes about a dead girl.

Alison's face darkened. "She sure thought she was hot stuff, though, with the way all the guys were drooling over her. Even Caleb, though I bitched him out good for looking at her like that." Her giggle was high-pitched. "Girls like that always end up the same way." She shrugged when she saw my shocked expression. "What? It's true."

I didn't bother to respond. I felt uncomfortable, like I wanted to crawl out of my own skin.

"Can you take Cora for a minute? I need to use the bathroom." Alison shoved the child into my arms and scurried away before I had a chance to agree. She was probably going to message half the town about my reactions to everything. I needed to remember to school my expression—and my answers—at all times. Because everyone in Fern River was watching, and reporting back to each other.

The nursery was operating in its usual barely contained chaos. Toddlers crawled and ran around the room, playing or throwing tantrums. I had been a nursery assistant at Little Darlings Daycare since eleventh grade. Not exactly what you would call a thoughtful career choice, but it was a nice way to pass the time until I got married and had my own babies.

The daycare's owner, Amy Franklin, whose mom, Leslie, was making my wedding cake, was outside talking on her phone for the fourth time that morning. Amy, like most people in Fern River, was a gossip of the highest order and had been practically buzzing with news of the body found at Jagged Point.

As for me, I wished I could lock myself away until it all blew over. I was already the topic of way too much conversation for my liking. And the last thing I wanted was for my name to be linked irrevocably with Jenn Moore's.

Alison came back and took Cora from my aching arms. "Mary-Beth messaged me a second ago. She said the police are going around and questioning everyone that was at the field party."

My stomach dropped. "Oh yeah?"

Alison nodded. "Wanting to know if people saw Jennifer talkin' to anyone . . ." Her words died off and she suddenly wouldn't make eye contact.

"Oh, okay," I remarked, making myself busy tidying up a pile of wooden blocks on the floor.

"I mean, should I mention what happened with you guys?"

I tried hard not to scream in frustration. "Nothing happened, Al, so not sure what there is to tell them."

Alison looked at me like I'd lost my mind. "We were all there, Lucy. We saw the two of them together. We saw what went down when you showed up. I know you said nothing was going on with Rhett and her—"

"I told you already it wasn't what it looked like." I sounded irritated. Probably because I *was* irritated.

"Sweetie, we both know how this town loves to talk. And Rhett sure did fuel the gossip mill with that little show he put on. I'd be ready to kill someone myself if it were me." She eyed me closely before putting a hand on my arm in feigned concern. "Why didn't you tell me you and Rhett were having problems? We could've had a good bitchfest before it got to all this. Maybe slashed his tires or burned his clothes." Her voice was much too loud.

I didn't like her insinuation. God knows what she'd tell the police when she was questioned.

My face scrunched up in a perfect semblance of confused befuddlement. "Rhett and I aren't having any problems. We're getting married next month. MaryBeth just wants drama. It's sad how she makes up issues to distract everyone from the fact that Lance dumped her two weeks ago. I heard it was messy." I raised my eyebrows, dropping that tasty nugget of small-town scandal in her lap and hoping she'd eat it up.

Alison's eyes widened. "Yeah, I heard about that." She frowned, clearly not as easily waylaid as I wished she'd be. "But I don't think it's just MaryBeth being MaryBeth. Everyone's saying it, Lucy. Half the town was there watchin' the two of them act like a couple."

Amy picked the perfect time to stride into the room, followed by the smell of stale tobacco and strawberry body spray. "Lucy, it's time for your break. Twenty minutes starting now."

Practically sagging with relief I hurried outside, beelining for the picnic area at the back of Amy's large backyard. I pulled my phone out to find the screen alarmingly blank. I still hadn't heard from Rhett. Not even with the news of *the body's* discovery. I thought that, at least, would bring him around. That our earlier argument would be forgotten now that the obstacle was officially gone. When had I gotten so bad at reading him?

I chewed on my nails, biting them to the quick. Then I stopped myself, staring down in horror at the mangled state of my manicure.

I knew I wouldn't be able to avoid the questions forever. The endless deliberations over *my* life. I clenched my hands into fists and pressed them into my thighs, the pain keeping my mind clear.

I was so damn angry. And upset. And betrayed.

And so, so hurt.

My eyes stung with tears. I wasn't the sort of woman who was used to heartache. I knew I lived a privileged existence. One I had always taken for granted.

If I wanted it, I got it. It's how things worked.

Until *she* came to town and screwed everything up.

Alison's question rang in my ears.

Why didn't you tell me you and Rhett were having problems?

Because I didn't know we were having problems. Not really. Of course, I'd suspected. I'd have to be an idiot not to.

But now I realized I had been living in self-imposed denial, all because I didn't want to face the very real facts shouting at me.

And I didn't do anything about it.

Not until it was too late.

* * *

After work I drove straight to Oakhill Street rather than go home. I'd told my mother I'd be home for dinner, so I didn't have much time. My parents had me on lockdown with everything going on. They didn't want me talking to anyone about anything. Yet, it was important to maintain a degree of normalcy, especially now that our town was the site of a murder.

I pulled up in front of the small yet well-maintained house with its bright yellow door and purple porch swing. I jangled my keys nervously as I walked up the front path and rang the doorbell.

A few minutes later, Ms. Olivia Clark opened the door with a look of surprise. "Lucy, it's so lovely to see you!" The tiny woman hugged me tightly. She was warm in all the ways a mother should be. In ways my own mother wasn't. She was already dressed in her uniform for her night shift at the nursing home.

"Good evening, Ms. Clark, it's nice to see you too." I peered behind her into the narrow, dimly lit hallway. "Is Rhett back from school yet? I know his last class ends at four on Thursdays."

"Oh, didn't he call you?" Her eyes widened slightly in alarm. "He's been here all day."

"What? He has an exam he's supposed to be studying for." I didn't try to hide the dismay in my voice. "Is he sick?"

"I don't think so." She glanced behind her with a look of concern. It was the face of a mother worrying she had let something slip. She was a good mom. Obviously she loved Rhett dearly and would do anything for him, but she worked two jobs and was oblivious to most things going on in his life.

"He's been so strange the last few days. Won't come out of his room. He hasn't been to school since last week," she confided. "Is everything okay between you two? You're not having second thoughts about the wedding? You're both so young, so it would be understandable, but I don't know what he would do if it didn't work out—" She stopped suddenly, as if realizing she shouldn't be sharing these thoughts.

I gave my future mother-in-law what I hoped was a kind smile. "We're fine. We've been playing phone tag is all, and I think he's worried about exams." I would die before I admitted to anyone, least of all his mother, that we were already having problems and we weren't even married yet. That I wasn't entirely sure if we were even still a couple.

"Oh, okay then. Well, you know the way. Why don't you try to get him to eat somethin'. He's starving himself up there." She clucked her tongue in maternal consternation.

"Yes, ma'am. Leave it to me." I patted her arm in female solidarity as I moved past her to make my way to Rhett's bedroom.

"He's so lucky to have you," Ms. Clark called after me.

"That's so kind of you, Ms. Clark," I called back, wishing her son felt the same.

I didn't bother to knock when I reached the door at the top of the stairs. Instead, I barged in hoping to . . . What? Catch him in the act of something?

I was being silly. Those days were behind us now.

Perhaps my paranoia explained why I threw open the door with all the dramatic flourish of a jilted lover on a soap opera.

However, what I found was the man I was supposed to marry curled up in a fetal position in the middle of his double bed looking like he hadn't showered in days. He stared blankly at the wall, not even registering my entrance.

"I've been trying to call you for days, Rhett. What in the hell are you doing? People are starting to talk." I didn't bother to hide my rage. All he had to do was act normal, and everything would be okay. Instead he was being suspicious as hell.

His eyes finally flicked in my direction. "Lucinda." He said my name flatly. Without emotion.

Hearing him say my full name was jarring. In all the years we had known each other, he had only ever called me Lucy.

"Your mom says you haven't been to school since last week." I put my hands on my hips in an imitation of my mother when she lectured my sister. I forced myself to relax my stance. The last thing I wanted was to be like her.

Rhett squeezed his eyes shut as if to block me out. "How can I think about school with everything that's happened?" he asked, his voice unnaturally monotone.

I glanced at the open door, knowing his mother was most likely in the hallway listening. Frowning, I marched across the room and closed it with a loud *click* before turning back to my frustrating soon-to-be husband.

"What's wrong with you?" I hissed, letting the full scale of my fury unleash itself. "Get up now!"

Rhett slowly sat up and ran his hand down his face. "Please stop, Lucinda—"

"I will *not* stop! Think about how this looks, Rhett. We can't have that, not with what's happened."

Rhett's cheeks flushed red and I saw a spark of *something* in his eyes. It looked a lot like disgust. "Oh, we can't have the neighbors talking, can we?" His lip curled. Finally, he looked at me. "But I'm not going out there and acting like everything is normal. Because it's not. It never will be again." His voice broke, his lips trembled. I knew he was trying to stop himself from crying.

I stared at him, hardly recognizing the man I was looking at. This person I thought was my savior had shown who he really was beneath his kind exterior.

I had been taught, since an early age, that my role in life was to find a man and settle down. To be a good Christian woman and raise my family with strong southern values.

My parents started setting me up with their friends' sons as soon as I was old enough to start dating. I knew I would be roped into their version of an arranged marriage if I let them.

I had so little control in my life, but when it came to Rhett, I, for once, put my foot down. And even though my parents thought I could do better, they were relieved I had at least picked a man that appeared to go along with the plan they had carefully constructed for my future.

I thought he was everything I needed. Sweet. Smart. And he adored me. I felt like someone saw me for *me* and not just my family name.

I had never stood up to my parents. He was my one act of rebellion, and now I was paying for it.

His attention had clearly been fleeting. I felt mortified every time I thought of him and Jenn together. And now I was stuck with someone who was proving my parents right. Yet I couldn't admit I had been wrong. I couldn't look my father in the eye and tell him that his disapproval was warranted. Instead I stood firm in my resolve—*for better or for worse.*

"We wouldn't be in this position if you were more in control of things," I snapped, crossing my arms over my chest. "In control of *yourself*," I added with enough bite for him to sense how furious I was. That seemed to get a reaction. I had never been particularly angry with Rhett before—I never had a reason to be—until a few months ago, when he showed me the kind of person he really was. Rhett rose to his feet, knocking a pillow to the floor.

"What is wrong with you? Is that all you care about? Jenn is dead, Lucinda. *Dead!*" His breathing was labored, his nostrils flared. "We need to talk about what happened—"

"Don't, Rhett. Just don't." My plea sounded more like a command.

"Just don't? Don't what? Talk about the things we said? About where each of us were?" He glared at me. "About who Jenn was to me?"

Those words took the air out of my lungs. He wasn't trying to protect my feelings at all—he was going straight for the jugular. At some point he had stopped caring about how I felt at all.

I wouldn't let him see how much he hurt me. I wouldn't give him the satisfaction. This man I had, until recently, trusted to put me first each and every time. He was a dirty, rotten liar.

"It's done now. There's no need to rehash it," I told him firmly with a strength that wasn't entirely genuine.

"Are you serious? You expect us to carry on as if the last week didn't happen? Things were said, Lucinda. Decisions were made. And now I don't know how to keep going after this." His eyes became wild. "This is *my* fault! She wouldn't be dead if it weren't for me!" He closed his eyes and let out a guttural groan, pressing his fist to his mouth.

I had no sympathy for him. I felt his betrayal like a stab to the gut. "You're right, this wasn't *her* fault. Not entirely. Yes, she was definitely vying for the Miss Teen Homewrecker crown, but *you* allowed her to wreck it. What happened to her . . ." My voice faltered. I took a deep breath. "We have to move on from this, Rhett. *You* have to move on from this. The best thing to do is to press on with the plans we made."

Rhett stared at me, his eyes filled with something inexplicable. "You think we're still getting married and settling down? Have you lost your mind?"

"Rhett . . ."

He took a step toward me, and I felt intimidated. No, I felt scared.

"You're telling me to just move on. As if the woman I love—" he faltered and my heart seized, "as if *Jenn* wasn't dead." He squeezed his eyes shut and when he opened them again, they blazed with an anger that disturbed me. I knew, in that moment, he wished I was the one on a mortuary slab. "How can you be like this? How can you be so calm and unfazed? You're acting psychotic."

I felt myself stiffen. "Psychotic? You mean like lying to your fiancée for months and messing up her whole life?" I challenged. "Or how about what happened that night? You weren't acting particularly sane yourself." I was rewarded when Rhett had the sense to look chastised. "We have a future together, Rhett. A future you seem hellbent on destroying. If you would just pull yourself together, we could get things back to how they used to be." I felt slightly panicked. I had to make him see reason.

What would become of me if this fell apart?

I didn't know who I was without the wedding, the marriage, the plans for a picture- perfect life. My chest constricted with anxiety.

I felt my world begin to crumble around me, and I was trying to hold it together with Scotch tape.

"We have a future, Rhett. A good one too. I know you don't want to be stuck in this tiny house with your mom forever."

I hated saying that—Ms. Clarke was a good woman and a good mom, but I felt like my grip on him was slipping.

His eyes were haunted, and I noticed how he didn't argue. He took a steadying breath and looked at me with a level of distrust—and disgust—I had never seen before. "Is there anything you need to tell me?"

I swallowed thickly. "Like what?"

Rhett stared at me for a moment longer before pressing the heels of his hands to his forehead like he did when he had a headache. "Maybe things are too messed up now. Maybe we shouldn't go back to how they used to be."

We stood facing each other. Both filled with our own versions of anguish. Both with our own versions of the truth. I wanted to shake him. I wanted to scream. He had come so close to ruining everything. And for what? For her?

I'd be damned if I'd let him burn down our white picket fence.

I took a deep breath, letting it out slowly. Neither of us would survive what lay ahead if we were at odds. We needed to put forward a united front. We loved each other. Everyone had to see it. They had to believe it.

I needed to believe it.

Because if not, things were going to get a whole lot worse.

I closed the distance between us and gently took his hands. "Rhett, you know what your mom said to me when I got here? She said she was worried about *you*, about *us*. She knows that our future is together, and without me, she doesn't know what you will do. What *she* will do."

I let that sink in for a moment.

He stared down at me for what felt like an uncomfortably long time. At some point in the last few months, I had lost my ability to read him. Or maybe he had written a whole new book in a language I didn't understand.

There was a coldness in him now. A flatness to his eyes as if all the feeling had been sucked out of him. They were the eyes of someone capable of things that would terrify me. People saw him as a nice guy, but they hadn't peeled back his layers like I had. They didn't see who he really was.

My mouth went uncomfortably dry. "Rhett?" I said his name again, haltingly. "You love me, right? You never meant for it to go this far. You would never knowingly hurt me, would you?"

He blinked slowly as if coming back to himself from that far-off place he had been in for too long. "No, Lucinda, I never wanted to hurt you." He sounded defeated. "I never meant for *anyone* to get hurt."

I forced myself not to notice that he never once said he loved me.

I put my arms around his waist and pressed my cheek to his lean chest, feeling the steady *thump thump* of his heart beneath my ear. "And you will never hurt me again," I said with total conviction.

I felt the deep rise and fall of his sigh. "No, I won't."

"This will all go away," I promised him.

I promised myself.

Rhett pulled back, his hands shaking. "But what about Jenn—?"

"Don't say her name," I pleaded. I pressed my palm to his cheek. "It's better that way."

Rhett shuddered. "This is bad, Lucinda."

"I know. But as long as we're together, we'll be okay."

"We should talk about it, though. About what happened—" His eyes clouded over, his lips pressed together.

"No." It was a whisper with all the force of a shout. "I don't want to talk about it. I don't need to, and I don't think it would be good for either of us."

"Things happened. Things we both regret—"

I put a finger over his mouth, silencing him.

"No."

The word felt like a grenade ready to go off.

"We say nothing. *You* say nothing," I told him before wrapping my arms around him again, squeezing him so tightly that it cut off any and all conversation. "We act like there's nothing *to* say."

After a few minutes, he lifted his arms and held me back. And we stayed that way for a long time as we tried to ignore the persistent phantom of the dead girl that lingered between us.

CHAPTER

4

Rhett

The Present

I RUBBED MY ACHING eyes and stifled a yawn. I had no idea what time it was or how long I had been sitting there. All I knew was that it felt like days. In reality, I had been waiting years for this moment to catch up with me. It was almost unbelievable how long I had gotten away with it.

I stared down at the table, at my hands clasped tightly together in front of me, and I thought of everything these hands had done to put me here.

I swallowed, trying not to think of *those* nights with Jenn. Of *that* night in particular. Of the chain of events I had set in motion. I had been so blind. Unable to see past the end of my nose to what was coming my way.

I would do anything to go back in time and take it all back.

Lucinda and her family had saved me once, but, man, they made me pay for it.

I had been paying for it for the past fifteen goddamn years.

The only thing I could be thankful for was that my mother wasn't alive to see this. Losing her five years ago to a brain aneurysm was one of the hardest things I ever had to deal with. She worked so hard to provide for me, and in the end she died before she could even retire, pulling shifts at the nursing home until the day she passed away.

But at least she was gone before my life imploded. She'd be heartbroken to see what Lucinda and I had become.

Footsteps echoed down the corridor outside the room. They seemed to take forever to arrive. My heart pounded in my chest, my blood pumping furiously through my body as I waited with bated breath for my past to rear its ugly head.

The door opened and I looked up as Chief Charles Young came in, accompanied by a plainclothes police officer. Chief Young carried a slim manila folder that looked as if it contained no more than a handful of sheets of paper and strangely, what looked like a Samsung tablet. The other officer brought in two paper cups filled with coffee. The men sat across the table from me, offering insincere smiles.

The camera whirred in the upper corner of the room, a red light blinking casually, as if this wasn't the most defining moment of my life.

Or maybe it wasn't.

Maybe that defining moment had come and gone the last night I had seen Jenn alive—scared and crying, but also angry. With me.

"Evenin'." Chief Young cleared his throat and gave me a grim smile. "Okay, I think we all know each other well enough, but for the record, I'm Chief Charles Young, and this is Detective Leonard Wright. Today is Thursday, April twenty-third, at 4:51 AM. This is a taped conversation with last name Clark C-L-A-R-K, first name Rhett R-H-E-T-T, date of birth September second, 1992."

Chief Young was an overbearing man with a head full of thick gray hair and a smile that unnerved me. I had always felt more than a little intimidated by the man.

Detective Wright slid a coffee across the table. "Thought you might be needing that about now." He was nondescript in the way police officers in small towns often were. Same crew cut hairstyle. Same bland, all-American looks. He probably completed the academy right out of high school like the rest of them.

"Thank you, Detective," I replied cautiously. He was right, I desperately needed some strong coffee. I was exhausted and thirsty. Though caffeine probably wasn't the best thing to settle my nerves, it would definitely keep me alert. I took the cup gratefully.

"Rhett, I've turned on the video recorder. I'm not the best notetaker in the world, and this will help us both out. That okay with you?" Charles inquired good-naturedly.

"Um, sure." I sipped the coffee, eyeing the two men. Chief Young took a sip of his own coffee before continuing. "I want to go over a couple of points first. We've brought you downtown to ask you some questions. You've been treated with the utmost respect, right?"

"Yes, sir."

"Great. And you don't need to keep callin' me 'sir.' Call me Chuck. It's what you've always called me. And there's no need to worry about anythin', I'm sure we'll get this cleared up in no time. I wouldn't normally be conducting this interview, I'd leave it up to my detective here, but we're short-staffed tonight and given the . . . *sensitive* nature of this investigation and who your family is," he gave me a pointed look, "I felt it important to be here." He let that sink in before continuing. "Detective Wright and I would like to talk to you about the death of Jennifer Moore. It was a fair few years ago—"

"Fifteen to be precise," Detective Wright added.

"That's right—fifteen years." The chief whistled through his teeth. "Time goes by in a flash, doesn't it, son."

"I . . . I guess so." Her name had a strange effect on me, as it always did. The hair on the back of my arms stood on end, and my stomach did a somersault.

"Well, I'd like to ask you a couple of questions. I know it was a long time ago, so your memory might be hazy on the details, but anything you can tell us would be helpful. An eyewitness has come forward that places you with Miss Moore on the night of her murder—"

"Shouldn't I wait for my lawyer?" I asked, feeling uncomfortable for interrupting him.

I knew I shouldn't be talking to these men. Cliff had made it clear that I should keep my mouth shut. Even though Chief Young was one of Cliff's oldest friends, and had always been polite to me, he had made it obvious that I was only Cliff's son-in-law. This man was *not* my friend.

Most of the people in this town regarded me the same way. I had no place among Cliff's cronies. I would never be inside their circle of trust. They were members of the good ole boys' club, and I was firmly outside it.

Fern River had been bought and sold long before I was even born. It was an unspoken rule that these men, including my father-in-law, pulled the strings behind the scenes. They guaranteed that the people they wanted were elected to local office. They made sure their friends and family never saw a speeding ticket. And the people that crossed them found themselves on the wrong side of the law.

I wondered where I now found myself.

Within their protection? Or without it?

But I had to trust that my connection to Cliff Herbaugh would once again prove its value. I couldn't let myself start doubting things now, or I'd lose my mind.

"Sorry. It's been a long night, and I don't want to piss off Cliff." I laughed nervously again.

Charles, I couldn't think of him as Chuck, laughed, too, and gave me a broad smile. "Son, we're just having a little chat, nothing to get your panties in a twist over. Lawyers are for guilty people, and you're not guilty of anythin' are you, Rhett?"

I shook my head, my gaze darting to the closed door and then to the camera, before looking at the chief again. "It's not about being guilty, but doing things the right way. And I still think I should probably wait, if that's all right. Cliff might not be too happy about me talking without any representation present, and he said that Glynn Walker was on his way."

Charles held my gaze, and I wilted slightly. It was stupid, but I felt like I had let him down somehow. It was probably my instinctual desire to please a male authority figure. Having grown up without my dad, I found myself craving the regard of the men I came in contact with. Because of this, it made it difficult to speak my mind.

"Absolutely, Rhett, that's no problem at all. We can wait. Though it's been hours. I know Glynn is clear across the state in Louisville trying another case. If Cliff called him early in the evening, it shouldn't take this long. Louisville is, what? Four hours from Fern River?" He glanced at the detective.

"Three and a half this time of night," Detective Wright added.

"I mean, it's not like Cliff would let his *favorite* son-in-law go down for murder, right?" Charles gave me a loaded look. "He loves Lucinda more than anything, and you're her husband and the father of his only granddaughter. And we both know how Cliff feels about family."

I nodded, my wariness growing. Chief Young was only following the rules. However, my mind couldn't tear itself away from what he had just said. He and I were both aware that I wasn't Cliff's favorite *anything*.

What was he trying to say?

The coffee felt like lead in my hollow stomach.

"There's no reason he'd want you out of the way, is there? Because, like I said, it's been hours. More than enough time to make that three-and-a-half-hour trip from Louisville, if you ask me." He paused and made a point to look at his watch. "Yet, he's still not here. So I wonder, what's the hold up? And speaking of our mutual friend, has he decided to wait at home for news? I thought he'd be down here tellin' me how to do my job by now."

The fact my father-in-law wasn't at the station hadn't been lost on me. He had told Lucinda he was on his way, but so far I hadn't heard his booming voice demanding action. It made me feel very, very alone, and more than a little anxious.

Charles picked up his coffee and took a long drink before turning to Detective Wright. "How long has Rhett been waiting now? Five hours?"

"Six, sir," Detective Wright corrected.

"Six hours." The chief whistled through his teeth again and grimaced. "Drink your coffee, son, you're going to need it." He watched as I picked up my cup again. "Someone here has to take care of you." He laughed again, and Detective Wright joined in. "Lord knows, no one else seems to be."

My brain went back over all the looks of disdain Cliff Herbaugh had given me over the years. The amount of times I had heard him muttering about how Lucinda could do better. How he made sure I felt uncomfortable in my own home—and his. His disappointment, all those years ago, when I told him I didn't want to study law anymore. That I didn't want to go into practice with him. That I planned to become a math teacher instead.

Did he really want me out of Lucinda's life that much? And if so, why make sure no one looked my way all those years ago, only to throw me under the bus now?

Is that why he was leaving me here to deal with this on my own? I had never missed my father-in-law's domineering presence more.

Family was everything to Cliff Herbaugh, second only to his pride. He had done a lot of things that would be classified as morally, and ethically, questionable to protect me—and Lucinda. Was he now regretting those choices?

Chief Young abruptly turned to the detective. "Can you go check to see if Glynn's here yet? And who knows, maybe Cliff decided to show up too." He gave me another broad smile. "We'll find out where they both are so we can get you back home to that beautiful family of yours as quickly as possible."

"Th . . . thank you, I appreciate that," I said, feeling worse with each passing minute.

Detective Wright stood up and left the room. We were quiet until the door shut, and then the chief reclined back in his chair.

"Sorry about Wright. He's not much of a talker and can be a bit of a stick in the ass. But you know what chain of command is like. It's all 'yes, sirs' and 'no, sirs.' I tell you, I'm getting too old for this shit. Being called 'sir' makes me feel like I have one foot in the grave." He chuckled, holding my gaze until I laughed along with him, though I didn't find much of this funny. "Come on, Rhett, that's the part where you're supposed to tell me I'm still young."

His features were relaxed, and I felt myself calm down a little. The chief had an easy way about him that invited confidences. It's why he was so good at his job. I knew I should probably remember that, but I was desperate for someone to have my back.

"Sorry," I remarked sheepishly, "like I said, it's been a long night."

The chief nodded. "I hear that. I'd rather be tucked up in bed listening to Tanya's snoring than having a late night chat with you. No offense." There was a pause before he changed the subject completely, and I felt off balance at the abrupt turn. "So, you're a math teacher, right?"

"Uh, yes, at Fern River High. Not the dream job for most people, but I love it." I took a slow breath, forcing myself to settle. My heart had been racing for hours and the adrenaline was starting to wear off, leaving me exhausted. Which could be dangerous if I didn't watch what I was saying.

"Wow, I tip my hat to you," the chief praised. "There's no way I could teach high school kids. The things we see at the parties we bust up—crazy stuff, my friend."

"I bet." I laughed.

"It feels like kids sometimes get in over their heads through no fault of their own, am I right?" His eyes hardened slightly. "Even good kids make mistakes, Rhett." There was a long, loaded pause. What was he getting at?

"So, let me get this straight, you and Lucinda started dating in high school, right? What made you decide to get married when you were still wet behind the ears?"

Was I supposed to defend our decision to get married young? We had been together for years. Why was this important now? I didn't know what he wanted me to say.

"I suppose you two were simply madly in love," he went on. "It couldn't have been a secret pregnancy you wanted to keep hush-hush." He considered me closely. "Or maybe it has to do with marital privilege in a courtroom. Because I'm sure Cliff told you two all about that." He chuckled when he saw my expression. Now him asking about our wedding made sense. "You look like you're going to pass out there, Rhett. I was only joking."

The chief was talking quickly, his words melting into one long sentence. I knew I wasn't supposed to reply; I was supposed to listen and keep quiet. I needed to wait for my lawyer. When I didn't respond, Chief Young continued, filling the silence. "Let me tell you, I've known Cliff Herbaugh a long time, and the day he told me his little girl was getting married at only nineteen was the day he got his first gray hair!"

Without warning, he let out another booming laugh that seemed far too loud for such a small room. I cringed at both his laughter and the memory of my father-in-law's face the day I asked him for Lucinda's hand in marriage.

I swallowed, my throat dry. "Lucinda always knew what she wanted, so there didn't seem much point in waiting. She hadn't wanted to wait, and neither did I." It was a romanticized version of how it had really happened. A rushed ceremony instead of the wedding of the year we had been planning for months. A quick job to silence all the talk. Because in the end, I owed Lucinda my commitment. In fact, she had demanded it.

And yes, Chief Young was right. Cliff had drilled it into our heads that married couples couldn't be compelled to testify against each other.

"I can imagine. The Herbaughs are an intimidating family, to say the least, am I right?" The chief picked up his cup and took a sip of what I could only imagine was now cold coffee. "You always knew Lucinda was the one for you, though, huh?"

"Yes, sir." I stared at the table in front of me and felt my shoulders slump. The lights in the room were too bright, and the spot behind my eyes began to throb.

"I can respect that. You get in with a family like the Herbaughs, you're set for life, right?"

"Right," I agreed before looking up sharply. "No, it wasn't like that."

Chief Young held up his hands in surrender. "It's okay, I get it. You loved her—Lucinda that is, right?"

"I did—I do!"

"You were only in a hurry to start your lives together, which is why you had the quickie wedding."

I nodded furiously, the movement making my brain feel like it was rattling inside my skull.

"You would never hurt Cliff's little girl—"

"Of course not!"

"You would never do anything to ruin the good thing you had going, and you'd do whatever necessary to keep it—"

"Absolutely!" Then I realized how that might sound. "Wait, that's not what I meant—"

He was confusing me. I couldn't even remember the question he had asked. Why did it sound like he was accusing me of something? And while it held some truth, not all of it was accurate. I did love Lucinda. Lord knows I had worked hard to convince myself of that.

Maybe some would say she had trapped me. But I had wanted the life she offered, hadn't I? Even when our mutual fantasy of having a large family of our own was shattered when it took so long to conceive McKenzie. I stayed during all those childless years because I believed it was what I deserved. Almost as if our dreams dying, one at a time, was some sort of cosmic karma.

Yet, after *that night*, I had to admit, I had been scared. I knew better than to go against her and what she wanted.

"Of course, I get it. She was young and beautiful, her family is powerful, nothing could compare to that."

I stared at him helplessly, not sure how to answer without making it sound worse. The Herbaugh family *was* powerful and they could, and did, do so much for me and my mom, but that wasn't the whole story.

It wasn't *our* story.

Lucinda's and mine.

Our story was thick with plot twists and side characters. It was never black and white—before *or* after Jenn came into our lives.

I had been surprised the first time Lucinda spoke to me. I had admired her from afar, never daring to approach her. When she became my girlfriend, I felt like I had won the lottery. I never really knew why she chose me out of all the boys who would have crawled over broken glass to be by her side, but I had counted myself more than lucky.

But I could admit now that I was forever searching for the high I had felt when she approached me that day in the Fern River High School hallway. The way my heart pounded and my veins fizzled at her nearness. The excitement of having something everyone else wanted.

I was always looking for the endorphin rush I only received when a pretty girl gave me her attention.

Unfortunately, our marriage had extinguished the flame instead of nurturing it.

"Long hair, tan skin, free to come and go as she pleased. Seemed like the kind of woman who took direction from the man in her life. Hard to say no to that, right?"

I nodded, and then shook my head, feeling my brow furrow. Who was he talking about? Lucinda could be described as many things, but she never took direction from anyone, let alone a man.

"You still love her?" he asked suddenly.

"Who?" I croaked.

Chief Young narrowed his eyes, like I was a fish flopping on the end of a hook. "Lucinda, of course. Your wife. Who else would I be talking about?"

I felt like I had messed up somehow. I scrambled to find my footing again.

"Of course." My voice sounded raspy.

"Even after all this time? It doesn't get stale? I know me and the missus needed to shake things up after a while, and we haven't been together since high school like you two."

I felt my back stiffen at the implication. "No, it's not stale."

He leaned in close, almost conspiratorial. "That Lucinda sure is a beautiful woman, but I've known her since she was born. I know how uptight she is. I love the girl like she's my own, but everyone knows she can be controlling. Cliff and I used to laugh that Lucinda was more dictator than homecoming queen. No wonder your head was turned when you saw Jennifer. Must be hard being second fiddle in your own relationship."

My heart began to pound so hard I was having trouble breathing.

I was so tired. If I could sleep for thirty minutes, I could organize my thoughts better. The chief made some notes in the file as he kept peppering me with questions.

"How did you two even meet? Miss Moore was in town for only a few months. From the sounds of it, you got to know each other pretty well in such a short amount of time. Though you were in college then, right? And plannin' that big wedding you were supposed to have. How did you even have the time to hang out with a new friend?" He regarded me levelly.

I dragged both hands down my face in a feeble attempt at blotting out her memory.

"So?" he prompted.

"So?" I was confused again.

"Lucinda's always been it, huh?" He raised an eyebrow, changing the subject once more. "You never wanted another woman? You're a one-woman man?"

I nodded, not trusting myself to speak.

We both knew the truth.

It was the reason I was sitting here, after all.

"I have to ask you, because I wouldn't be doing my job if I didn't, where were you on the evening of July 12, 2010? I know it was a long time ago, but try and jog your memory."

"Uh, I was with . . . Lucinda."

The chief wasn't smiling anymore. He was very, very serious. "That's right. She was your alibi." He sucked on his teeth noisily as he seemed to deliberate. "But maybe that's not how things actually were."

I started to protest, but the chief held up his hand. "I'm not sayin' you lied or anything, but sometimes, in the heat of the moment, stories get messed up in our head. What sounds like fact maybe isn't." He never gave me a moment to think as he went on. "So, I'm asking you to think long and hard about where you were that night. Whether what you said back then is the truth or not. I know fifteen years is a long time ago, but it's amazing what you actually remember later."

The last thing I wanted was to think about that night. And I sure as hell wasn't going to share those memories with Charles Young. I wasn't a *complete* idiot.

"More coffee, that's what we need." Charles slammed his hands down, making me jump. I hit the table, knocking over the paper cup. The last remnants of black liquid spilled onto the file he had brought with him.

He quickly picked it up, shaking it dry, cursing under his breath.

"Sorry about this," he muttered before opening the file and spreading the contents on the table. I froze at the sight of *her* face staring back at me.

"Let me go get some napkins and some fresh coffee while you keep jogging that memory of yours. I'll be right back."

Chief Young left the room, leaving me alone with the black-and-white image of Jenn's dead body, bent at an awkward angle in the thick brambles at the side of the road. I knew that stretch well. I used to drive it almost daily but refused to visit it now.

Without thinking, I reached out a trembling finger, my throat squeezed tight, and placed it on her cold, gray cheek.

Even in death she looked beautiful. But the dried blood caking the side of her face told a story of violence and suffering that made me sick inside.

Tears dripped onto her image as I took long, gasping breaths. I picked up the picture and brought it closer to my face, wishing I could smell her floral body wash one last time, or feel the softness of her hair against my bare chest. If I thought hard enough, I could still hear her voice and her teasing laughter.

The way she made me feel alive.

Important.

Desired.

Like I was the one in control.

I hadn't seen her face in over a decade, but her image lived vibrantly in my mind every day.

As usual, the guilt I felt when I thought about her rushed through me in waves. She had brought me to life, and I had brought her only death.

The door opened suddenly, yanking me from my memories. Glynn Walker stormed into the room and saw the picture in my hand.

"Put that down and pull yourself together," he barked.

I dropped the photo as if I had been burned.

Chief Young stepped inside and closed the door behind him. He sat down again, indicating for Glynn to do the same. He held a ceramic cup in his hand—not the paper cups from earlier—and he had only one for himself. He looked at me as he took a long gulp.

It was then that I knew I was really in trouble. That this whole thing had been a setup to break me. And that even Glynn Walker might not be able to get me out of it.

"Look, if you're not going to charge my client with anything, then you need to release him immediately," Glynn said with irritation.

Chief Young looked through the file and pulled out a piece of paper and handed it to Glynn. "Well, here's the thing, Mr. Walker, we have an eyewitness that not only places your client with the victim the night she was murdered, but they also say that Mr. Clark is the one that killed her."

Glenn Walker snorted, barely glancing at the paper in his hand before tossing it on the table. "That's all hearsay and circumstantial at best. It will never hold up in court. You know that. I know that. And there's no way the commonwealth attorney will agree to charges based on an eyewitness and a shoddy confession about events that happened fifteen years ago." Glenn Walker looked over at me with a smugness I wasn't sure was earned.

"I agree, Mr. Walker. You can't build a case on a single witness statement. That would be ridiculous," Chief Young said. He tapped the screen of the tablet I'd noticed earlier and then pushed it toward my attorney. The smugness faded instantly.

"Where did this come from?" Glynn watched the screen, his mouth pressed into a thin line.

"The eyewitness, of course," the chief responded.

"Don't you find the timing suspect? Why wasn't this handed over years ago?" Glenn demanded, glancing at me but not meeting my eyes. The confidence had leeched out of him.

"What is it?" I whispered, peering over his shoulder.

"Let him have a look," Chief Young said nonchalantly.

Glynn slid the tablet toward me, and I pushed play. Old grainy footage began playing, showing a place I knew all too well. I was on the screen, only younger. And there was Jenn. She seemed so young and vulnerable, and I stood before her looking like the worst kind of man. The kind that would hurt a defenseless girl.

This video did a damn good job of making me look like a monster.

I knew exactly who had made this video too. At the time I had barely registered him recording the heated fight between Jenn and me. I was too lost in my own hurt feelings and pride.

But now, it painted a very bad picture.

I turned it off, unable to look at the horrific image of blood spattering the rocks. I didn't need to watch it, anyway. I had lived it. The memories of that night had tattooed themselves on my soul.

"Sure, it may seem strange, but it doesn't change that this video, paired with the physical evidence we now have that connects your client to the victim, and potentially, the murder scene, tells a very compelling narrative. And our friend the commonwealth attorney thinks this provides a strong foundation to build a case. Everyone is eager to get this cold case off the books."

"What?" I rasped, barely audible.

The chief looked pleased. "I'm afraid it's true, Rhett. We have enough here to arrest you—"

Glynn put a reassuring hand on my arm. "Don't say anything, Rhett." He turned back to the police chief. "Are you arresting my client? Otherwise, this can be construed as intimidation—"

The chief got to his feet and took out his handcuffs. "Yes, that's exactly what I'm sayin'. Rhett, I need you to get to your feet and put your hands behind your back."

The words *You have the right to remain silent* thudded in my ears. I thought I heard talk of bail hearings and being held until the judge could schedule it. Cliff's name was dropped more than once, but I could barely follow what was happening.

It had been fifteen years since Jenn had been murdered. Fifteen years of carrying the guilt and the burden of her death on my shoulders. I was almost relieved that this was finally coming to a head.

As I was led back to my holding cell, I wondered what Jenn would be doing now if she were still alive. The life she might have led if it hadn't been snuffed out so brutally.

If she had never met *me.*

I had years to do the right thing, but I never did. I was a coward. I always had been.

My mom once said that women changed men for the better, but I believed the opposite. Women made you do crazy, unimaginable, violent things. They made you do unforgivable things that forced you to become a stranger, even to yourself.

Jenn had met me at a time in my life when I had no control over anything. My future had been mapped out by everyone else. But Jenn had given me a taste of what it would feel like to be the one in charge. She was timid and demure. She needed *me.* With Jenn, I had found the control I had been craving, and in the end it had killed her.

Jenn was dead because of me, so maybe it was time that I paid for it.

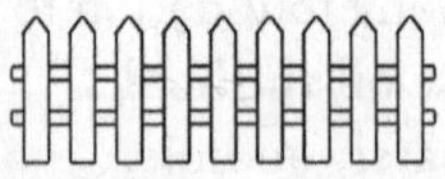

Today 8:18 AM

Hey Amy, have you spoken to Lucinda recently?

No, why? Is this about Rhett getting arrested?

Caleb's mom said the police were at their house, walked him out in handcuffs!

My aunt Kay heard Rhett resisted arrest and was tased in the street!

I always knew him getting mixed up with that girl was bad news. Ruining a guy's life like that, the tramp deserves what happened to her.

Come on Al, everyone knows Rhett's guilty. He's Cliff Herbaugh's son-in-law, so of course he's gotten away with murder! Don't ever trust a "nice" guy.

CHAPTER

5

Jenn

The Past

Mid-May—Fifteen Years Ago

THE SHEETS WERE scratchy. The pillow was as flat as a pancake. The room temperature fluctuated between freezing and sweltering.

But it didn't bother me. I was grateful I had a roof over my head for ten dollars a night. It was a hell of a lot better than the budget motels I had been staying in since leaving home.

I suppressed a shudder at the memory of the stained comforters and TVs bolted to the floor. The sounds of sex and violence on the other side of the wall.

I had never felt so alone. Or so vulnerable. I started to doubt my reasons for running away. Maybe it wasn't so bad. It couldn't be worse than what I encountered out *here*.

But then I remembered. And that was enough for me to put my thumb out and hitch a ride to another town. Another state.

Far, far away from the pain I left behind, and never look back.

I quickly got dressed, making sure to slide my three silver bangles onto my right wrist. My one reminder of home.

I tied my hair back in a ponytail and quietly left my room, hoping to avoid Ms. Cora Stanley, the owner of the B&B. She was a nice enough lady, but she was a little too interested in where I came from. She seemed nervous having an "unattached young lady" staying in her establishment.

"Don't you have a man to travel with you?" she asked me that first night.

"No, I'm alone," I told her.

Ms. Stanley had tutted under her breath before narrowing her eyes. "This isn't one of those hourly places off the highway. I don't condone sin under my roof."

I had to swallow a laugh. I knew she was serious. She had the look of someone who had never had a good sinning in her whole sorry life.

"I promise I only need a place to sleep," I said with all the solemnity of the God-fearing church girl I used to be.

After that she had taken to writing a daily Bible passage on the breakfast board in the dining room. I half expected her to kidnap me and force me to church. But she was harmless. And I knew she meant well. That didn't mean I wanted to be drawn into any prolonged conversations with her.

It was a pretty day, and I wanted to do a little exploring. I hurried out the front door and down the sidewalk. It was early, only a little after eight in the morning, so the streets were remarkably quiet.

Fern River was nestled in the rolling tulip-tree scented hills of Kentucky. The kind of town that moved at its own pace, lazy but deliberate. Cobblestone streets and old red brick storefronts lined the small, well-maintained town center.

I felt invisible here, like I could blend in and go unnoticed, and for the first time since running away I felt like I could relax—at least a little. The town was almost picture-perfect, something my mother would have called quaint. A place where she would have loved to live. But my mom, along with the rest of my family, would never leave the place they were from. Their world was small. Maybe that was why I liked Fern River so much. As tiny as it was, it still felt bigger than anything I had ever known. Not that I planned to be there long enough to appreciate it.

I headed to the pretty downtown area. There wasn't much there, but every shop appeared to have a purpose. The ice cream stand seemed to have a permanent line, and there was a small fountain that kids were running in and out of. The library doors swung open and closed continuously, and the hardware store looked busy, indicating that for a small town, it had life to it.

I passed a brick building that housed the local police department, then a bait and tackle shop, and finally I stopped outside Crème Dulce Bakery, a cute little café.

I put my hand in my pocket and pulled out a twenty dollar bill. On a whim I went into the bakery and bought a ridiculously expensive cinnamon roll and then sat on a wooden bench in the small park by the movie theater. The marquee advertised a new action movie and an animated film I had seen commercials for on TV.

I loved to people watch. It was the best way to get to know a place. I could figure out most everything I needed to know about a town by observing the people who lived there.

Fern River didn't seem to be the sort of town that liked hustle and bustle. People took their time, even when they looked busy. They stopped and talked to each other. Everyone seemed to know everyone else.

I watched a small group of teenagers laughing as they walked together down the street. I felt a tug of longing in my chest for something I'd never had.

"Hey, Jenn."

I glanced up to see Rhett, the man I had met a week ago when I arrived. The one who had bought me a pistachio ice cream cone.

My heart did a little flip.

We had messaged back and forth a few times, but I hadn't seen him in person since. Even though I had looked out for him every time I left the B&B.

Even over text he seemed like such a nice guy. He was friendly and eager to help out the new girl in town.

"Hey." I smiled.

He smiled back and I noticed he had an adorable dimple in his left cheek. He really didn't look like a "Rhett." The name reminded me of Clark Gable, my mom's favorite old time actor, and he was as far from dark and brooding as you could get.

This Rhett had light-brown hair that was a little on the curly side. His nose was too big and his chin too pointy. He was tall and gangly as if he had yet to grow into his limbs. But he had that smile and a goodness about him that felt genuine.

"Oh, nice choice. The cinnamon rolls at Dulce are the best," he exclaimed.

I looked down at my half-eaten pastry then on a whim I patted the bench beside me. "Well, you better help me eat it, then."

His eyes widened slightly. "Oh, I wasn't expecting you to share your breakfast. It's okay, you enjoy it."

He had the look of a happy puppy, and I had always been a sucker for a puppy.

"I'll enjoy it more with company," I said, breaking off half of the remaining cinnamon roll and holding it out to him.

He hesitated and cast a quick look around, but then sank down beside me, taking the pastry and shoving it into his mouth. "Thanks," he mumbled, his mouth full.

"Man, someone was hungry." I chuckled, enjoying the way Rhett's cheeks colored in what I guessed was embarrassment. He really was cute.

"I guess so." He looked around again."I hoped I'd run into you."

"Oh yeah?" I couldn't keep the anticipation out of my voice.

"Yeah." He gave me a sweet smile that I had to return.

"You could have told me that when you messaged me. We could have made plans," I told him, holding up my ancient Nokia.

"I know." He ducked his head before giving me a bashful sideways glance. "But I always get awkward around beautiful women."

I didn't even try to stop the grin this time.

He thought I was beautiful.

He moved a little closer, our arms brushing. I noticed he didn't move away. We stayed pressed up together on the old wooden bench like a lovey-dovey couple. The kind I always dreamed of being a part of.

"So, uh, how are you liking Fern River?" he asked.

It was my turn to look around. "It's nice. Really quiet. "

Rhett grimaced. "Unless you want to go hunting or fishing, there's nothing really to do. Though there are some great places if you like hiking." His face lit up.

"I like that there's not much going on," I told him. "I hate cities. The noises, the smells, the cars."

"If I lived in an interesting big city, it'd be hard for me to leave," he replied wistfully. "Though, if you're looking for a marginally good time, we *do* have a bowling alley over on Chestnut Ridge. They recently got their liquor license and don't card. It's where people under twenty-one go to get cheap beer."

"I'm not much of a drinker," I confessed. "I just turned eighteen. I have to admit I've never done the whole underage drinking thing."

He smiled again, and I couldn't get enough of the way it made the dimple in his cheek pop. "Yeah, I've never been into it either. I'm only nineteen myself. I figure I have all the time in the world to get shitfaced when I'm legal."

"I love bowling, though. I was in a ten-pin league back home," I found myself saying.

"Oh yeah? I'm horrible at bowling. I still have to use the bumper rails," he said self-deprecatingly.

I finished the cinnamon roll and threw the napkin in the trashcan. "Maybe you need a good teacher," I said. Our eyes met, and I knew I wasn't imagining the little spark there.

"Maybe you're right," he agreed.

It felt wrong to flirt with him when I had no intention of staying in town longer than a week or two.

But didn't I deserve to feel good for a little while?

Didn't I deserve to be a teenager flirting with boys and not having a care in the world? My life had been so hard. It would be nice to feel normal.

"Should we go bowling, then?" I asked.

Rhett's eyes clouded slightly. "I uh—" My stomach clenched at his obvious reluctance. But then his face brightened. "Maybe we could go hiking instead."

"Hiking?"

He nodded. "There's this great place outside town. I actually walk up there all the time, no car needed. It's called Jagged Point. During the day, especially in the middle of the week, it's pretty quiet. What do you say?"

"Sounds fun," I said with a little too much enthusiasm. "When do you want to go?"

"Oh, umm . . ." There was that hesitation again. He was the one that suggested meeting up, and now he acted unsure.

"It's okay if you don't want to." I felt the need to let him off the hook.

He grabbed my hand. "No, I really want to. It's only that—I'm so busy. I'm pre-law at college and I have exams coming up and . . . Yeah, it's hard to do anything at the moment." He looked apologetic.

I couldn't help feeling disappointed. "I get it. You don't need to worry about me," I assured him.

He frowned, lost in thought. "You know what, let's go tomorrow," he said firmly. "Who cares about studying."

I felt the buzzing of unfiltered joy. "Well, if you're sure, I'd love to go hiking with you."

Rhett squeezed my hand. "I'll text you directions. Like I said, it's an easy walk."

I didn't ask why he couldn't pick me up. Or why we couldn't walk together. I was simply happy he wanted to hang out together.

We were interrupted by the shrill sound of a phone ringing.

He pulled his Blackberry out of his pocket and looked at the screen. "I have to take this." He abruptly got to his feet. "I'll message you later."

He looked at me for one lingering moment, and I wasn't sure if I was imagining the longing in his expression. But then he was rushing off, the phone pressed to his ear.

I heard him apologizing to the person on the other end for being late before he was out of earshot and I was left alone again.

I watched as he ran across the street to a beat-up white Honda Civic parked in front of the library.

It felt silly to be sad that he left so quickly. I didn't even know him, and yet it felt good to have a small connection. It had been a long time since I'd had that with anyone.

I sighed, feeling unreasonably despondent. But then he turned around and waved, and I could see his sweet smile again. I lifted my hand and waved back, the heavy load in my chest lightening, if only a little bit.

I felt like, perhaps, I had made a friend.

I watched as he sped down the street like he was wanted for murder.

One thing was for sure, I wanted to see him tomorrow. And he might be the distraction I needed.

Perhaps Fern River could become something like home.

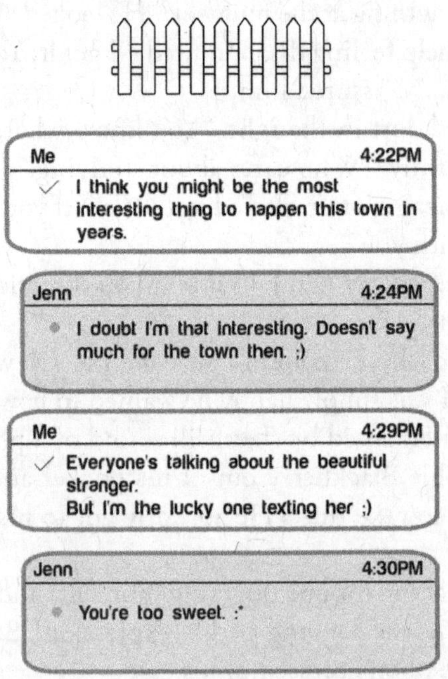

CHAPTER

6

Lucinda

The Present

I HADN'T BEEN OUT here since I was a child.

I avoided it at all costs.

I thought about Rhett and wondered if he still wandered the gravel path. Whether he ambled along the tree line, remembering a woman that was long gone but never silent.

I didn't know what made me drive out to this desolate spot after Mom and McKenzie had fallen asleep. But I felt compelled to. It was an irresistible urge I knew I couldn't fight.

Maybe I was looking for the serenity and solitude that my husband claimed he found there one upon a time.

Maybe I was hoping I could face the darkness that lived there and come out victorious.

Whatever the reason, here I was. In the woods. Alone. In the dark.

Probably not my smartest idea if I was being honest. Yet I knew what the real danger in these woods was, and it wasn't the bears or bobcats.

I pulled the flashlight from my pocket and turned it on, making my way along the twists and turns of the now overgrown trail. The county used to maintain it. The gravel would be replaced regularly and the weeds chopped back.

Now . . . ever since *the body*, no one bothered. As if it had been a collective decision to try to forget it ever existed.

I wished it were that easy for me.

The air felt heavy and thick in a way that had nothing to do with the temperature or weather. This was a space that had *seen things*.

I never understood how Rhett found peace in such a place. In trees and rocks laden with a morbid past.

A past even more morbid now because of Jenn.

I shivered as the memory of her skittered across my brain. A whisper of a breeze whistled in my ears. The sound of laughter echoed off the boulders.

And inexplicably, I swore I could hear the tinkling of windchimes.

I started to walk faster, but it quickly built to a run as my need to get away from there overtook me. It was a fast-paced sprint as I traversed the mile it took to reach the end.

I stumbled over roots, barely staying upright, until I reached the cliffs.

With my lungs on fire, I looked out over the valley, instinctively knowing the direction of Fern River.

It was beautiful in a cold, foreboding way. Stars shone overhead, the full moon lighting up the sky so I didn't need the flashlight now I was out of the thick of the woods.

I stood there for a long time. Until my breathing slowed and my limbs stopped quivering, as I watched the town below.

And I felt the embrace of ghosts that would never leave me.

* * *

I stared at the glowing numbers on my alarm clock. Watching as the minutes rolled by.

I had been lying in bed since midnight trying to rest, but my mind wouldn't stop its manic race from one worst-case scenario to the next. With a frustrated sigh I sat up, giving up on sleep altogether.

Mom was sleeping on the sofa bed in McKenzie's room. We hadn't spoken much when she showed up. She made me a cup of chamomile tea and instructed me to sit in the living room.

"Put your feet up and watch something to get your mind off all this," she said. She handed me the remote control after turning on a reality dating show that under normal circumstances, I would have been happy to watch.

But not today.

"Sorry, Mom, watching people jump in and out of each other's beds like horny rabbits is not my idea of a good time right now," I'd snapped, my voice rising, "or did you forget my husband is being interrogated by the police for murder. He's not down there making ori-fucking-gami!" The rage came quickly and wasn't entirely connected to the situation.

I wasn't mad *about* my husband, I was mad *at* him.

Mom had looked taken aback by my hostility. After that night all those years ago, I knew she was unnerved by me. In fact, she often appeared on edge around our entire family.

There had been so many times I'd longed for a relationship with her where I could tell her my secrets and she'd love me anyway. Because, deep down, I was still a little girl that craved the affection and approval of her parents.

But that wasn't the way things were—and they never would be.

"Maybe we should call Bailey. She'll come over and sit with you. She's worried about you and Rhett. She's absolutely beside herself," Mom said.

"I don't *need* Bailey. You and I both know being helpful is not exactly her strong suit."

Mom had opened her mouth to speak, but I held up my hand, cutting her off. I inwardly flinched at the panic on her face.

She had once been such a force. She had been strong and in charge. Everyone knew who held the true power in my parents' relationship—and it was Mabel Jean.

But over the years she'd become more diminished. She was skittish and overanxious. Now, she backed down much too easily, avoiding a fight rather than jump into one the way she used to. And there was a look of pure fright that would appear on her face that was the strongest indicator something had fractured within my once indomitable mother. The only person that could make her smile anymore was McKenzie.

It made the guilt even worse.

"I'm sorry, Mom," I said wearily.

Mom patted her hair nervously. "Oh, it's fine. It's a stressful time for everyone."

"I know you're only trying to help. I'll call Bailey tomorrow."

"Yes, well . . ." Mom looked around uneasily. "I think I'll go check on McKenzie."

"You don't need to do that." I pointed to the baby monitor perched on the coffee table.

"Oh, right. Well, I still think one of us should be up there in case she wakes up and wonders where her daddy is." Before I could argue anymore, Mom disappeared up the stairs and I heard the door of my daughter's room open and shut softly over the static-y airwaves.

I knew she was only offering so she could get away from me. I wished I would stop letting my parents' dismissal bother me so much.

Then, I had walked to the kitchen and dumped the contents of my mug down the drain and grabbed the car keys and left for Jagged Point before I could talk myself out of it.

Going there had been a bad idea. It brought those memories far too close to the surface. I worked hard to suppress them. To pretend they never existed in the first place.

I was really good at make-believe. It's the only way I had been able to stay married all these years.

But right now, I was torturing myself with second-guessing. I needed to get my head together. And driving out *there* hadn't helped a thing.

It had only reminded me why I avoided the place to begin with. It was too dark. Too silent. Like it sat there in judgment of all my mistakes. The trees and rocks knew my secrets and sometimes, when the wind blew, it felt like they were trying to reveal them.

I returned home quickly then went straight to bed, leaving every light blazing, terrified that the darkness had followed me home.

But I hadn't slept.

I stupidly thought I could put my demons to rest for at least a little while.

I was so very, very wrong.

And as the minutes ticked by, Rhett still hadn't come home.

Lately, I had grown accustomed to his empty side of the bed. He was often late coming home from work for one reason or another. Or he would stay up long after me, sometimes into the early hours. I had become used to the loneliness, accepting that was the way it was going to be. But this was different. This felt like something final.

Lying in bed now, staring at the ceiling, I thought of all the ways this could go. The only conclusion I came to was that this situation needed to be managed very carefully.

Just like last time.

Because, no matter what, I was determined that the memory of Jennifer Moore wouldn't come back to haunt me.

I stared out the bedroom window at the hazy early morning light. Dawn was coming hard and fast, and I felt unprepared for the day ahead. I knew Kenz would ask for her daddy first thing, as she did every morning. She'd expect Rhett to feed her waffles and sing "Here Comes the Sun" by the Beatles on repeat until it was time to go to daycare.

I'd rather be interrogated for murder myself than sing *anything* that many times.

But Rhett had always been better at the whole parenting thing than I was. In truth, he was a much better father than he was a husband. Being a dad came so naturally to him.

He and McKenzie had an easy bond that felt alien to me. As much as I tried, I couldn't connect with our child the way Rhett did. In the early days I had suffered from postpartum depression, and caring for McKenzie felt overwhelming. Rhett had swooped in and taken over, giving our daughter all the love and devotion that felt so difficult for me to provide. But once I was myself again, I tried to pick up the pieces only to find I wasn't needed. My role had been usurped, and it was clear Rhett didn't plan on giving it back.

Maybe I should have fought harder for it, but Rhett made it seem like he was doing me a favor. After all, how many women had husbands who were so hands-on with parenting? While my friends struggled with fussy babies and little sleep, I was fresh-faced and well-rested because Rhett took over everything.

"You sleep in. I'll make Kenz breakfast."

"Why don't you get a manicure, Lucinda? McKenzie and I are going to the park."

"I know you hate Disney movies. Why don't you read a book in bed? I'll put Kenz down."

Before I knew it, I had become extraneous.

My phone lit up on the bedside table. I answered without looking to see who it was.

"Rhett?"

"No, Lucinda, it's your father. Where's your mother?" My dad's voice sounded gravelly from what was most likely too little sleep.

"She's with Kenz." I braced myself. "Is Rhett with you?" I could only imagine how awkward that would be for both men.

Dad had never cared much for Rhett. Despite pushing me to find a nice young man and settle down, he hadn't wanted that man to be Rhett. Especially after he turned his back on my father's plan for him and decided to become a teacher instead of a lawyer. Dad had no patience for people who didn't keep their word, and Rhett had shown his meant nothing.

Dad had lost both his parents as a boy and because of that, his family was his first, and most important, priority. He was protective to a fault and his desire to pave a smooth path for me had definitely made my life more comfortable, if not easier. Because in his need to keep me safe, he also kept me under his thumb. I had learned from an early age that it was better to accept my fate than fight it. Trying to forge my own path never got me very far, anyway.

Even still, my father was a man with a strong moral compass, yet he was also the same man who got me out of my first speeding ticket. For Dad, most things were black and white—except where his wife and daughters were concerned. Then things were a hazy shade of gray.

There was nothing he wouldn't do if he felt his family's well-being—and his reputation—was on the line. It made him wildly unpredictable in the worst possible way. But it also comforted me to have the steady reassurance that no matter how bad it got, Dad was there to take care of it.

"No," Dad said. "He's still at the station. Lucinda, he's been arrested."

I sat down heavily on my bed, not sure what to say. "Okay."

"I just got off the phone with Glynn. He's still down there—"

"Wait, you're not with him?" I frowned in confusion. "Where are you?"

I heard my father's exasperated sigh on the other end. He hated to be questioned about anything. "Well, I wasn't going to stand around at the police station with my thumb up my ass. There was nothing I could do. Chuck wouldn't talk to me."

Normally, Chuck wouldn't make a move without consulting my father. He ran every case by Dad, wanting his advice. They had been best friends since elementary school. But clearly, if Charles Young was keeping his lips sealed, this was serious. Uncle Chuck only played by the rules when too many eyes were on him.

"I *was* able to speak briefly with Betty Poole," he went on. "She's the pretrial services officer, but she wasn't any help. I was all but frozen out."

I knew he wasn't used to not being able to wield his power and influence. He had built his career on his connections, and they had failed him. It seemed to have rattled his confidence.

"What does that mean, Dad?"

"It means that this is serious. If Chuck isn't talking to me, it means people will be paying close attention and my hands will be tied. I don't like not knowing what's coming. It's not how I operate. I like to plan for every outcome." His frustration at his impotence was palpable.

"What can I do?" I asked, my voice firm with resolve. I wasn't the kind of person to fall apart. Ever.

"Not much at the moment. Rhett's being held until his bail hearing. I asked Betty why the wait, and she gave me some song and dance about Harry Balfour being down in Georgia until Tuesday. She claimed she couldn't put it on the docket until after the judge was back. I can tell you, it's bad for Rhett that he's been assigned the case. He's hated me ever since I had him thrown out for contempt when he was a shitty defense attorney."

I had heard the story before. There were only a few people in Fern River impervious to my father's charms and influence, and Judge Balfour was one of them.

"But maybe," Dad continued, "this will give that husband of yours time to think about his actions."

My dad was a "tell like it is" man. You always got the truth from him, whether you wanted it or not.

"Listen, Lucinda, you were Rhett's alibi fifteen years ago. It was one of the main reasons I was able to dampen the heat on him so quickly. Chuck believed me—and you—when you said the two of you were together. I stupidly never asked if there were holes in that story. Whether anyone could contradict what you told me. But, I'm asking you now. Were there any times you and Rhett weren't together? Could someone have seen him? Could this supposed eyewitness be legitimate?"

"I'm not a liar, Dad," I insisted, inserting enough offense for my dad to know how upset I was by the question.

Another silence. This one was longer and heavier than before.

"It sounds like this eyewitness is credible and they have evidence—"

"I'm sure they do," I scoffed, my voice laden with sarcasm.

"Lucinda, I think you need to start preparing yourself," Dad said. "I've always done everything I can to protect this family—*my* family. Because you were committed to that man, I kept him out of it. I used *my* name and *my* connections to make sure he never saw the inside of a courtroom—against my better judgment. I shouldn't have bothered. It would have saved us all a lot of grief. Because if the evidence is as strong as I suspect, then Rhett might be on his own this time. I'm not sure there's anything I can do now."

Part of me knew this day would come. My dad was talking about wiping his hands of all this. Of *Rhett*.

"What makes this different from before?" It was a simple question, but a pointed one. I never contradicted my father. I trusted him completely. But I wondered what his motives were at this point.

"Lucinda, you know I'll look out for you and Kenz. Rhett may be *your* husband, but he's not my blood. He's done nothing but hurt and disappoint you and put my family at risk. I only ever wanted you to be safe and happy and I thought he could, at the very least, give you that. But I was wrong. I should have listened to my gut and not your tears. Then we wouldn't be here," Dad reminded me coldly.

"Is that your father on the phone?" My mother appeared in the doorway holding a sleepy McKenzie. They looked so natural together. As if *they* were the mother and child. My mother so easily slotted into the role of McKenzie's caretaker, and my daughter gravitated to her with adoration.

I nodded to her, holding up a finger impatiently, focusing on my dad.

"Glynn will call you about the time of Rhett's bail hearing. I'm assuming you'll want to go—" Dad was saying.

"Of course I do!"

"Okay, well, I'll see you later today. I'll come by to check on McKenzie, make sure our girl's doing all right. I'll get to the courthouse early Tuesday so I can try to have a word with Harry before he enters his chambers. I doubt he'll talk to me, but I can try. I'll be damned if I'm going into this blind. I need to know what direction this is headed."

"Great." My voice was hollow, just like I felt.

"And, Lucinda, keep your mouth shut. The best thing is to remain silent. Don't talk to anyone about what's going on," Dad instructed gruffly. "This is family business."

"I've been through this before and got the crummy T-shirt, Dad," I retorted before handing the phone to my mother and taking my daughter from her arms.

McKenzie laid her cheek against my chest, and I relished in the feel of her solid warmth. "Daddy," she murmured, sucking on her fist in the way she did when she was hungry. I swallowed down the pain I felt at how she always called for him and never me.

"Daddy's not here. It's just Mommy." I carried her from the room, leaving my parents to talk.

"Daddy," McKenzie repeated, this time more insistently. She only ever said a handful of words, with *Daddy* being the most frequent. Lately when it wasn't *Daddy*, it was *Nanna*, showing her preference for my mother if Rhett wasn't available. Even with my own child, I was never enough.

"Well, Daddy has made a big ole mess that Mommy has to clean up," I replied sweetly, knowing she didn't understand a word I said.

It was nice telling truths to someone who would never repeat them. McKenzie was the best secret keeper there was.

"How about chocolate chip pancakes for breakfast?" I asked her, making sure my voice was as perky as possible. Nothing like bribing your toddler with sugar to get her to hang out with you.

Her eyes, the exact shade of mine, lit up. My daughter was a tiny carbon copy of me. Rhett may be able to claim her affection, but no one would ever doubt she was mine.

Pushing all the ugliness from my mind, I went about my morning as normally as possible.

* * *

I sat in the stiflingly hot office of my husband's defense attorney. It looked as if it had been staged like a magazine spread. Expensive desk and chairs. Plush couches in a traditional dark plaid fabric. Gleaming hardwood floors and overly patterned curtains.

On prominent display was a large, framed diploma from University of Virginia Law School. Glynn Walker was a man who would show that off. I got the sense he was all talk and didn't have a lot to back up the pretension. A decent lawyer didn't have to show off so much.

My dad's office by comparison was bare, with only a wall full of law books and a heavy desk made of walnut in the center of the room. The only personal touch was a framed print stating, "A good lawyer knows the law. A great lawyer knows the judge." This mantra had served him well, and his trial record spoke for itself. He didn't need to be flashy.

I sat back in my seat and faced off with Glynn Walker. "Can I visit him?"

"No, family aren't permitted visitation to a holding cell, which is what he's in. You'll see him at his bail hearing on Tuesday. I expect his bail to be high, given the charges. But he's not a flight risk and he's a first time offender, so I don't think he'll be remanded to custody until the trial." He was cut and dry. He lacked any sort of bedside manner, which is probably why he was a lawyer and not a doctor.

"Can't my dad—?"

"Not even the great Judge Herbaugh can get around this one," Glynn intoned darkly, cutting me off.

I smarted from the chastisement. "Okay, fine. He'll be home soon enough anyway."

Glynn raised a bushy eyebrow. He looked like he'd slept in his car, despite his high-end surroundings. His hair was slightly too long, and he needed a shave. His suit was rumpled even though it was pricey. "As I said, I'm assuming they'll grant bail, but we'll have to see what kind of mood Judge Balfour is in. Hopefully, he'll be magnanimous after his two-week vacation."

I crossed my arms over my chest. "I know Judge Balfour can be a bit of a ball breaker, but I'm sure he'll be reasonable."

Glynn peered at me like I was an idiot. I wanted to poke his eyes out. "It's really bad luck that of all the judges in the county, Rhett's case landed on Harry Balfour's desk. I'm sure you know he and your father have a bit of a history."

"So I've heard," I said tightly.

Glynn stared at me a little longer before opening a file on his desk, his eyes scanning the papers in front of him. "I have to be honest with you, Mrs. Clark, the evidence against your husband is significant."

I sat up straighter. "What does that mean?"

"Does the name Martin Richards ring any bells?"

I frowned, playing dumb. No way I'd reveal anything to a guy that looked like he would mansplain my menstrual cycle. "Martin Richards?"

"His friends call him Marty."

The image of a tall man with intense blue eyes instantly came to mind. As well as a scar that contorted his handsome features. I could almost smell the sweet, musky scent of weed and wood smoke that always clung to his clothes. I could still hear his deep, cruel laugh.

And I could feel the way his eyes seemed to follow me everywhere. How he saw more than I wanted him to.

"Marty? What about him? I haven't thought about him in years."

Glynn closed the file, crossing his hands over top of it. "Rhett tells me they used to be friends. That Mr. Richards worked for your parents for a while."

I chewed absently at my thumbnail. "I wouldn't really call him and Rhett *friends*. He hung out with my husband for a few months. But it's not like they were close. He was new in town." My frown deepened as my mind went through details, trying to determine which I should share . . . and which I shouldn't under any circumstances. "I can't remember where he came from, but he moved here around the same time as . . ." My voice trailed off.

"Around the same time as Jennifer Moore," he finished for me. "In fact, I hear it was within a week or two of her coming to town," Glynn volunteered with a knowing look.

I cleared my throat. "Yes, that's right." I fidgeted in my chair restlessly. "He worked for Sal Stanley, you know, the landscaper. He was part of the crew working at my parents' house. He came with the usual crowd of transients that move to the area every summer for cash-only work—" I stopped suddenly. Glynn met my eyes and gave me a small nod. "He's the eyewitness," I stated, saying out loud what we both knew.

"Seems so. He says he was with your husband the night of Miss Moore's murder and that the two of them were driving around smoking a joint and drinking when they picked her up."

"What?" I gripped my hands together in my lap. "Marty Richards is saying he and Rhett were with Jennifer that night? He's lying!" I sounded so sure. So emphatic.

Glynn raised an eyebrow and pulled a paper out of the file. "And you would know that because you were his alibi."

I cleared my throat again. The room felt close. The air conditioning was obviously not turned on high enough. "That's right." The words barely squeaked out.

Even to my ears it sounded like a lie.

Glynn looked at me again. "Except Marty produced evidence that contradicts that. A T-shirt with both Rhett *and* Jenn's blood on it." I tried to control my reaction, but Glynn wasn't even paying attention to me. "It sounds bad, but I can argue there was no chain of custody. Sure, the prosecution says Marty kept it in a Ziploc bag for all these years, but come on. No reasonable jury—or judge for that matter—will simply take his word for it. And if Judge Balfour isn't feeling particularly ornery, maybe he'll throw it out."

"You don't sound convinced," I surmised, my words careful.

"Judge Balfour isn't known for being particularly agreeable *or* reasonable, particularly where your father—or those connected to him—are concerned. So we have to hope that his vacation mellowed him out enough for him to listen to my very sensible argument." Glynn's smile was more of a wince.

"Okay, what else is there?" I asked.

Glynn sat back in his chair. "Mr. Richards also has videos on an old phone showing the three of them together, with Rhett wearing that very same T-shirt. The footage depicts a violent argument between Miss Moore and your husband that's time stamped the night of her death. Marty has told a convincing story of how Miss Moore rejected your husband's advances and he murdered her, bludgeoning her to death with a rock and leaving her body in the brambles out by Jagged Point next to the turnoff onto the main road. The police found this interesting because investigators never released a cause of death. Nor the exact location where her body was found." He pursed his lips. "So, this paired with the shirt makes your husband look very, very guilty."

"Why is this only coming out now, though? It's been years and he's never said anything. That has to look suspicious," I asked, testing him.

"I agree, and that's something I will argue when this goes to trial—because Lucinda, this *will* go to trial. There's no way this will be thrown out with a pretrial motion. They've pressed charges, and there's enough here for the prosecutor's office to build a good case against Rhett." He sat back in his chair. "But as to your question about why now, Mr. Richards is not saying much other than the truth has been preying on him and he finally wants to come clean about what he knows. He's painting it that he's offering up details as a way of assuaging a guilty conscience. Given he only lives over in Floyd County, about thirty miles from here, he'll be testifying in person at the preliminary hearing."

I had hated Rhett's friendship with Marty. Marty was the complete opposite of my once dependable, mild-mannered fiancé. He was wild and reckless. Maybe even a little exciting. Yet, there was something dark and disturbing about him as well. He had opinions I definitely didn't agree with that rubbed off on Rhett. It had caused a lot of conflict between us at the time.

I honestly couldn't even remember how they had met. It seemed one day Marty was there—sticking his nose into our lives and stirring up trouble—and the next he wasn't. And the void he left behind was far too noticeable.

"If I remember correctly, Marty left town right after the . . . the death," I added. "Maybe he's trying to make Rhett look guilty to cover *his* crime. He knows all these details, after all."

Glynn gave me a wily grin. "My thoughts exactly. This evidence, while interesting, is also circumstantial, and I can build a case of reasonable doubt. But I've heard a lot about the prosecutor. He's come all the way from Atlanta, and his trial record is one of the best on the East Coast. He knows what he's doing, and Rhett wouldn't have been arrested if the commonwealth's attorney didn't think he had a damn good case." Glynn shrugged in a way that infuriated me. "And we can't underestimate Judge Balfour's grudge against your father."

I rubbed my forehead like I did when I started getting a migraine. "I can't believe this is happening."

Glynn attempted a sympathetic expression, though it only made him appear constipated. "I'll do whatever I can for you and your family." We both knew his words were merely lip service. We were his paycheck. Nothing more, nothing less.

I wasn't in the mood to engage in niceties neither of us meant. "I'm sure my father is paying you handsomely for the privilege."

Glynn gave me a tight, closed-mouth smile. "Right, well, I think that's all for now. I'll call you to set up a time to go over that statement you made fifteen years ago. You can't be made to testify against your husband, but your official statement will be pored over with a fine-toothed comb, and I need to know it inside and out. We can discuss whether you going on the stand will help Rhett. And Lucinda," he forced a smile, "one positive is the pretrial assessment is in Rhett's favor. Ms. Poole reported that he isn't a risk to the public, nor does she believe he'll leave town. So at the very least, he'll be able to come home until the trial."

I got to my feet, eager to leave. "That's something, at least. I'll see you at the hearing."

Glynn had already turned to his computer, lifting his hand in a distracted wave.

I pushed open the heavy oak door of his office building, which was situated in the heart of downtown Fern River, and let it swing closed with a thud behind me. My thoughts were consumed by a woman who had been dead for years and still had the power to wreak havoc on my life.

The day was warm and the scent of fresh-brewed coffee drifted from the café down the street, mingling with the scent of honeysuckle from the nearby park.

My nerves were fried after the meeting with Glynn. Because as much as I came across like I wasn't concerned, deep down, I was.

I had never really known Jenn. Not until it was too late. We circled each other for only a brief period of time. When our worlds did intersect, it hadn't ended well. In truth, at the time, I had hated her, and whether that was fair or not wasn't the point. I didn't forgive easily. I hadn't then, and I definitely didn't now. And the years hadn't eroded the betrayal I had felt so acutely at the time.

However, for Jenn, I hadn't been a consideration. Perhaps she hadn't meant to mess up my life, but mess up my life she had.

And the thing was, I knew about Jennifer Moore long before she knew about me.

"Lucinda?"

I braced myself as I turned around. "Gail, hello." I tried to sound polite, but I was pretty sure I wasn't very convincing.

Gail Travers was one of Rhett's fellow teachers at the high school. She had been to my house, along with several other teachers, numerous times over the years for Christmas parties and backyard barbeques. I always made an effort when it came to Rhett's work friends, but some of them bothered me more than others. And Gail's wholesome "aw-shucks" demeanor grated on me.

She was fresh-faced, pretty, and always appeared ready to run and hide underneath a chair. She was modest and soft-spoken. I bet her students ate her up for breakfast.

"I wanted you to know none of us believe Rhett is guilty," she said in a hushed whisper, her eyes darting around as if worried she'd be overheard.

I gave her a thin-lipped smile. "That's nice of you. I'll pass along your well wishes to him."

"Oh, please do. I want him to know we're all thinking about him." She tucked a piece of strawberry-blond hair behind her ears. She looked young. In fact, she didn't seem much older than the kids she taught.

"I'm sure he knows," I replied, trying not to choke on her good will.

Gail lifted one of her grocery bags. "Well, I'd better get these home. Don't want the pistachio ice cream to melt."

"You sure don't," I retorted with a sarcasm Gail didn't pick up on.

"Take care, Lucinda. I'm praying for you and McKenzie."

Just what I needed: thoughts and stupid prayers. "Thanks, Gail."

She all but ran in the other direction, leaving me wondering why she bothered to talk to me in the first place.

I crossed the street and stopped to get out my keys. When I looked up, I realized I was standing in front of the empty shop where Crème Dulce Bakery once thrived. It had closed down five years ago when Leslie, the owner, had suffered a stroke. Nothing had taken its place, so it was now an abandoned reminder of what I once thought were happy memories.

I recalled that day we sat together, sampling cake for our wedding. Rhett and I had been young and full of hope for our future. I had never felt so completely sure of myself—*of us*.

It was a snapshot of a time that couldn't last. As wonderful as that day had been, it was also the day I felt the first seismic fissures in our relationship.

I remembered that initial stab of jealousy like it was yesterday. The swirling darkness that surged from the pit of my stomach and morphed into red-hazed fury.

I had been on my way to spin class and realized Rhett still had my phone in his pocket. He would usually hold my things for me because I hated carrying a purse. Back then we had operated like a single organism.

We were RhettandLucy.

There was never one without the other.

I had no reason to doubt him or his love for me. It's why I was so sure of our future together.

That day I had rushed back toward the bakery hoping to catch him before he left, when I saw him by the ice cream stand. He was purchasing two cones. I felt a tremor of annoyance. I had told him I couldn't eat ice cream. I was trying to watch my weight before the wedding. What was he thinking?

But the ice cream wasn't for me.

I watched as my fiancé sat beside a redheaded woman I had never seen before. He handed her the dripping cone and smiled at her in a way he only ever smiled at me.

She angled her body close to him, touching his arm.

I should have marched over there and introduced myself then. I could have held out my hand, given her a smile, and let her know, oh-so politely, that he was spoken for. But I didn't.

Instead, I hid around the corner of the bakery and watched him talk to her. His eyes didn't leave her face. They sat so closely that they practically thrummed with intimacy. Their legs brushing purposefully. Before that day, I had never wished violence on someone I had never met.

And, unfortunately, it was the first of many times I would feel that way.

Jennifer Moore brought out a brutality in me that once unleashed, couldn't be contained.

And I had been paying the price ever since.

CHAPTER 7

Rhett

The Past

Late May—Fifteen Years Ago

"So, Rhett, how are classes going?" Mr. Herbaugh asked without even looking at me. It was after seven and thankfully, the evening was nearly over. Drinks at the Herbaughs was always something to get through rather than enjoy.

"Good, sir. I have my final exams coming up that my teachers think I'm going to ace, so I'm not too concerned about them."

It was all lies.

I was failing.

I was falling asleep in class and while studying. I could barely get through a paragraph in the expensive, overly wordy law books that Mr. Herbaugh had bought for me without wanting to scratch my eyes out.

I felt my cell phone vibrate in my pocket with an incoming message, and as was the norm recently, I knew it would be Jenn.

I was itching to read it and see what she had to say. Even sitting here, being grilled by Clifford Herbaugh, I felt the buzzing of excited anticipation. Knowing she was waiting somewhere to hear from me filled me with a heady power. Jenn had a way of making me feel like I was in charge. She looked to me to dictate the pace of our friendship. I had never been in a position to make decisions in a relationship before, and I was finding it oddly addictive.

We had been hiking up at Jagged Point for weeks now. Our time together felt loaded with a gradually building tension that neither of us could ignore. I spent at least three days a week at the cliffs with her. And when we weren't together, we were messaging back and forth. Sometimes our conversations were surface level, and other times I found myself telling her things I had never told anyone else, not even Lucy.

Jenn had become important to me. So important that I was becoming less patient with Lucy's family and their heavy handedness in our lives.

Mr. Herbaugh was clearly perturbed by something I said, or hadn't said. It didn't take much. He had always made it obvious that he didn't like me. That he thought Lucy could do better.

At one time it had mattered that Lucy didn't agree with him. That she believed in me and thought me worthy. But lately, her opinion mattered less and less to me.

"Well you *should be* concerned—failing to prepare is preparing to fail, and having such a lax attitude will get you nowhere."

"Oh, Dad, of course he's studying." Lucy laughed. She stared at me, her eyes wide as she sipped her Shirley Temple. Her unspoken communication was obvious.

Tell him what he wants to hear.

My phone vibrated again. The feeling of it against my leg was comforting. Like Jenn was there with me. Her presence was a balm for my battered ego. She made me feel better when Lucy—and her family—wore me down.

We were sitting in the living room, in front of the grand wooden fireplace. It wasn't lit—it wasn't the season for it—but it was Mabel's spot for entertaining. Artwork hung on the walls, flowers and landscapes between portraits of long-deceased family members. It was decorated with red maple furniture and fussy floral curtains that probably cost more than my mom's monthly salary.

The home I shared with my mother was the complete opposite in every way, with our sagging sofa, large rug that covered the hole in the carpet, and our one luxury, the high-definition flat-screen television for my mom to watch *Family Feud* on during her lunch break.

My mom had never been to Lucy's house, despite Mabel's invitations, and I honestly never wanted her to go there. I couldn't wait for the day I could buy her a house just as nice as this one. One she didn't have to rent, but with her name on the deed. I owed it to her to give her the one thing she could never get for herself.

I realized that Mr. Herbaugh was still looking at me expectantly, waiting for an update. I shouldn't need to say the words. I had made sure to tell him often enough how much his help meant to me. How much I looked forward to following his plan for my life. Even if saying the words felt like razor blades on my tongue.

But, as with everything with Clifford Herbaugh, he expected verbal recognition. He wanted to be told exactly what I had been doing. Exactly how hard I had been working.

Which made it all the more awkward because I was lying. I *was* wasting the opportunity. And all because his profession bored me to tears.

"Yes, sir, Lucy's right. I've been studying nonstop, of course." I swirled my alcohol-free old-fashioned. I didn't know what the point of drinking it was if I couldn't at least get a buzz. I needed one to get through this interrogation.

"*Lucinda*," Mabel interrupted with a disapproving look from where she was sitting across from us. "She's not a puppy or a doll. She's a woman, and her name is *Lucinda*."

"I like it when he calls me Lucy, Mom." Lucy's voice was high-pitched and nervous. I knew how hard it was for her to speak up to her parents. I should appreciate the effort she made, but honestly, this evening had exhausted me too much to care.

"If I wanted to name you Lucy, it would be on your birth certificate. I'm sure Rhett understands why it's important to call a young lady by her proper name." Mabel gave me a frosty smile.

"Yes, sorry, ma'am. Lucinda it is."

We finished our drinks and the evening came to a close. After exchanging tense goodbyes with my future in-laws, Lucy saw me out. There was no dinner tonight, which I was thankful for. I couldn't sit through another hour or two of question and answer time with the Herbaughs. I'd rather be anywhere else, preferably with Jenn Moore.

"Rhett!" Bailey came bounding down the stairs and launched herself at me. I couldn't help but laugh as I wrapped my arms around Lucy's sister, giving her a tight hug.

"Be careful, Bailey, you'll hurt him jumping on him like that," Lucy admonished.

"It's fine, Bai. I'm big and strong. I can handle you." I gave her a wink, making her giggle.

Lucy rolled her eyes but didn't say anything else.

"You still want to play basketball after school tomorrow?" Bailey asked me, her eyes sparkling.

"I wish I could, but I have to study." Truth was I planned to see Jenn at Jagged Point. We were going hiking again. I had been looking forward to it for days.

Bailey didn't try to hide her disappointment. "But you promised," she whined.

"Bailey, you heard him. He's busy. Leave him alone." Lucy scowled at her sister.

"Fine, whatever," Bailey retorted, but I noted the sadness in her expression.

I grabbed her hand briefly. "Another time, Bai. You know I love hanging out with you."

Her face brightened. "Okay, how about Friday?"

"Sure," I answered, already knowing that wouldn't happen either. But I'd make up an excuse, and she'd understand. She was just a kid, so she trusted me unconditionally.

After Bailey headed back upstairs, Lucy opened the door for me. "Do you want to do something? We could go for a drive," Lucy suggested, her eyes hopeful.

I rubbed the back of my neck. "Honestly, I'm beat and need to get some sleep. Also, I told my mom I would help her with some stuff when I got home."

"Oh, okay." Lucy looked hurt, and I felt guilty for lying to her. I considered taking her for a drive. We used to do it all the time. Pulling over on an out-of-the-way road to kiss and talk. We hadn't done that for a while, and I knew it was my fault.

I had been preoccupied, primarily with thoughts of Jenn, and though I knew it was wrong, I wasn't ready to stop yet. Jenn made me feel calm, while Lucy stressed me out.

"Breakfast tomorrow as usual, though?" I asked instead, placating her.

"Sure, tomorrow," she replied, her voice sad even as she tried to hide it from me. She gave me a quick kiss on the cheek, barely touching her lips to my skin, and closed the heavy wooden door behind her.

I strode to my car, glad to be getting out of there. I took in a huge lungful of air, feeling like this was the first proper breath I had taken all night.

It was dark now, and I couldn't wait to get home. I wanted to lie on my bed and text Jenn, as had become my nightly routine. Sharing stories and confidences that felt safely contained within the confines of the phone screen. It was shocking how quickly I became dependent on our evening messages.

As I pulled out my car keys, I heard footsteps on the gravel. Confused at who it would be this time of evening, I was surprised to see one of the guys on the landscaping crew coming from around the side of the house.

He stopped in his tracks when he saw me. There was a moment of panic on both our faces. His because he had clearly been caught doing something he shouldn't, and mine because the guy was much bigger than me.

He had an ugly scar that ran down his face all the way to his lip that made him look scary as hell, especially in the dim light. I didn't know much about any of the staff that worked at the Herbaughs', but he didn't seem like he fit in with Sal's guys.

"I forgot my stuff." He pointed to the backpack on his shoulder, and his expression relaxed when he saw me more closely. "Oh, I thought you were one of the assholes that live here."

I should have said something about his characterization of my future in-laws, but after the round of "put Rhett on the spot" I had just endured, I wasn't feeling particularly magnanimous. "Nope. No assholes here." I chuckled.

The guy grinned and held up a crumpled baggie. "I actually forgot my weed. I stashed it in the pool house. I need a toke if I'm going to get through hours of listening to Sal talk about his mother's gout."

I held up a hand. "I get it, no worries, man."

"Any chance I could get a lift?" he asked.

I hesitated, but only for a moment. The guy looked fierce, but he seemed harmless enough. "Sure thing, hop in." We climbed in my car, and I started the engine. "I'm Rhett, by the way."

"Marty," he said. "I heard about this cool overlook outside of town. I was told it's where the locals go to hang out. I was going to head up there and have a beer and smoke this bag, if you want to join me?"

"You're talking about Jagged Point," I told him.

I pulled out onto the long stretch of road in front of the Herbaughs' house and headed back toward town.

"Yeah, that's it. Jagged Point," Marty said. "I've heard some wild stories about that place. Murders and stuff." He gave me a wicked grin.

"It definitely has a colorful past. Two hikers were found dead up there years ago. No one knows if it was natural causes or if they were killed." I played it off as insignificant, but people still talked about the long-ago deaths as if they happened yesterday.

"Gruesome." Marty didn't sound bothered by it. "And that's where you locals go to hang out? That's some morbid shit, Rhett."

"I guess so," I replied, realizing how strange it must seem to an outsider.

"So, you game to hang out with the dead folks?"

"Oh no, I'm good, thanks. But I can drop you off there. It's not far. There's probably people hanging out, and it's not a long walk back to town. I do it all the time." I had an early start the next day. I knew I should get home and have a good night's sleep. Mr. Herbaugh's questions about my grades had me on edge. And, of course, there was Jenn and her messages waiting for me.

"Okay, cool, I appreciate it. Mind if I open a window, then?"

I shrugged. "Go for it." The smell of weed hit me as he lit his joint and I jerked my head in his direction.

"Shit, not in the car or my fiancée will kill me!" I yelled, waving the smoke from my face. I opened the center console and grabbed a can of air freshener, squirting it heavily into the air. The sickly scent of watermelon mixed with the musky smoke made me want to gag.

Marty seemed unconcerned. "Sorry, my bad, man." He laughed. "Shit, you're acting like your fiancée has your balls in a vice." He threw the joint out the window.

"Thanks, it's just that Lucy hates this stuff," I explained anxiously. I was supposed to pick Lucy up in the morning and take her to breakfast. If she smelled weed, she'd freak out. I sprayed more air freshener for good measure.

"I think that's enough, buddy." Marty coughed. "All I can smell is chemicals. No one's gonna know someone smoked weed in here. Chill out." He shot me a sideways glance. "That woman of yours is a little uptight, huh?" I wanted to tell him no, but I also couldn't deny it.

When it was just us, Lucy was a different person than when she was with her parents.

But she did always seem stressed out.

I used to like the way she wanted things to be perfect and how she worked hard to get what she wanted. I appreciated that she wanted to please her parents, who expected a lot from her, because I felt the same way about my mom. The difference was that my mom wouldn't unleash a lifetime of guilt if I went against her.

They say opposites attract, and we balanced each other out well. Or at least, I used to think we did.

Though lately, I wasn't so sure.

"She's just . . . I don't know . . . I mean," I stumbled over what to say. I didn't want to insult Lucy, or her family, but if Marty had worked for the Herbaughs for any length of time, he had to already know what they were like. "Yeah, a little, I guess," I admitted.

"I get it. She must be worth it, though."

"She is," I agreed, saying it with more force than I meant to.

As we drove to Jagged Point, my thoughts drifted to Lucy and the wedding, and the never-ending list of things to do. We seemed to have done so much, and yet Mabel came up with new tasks every day.

Sometimes I wondered if Lucy felt as suffocated as I did. Her parents were pretty hard on her, but she took it without complaint. Yet there were times, when she thought no one was looking, that I saw the mask slip, and I knew it got to her. The pressure and expectations from them could be overwhelming, and I had a feeling, sometimes, that maybe we were rushing the wedding so she could escape that house.

Then, because I couldn't help it, my thoughts turned to Jenn Moore.

She seemed to hang on my every word as if *I* were the one with the answers. She found me interesting. She liked my stories. She never rolled her eyes or made me feel stupid about my opinions.

"What has you smilin' like the cat that got the cream?" Marty asked. I glanced at him; the long scar made him seem more disfigured in the dim light of the car.

"Nothing, just thinking . . ."

"Thinkin' never made me smile like that. You thinkin' about that woman of yours? She's beautiful—if you don't mind me sayin'. I've seen her out at the pool in a tiny bikini. A woman that beautiful wants to be looked at, so I've definitely had my fill." He laughed again and punched my arm, making me swerve.

It felt wrong to let him talk about Lucy like that. I should probably be pissed off that he admitted to ogling her without her knowledge. But at the same time, he was right. Lucy *did* like to be looked at and admired. It's why she entered those stupid beauty pageants.

I felt a flash of anger at the thought of her lounging around, practically naked, with men there to see her. What did that make me look like when she showed off her body to strangers?

"Hopefully she'll take that stick out of her ass and not end up like her stuck-up mother," Marty went on.

He didn't care that he was insulting my future mother-in-law, and I couldn't help but choke on a laugh.

"You've met Mable, then?"

"I was there when she bitched Sal out for emptying the grass clippings in front of the kitchen window. You would have thought we had put a body in the wood chipper the way she went off on him."

I pictured it clearly in my head. I knew exactly how Mabel could be. "Yeah, she can be tough on people."

Marty sneered, resting his booted feet up onto the dashboard. "If you ask me, a woman like her needs knocking down a peg or two. Talking like that to Sal, who operates his own business. What the hell has she done with her life other than marry some rich guy and pop out a couple of kids. She doesn't know what the fuck she's talkin' about. Stuck-up bitch."

I wasn't sure I had ever heard someone speak badly about the Herbaughs, and certainly not about Mabel. But he wasn't wrong—Mabel *was* stuck-up, and it was refreshing to hear someone say the truth for a change instead of kissing her ass.

Marty seemed like the kind of guy that said whatever came to mind, offensive or not. I appreciated that. In Fern River, people spent entirely too much time worried about what others thought. Monitoring their words in case someone might get upset. It was nice being around someone with no ties to this place and no allegiances either.

We reached Jagged Point a few minutes later. I slowed down and pulled my car over. Marty climbed out, picked up his bag and slung it over his shoulder.

"You sure I can't tempt you with a beer? Just one? It might loosen some of that tension in your shoulders. You look stressed enough that if someone put coal up your ass, it would turn into a diamond." His mouth twisted into a crooked grin. He reached over and gripped one of my shoulders and gave it a small shove. "You need to loosen up."

I laughed, realizing he was right. I was always like this whenever I went to Lucy's house. "You know what, a beer would be good. Just one, though, because I'm driving." I turned the ignition off and got out of the car, joining him on the gravel path. Together, we began the mile-long trek up to the overlook.

As we walked I checked my phone while I still had a signal, elated to see two messages from Jenn. Giving Marty a sideways glance, I surreptitiously sent one back to her.

Jenn—I stopped at the ice cream stand today. I tried that new flavor you suggested. Delicious!:-)

Jenn—Maybe we could grab one together tomorrow??

Me—I should have some free time around lunch. I'll grab a couple cones and meet you at Jagged Point?

She replied almost immediately, and I smiled, happy she had been waiting for my reply.

Jenn—How are you going to drive with two ice cream cones? Lol.
Me—For you, I will find a way!
Jenn—:-)

I should have felt guilty. I was making plans, again, with a woman that wasn't my fiancée. I was essentially juggling two women and instead of feeling horrible, I felt an odd rush.

After all, I could see Lucy in the morning and Jenn in the afternoon. Their paths would never cross and I would stay in the clear. Then, I could study for my upcoming test tomorrow evening. I was keeping all my proverbial ducks in a neat and tidy row.

But, deep in the pit of my stomach, I knew it was wrong. I was a good guy. Everybody thought so. But what harm was I really doing? I shouldn't have to explain myself to anyone. For once, I was going to enjoy myself and not overthink it. Besides, Jenn was only a friend and Lucy couldn't tell me who I could hang out with.

The trees grew thick above us, and overgrowth swallowed the path in places. The inky night seeped through the foliage, making it hard to see. But I had run out to the overlook so many times I'd know the way with my eyes closed.

The gravel crunched beneath our tennis shoes. The air around us was thick with the constant drone of cicadas as they scratched and creaked like an old vinyl record.

"So tell me more about the people that died up here," Marty said, snapping me back to the present.

"There were two hikers a few decades back. Some say they lost their way and died of dehydration. Others think they were attacked by some feral mountain men rumored to live out here somewhere. No one really knows, and it was so long ago that the people who *might* know aren't around anymore. Aside from that, this place is notorious for accidents. Sure, it looks all pretty and serene, but it's dangerous if you don't know where you're going. People have actually fallen over the edge of the cliffs and died."

Feeling hot and sticky in my button-up shirt and polyester slacks,

I rolled up my sleeves and wiped my forehead with the back of my hand.

"Do you know where the bodies were found? The hikers, I mean," Marty asked a little too excitedly. "We could go take a look. I bet there are other bodies around. Bones buried in the dirt beneath your feet."

I pointed farther down the path. "I'm not sure. I was told it was that way somewhere, but I couldn't tell you the exact spot. One summer, my friend Jeremy and I tried looking and almost got lost. We didn't go far off the path, but all these trees look the same and it's easy to get turned around. We did find a deer carcass, but nothing human. Though I wouldn't be surprised if there were other bodies out here. Some say this whole place is a graveyard. Like I said, people have accidents and go missing from time to time."

"I'm surprised people are still allowed up here. You'd think they'd cordon it off as a hazard to the public or something," Marty remarked.

I shrugged. "They added some warning signs down at the end before you get to the overlook. Removes liability if people are still stupid enough to walk along the edge."

Unsolved death left a scar on the soul of a place, and Jagged Point was no different. You felt it here. In the air. In the dirt. A pallor of gloom you could never quite shake.

The air was thick and heavy, but it was more than the humidity that was making me sweat. There had always been something about this place that held a ghoulish fascination for me. It was beautiful, but it also felt like were never quite alone. As if there was something—*or someone*—watching you from the trees.

Like ghosts had congregated in silent observation as you made your way along the path. Sometimes you could almost hear them whispering.

If you listened hard enough, you could hear your name being called from the depths of the trees.

Which is why I always wore headphones here. Everyone knew it was a bad thing to hear your name on the wind and even worse if you responded.

Once at the overlook, we stopped to catch our breath. Surprisingly, we were alone. Marty pulled out a couple of bottles of Coors from his bag and cracked them open using his lighter before handing one to me. We clinked them together and each took a long drink.

From our viewpoint, we could see the whole town and beyond. It seemed so small and inconsequential from up here, and yet, I knew Fern River was the beginning and ending of everything that made up my world.

"Real pretty," Marty said, still sounding out of breath.

"Yeah. This is my favorite spot in the county." I took a big gulp and watched as Marty rolled another joint then put it between his lips and lit it. The pungent smell filled my nostrils, and I found myself relaxing for the first time in forever.

"Can I ask you somethin'?" Marty took a long drag and stared out over the valley below.

"Sure," I replied without taking my eyes off the view.

"How'd *you* get with a woman like that?"

I turned to look at Marty in surprise, not sure if he was joking. "What do you mean?"

Marty held the joint between his fingers, a smirk on his lips. "Not to be an asshole, but you two don't strike me as comin' from the same side of town, if you know what I mean. She's Miss Prim and Proper and you're . . . Well, look at you. You ain't the usual college boy type, are ya."

I laughed, and it felt like a real one instead of something forced. I didn't take offense, though maybe I should have, but Marty was right. On paper Lucy and I should never have been together. I *was* kind of a dork. Always had been. But how to explain that to him so he'd understand?

"We've been together since sophomore year of high school. We hit it off, I guess. I was shocked as hell when she spoke to me. But she was the most popular girl in school, and it felt pretty damn good to have someone like her want to date me." I drank more of the warm beer, enjoying the taste of it way more than the booze-free cocktail from earlier.

"It doesn't hurt that she's got tits and ass for days, right?" Marty added with a salacious grin.

I choked on my beer, and he laughed as I spluttered. I wasn't entirely sure how to take the comment. I didn't like how he kept talking about Lucy like that, but it was obvious he meant it as a compliment.

"Oh, come on, don't act like a fuckin' grandma. Pretty girl like that would make any man hard as a rock." He grabbed his crotch to make his point. "You must be a walkin', talkin' hard-on with that chick in your bed. I salute you, my friend."

"Sure," I replied, my cheeks heating uncomfortably.

"Man, the things I would do to a woman like that. You gotta take charge, show her who's boss. You get me?" Marty licked his lips.

"I get you," I responded weakly.

Marty nodded to himself. "If you let a woman think she's in control, you'll be doin' it missionary style for the rest of your goddamn life. Grab her by the hair and bend her over, my man. Otherwise you'll be lickin' *her* boots instead of her lickin' yours."

I stared at him open mouthed, unsure how to reply. Who really thought like that? Did all men have these kinds of ideas? Growing up without a dad, I didn't have much of a man's view of the world. I only had my mom to teach me how things worked. As I listened to Marty, I realized how much I had missed. How much I didn't know. Because the way I looked at things may not be the way other guys did.

Maybe a man like Marty could teach me a thing or two.

"You want a hit?" Marty asked, holding out the joint.

This time I nodded and took it. I had smoked weed once before, but Lucy didn't like it so I never had again. I took a drag, choking on the thick smoke but also enjoying the instant dulling of my senses. The weed made my thoughts feel heavy, and I couldn't stop thinking about Marty's comments about Lucy.

I had never talked about Lucy like that. She'd be horrified to hear Marty objectify her. But I found myself chuckling dryly and agreeing when I probably should have told him to keep his mouth shut.

But maybe, in some crude way, Marty had it right. I didn't subscribe to patriarchal bullshit, but sometimes, with Lucy, and particularly her family, I *did* feel emasculated. I had lost control of my life somewhere along the way, and I knew it had set the tone for how our lives would be together. Marty's off-color remarks only highlighted how little power I had.

Perhaps what I needed was to assert myself more and stop letting Lucy's parents run the show.

Then I'd grab Lucy by the hair and show her who's boss once in a while.

I wasn't sure I liked having that thought bouncing around in my head. It felt wrong.

But also oddly liberating.

"What brings you to Fern River?" I asked Marty, feeling like I should change the subject.

"Just passing through," he said. "Earning a few bucks before moving on again."

I wondered what that kind of life would be like. Jenn lived like that, and it seemed Marty did too.

I had been raised to think there was a certain order to things. You graduated from high school, went to college, got married, got a job, and settled down. I knew Lucy had been conditioned to think the same thing.

"But what if there's more to life than that?" I murmured to myself.

"What?" Marty looked at me questioningly.

"Nothing," I muttered, embarrassed I had said my angsty inner thoughts out loud.

"Truth is, I'm searching for someone," he continued. "Been on the road for a while now, looking for her."

"Is it an ex or something?" I asked.

"Or something." He gave me a sly grin. "Women these days don't know a good thing when they have it." His expression took on a tinge of anger. "I'd like to go back to how it used to be. When men were men and women were women, none of this modern feminist bullshit."

I thought about my own mom. She worked hard to provide for me, but growing up, I hated that she never had time to bake me cookies or iron my clothes before school. It pissed me off that she was never around when I needed her.

Wasn't that why I was working so hard? To one day have my own kids and give them everything I had missed out on? So my wife didn't have to go to work and could stay home. I wanted the kind of life Marty was talking about, where a woman could be traditional and the man could be the one providing.

And wasn't that partly what drew me to Lucy?

She was strong-willed and smart, which I respected, but she was also content to focus on being a good, traditional mother. One that baked cakes, packed lunches, and went to the park after school. She had loose ideas for a career, but she also seemed to want the same things out of a family and marriage I did, so I knew she wasn't really serious about any of them. The main thing was that she felt like she had options, even if deep down we both knew what she was going to do with her life.

"I don't know, man, that doesn't sound very progressive." I didn't want to offend him, but I couldn't *not* say anything.

"Progressive?" Marty snickered and handed the joint to me. "Let me tell you something about progression, my friend—it's ruining America. What's wrong with a woman staying home and making babies? If women go to work, who's home to take care of your kids? Do you really want someone you don't know raising your kid so your woman can feel 'progressive'?" He made the air quotes with a look of disgust.

I frowned uncertainly. "And what if the man walks out and leaves his family behind? What then? Is he really being a man?"

"You ever think about why he would do that?" Marty asked aggressively. "What it takes for him to give up his wife and kids and walk away from everything he worked hard for? Maybe it's the woman's fault he's so unsatisfied at home. We need to stop blamin' the men and look at why they run. These women have their men by the balls, and one day they snap and need to get the fuck out. It's not their fault. It's *progression*." Marty was like a preacher in his pulpit shouting about fire and brimstone. His passion—his *rage*—was felt in every word.

Everything he said sounded like something out of a bad movie, and yet it actually made a weird kind of sense.

Mom always said that Dad ran off with another woman, and I never questioned why. He was simply the asshole who abandoned his family.

But maybe I should have. What had Mom done to drive him away? Maybe she wasn't the kind of wife my dad needed. Mom never missed a shift of work no matter how sick or tired she was, but how many awards ceremonies had she not attended? How many field trips? Had my dad felt like that? Like his needs were always coming second to hers?

Maybe the real problem *was* this "progressive bullshit" Marty was talking about. It was definitely food for thought. Just not a thought I'd ever say out loud to anyone else.

"I do love a strong woman, though—one just like yours." He winked as if we were on the same page. "Nothing better than breaking her. Like a wild horse, you have to ride 'em till they don't have a mind of their own anymore." He laughed hard at his joke. I laughed, too, though maybe I shouldn't have. "It's the best rush there is. Better than beer. Better than drugs. Better than just about anything."

There was a gleam of something dark in his eyes that sent a shiver of trepidation down my spine.

"Women like that don't think that's how they want to be treated, but let me tell you something, Rhett, that's a lie they tell themselves. They *want* to be tamed. They *want* to be controlled. They want you to be the man and put them in their place."

My muscles felt tense as Marty's words took an insidious hold one small piece at a time.

"Women want to be chased. No matter how far or how fast they run, they want to know that *you* will find them—that *you* will hunt them down no matter where they go."

My breathing was shallow and I felt dizzy. I let his words infect me like a disease.

"A woman like that needs to know she will always belong to you. And she'll love every minute of the life you give her, because *that's her place*."

Marty was staring directly at me, his expression serious. He was so forthright that it unnerved me at the same time it made my skin crawl.

And yet, I found myself agreeing with at least *some* of his sentiments, regardless of how they made me feel.

Women did love the thrill of the chase, didn't they?

And what was wrong with more traditional roles? Wasn't that why I was putting myself through law school? So I could provide for my mom and Lucy? So I could be the man of my household?

And if that was true, then what right did Lucy, or any other woman for that matter, have to tell me what I could and couldn't do?

This time, it was my own dark thoughts that unnerved me.

The truth was I knew Lucy would never be content letting me run the show. Her mother was the same. Even though Mr. Herbaugh made the money, it was Mabel who ran the house. I had no doubt Lucy would be the same way.

But Jenn seemed different. There was an innocence about her that was incredibly attractive. She appeared timid and unsure, even as she was trying to figure out her life on her own. I could tell, from the conversations we'd had, that she really wanted someone to direct her.

She and Lucy were complete opposites. Jenn needed someone to guide the ship, and Lucy was already steering it.

Marty suddenly clasped me on the shoulder. "You need another beer, buddy." He pulled another bottle out of his backpack and handed it to me. "Man, this thing is high up," he said, peering down from the top of the cliff.

I followed his gaze. I felt dizzy as I stared at the tiny matchbox town below. "It's more dangerous up here than people realize. It's not just a pretty view."

"I'm sure it is." Marty threw his empty bottle over the edge. I jumped at the sound of it shattering on the rocks below. "This is a good time, man. We should do it more often."

I smiled. "Definitely."

The conversation with Marty had my mind in turmoil.

Maybe I needed to start telling Lucy how things were going to be instead of the other way around. Then maybe Mr. Herbaugh would respect me more.

Everything Marty said felt so wrong. I thought of myself as a modern man who believed women deserved to be treated as equals. That Lucy would be my partner because that's how it should be. I was raised by a single mom who did everything for me.

I was an enlightened man, goddamn it!

And yet, somewhere deep down, the rightness of Marty's words were heavy and sticky like tar.

But like any radical idea, once it took root, there was no getting rid of it.

I just didn't know what it meant for Lucy.

Or for me.

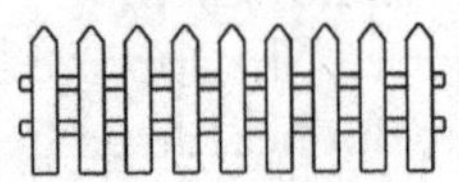

Lucy 10:00AM

- Where are you? I've been trying to reach you for hours!

Lucy 10:05AM

- Rhett? You were supposed to pick me for breakfast. We had plans!

Lucy 10:42AM

- I just went by your house and no one was home. Where are you? Are you hurt? I'm starting to get worried!

Lucy 11:23AM

- Why aren't you responding? You're becoming so unreliable!

CHAPTER

8

Lucinda

The Past

Late July—Fifteen Years Ago

I WATCHED RHETT THROUGH the large picture window. He was so lost in his own thoughts that he didn't feel the heat of my eyes as he paced through the trees.

He's completely oblivious.

I had never felt such bitterness toward Rhett before.

Such anger.

But the feelings, now unleashed, couldn't be tethered, and they flapped around inside me, threatening to decimate every semblance of happiness I had worked so hard for.

Rhett was clearly in his own world, wandering around the small apple orchard to the south of my parents' house, his face covered with cuts and bruises, blind to how horrible he looked.

We told everyone he had fallen in some brambles while out on a run. My father saw through the lie right away.

I leaned closer to the glass and frowned as he braced himself against a tree, his head hung low, his eyes closed as if in pain. I knew I wasn't imagining the tears that slid down his cheeks.

We had sworn not to talk about that night. It was easier for us both to ignore what happened than to face it. To face our actions.

Rhett wore his heartache like a flashing neon sign. He didn't try to hide it. His face was etched with the grief of a man who had fought, and then lost, something important. Something that mattered to him. And when that something was another woman, it was hard for me to feel anything but agony that quickly turned to rage.

I wasn't sure what devastated me more. That he was so cut up about her being dead, or that he was, yet again, willing to risk us—*our lives*—because of her. Because he was making us both look guilty as hell.

Why wasn't I enough for him?

What did she have that I didn't?

The questions had been eating me up since the day I saw them together eating those goddamn ice cream cones. I had never felt so inadequate in my life.

It was such a disappointment to realize the man you loved was no different from every other male on the planet. That he was capable of betrayal and subterfuge all in the name of a pretty face. Damn the consequences.

Or the destruction he left in his wake.

When I had chosen Rhett, I really thought he was better than that. That I would never have to worry about him straying.

It seemed he wasn't the only idiot.

"What's he doing?"

I didn't bother to turn around. I wasn't in the mood for Bailey's nosy intrusion.

"What does it look like?" I snapped. "Haven't you ever seen someone getting some fresh air before?"

I glanced at my little sister, who had pressed her hand to the windowpane as she watched Rhett.

"He looks upset." She cocked her head as if examining him. "What happened to his face?"

"He's fine," I replied dismissively.

"He doesn't look fine." She paused, her expression unsure. "Did he get in a fight?"

"No, of course not! It's Rhett, for God's sake." I snorted as if the idea were absurd. "Unless you count falling into a blackberry bush."

"He seems really sad, Lucy."

I didn't know how much Bailey was aware of Jennifer Moore and the chaos she had wrought in our lives. I hoped she was too young to listen to gossip and speculation. But she was a teenager, and teenagers talked as much as old women.

"He's fine," I repeated, firmer this time. "He's just stressed, with college and the wedding, and . . ." My voice trailed off and I didn't bother finishing the lie. There were so many lies.

Bailey's expression was still troubled, and I realized I wasn't fooling her. She had been there that night. She'd heard the fight. I didn't feel like playing a round of "pretend everything is hunky-dory."

"Can we drop it?" I asked tiredly. "Rhett's fine. I'm fine. We're all fine."

Bailey placed her hand reassuringly on my arm and I stared down at it, confused by her sudden gentleness. We were sisters, but we weren't close. Though I sensed she would have liked us to be. Even though our age gap wasn't that large, we had never gotten along. But she *was* my little sister, and I was supposed to be a role model. Someone for her to look up to. Unfortunately, that only made her another burden. Another responsibility that my parents held me accountable for.

But was that really her fault?

I felt myself soften.

"I think you should go talk to him. Or maybe I can. Remember what Dad always says, we protect family, no matter what—" Bailey began, and just like that, she was back to being my annoyingly meddlesome little sister.

"Rhett doesn't need protection. He'll be *fine*," I stated once more for emphasis that was more for my benefit than Bailey's. She looked as if she didn't know what to say. That made two of us.

"Lucinda, where's Rhett?" My father's booming voice startled Bailey and me.

Dad strode into the room, his thinning hair plastered to his forehead, his expression stern and foreboding.

Physically, he didn't look much like a man who commanded respect. He was relatively short, coming in at only five foot four, with a thin, wiry frame. At a glance he resembled someone who was bullied by the quarterback.

But everyone knew my father's strength was in his head, not his body. He had worked his way up from nothing—having come from humble beginnings—and put himself first through college, then law school. He was quick on his feet, and according to people in town, could make you believe the sun was blue and the grass was yellow if he had a mind to. He could smile and put you at ease all the while planning the ways he would ruin you.

His friends were many. His influence, far reaching. His was a power born from hard work, and he expected the most from those around him.

Particularly his children.

He looked momentarily taken aback by Bailey's presence. His gaze shifted quickly between the two of us.

"Bailey, what are you doing here?"

"I was talking to—"

"You need to get to your tutoring session." He cut her off abruptly. "Mr. Orndorff is waiting for you in the dining room." Dad gave my sister a stern look. "And for God's sake, try and get through the hour without arguing with him, please. Your mother is in bed with a headache, so do as you're told, for once." He sounded uncharacteristically tired. His words were more of a plea than an order.

Guilt bloomed in my chest. This mess was taking its toll on all of us.

I expected Bailey to argue, as she was prone to when asked to do anything. She was a typical teenager and no one was exempt from her attitude or her temper, even our intimidating father. So I was surprised when she hurried off without a word.

As soon as the door shut behind her, Dad rounded on me, his eyes flashing. "We need to have a talk, Lucinda."

"Okay, Dad, what is it?" My stomach lurched. There were so many secrets floating around. Which ones had he discovered?

"I need you to tell me the truth, because after everything, I'm not sure that man of yours is the kind of person I want to put my neck on the line for." He stared at me for several long moments, and I knew then that I could fool many people, but I would never be able to fool him.

In the week since Jenn's body had been found, the rumblings around town had grown louder. So far I had furiously ignored them as best I could, immersing myself in wedding preparations for a ceremony I insisted was still happening.

I felt everything inside me tense. "I know it looks bad—"

"It doesn't look bad, Lucinda. It looks *criminal*."

Dad took a cigar out of his pocket and rolled it between his fingers. He'd never light it up in the house, Mom would kill him if he did. "I know Rhett was involved with that woman. We've had this discussion before, Lucinda. Don't pretend like we didn't. I thought you had more pride than this." His bluntness took the wind out of me.

"What woman?" I said, the two words barely squeezing out of my too-tight throat. I wasn't sure why I bothered acting oblivious. I remembered the conversation well. Dad knew all about Jenn and Rhett. My shame wasn't news to him. Yet here I was trying to save what little face I had left. "I don't know who you're talking about."

Dad looked like he might self-combust at any moment. "You know damn well, what woman," he hissed, "Jennifer Moore!" He glared at me. "I need you to quite playing dumb—this is serious." I stared at him in a horror I couldn't hide. "I told you I had heard from Tanya Young that Rhett was seen around town with her. He wasn't hiding it," he seethed, making me shrink before him. He wasn't even trying to protect my feelings.

"And I told you I'd fix it." I gave up pretending I didn't know what this was about. I tried to sound steady and confident but my voice was far too small. My cheeks flushed in mortification.

"This has gone beyond him bowling with some slut. Everyone in Fern River is saying he was carrying on with her right under your nose. Under *all* our noses." My father didn't shout. He didn't need to. His words were bullets and they hit their mark.

He had been so sure marrying Rhett was a mistake. Yes, he had publicly shown his support, but behind closed doors he hadn't minced words.

"That boy wasn't raised with the same values as you were. Promises and vows mean nothing to someone with no ethics. I've seen men like him in my courtroom hundreds of times. He only cares about himself. Mark my words."

But because, for once, I wanted to choose something for myself, I had stuck by him. I had gone all in, believing that Rhett loved me and would look after my heart.

Clifford Herbaugh had been right.

And now I was scared this would be a reason for my parents to exert even more control over my life. I could practically feel the walls closing in around me.

* * *

"Judge Taylor's boy is coming by to take you out this Friday at seven sharp," my mother announced from my doorway.

I looked up from the book I was reading, feeling a keen sense of dread sink in.

Every few weeks, my parents arranged for the son of one of their well-connected friends to take me out on a date. It was always stiff and awkward. Either the boy was as unhappy about the arrangement as I was—or even worse, they thought they could get something out of it.

I was only fifteen, but I had become adept at fending off unwanted sexual advances with a smile and a laugh. I had to make sure to never offend; otherwise, it would get back to my father. I couldn't make him look bad in front of his friends. There were some fates worse than death.

"Kyle Taylor?" I asked, unable to hide my dismay. "But he's a total jerk!"

Kyle was a senior who liked to talk loudly about his many conquests. There were rumors he had gotten a girl pregnant and his dad had paid her off to leave the county to have it and give it up for adoption.

The thought of going out with a guy like that was petrifying.

"Greg Taylor is a candidate for the state supreme court. He's an important connection for your father. So it's imperative you make a good impression."

I knew what kind of impression I would be expected to make.

My mother went to my closet and pulled out a dress with a short hemline but modestly cut. It accentuated my developing figure in all the right ways.

I was aware of what a boy like Kyle Taylor would think if I went out with him dressed like that. It didn't matter if I said no; he'd see that stupid dress as a yes.

I felt cold inside.

"Maybe I could wear something else—"

Mom's face hardened. "Your father and I are hoping you and Kyle hit it off. It would be nice to have a young man from such a respectable family connected to the Herbaughs."

Then she left, leaving me no choice.

Because I never had a choice.

* * *

It was only two weeks later that I noticed Rhett in the hallway of our high school.

Sure, I knew him, but our social circles never intersected. He was goofy and sweet and the exact opposite of Kyle Taylor and his grabby hands and invasive tongue.

I thought he was different.

I thought wrong.

I liked to think that if my father knew how bad those dates were for me, he would have stopped pushing me to go on them. But I'd never know because my mother made it clear it was my duty and I would perform it with a smile on my face, so I never said a word.

I loved the look on her face the first time I brought Rhett to the house. The disapproval was instantaneous. But given all the ways she exerted control in her own life, she shouldn't have been surprised that her daughter was watching and taking notes.

"Was it Tanya again?" I asked when he didn't answer me right away.

"Does it matter?" Dad countered. "Everyone in this goddamn town has an opinion about Rhett and they all agree he's not a man to be trusted."

"Look, I thought the same thing for a while. But I was wrong. I know what I said before, but I've spoken to him. He wasn't sleeping with her, Dad. They were just friends." I hated lying for Rhett. Especially to my father. But what choice did I have? "Rhett would never do that. He loves me." I swallowed, the words bitter in my mouth. "People are just trying to start drama. It wouldn't be the first time rumors based on lies ruined someone's life. "

This time *neither* of us believed me.

"You're telling me not only is Tanya Young lying, but half the town too?" My father's eyes flashed with something terrifying. "I've heard it from my friends, Lucinda, not a bunch of ignorant teenagers with nothing better to do. I trust these people." My stomach dropped. "And if they tell me your fiancé is screwing around behind your back, then I believe them." His gaze was steady and unwavering. "He made you look like a fool. Made all of us look like fools. I couldn't let that slide." I noticed the tick in Dad's jaw. A sign his blood pressure was rising.

"Did you say something to Rhett?" I asked my father. I watched him closely and knew he was containing a rage that would be terrifying when released. "What did you do, Dad?"

His expression was completely unreadable. "I will always look after my family, Lucinda." Why did the words feel so cryptic? "People are talking. A lot of people. And yours and Rhett's names are in their mouths. That's a problem. Chuck needs to find that woman's killer, and Rhett sure has made himself look picture-perfect for the role. Though, to be honest, you're not looking great either."

Dad didn't try to hide his distaste. If there was one thing he detested, it was sloppiness. If Rhett had been having an affair, that was bad enough, but he hadn't been smart about it, which made it worse. And his daughter being implicated in a murder would push him over the edge. He could be rational about most things, but needing to protect his family brought out a viciousness in him that was unparalleled. People knew not to mess with Mom, Bailey, and me. Dad's fury was legendary.

"He wasn't sleeping with her." I said it firmly, the fire in the pit of my stomach searing my insides. "They were friends. He was being nice." I swallowed again, my mouth dry. "I trust Rhett, Dad. We're getting married." Even though the man in question didn't deserve my loyalty.

Dad watched me closely. I knew he was analyzing me the way he analyzed people in his courtroom. Looking for holes in my story. Weaknesses.

"Then you're an idiot, Lucinda. A man is never *just* friends with a woman." He shook his head in disappointment at my perceived naivety.

Humiliation clawed at me. And when I thought things were bad enough, he dug even deeper.

"Where were you last Saturday night?"

I tried to laugh, but it was without humor. "I can't remember where I was yesterday, let alone last Saturday."

Dad didn't appreciate the joke. "You need an alibi, Lucinda. Where the hell were you?"

I looked out the window again, my eyes searching for the man I had pinned my future on. "Rhett and I were together. At his house."

There was a loaded moment of silence as I felt my father weighing up my words. "Together? Are you sure about that? This is very important. So think long and hard before you answer."

I drew myself upright in indignation. "Of course I'm sure! Are you calling me a liar, Dad?"

Yes. Yes, he was. And he was right.

I was a liar.

We stared at each other, locked in a battle of wills I usually lost. But this time, I had something on the line. My gruff father softened ever so slightly. "It would be much better if you weren't with him," he reasoned.

I frowned but didn't say anything. Too scared to open my mouth, to spew more dishonesty.

"You don't need to be his alibi." Dad spoke to me as if I were a toddler. "The police are already looking at him. It's easy enough to keep you out of the conversation. No sense sweeping up the mess of a man who was quick to hop into bed with a woman that wasn't his fiancée. He's quite literally made his bed. Let him lie in it."

"Stop talking about him like that. We're getting married, and nothing will stop us!" Hot tears poured down my cheeks. I inwardly cringed at how immature I sounded.

But for better or for worse, I would stick by Rhett. I had stubbornly made my choice. It was bad enough that I looked like a betrayed woman. I'd be damned if I'd be a jilted one as well.

The town needed to see that my faith in Rhett was warranted. That we would stand by each other no matter what.

"We were together, Dad. All night." I gritted my teeth and willed him to believe me.

Dad finally looked away as if he couldn't take the sight of me a moment longer.

"Well, if you're sticking by him, then we'll have to make sure the police look elsewhere." He sounded resigned.

I knew he would do whatever it took to keep his family's name out of this potential storm. It was what made him so reliable.

"I'm sure Chuck will be by at some point to chat with you two about all this. Better here in our home than people seeing you and Rhett at the station."

"Chuck wants to talk to Rhett and me?"

My father looked at me like I was an imbecile. "Of course he does. This is a murder investigation, Lucinda, and there are rumors going around about the two of you and that girl. Sounds like both of you made a spectacle of yourselves. If it were me, I'd let Rhett deal with this on his own, see how far he gets without the Herbaugh name behind him."

"Please, Dad," I begged, the words exploding from me automatically.

"You're my daughter and I'll do what I can. For *you*. Now, Chuck's a good policeman, so he's got to follow the general order of things. People know there's a connection, so Chuck knows there's a connection. But I'll make sure all he sees is a dead end. You and Rhett were together that night. You can vouch for each other. End of story. Just make sure that man of yours knows his part to play." Dad met my eyes. He was good at surmising a person's character. It's why he was a judge. A well-respected one at that. He knew people. He could read them like an open book.

But did he really know me?

Could he read *me*?

I was better than most at keeping secrets, but not from him. It all depended on how much he wanted to know.

And for whatever reason, I had a feeling he didn't want to dig too deeply. Maybe he was scared of what he'd find.

With a final look that was more loaded than I wanted it to be, Dad left me alone.

I wrung my hands together nervously, a bad habit from my anxious beauty pageant days.

Were Rhett and I suspects?

That was a problem.

A huge, gigantic problem.

In a pique of rage, I picked up a crystal vase from the table and threw it against the wall, watching it shatter into a thousand tiny shards. They tinkled as they fell to the floor and I could only watch, numb, as the anger abated and was replaced with a cold *nothingness.*

At that moment I hated Rhett.

More than I ever hated *her.*

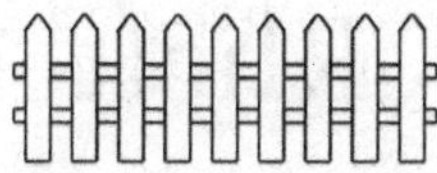

Alison

I saw Rhett at the bowling alley last night. He seemed like he was having a real good time.
Hope everything is good with you two!

6/22/08 4:35PM

C H A P T E R

9

Rhett

The Present

I SAT UNCOMFORTABLY ON the wooden chair, feeling the heavy weight of Lucinda and her family staring at my back.

The courtroom was too warm, and a light sheen covered everyone's faces, despite the air conditioning.

"All rise," the bailiff's voice called from the front of the courtroom, and I rose to my feet alongside Glynn.

Judge Balfour came out of his chambers and shuffled up the stairs to his bench. He was a gaunt man with barely a wisp of gray hair on top of his smooth head. His glasses were an inch thick and his skin was rumpled like a piece of paper. Glynn had already warned me not to be fooled by his aged appearance. Judge Balfour was apparently no-nonsense in a way that didn't bode well for someone used to getting by on his in-laws' reputation.

"Here ye, here ye, here ye, the Circuit Court of Chadwick County is now in session, the Honorable Judge Balfour presiding." I glanced over my shoulder, seeking out Lucinda, desperate for a friendly face. I really wanted to see our daughter—it was the longest we had been apart—but this was not the place for a child.

Lucinda was sitting with her dad. Her mother, Mabel, must have been looking after McKenzie. I doubted she wanted to be anywhere near this courtroom, or me.

Bailey sat between Lucinda and their father. The younger woman met my eyes and gave me a friendly wave.

I waved back, but then Lucinda gave her a loaded look and Bailey turned away.

Lucinda appeared tired. There were dark shadows beneath her eyes, her skin sallow and drawn. I willed her to look at me. As if we could still communicate silently the way we used to. But time, and betrayal, had eroded that intimacy.

Yet the secrets that cleaved us created a bond that had proved impossible to sever.

And of course I loved her. Or at least the memory of how she used to be.

But that love had morphed into something parasitic, feeding off me until there was nothing left.

Finally, as if sensing the weight of my gaze, she looked at me, her expression shuttered.

"It will be okay," I mouthed. It was a lie, but I was good at that.

She stared at me, making no indication she understood what I had said. Her face was blank and unreadable. It chilled me.

"Ladies and gentlemen, please be seated." Judge Balfour's rough voice grated my ears.

I swallowed around the lump in my throat, my body filled with apprehension as I sat back down.

"Good morning and welcome to the fifty-eighth district Circuit Court of Chadwick County. Today is the detention hearing for case number KY2024-40003, Chadwick County vs. Clark." He looked down at the docket briefly before acknowledging the courtroom again. "This is to determine whether Mr. Clark should be granted bail or remain in custody during the pretrial period. I've read the pretrial assessment completed by PSO Poole as well as the petition put forth by the defense regarding Mr. Clark's constitutional right to bail. What is the defense's statement?"

Glynn stood up. "Good morning, Your Honor, and may it please the court, my name is Glynn Walker on behalf of Mr. Clark and the claims against him are ludicrous. The defense believes that Chief Charles Young is grasping at straws as he desperately tries to close a cold case before he retires next year."

Glynn gave me a quick, smug glance before addressing the judge again. "As presented fifteen years ago, my client, Mr. Rhett Clark, had an alibi for the night in question, and this has not changed. My client presents no risk to the greater public. He has been an upstanding member of the Fern River community for most of his life. He is a respected teacher. He coaches the girls' tennis team. He is the faculty adviser for the debate club. We have three pages of character testimony from his friends and colleagues that provides a clear picture of the well-regarded man Mr. Clark is."

Glynn was all solemn seriousness. "He is a man well-liked by the people of this town. Mr. Clark and his wife live here with their young daughter. Mrs. Clark's family is here. He is not a flight risk. I request that Mr. Clark be granted bail immediately under his father-in-law's reconnaissance."

Judge Balfour's expression was fierce. "Your petition is noted. And for the record, the court is aware of who your client and his family are. However, this is *my* courtroom." He leveled me with his cold gaze. "And Mr. Clark, your name, and your *family*, only matters for the paperwork."

Judge Balfour stared at my attorney and me for a few beats longer before directing his attention to the other bench, where a man and woman in almost identical dark blue suits were sitting.

"What do you two have to say about this? I have read your brief, and while it is compelling for trial, given Mr. Clark's spotless record, as much as it pains me, I'm not seeing why I should deny the request for bail. I don't make it a habit of keeping a family man in custody at the taxpayers' expense; it's not good for my electoral prospects. So, unless you can provide anything worth my time, I am ready to make my decision."

Both prosecutors stood, but it was the tall man with light gray eyes that spoke. "Your Honor, Daniel Ranger and Anne Massey here to present the case for the county. While the commonwealth attorney's office concedes that Mr. Clark has no prior offenses, the nature of this crime, as well as his access to significant funds to aid in his ability to leave the jurisdiction, makes it imperative that he stay in detention."

His co-council handed him a piece of paper, which he read before speaking again. "As stated in the bench brief we submitted to the court, we have video evidence that puts Mr. Clark with the victim on the night of her murder, and an eyewitness to corroborate it. This proves Mr. Clark's current alibi provided by his wife, Lucinda Herbaugh Clark, was, in fact, fabricated."

"I must say, I was very interested in this new evidence," Judge Balfour said.

"Your Honor, we also have in evidence a bloodied T-shirt belonging to Mr. Clark that contains both his and the victim's DNA, which he is seen wearing in the phone footage. The video clearly shows Mr. Clark with the victim engaged in a violent argument that further points to Mr. Clark's volatile nature."

I looked up at Glynn, hoping he would say something, but he stayed silent.

"This, paired with the eyewitness testimony of Mr. Martin Richards, a known associate of Mr. Clark, and our case demonstrates that the accused is responsible for the brutal murder of Jennifer Moore," Daniel Ranger finished.

Judge Balfour peered at my attorney over the rims of his black-framed glasses. "Mr. Walker, do you have anything to say about all this?"

"Your Honor," Glynn began with a small laugh, "If I may, this so-called eyewitness testimony is nothing more than the product of a soured friendship and bad blood. My client and Martin Richards were casual acquaintances, nothing more. And Mr. Richards left town rather abruptly after the murder of Miss Moore, which I must say, is highly suspicious."

Glynn was clearly giving it his all, which I appreciated. "If what he states is true, why did he not provide this information to authorities fifteen years ago? I would argue that this lack of transparency makes his testimony completely unreliable."

He threw a sideways glance to the prosecution before continuing. "Your Honor, while new physical evidence, if credible, would certainly be worth exploring in the hope of finding the *actual* murderer of Miss Moore, it is also circumspect given that it was provided by this same individual who, we will establish, has a personal vendetta against my client. In fact, the evidence itself does not imply murder at all but more a case of a relationship with the deceased, which Mr. Clark has always admitted to. My client acknowledges that he and Miss Moore were engaged in an adulterous affair, which makes the existence of this so-called evidence easily explained."

While I knew what he was saying could help me, I also knew every word would be a knife to Lucinda's heart, and her back.

"Your Honor, we strongly feel that it is in the best interest of the public that Mr. Clark be held until the time of his trial. He is being tried for first degree murder. Despite his clean record, this demonstrates the danger he could pose to the community," Mr. Ranger argued calmly.

The courtroom was silent as Judge Balfour read through the docket in front of him, flipping through the pages and pages of briefs both Glynn and the prosecution had submitted. He took his time, seeming to carefully consider everything. Finally, with steepled hands, Judge Balfour gave his ruling. "After carefully reading all the information submitted to the court, I have decided to grant bail for Mr. Clark." I heard whispers from the galley behind me.

Mr. Ranger got to his feet. "Your Honor, as stated, we have significant concerns about granting bail to Mr. Clark. If we may—?"

"No, you may not," the judge cut him off abruptly. "I am granting bail for Mr. Clark because I do not believe him to be a flight risk, and I have yet to see anything that suggests his release is a concern to the public. However, given the serious nature of the crime, as well as the complexity and involvement of individuals in the greater Chadwick community, I will set bail at five hundred thousand dollars and under the condition that he is on home remand until the time of his trial."

I heard Lucinda gasp behind me.

Five hundred. Thousand. Dollars.

Even though Glynn had explained that we'd work with the local bondsman and only have to pay 10 percent of the total bail amount, that was still more money than we had in our savings account.

Maybe we could take out a second mortgage, but even if we did, we'd never get the money in time to prevent me from spending a considerable amount of time behind bars. There was no way we could pay that amount on our own so I could get out before trial.

Glynn immediately got to his feet. "Your Honor, that amount is exorbitant given that my client has no prior offenses."

Judge Balfour seemed unconcerned. "That is the amount. It will not be reduced," was all he said.

As much as I hated it, my father-in-law was my only hope. I despised that, once again, Clifford Herbaugh was the only one who could save me.

The man hated me.

Had always hated me.

Fifty thousand dollars was a lot of money, even for the Herbaughs, but they would put it up.

If only to show the community they were sticking by me. They'd never share their disapproving doubts out loud. I was their daughter's husband, and they were well-known for putting family first, no matter what.

Because we all knew that if it wasn't for Lucinda, Cliff would have thrown me to the wolves a long time ago.

And smile as they devoured me whole.

* * *

The car ride back to Lucinda's parents' house was silent.

I had been disappointed when Bailey left to go back to work. I could have used her as a buffer right about then.

Since leaving court $50,000 lighter, Cliff had been a pot of boiling water ready to bubble over. And there would be no escaping him either. Since my father-in-law had put up the bond, he had insisted that I stay at his house.

"You were released on my *reconnaissance. That means* my *name,* my *word, is on the line. You'll stay with Mabel and me until all this concludes one way or another," my father-in-law insisted with his jaw clenched as we stood in the hallway outside the courtroom after the hearing.*

So I wasn't given a choice. I had given up my passport to the court. I couldn't go home. I was stuck. And I doubted the school would let me come back while all this was hanging over my head. The case hadn't even gone to trial yet, and it already felt like I had lost everything. Potentially my job, my home, and I was pretty sure my wife too.

I wasn't sure if Lucinda and McKenzie would be staying with her parents—though I sincerely hoped so. I couldn't imagine her leaving me to deal with them alone. But given how angry she must be, I couldn't rely on her goodwill either.

Back at their house, Cliff pulled the car to a screeching halt and got out without a single word to Lucinda or me. He stomped across the gravel path and went inside the house, slamming the door behind him.

Lucinda and I got out of the car, neither of us saying a thing. I reached for her hand, but she rebuffed me. I trailed slowly after her, feeling like I was heading down the green mile.

I was eager to see McKenzie, but Lucinda told me that Mabel had taken her to the park. I had no doubt she had done it to keep me away from my daughter, but for once I didn't mind. As desperate as I was to see my little girl, I knew it was important that Lucinda and I talk alone.

The entryway of Lucinda's childhood home was gloomy. The dark wood paneling and deep green carpet had always given off an ominous air, but now it felt fitting given my mood. Lucinda started up the stairs and I followed her, my head hung low. It had been years since I had followed Lucinda up these stairs. Back then we had been young and in love, but now we were older and barely tolerating each other.

Part of me longed for the connection we used to have. It made my life so much easier when I knew she had my back no matter what. But as we entered her childhood bedroom, I knew those days were long behind us.

She closed the door with a decisive *click*.

When Lucinda turned to look at me, her face was flushed with pure, unadulterated rage.

A look I hadn't seen since the night Jenn died.

I braced myself against her wrath. I felt my own indignant fury arch up to meet hers. This wasn't all my fault, goddamn it. Maybe my *loving* wife should look at herself once in a while. After all, I wouldn't have messed up so badly if she hadn't given me a reason to.

"Do you have any idea how humiliating that was for me?" Her voice was like fire, her words incinerating me. "Even from beyond the grave, she is still between us." Her voice hitched, and I watched her take a deep breath to get herself under control. "Glynn just shared your affair with everyone in that courtroom. With the whole town."

"Lucinda—"

"I'm not finished!" I sat down on the edge of the bed, waiting for her to tire herself out and leave.

"My dad is furious. He wants to leave you to deal with this on your own. Marty has come forward, and we both know he has information that can send you up the river. You need to be realistic. This looks very, very bad for you because you were messy." She spoke matter-of-factly. The anger that was there before was completely gone now. "Everything is pointing at you, and it will take more than a good defense to turn it around."

My face tightened with frustration but I kept quiet, knowing anything I said would be like throwing a match on gasoline.

"What would you do if I didn't keep convincing my family to save you?" Her tone was harsh and even. She looked exhausted, but I knew that had never stopped her before. "When you speak to Glynn tomorrow, the best thing to do is stick to the story. We'll just have to see if it's enough."

"Lucinda, maybe it's time we talk about what really happened that night and what we did—"

"There is no *we*," she snarled. "There is only *you* and *your* mess." She poked her finger at me and I fantasized about grabbing it and snapping it right off.

"Lucinda—" Her name tasted like poison in my mouth.

"Do you still love her?" Her lips twisted as if she was in pain.

"Say her name, Lucinda." I didn't give her time to brace herself. "Her name is Jenn." The impact was instantaneous. It was the one weapon in my arsenal that always hit its mark and one I would only employ when absolutely necessary.

Lucinda looked away from me, and my momentary victory fell flat. "She made you an idiot back then, and she's making an idiot of you now." She didn't sound angry anymore—just disappointed. "My family will not keep suffering for the choices *you* made. *I* will not keep suffering because of *you*."

I both loved and loathed Lucinda.

She was a mother, a wife, and the villain in my long, complicated story.

She had given me everything, while simultaneously taking everything away. We were each other's worst enemy.

Her hair fell wildly around her face, revealing more about her state of mind than anything else. She was usually impeccably put together. "She's in the past. We've moved beyond what happened—"

"Have we?" I sneered. "Because from where I'm standing, it doesn't look like either of us have moved beyond anything. Certainly not from Jenn." I said her name again to create ultimate carnage. Lucinda and I had always existed in this precarious place between her will and mine—with me usually coming out the loser. Things had been different with Jenn, which is what had made her so special. Lucinda knew that Jenn offered me something she never could.

Control.

Neither of us said anything for the length of time it took for us both to get ourselves together. Finally, she smoothed back her hair. "I'm going to the park to meet up with Mom and Kenz. Get your shit together, Rhett. I'm tired of being this family's backbone." She hit me right where it hurt. In my figurative manhood.

I thought about grabbing her and shaking her. Maybe I would squeeze her arms hard enough to bruise. I imagined all the ways I could make her sorry for saying such awful things to me.

But the dark thoughts stayed tucked away inside.

Lucinda turned and left the room, slamming the door so hard that a photo fell from the wall and smashed on the floor. I flinched as I stared at the glinting pieces on the ground. It was a photo of Lucinda and me in high school.

Before Jenn.

Before Marty.

Before the biggest mistake of my life.

* * *

July 12—Fifteen Years Ago

"Here, buddy." Marty passed me the joint. I reached over to take it, swerving slightly into oncoming traffic.

"Shit." I overcorrected to get back in my lane. Marty cackled in delight as my tires caught the gravel on the verge and spun slightly, fishtailing dangerously. With shaking hands I took a small drag and handed it back to Marty.

"Calm down, Rhett. You'll get us both killed." Marty pulled on the joint and rolled down the window to blow out a thick plume of smoke. He looked at me and raised his eyebrow. "What's got you all messed up this evening? Woman trouble?"

I laughed. "That's an understatement, man."

"That lady of yours seems like a lot of work. I told you how to handle her." He made a crude gesture. "Bitches like that only ever respond to a strong hand, know what I mean?" He toked on the joint as he braced his feet on the dashboard. I wanted to tell Marty to move his muddy boots, but I knew he wouldn't listen anyway. He did what he wanted, when he wanted. Which was one of the things I respected about him.

"That's not the one I'm talking about," I muttered. The horrific fight Lucy and I had tonight wasn't what was pressing on my mind. She wasn't the woman I was consumed by.

Marty nodded knowingly. "I heard you were playin' around behind the back of that fine piece of ass. You've got balls, my friend. Big fuckin' balls." However, he spoke as if he wasn't giving me a compliment. In fact he looked kind of pissed off.

"Yeah, I guess so." I shrugged, glancing at him nervously. Why did I want Marty's regard so badly? I wanted him to think of me as his equal. Like I was as much a man as he was.

Marty bared his teeth in a feral grin that put me on edge. "I want to hear all about this new piece. How'd you even meet her? What the hell you thinkin' screwing around with some girl while your nuts are in some other lady's purse?"

My mood darkened even more. "Yeah, well she's avoiding me now anyway."

Marty laughed but it sounded brittle. "You fuckin' kiddin' me? What the hell is wrong with you, man? You keep fucking it all up. It's like you can't help but be a little bitch."

I felt myself freeze at his ridicule that lately held a note of something more cruel. "I'm not fucking anything up!"

"From where I'm sitting, all I see is a guy tryin' to mess around with two chick and yet here you are, a sad sack whining about your

problems like a little fucking bitch." He flung the words at me like knives. Neither of us spoke for a few minutes, bad blood stewing between us. But then he pointed to the convenience store in front of us. "Pull over here. I want to get some brews."

I did as I was told. I waited in the car as he went inside.

The argument with Lucy had been bad. We both said things we'd never be able to take back. But I had made my choice. I knew Lucy would never forgive me. Not that it really mattered. Lucy's opinion about my life was no longer an issue.

I deserved to be happy. It was time for me to put myself first.

Lucy's feelings didn't really enter into any of it.

Marty came back a few minutes later and climbed into the backseat this time, spreading out his legs, lounging with his twelve pack like I was his chauffeur. Then we were on the road again, heading out of town—toward Jagged Point. Marty opened a can and handed one to me. The last thing I needed was a DUI, but I took it and drank deeply, wanting to drown my sorrows. Everything had gone to shit, and I wasn't sure how to fix it.

"I told Lucy I don't want to get married. I'm thinking of leaving town," I said suddenly. God, Lucy would hate me even more if she knew I'd told him that. She loathed Marty for some reason. The intensity of her hatred grew the closer he and I got.

Marty let out a low whistle. "You're a braver man than me. That Lucy, she's a wildcard. Who knows what she's gonna do now. I've seen murder in that woman's eyes, and it's scary as shit." Marty didn't sound scared. That anger I had seen earlier flared back to life.

"Lucy wouldn't hurt me—"

"I'm not talkin' about you, man. I'm thinkin' of Jenn," Marty interjected with venom.

I glanced at him in the rearview mirror. "I don't think I ever told you her name."

Marty took a long drink of beer, his face hard. "Whose name?"

"Jenn Moore."

What was he hiding from me?

"Do you know her or something?" I asked.

"Moore, huh? Interesting." He appeared thoughtful, and I noted that he didn't answer my question. My head was muddled, and I didn't want to spend time wondering about Marty's change of mood, or his secrets.

"Lucy wouldn't hurt Jenn," I repeated, needing reassurance.

"I wouldn't be so sure about that. A woman scorned and all that. I told you to lock her down while you could. Now, I don't think you could even if you tried," Marty retorted nastily. "And what about Jenn? You're puttin' her in the damn lion's den. What sort of man sets his woman up like that?" He spat onto the floor of my car. "You're fuckin' weak."

I was stung by his derision.

I didn't have time to answer because that's when I saw her. I turned the steering wheel sharply and stopped alongside her.

She was walking, her head down, sweat dripping from her forehead, her book bag heavy on her shoulders.

I beeped my horn and she looked up. Everything inside me went perfectly still.

I could tell she was leaving.

An ugly fury unfurled inside me.

She was leaving town.

Leaving me!

I couldn't let that happen.

I wouldn't.

I rolled down the window.

"Hey, need a ride?"

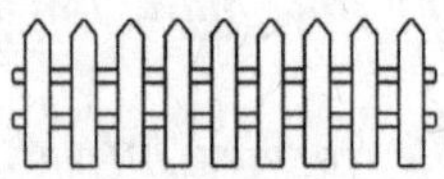

Today 8:18 AM

Jer, heads up, Rhett was arrested for murder.

Fuuuucckkk.

About time too. He became such a dick after marrying Lucy.

It'll be nice to see that asshole knocked down. Jenn should have listened and stayed away from that clown.

Maybe it was Lucy? We all know what a psycho she is. Or that Marty dude. He was a weirdo.

Jenn Moore fucked around and found out if you ask me.

Sure man, whatever. I think Lucy and Rhett did it together. Those that kill together, stay together.

CHAPTER

10

Jenn

The Past

Early June—Fifteen Years Ago

IT FELT LIKE I was being watched.

I couldn't shake it.

Perhaps I could put it down to the fact that everyone in Fern River seemed to be paying attention to what I was doing.

I couldn't go into the grocery store without conversations stopping and eyes drifting over me in a way that let me know I was the source of their gossip.

I thought I could be invisible here, but it now felt a little too much like what I had run away from.

But that wasn't it.

That wasn't why I felt a nerve-racking paranoia with my every movement.

I felt as though I were running out of time. As if any moment this new life I was trying to carve out for myself would be blown apart.

Because of a past I couldn't get away from.

I sat in a booth at Ryder Creek Bowling eating a basket of fries. I covered them with ketchup, turning them into a pile of mushy potatoes.

"What's a hot girl like you doin' all by herself?"

I felt myself stiffen. I was used to unwanted attention. I had been on the road long enough that I had become adept at fending it off. But here, in this tiny, claustrophobic town, it felt like I was being backed into a corner at every turn. The scrawny guy wearing a backward baseball cap and basketball jersey was smiling at me, a toothpick between his lips. He had the predatory smile that I had come to associate with men who expected something from women.

"Just hanging out," I said quietly, trying to make myself as small as possible.

"Never seen you before. Where are you from?" he asked, leaning against my seat, his body a little too close for comfort.

"Oh, here and there," I said, avoiding his question. I gave him a quick smile, hoping to placate him. I knew better than to make a man angry, so I made sure to keep my face neutral.

Why couldn't people mind their own business?

Why couldn't men leave women alone?

Why did simply existing serve as some kind of proposed invitation?

Why did we always have to give an explanation for where we were going or who we were with?

It was enough to make anyone want to scream.

He laughed, but there was a hardness to it I knew I shouldn't ignore. "Come on, sweetheart, just give us a smile. I can imagine those full lips of yours are good for all kinds of things." He wiggled his eyebrows. Did he think he was being funny? "It's a joke, okay?" He sat beside me on the same side of the booth, trapping me in with no room for escape. "I'm Jeremy Majors. I work here. I'm not trying to be a creep or anything."

For a guy not trying to be a creep, he was failing miserably.

I knew I had to play this carefully. I chanced a quick look around. No one was paying attention to us, and we were situated in a secluded corner of the bowling alley. I should have thought better about where I was sitting.

Not feeling like I had any other option, I introduced myself. "Jenn Moore."

"Nice to meet you, Jenn Moore." He sucked on the toothpick noisily. "You gonna bowl?"

I looked around the surprisingly busy bowling alley. It was something straight out of the 1970s with wood-paneled walls and orange and yellow plastic-covered booths. A couple of old-school pinball machines were shoved in a corner next to a battered pool table and an ancient Pac-Man arcade game. The only thing that appeared modern and up-to-date were the lanes themselves. Modern score screens hung from the ceilings, and the ball returns gleamed like they were brand-new.

"I was thinking about it. But I'm waiting to see if I have company." I had hoped to run into Rhett. While it was nice meeting him up at Jagged Point, what I wanted more than anything was to spend time with him doing other things. What I longed for was for us to go on an actual date. I wasn't so clueless that I didn't feel the heat between us or see the way he looked at me.

Sure, we were friends, but it was a friendship that begged to be something more.

Yet, every time I brought up meeting somewhere that wasn't in the middle of the woods, he made an excuse. But I knew he went bowling with friends during the week. He had mentioned it in passing only a few days ago when we were sitting together on top of the rocky overlook. I held on to all the tiny details he gave me, tucking them away, knowing they were important.

So, yeah, I came to the bowling alley because I thought I might run into him. Because our time together was never long enough. Did that make me pathetic? Probably, but I didn't care.

I pulled out my phone and looked at our last text exchange from only an hour ago, liking the bubbly warmth it caused in the center of my chest.

Rhett: You never finished telling me that story about the time you brought home a skunk thinking it was a stray cat. I guess we'll have to meet up tomorrow so you can tell me the rest.:-)

Me: Absolutely! It's not like I have a full schedule, LOL.

Rhett: So it's a date then. I'll meet you at lunchtime in the usual spot. I'll even bring your favorite cinnamon rolls.

Me: You sure know the way to a girl's heart.:-*

Rhett: Or maybe just yours.;-)

"The first game is on the house. No sense wasting the day away waiting for someone who might not show. I can keep you company." Jeremy was clearly not put off by my efforts to disengage. In fact, he slid closer to me, boxing me in even more.

I wiped my hands on a napkin. "I think I'd like to bowl actually." I hesitated before making my position clear. "Though you're working, so it's probably better I play this one by myself." I held my breath, waiting to see how he'd respond.

Jeremy's face darkened slightly. He loomed over me, and I wanted to cower into the corner. "That's how it is, huh?" He looked around as if to see how many people were nearby. Thankfully, a couple came in and called out hellos to Jeremy. He shrugged and slid out of the booth. I tried not to sag in relief. "Whatever, come on then, I'll get you some shoes."

I stood up, tucked my phone back in my pocket, and followed Jeremy to the counter. I took off my battered sneakers and handed them to him, and he put them on the shelf before spraying a pair of bowling shoes with disinfectant. "Here ya go. You can have lane three."

He seemed to have gotten over his hurt feelings at my rejection. I felt myself relax just a little. "Don't get too bothered by the group over there." He pointed to a group of older men and women. "They're from the Baptist church on Lee Drive. They come here every Tuesday evening for Bible and Bowling. They're an excitable bunch."

"Duly noted," I said before making my way to the open lane. I looked over at the people in lane four, thinking back with fondness mixed with regret to my own days of bowling with my Bible study group.

I picked up the heaviest bowling ball in the ball return and lumbered my way to the edge of the lane. Swinging it between my legs granny style, I smiled to myself as I thought about the last time I had played. It had been the first time I had rolled a strike. The momentary pride at the accomplishment was quickly overshadowed with what happened afterward.

I rolled the ball as hard as I could toward the pins, and it ambled along, knocking over all but two.

"Nice"

I practically jumped out of my skin at the sound of the familiar male voice so close to me.

Rhett grinned, gesturing toward the lane. "Care if I join you?" He handed me a cup with a straw.

"Thanks." I took a drink, enjoying the fizzy sweetness on my tongue. "Vanilla Coke, yum!" I took another long drink. "How did you know it was my favorite?"

"You mentioned it one time." He answered with a shy smile.

It seemed I wasn't the only one that paid attention to all the details. He had no idea how that made me feel important and wanted. It had been a long time since I had felt that way—if ever.

I put the soda down. "Finally up for a game?" I asked teasingly.

Rhett chuckled. "Sure, why not?"

"That's great!" I exclaimed with perhaps too much excitement, but Rhett seemed to like my reaction. I wanted to hug him but wasn't sure if I should. "Here, let me take my second turn." I rolled the ball again, knocking down the remaining pins.

"A spare, awesome!" Rhett enthused, giving me a high five.

I sat down and watched him bowl, getting a strike with little effort. When he turned back around, I jumped to my feet and this time gave into the urge and hugged him. "Good job, Rhett." I squeezed him tight.

Neither of us let go right away. He hugged me close, his hands pressed to the small of my back, the heat of his palms searing my skin. My heartbeat quickened, and I could hear his breathing deepen.

I pulled back slightly and looked at him. "I'm really glad you're here. I've . . . I've missed you," I told him.

"We just saw each other yesterday," he reminded me with a twinkle in his eye.

I ducked my head, feeling embarrassed by my admission. He tilted my chin up with his finger. "I missed you too. All the time," he whispered.

I swallowed thickly, feeling things change between us with those simple words.

I felt safe around him. Maybe it was because he was the opposite of everything I knew. Or that with his sweet smile and warm eyes, he didn't seem like a man to be feared.

"I've never had all this," I murmured, unable to look at anything but him.

"All of what?" Rhett asked, frowning slightly.

"This. Fun outings with friends. A boy buying me my favorite soda. Being able to do the normal teenage stuff." I felt my throat tighten with tears. I had missed so much. I hadn't realized it until Rhett.

Rhett tucked a piece of hair behind my ear. "Well then, I guess it's my job to make sure you experience it all."

"I think it might be too late for the prom and class ring." I laughed a little, even though the truth was depressing.

"You're telling me no guy ever gave you his ring to wear? I find that hard to believe, a beautiful girl like you." Rhett's compliments hit me right in the center of my chest.

I shook my head. "Nope. I never really dated." I hated how babyish I sounded.

Rhett lifted my hand, tracing the length of my ring finger with his thumb. "Doesn't seem right. Though I like it no one had you first," he murmured.

There was another beat of silence as we held one another. The noise of the bowling alley faded into the background as our breaths caught and held suspended as if the air itself was waiting in anticipation.

That feeling of being watched creeped slowly across my skin. I glanced over Rhett's shoulder and saw Jeremy staring at us, a thunderous expression on his pock-marked face.

I quickly looked away, burrowing myself into Rhett's protective warmth.

"Rhett, hello!" Rhett pulled away so fast I stumbled and had to catch myself from falling over. I saw an older woman with smooth blond hair approaching us. Her greeting may have been for Rhett, but her eyes were on me.

"Hi, Mrs. Young," Rhett replied, glancing my way before taking a noticeable step away from me.

"Hi, Rhett!" A woman with obviously dyed red hair waved enthusiastically from the group of middle-aged women avidly watching us.

Rhett lifted his hand in a halfhearted wave.

"Ignore Celia," the blond woman said with a roll of her eyes. "I was just telling Chuck the other day we haven't seen you in ages. He tells me you're studying pre-law now. Good for you. I'm sure Cliff is pleased." She looked pointedly at me again. "Your mom, too, I bet."

Rhett seemed very aware of the woman's keen observations. There was a strange undercurrent to the interaction. It felt loaded with all the things not being said.

"I'm working hard," Rhett told her with one of his warm smiles.

The woman put her hand on her hip. "Though clearly not *that* hard if you can take a break to go bowling." She laughed, though there wasn't an ounce of humor in her words.

It was all judgment. Every small town was the same, local busybodies and gossips who liked to make everything their business. They were both the worst and best part of any community. Friendliness tinged with malicious examination.

Rhett laughed too. "You know what they say, all work and no play . . ." He didn't bother to finish the sentiment.

The woman turned to me. "Since Rhett seems to have forgotten his manners," she said and held out her hand. I shook it tentatively. "I'm Tanya Young, the chief of police's wife. And you are?" The implication was clear. She was watching me and reporting back.

"I'm Jenn Moore." I didn't offer anything else. Not to be rude but because my throat seemed to close up.

"And how do you know our Rhett?" She patted his arm and his smile became a grimace.

"He's been nice enough to keep me company and show me around since I'm new in town." Given Rhett's furtive glance, I got the impression I should make an excuse for us being together. I felt like I was tiptoeing through a minefield, but I didn't know who had planted the bombs. I went along with it, for his sake more than anything else. He must have his reasons.

"He *is* a gentleman. Always has been. That's why we can't wait until the we—"

"It was good to see you, Mrs. Young. But I have to get going," Rhett interrupted abruptly.

Mrs. Young seemed taken aback by Rhett's bluntness, but she covered it well.

"Of course. It was nice seeing you. Be sure to pass on my regards to Lucinda, won't you." She glanced at me again and didn't bother to say goodbye before returning to her lady's group.

"Shit," he muttered under his breath.

"Is everything okay?" I asked.

Rhett's expression hardened. "Everything's fine." He looked at the group of women, who were making it obvious they were talking about us. That feeling of being watched amplified until it was like spiders crawling over my skin. "I'm really sorry, but I have to go."

"But you just got here." I was confused.

Rhett rubbed the back of his neck. "Yeah, I have a lot going on. I don't have time to bowl right now."

"You're always in such a rush," I teased, attempting to cover up my hurt feelings. "You need to take some time to relax."

Rhett's eyes flashed with something dark. "I'm busy, Jenn. I told you I was in college—"

"Studying law. I remember. I also remember you saying once that you didn't like it." I was being pushy. I felt it. He felt it.

"Pre-law," he corrected, "and it's tough."

"I'm sure it is. I didn't mean to keep you from it." I swallowed, familiar feelings bubbling up inside me. It reminded me of home.

"You have no idea," he said with a note of frustration.

"It's only that you're obviously doing something you don't want to do, and well, have you ever thought about why you're doing it? About who you're doing it for?" I had never been a bold person. I wasn't the kind of girl to speak my mind—it had never been my place to speak out. But I cared about Rhett, and I didn't like seeing him so worried. I felt it was my duty as his friend—or whatever I was to him—to try and make him feel better.

Rhett's eyes narrowed. "I'm doing this for *me*, Jenn. And to give my mom a better life. That's all I want to do."

I cocked my head, not wanting to poke the bear but also not wanting to back down. I had been doing that my whole life. It took a lot of effort and bravery on my part to say what I thought. My voice had been silenced for so long, it was difficult making it heard now.

"Are you really, though? Have you thought about what's the best thing for you? Because you seem stressed every time I see you—"

Rhett laughed dryly, his face hard. "Unbelievable," he muttered under his breath. "Have you ever been to college, Jenn? Do you even know what it's like? How stressful it can be?" His words were dismissive and hurtful.

"No, I haven't." My voice was small. I felt even smaller.

"Then maybe you're not the right person to judge what's best for me."

We were both shocked by his words.

Not just his words.

It was what he didn't say that dripped with offhanded cruelty.

"I guess I'll see you whenever then." I couldn't hide the tears thick in my throat. I had to bite back what I really wanted to say. That I didn't deserve his nastiness. That I was only trying to help him. But I had learned my lesson the hard way. When the dragon roared, I needed to back off and make myself as tiny as possible.

I turned back to my lane. I didn't want to play anymore. I wanted to leave immediately. Heat crawled up my chest, and I wiped away the tears that had already fallen. I was never good at holding them back. My mother used to tell me I had to learn to hide my feelings better. She had figured out that the best way to survive was to keep a smile on her face and the sadness tucked up inside. She was quite the role model.

Rhett reached out to take my hand. "I'm sorry. I'm being a jerk. I know you're only trying to be helpful." He glanced at the group of gossipy women again and quickly dropped it. "This town talks, Jenn. And there's nothing people love more than a scandal, even if there isn't one."

"Why would there be a scandal? We're two friends hanging out together and playing a game of bowling." He was hiding something, but after the way he had reacted, I didn't want to pry much further and push him away.

Rhett pressed his lips into a thin line. "A man and a woman together, even if it's innocent, is *always* a scandal in a town like Fern River."

I sighed heavily. "All small towns are the same. Where I came from, nothing was private." I laughed halfheartedly. "But this *is* innocent. There's nothing to see here."

He looked at everything but me. I worried that I sounded desperate.

But I liked him. And I needed friends. I was starting to feel lonely from my time on the road. Being a young girl, having to be on guard twenty-four seven, left me feeling on edge.

And the constant paranoia of being followed and watched was starting to get to me.

Rhett appeared startled. "You still want to hang out with me? Even after I've been such an ass?"

I put my hand on his arm. "Of course I do. I'd love it, actually."

His expression cleared, and his grin was sincere and blinding. "Do you want to go hiking again?"

I nodded. "Absolutely."

"Meet me back up at Jagged Point tomorrow afternoon. The walk isn't too long, right?"

I didn't want to tell him that I hated walking the isolated stretch of road by myself. That I felt exposed and hyper-vigilant. I wanted him to offer to pick me up and go out there together.

But I didn't want him to change his mind.

"I'd love to. The overlook is one of the prettiest views I've ever seen."

"Maybe not the prettiest," he murmured, his eyes lingering on my face in a way I knew meant he wasn't talking about the cliffs.

I blushed but felt better that it seemed we were okay again.

"I'll be back from school around one o'clock. I'll head straight there." His expression brightened, and I loved that I was the one that did that.

"Sounds good," I said with enthusiasm. "Give me a call when you're on your way. I bet I can beat you to the top."

Rhett chuckled. "That sounds like a challenge." He winked at me and I melted a little. "Okay. I'll call you."

"Promise?"

He nodded but didn't say the word. It seemed obvious that he omitted it, but I ignored it all the same.

He looked around uncomfortably. "I've really got to go. I'll see you tomorrow, though."

As I turned to the door to watch him leave, I saw something I hoped was a trick of my imagination.

Because, for a moment, I saw a familiar figure. A shadowed face staring back at me from the other side of the room.

The same cruel smile I thought I'd left far behind. I took a deep breath, closed my eyes.

When I opened them, *he* was gone.

"You think you can outrun me, Jennifer? I'll hunt you down like a deer. You think you're so smart, but I'll always catch you."

The memory of his words embedded themselves in me like a hookworm. I knew I should be wary. That perhaps I *wasn't* seeing things.

I was a rat in a cage. I knew that no matter how far I fled, he was always there, right behind me, nipping at my heels.

I could almost hear the ticking clock counting down to my doom.

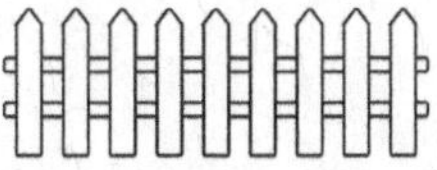

Message

I love talking to you. I'm so glad you came to Fern River.
-Rhett

Options **Back**

CHAPTER

11

Lucinda

The Present

I HAD JUST SPENT the last three hours going over my alibi statement with Glynn. He had grilled me within an inch of my life, yet even he was impressed with how calm and unruffled I remained. My story never wavered.

No one would know that every word was a complete lie.

I thought I'd be more exhausted afterward, yet there was something exhilarating about telling a story that others believed, even when it was all bullshit.

As I was leaving I ran into Alison Schaffer, my old high school friend who was now married to Rhett's friend Caleb. We hadn't spoken in years. After everything that had happened with Jenn, she, like many of my old friends, kept a wide berth.

My last name may have saved me from becoming a suspect, but it had cost me a lot of friendships.

"Hi, Al," I called out when I realized she was coming over to speak to me.

"I heard about Rhett," she said by way of greeting. She didn't even bother with a hello. She never had been great in the whole manners department.

"I'm sure you have." I didn't bother to smile or be polite. What was the point?

"You know everyone thinks he did it," Alison said with a shrug. "And that your dad covered it up."

I suppressed a sigh. Alison had always been a shit stirrer. And she never minced words. She used to say that she had no filter. I thought that was just her excuse to be a bitch.

"That's ridiculous," I told her tiredly.

"Just tellin' you what everyone is sayin'." Alison hadn't aged well. Five kids and a husband that drank every night did that to a woman. She looked haggard and bitter. "I said it then and I'll say it now, that girl got what was comin' to her."

I glanced around, surprised Alison would be voicing such an awful thing out in the open. "I don't think that's fair—"

Alison licked her dry, cracked lips. "I hated how she came to town and acted like everything belonged to her, even the guys. Jeremy went crazy over her. Caleb, too, if I'm bein' honest. Fern River is no place for someone like that. It was disgusting how Rhett took up with her with no thought to anyone else. It's no shock she ended up dead."

Her words were spiteful and I recoiled slightly at the hostility she exuded.

I had always suspected she had a crush on Rhett, and it seemed my instincts were right. Alison was your typical small-town mean girl with even smaller opinions.

Not wanting to enter into any sort of talk about Rhett and his upcoming murder trial, I made an excuse to leave and headed home.

Leaving the house probably wasn't a good idea when that was what I had to put up with when I did.

Now, I was alone for the first time since Rhett had been released. Actually, it was the first time I had been alone at my parents' house since I was a teenager. It felt strange rambling around the big house, seeing pictures lining the walls that commemorated every step of my life.

Staying in my childhood bedroom, it was so easy to hand over the reins to my parents. But I knew if I was going to survive what came next, I had to keep as much control as I could.

I was no longer Lucy Herbaugh, beauty queen, straight-A student, devoted girlfriend, then fiancée, then wife of Rhett Clark.

Now I was someone different. Someone darker. Someone angrier.

I knew Rhett hated being here and on some twisted level, I enjoyed his discomfort. Protecting family was the most important thing to my dad. He was ruthless in ensuring his girls were taken care of. He may be formidable, he may be scary at times, but I never doubted his love for us, or his drive to protect his reputation. They were both all wrapped up in each other.

I wished Rhett had even a fraction of my father's loyalty. But one thing I had learned about my husband over the years is that he protected his own feelings first and foremost.

Now our marriage was strained to the point of breaking. Rhett and I existed side by side in a facsimile of how our life used to be.

On the outside, everything looked normal.

But inside, we were decaying more and more each day.

Rhett wasn't the only one trapped in a life he couldn't get out of. He thought I was his jailor, but in truth, he was mine. The specter of the man I wanted him to be kept me frozen in place, too afraid to leave. I hated that I still hoped he'd love me in the way I thought he used to.

That one day I'd be enough.

Rhett and I hadn't really spoken since the day of his bail hearing. Our conversations lived entirely in the realm of his attorney's office.

Within these walls we interacted with McKenzie, but never each other.

We slept side by side in bed every night, but didn't touch.

There was a wall between us that neither of us were in a hurry to climb.

Rhett seemed terrified—his fate held in the balance. But his terror wasn't for what he'd leave behind. It wasn't for the life of his wife and daughter, who would forever be tainted by association. He didn't, for one moment, consider the ramifications of this on anyone but himself.

Rhett was still at Glynn's office preparing for his preliminary hearing, which was scheduled for two weeks away. I had claimed I wasn't feeling well, so left after my part was over. McKenzie was spending the day with my mother, who had swooped in, once again, to play surrogate parent to my child, who was becoming more and more reliant on her grandmother as her primary caregiver.

It didn't feel great. As if I were unable to perform the two roles I was supposed to inherently do well. Being a mother, and being a wife.

Yet I couldn't ignore how relieved I was to be by myself. Away from the parody of marriage and motherhood for a little while.

I let myself out onto my parent's expansive back patio. It was made of decorative brick that curved and swept along the length of the backyard in perfect harmonious lines. An outdoor kitchen had been built off to the side that I was pretty sure Mom and Dad had never even used. A hot tub was tucked away, hidden behind large butterfly bushes, housed within a gazebo of glass and wood.

My much smaller home felt inadequate when compared to the tastefully designed and decorated home of Clifford and Mabel Herbaugh. I thought I had assembled something different for my life, but it seemed my world was only a smaller, less impressive version of my parents'.

Nothing came free for a Herbaugh. Not love. Not affection. Not respect. We had our parts to play, and we all did so perfectly. The alternative was something too horrible to think about.

Being back here, wandering the grounds as I had done as a child, I felt the same desperate longing for validation I once had. A longing that had never really gone away.

I thought I had done everything right, yet I had failed spectacularly at the same time.

The air had an unseasonal chill to it, and I had forgotten to put on a jacket. I reached behind one of the ornate planters filled with my mother's begonias and found the pack of cigarettes I had hidden there months ago during one of our visits. My secret vice reared its head most often when I was with my parents, and I was thankful for my foresight now.

I fished the lighter from the half-full box and lit one, taking a deep drag into my lungs. It was a nasty habit that I hid very, very well. Not even Rhett knew how, when I was particularly stressed, I snuck away to have a smoke. Or two. Or three.

I blew out the smoke, watching it drift away into nothing.

I stared down at my phone, opened my contacts and scrolled down until I reached the one labeled "Rabbit." My thumb hovered over the screen.

It was a cyclical pattern.

Think about calling.

Talk myself out of it.

Berate myself for not deleting the number years ago, the guilt clawing up my insides.

A few months later, I'd think about calling again. And eventually I'd cave. The connection was important to keep, and I was careful about never crossing the line I had drawn in the sand. But I needed to know I still had a key to my prison cell out there.

But this time was different. The need was bordering on anguish.

What would Rhett say if he knew? Why did I still feel horrible at the thought of his pain after everything he'd done?

I read the last message I had received and felt something like relief.

Rabbit: I'm still here. You don't need to keep checking up on me.
Me: I'm trusting you. I hope it's not misguided.
Rabbit: I'm not going anywhere. Your monthly gifts make sure of that.

That was from four months ago. My misgivings were evident, yet I took solace in the fact that I was the one calling the shots. The dynamic was hard won, but the battle had been worth it.

I knew I was being incredibly self-destructive by holding onto this. But it was my favorite flavor of mistake.

I stubbed out the cigarette and hid it beneath a planter. I stood up to go inside when I saw the gate at the side of the house slowly open.

Feeling a flash of irrational fear, I looked around for a weapon, settling on a heavy rock at my feet.

Jenn Moore's tear-soaked face flashed through my mind. Dirt mixing with blood on her goose-pimpled flesh.

No, I would *not* think about that.

The gate pushed open, revealing who it was, and I dropped the large rock. It landed in the decorative pea gravel with a thud.

"What the hell are you doing sneaking around Mom and Dad's backyard?" I demanded, trying to get my breathing under control. I watched as my baby sister jumped, clearly not expecting to find me here.

"You scared the life out of me," she shrieked, pressing her hand to her chest.

"Scared *you*? I'm not the one prowling around like a burglar. Why wouldn't you ring the doorbell like a normal person? And more importantly, why aren't you at work?" I glared at her, feeling perturbed.

Bailey glanced around before sinking down into one of the patio chairs with a heavy sigh. "I called in sick. I guess I should have knocked, but I didn't know if Rhett would be resting."

I raised an eyebrow. "You mean you were avoiding Dad."

She glanced up at me and grinned, her brown eyes wide and guileless. "Is it that obvious?"

Looking at her, you'd never know we were sisters. We were opposites in every way. Her hair was brown, where mine was almost white blond. Her eyes were also brown, mine were a clear, vivid blue. People always said I got the looks in the family. But my sister made up for it by being sporty and outgoing, impulsive and passionate. She was always one to act first then think later. When we were younger, I found her eager to please nature aggravating. Now, as adults I still found it aggravating, but I hid it better.

"So obvious we'll start calling you captain," I joked.

Over the years, the relationship between Bailey and our dad had become fraught. Whenever they were in the same room, an argument ensued. Mom, however, mostly avoided my sister. Her affection was more distant, and I knew it affected Bailey as much as it affected me. Our mother's brand of parenting involved steely judgment and unreasonable expectations. In Fern River, everyone loved Mabel Jean. Yet, her own daughters' feelings for her were more complicated.

Bailey waved her hand in the air between us. "Anyway, is the general home, or is the coast clear?"

"You're good. Rhett and Dad are at his lawyer's office, and Mom is at the park with McKenzie."

"Phew!" Bailey sat up in her chair and grinned. "I couldn't deal with them today. I haven't been able to relax in days, you know, with everything going on."

"*You* can't relax?"

Bailey cringed. "Sorry, I know it's nothing compared to what you and Rhett must be going through. I wanted to make sure you were both okay. I've been so worried about Rhett. I hate that he's going through all this. Do you want to talk about it?"

She sounded agonized, her pain obvious. She and Rhett had always been close. When she was a teenager, he'd make it a point to spend time with her, even when she was annoying the crap out of me. Her constant demands for his attention didn't seem to put him off. He didn't have any siblings and had always felt he missed out on having someone younger looking up to him.

So, any irritation I felt faded at her genuine concern. She had no idea that Rhett's current situation was self-inflicted.

I sat beside her, feeling my limbs sag as the exhaustion I had kept staunchly at bay seeped into my bones. "Not really, Bai. It's been easier *not* to talk about it." I pulled at a loose thread on my blouse. "At least that's what our attorney says we should do. Don't want us tainting our testimony by corroborating." I looked around the large backyard. "I try not to leave the house if I don't have to. Every time I go into town, I feel everyone looking at me. And you know there are certain people that are loving all this."

Bailey grimaced. "It's pretty bad at work. Everyone either offers fake sympathy or wants details. It's awful."

"I figured it was better to keep to myself. Otherwise, Rhett won't be the only one in a courtroom." I shared a side-eyed glance with my sister, and we both chuckled uneasily.

Bailey chewed on her bottom lip, her eyes glassy. "I wish there was something I could do."

"There's nothing anyone can do, unless you could invent a time machine so I could go back fifteen years and stop that bitch from ever coming to Fern River in the first place." If the voracity of my anger surprised my sister, she didn't show it. In fact, she smiled, as if she appreciated my ire.

I pressed the heels of my palms to my eyes, willing the painful thud to dissipate. "I shouldn't have said that. It's not her. Well, at least, not *just* her. It's Rhett too. It's everything."

Bailey watched me with a mixture of concern and apprehension. It was times like this that I wished we had the kind of sisterly bond where I could tell her everything. But that wasn't our reality.

"You shouldn't blame him, Lucy. He loves you. And you love him. You've always loved him. Remember, *she's* the one who got between you two. None of this would be happening if she had kept her nose out of your relationship."

I wanted to tell her that while I appreciated her defending me, it wasn't that simple—she had no idea how deep this went. But instead I said, "Be thankful you don't have a man in your life making a mess of things."

Bailey had never gotten married, but she had a job she loved, working as a domestic violence advocate at the local women's shelter. Her days were spent accompanying women and children to court and devising safety plans for those fleeing abuse. I often wondered how she could be happy with such a stressful job, but she insisted it was her calling. Though she wasn't the only one who donated to worthy causes.

However, my philanthropy was a bit more selfish.

Regardless of reasons, she always seemed content to play the doting aunt to McKenzie and spend time with Rhett and me.

Bailey's face hardened before relaxing into a smile. "Yeah, I guess so." She looked like she wanted to say more, and if I was a better sister, I would have asked, but I was too lost in my own problems to give it much thought.

"So, anyway, look what I dug up last weekend when I was going through some of the boxes from when I moved out." She pulled a decorative wooden box out of her purse and held it out to me. I could see the initials *LAH* on the top.

My insides froze.

"Why did *you* have it?" It came out as a raspy whisper. I cleared my throat and forced a smile. "I thought I threw that out."

Bailey gave me a confused look. "Why would you throw it out? This was your memory box when you were a teenager." She gave me a sheepish look. "Okay, so maybe I took it and hid it in my closet when I was sixteen. I never really grew out of wanting anything that reminded me of you."

"That's . . . sweet?" It came out more as a question because I didn't want to tell her how irritating I found it. Bailey always had sticky fingers. Our father used to call her his little magpie.

Though, when it came to my things, if it mattered to me, she was drawn to it. I would find my jewelry, my clothes, my *diary*, hidden away in the nooks and crannies of her room.

We'd have explosive fights and then she would return them, only for the same items to go missing again months later. Mom and Dad knew how annoying it had been—their things had also gone missing from time to time—but they had hoped she would grow out of it.

"Yeah, well, I've always been overly sentimental." Bailey laughed as if it were all a big joke. I wanted to snatch the box from her and set the damn thing on fire, but didn't dare. My reactions, especially from here on out, had to be measured. Controlled. Even around my own family.

Especially around my family.

"I wasn't sure what this was." Bailey lifted up a scrap of sequined fabric.

I couldn't help but grin. "That's from my pageant dress freshman year."

"That was the first year you won the Young Miss Fern River Fair, right?"

I couldn't help but glow with pride. "That's right. The first of many wins, I might add."

Bailey spread out the small scrap of material on her knee. "Where did the rest of it go?"

I chuckled. "That was the piece MaryBeth Rutz ripped from my sleeve after losing."

Bailey's eyes widened with a smirk. "And you kept it? Why?"

"Because I hated MaryBeth, and I wanted to remember the look on her face when the judges said *my* name and not hers." Even to this day, the memory warmed me up inside.

Over the years, I had developed a nasty habit of collecting enemies. And just as good a habit of defeating them.

Bailey continued to rummage through the box. "Awww, look."

My stomach dropped.

"Rhett's class ring," I said quietly, watching as Bailey slid it on her finger and held it up to the light. The gaudy gold band hugged a chunky blue stone with an embossed *FR* on the top for Fern River Highschool. I had felt so special when he asked me to wear it our junior year.

And devastated when I saw it around someone else's neck years later, having never realized he had taken it back.

"Take it off, Bailey," I commanded a little too harshly.

Bailey was admiring it as if it were a ten-carat diamond.

"Bailey, give it to me. Now!"

I reached over, grabbed her hand, and wrenched it off.

"Ow, Lucy, what the hell?"

Before I had time to defend my overly aggressive behavior, the patio door opened and Rhett came out. He looked haggard. He came up short when he saw Bailey and me.

"Oh. Hi." His words were deadened.

I quickly tucked the ring in my pocket.

Bailey went over and gave him a hug. "Rhett, how are you?"

He wrapped his arms around her, closing his eyes briefly. "I've been better." He glanced at me, then looked away.

"Lucy says you were meeting with your lawyer? How did it go?"

Rhett looked worn down, like he was at the breaking point—spending the afternoon with my father and his lawyer would do that. "Fine, I guess." Rhett let out a beleaguered sigh that made me want to scream. "Though I'm not sure Glynn is worth the money your dad is paying him. He doesn't seem very confident about my case."

I had no doubt that my father paying for his defense was grating on him. Well, tough cookies. We were in this mess because of him. His feelings had little say in any of this anymore.

"He's been talking to some people who say though the prosecution's case is built on circumstantial evidence, it's still very strong." Rhett's eyes burned into mine. "He has Marty's witness statement. Says he's in town." He paused. "Did you know that?"

"Why would I know that?" I answered a little too defensively.

We stared at each other while my sister looked between us in confusion, clearly sensing the tension. "Well, I'm sure Dad made sure you have a decent lawyer. He'll get you off." Her voice was a little too perky for the situation. "Not off, but prove it wasn't you. Right, Lucy?"

Rhett and I were still looking at each other. Neither wanting to concede an inch. When had we become this combative?

Oh, that's right . . . when we were nineteen years old.

"We'll see," Rhett said. "It's all down to what the judge and jury believe. And it sounds like Judge Balfour has an ax to grind with your father, which doesn't bode well for me." He shrugged, finally breaking eye contact. "Maybe it's all as it should be."

Bailey took his hand, her eyes full of tears. "Don't be so defeatist, Rhett. This is all a big mistake. Everything will be okay. You didn't do this. Everyone who knows you knows that." She seemed more cut up about Rhett's predicament than I was.

But then, she didn't know what I knew.

He gave my sister a weak smile. "I appreciate your confidence, Bai. You always make me feel better." Then his entire body drooped. "On my way home, I got a call from Sherry."

"Your principal? Why?" I asked.

"Apparently, they're not comfortable having a man about to stand trial for murder showing up and teaching sixteen-year-olds math. They've put me on administrative leave for the foreseeable future." He sounded like a man ready to roll over and show his belly.

"I guess that makes sense. I mean, what did you expect them to do?" I replied.

"I don't know, but a little support would be nice, Lucinda." He didn't try to hide his bitterness. I opened my mouth, but my husband turned away from me before I could speak. "It was nice seeing you, Bailey. Come back and see me soon. I could use some positivity in my life," he said, the cutting remark aimed squarely at me. Then he went inside and slammed the door behind him.

Bailey looked uncomfortable. "He doesn't seem good, Lucy. And honestly, neither do you. Are you guys okay?"

"I think we just need some time alone," I told her pointedly, and thankfully she got the hint.

"Okay. I'll head out then." She stood up and went back toward the gate.

I followed her. "Aren't you going inside before you leave? Dad probably came back with Rhett. He'll be in his office—"

"God, no. I'm going to sneak out the same way I came in." She blanched. "Otherwise, I'll be forced to sit through a lecture about whatever I've done wrong this week." This time we shared a genuine laugh at our father's expense.

"Fair point," I conceded. I walked Bailey out, and she gave me a quick hug.

"You'll fix this, Lucy. You always do. And if you can't, Dad definitely will. Dad can fix anything."

I held out my hand and Bailey looked at me in confusion. "The box."

My sister opened her purse, pulled out the wooden box and handed it to me with a grin.

"Is there anything else you've hung onto that I should know about?"

Bailey rolled her eyes. "It's not like you even knew it was gone, so obviously it wasn't that important."

She slipped out the gate without really answering me.

I watched as she walked to her car and gave her a wave as she climbed in and drove off a few seconds later.

My sister was right. I was going to fix it. And it was going to start with retracing our steps very carefully.

It was time to plug all those holes.

* * *

The Past

July 14, 2:10 AM*—Fifteen Years Ago*

I was shaking uncontrollably. I couldn't stop.

I couldn't believe everything that had happened.

Rhett wouldn't look at me.

He wouldn't say a word.

I tried to touch him, but he pushed me away. It was becoming much too easy for him to treat me like this.

His face was battered. I tried to clean his cuts, but he kept pulling away. I could tell he was in pain. But I knew it wasn't the injuries that had him groaning in agony.

I hadn't seen him in over twenty-four hours. Part of me was shocked to see him at all. After how things were left between us, I figured he had left town. But then news spread about the body found up at Jagged Point and I suspected—and hoped—he'd come around eventually.

When he showed up at my house looking the way he did, I took him inside and snuck him to my room before my parents could see him. Neither would be happy he was there.

I wasn't sure whether I was glad to see him or not. The jury was still out on whether I had forgiven him. Or if I ever would.

There was no talking. He laid down on my bed, as if he still had a right to, and turned his back to me. It enraged me how he acted as if he hadn't so recently tried to break my heart and stomp all over it.

He had shown his hand. I knew the truth.

It was hard to accept how much he was truly capable of.

I had seen inside his ugly heart, and it devastated me.

But that didn't mean I wouldn't do what needed to be done.

Even though we hadn't said our vows yet, promises had still been made. And, unlike Rhett, I kept my word.

"I'll be back in a little bit," I told him, getting up from my bed, where we had been lying like two corpses since he had arrived.

Rhett didn't say anything. He didn't ask where I was going.

I didn't think he really cared.

He was too lost in his own misery.

But it was time for me to start cleaning up the mess we found ourselves in.

So I shoved the piece of discarded clothing Rhett had taken off into my purse and left my room without another word.

I hurriedly got in my car and drove to the other side of town. I parked surreptitiously around the corner of a run-down two-story house with peeling paint and missing most of its shutters. I knew he had been renting the place for dirt cheap from Jim Dellinger, a local slum lord. It had stood abandoned for over a decade because no one else wanted to live in a place with dirt floors and a porta potty in the yard due to no indoor plumbing.

I didn't have to knock on the door. He was already sitting on the porch.

"I figured you'd turn up here sooner or later, little rabbit." Marty spit tobacco juice into a Folgers can before pulling the wad from his lip and disposing of it. His face, like Rhett's, was black and blue. But unlike my fiancé, he seemed to have come out the victor.

Seeing him like this, I put some of the pieces together. If I asked him about what happened, would he, unlike Rhett, answer my questions?

In the end, I decided it didn't matter. All that mattered was hiding the evidence—and keeping myself out of it.

I pulled the shirt out of my purse and held it out to him. "You need to hang onto this for me." I was relieved that my hands were steady as I handed him the bloody fabric I'd put in a Ziploc bag.

Marty frowned in confusion. "What is this?" he asked as he examined it through the clear plastic. "Is this Rhett's shirt?" He looked at me sharply. "What crazy shit are you pulling me into, woman?"

"It doesn't matter, Marty, just do as I ask. I'll explain everything later."

His expression changed from casual nonchalance to dogged focus. "Is this about Jenn?" he demanded. He looked at the shirt again, staring at it with a face full of fury.

I took a step toward him, letting him see, just for a moment, a sliver of vulnerability. It was dangerous to give a man like Marty Richards a glimpse of anything authentic. You couldn't trust what he'd do with it.

I also knew that for whatever reason, he would do as I asked.

But his anger confused me.

I peered at him closely. "Why do you care?"

Marty glanced at me, his eyes full of fire. "Why are you giving this to me?" he countered, his jaw twitching with barely restrained anger.

I dropped my voice to a whisper and met his intense blue eyes. "Because my dad can't know about it, and there's no one else I trust to handle it. Please, Marty. I need your help. You're the only one I can turn to."

He hesitated. He seemed to be experiencing some kind of internal battle I didn't understand.

"Why can't you handle it yourself?" Marty challenged, his voice clipped and hard, his hands now shaking.

A good question that only had one answer.

"Because I need my hands clean of all this. It could ruin me."

A man like Marty would understand the desire for self-preservation. It was one of his defining characteristics.

I glanced around, relieved the street was empty. "Marty, please don't make this difficult—I need you." I saw the moment he caved. My ticket to his acquiescence.

Marty hesitated for only another moment, but then he shoved the shirt into his back pocket. "Fine. But this isn't for Rhett." The way he said my fiancé's name let me know exactly what he thought of him

"It's for me," I reassured him.

Though I wasn't sure I was the one he was doing it for.

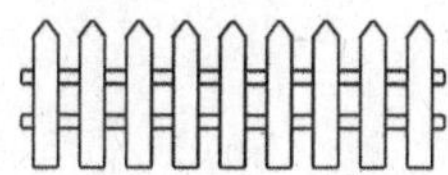

Marty 9:17PM

• Scored some dope, you down?

Me 9:22PM

✓ Sounds good, man. Give me an hour and I'll pick you up.

Marty 9:30PM

• Ball up and tell your woman you've got to go and to keep her mouth shut and her legs open.

Me 9:35PM

✓ Ha! Good one! Be right there.

CHAPTER 12
Rhett

The Past

Late June—Fifteen Years Ago

THE WORDS WERE beginning to blur together.

Even though exams were over, I was getting a jump start on my reading for next year. I knew it's what was expected of me. I was pretty sure I failed at least one of my tests and the disappointment from everyone would probably drown me.

It felt like I was studying nonstop, though this should have been my time to have a break. But I couldn't let up. It was the only way to keep my head above water. And when I wasn't cramming information into my skull, I was with Jenn. She was the only bright spot in my never-ending spiral of stress and guilt.

Because I still had a wedding on the horizon. One that I was expected to help with.

Feeling overwhelmed, I knew I needed to get out.

I pulled out my phone and typed a quick text.

Me: Meet me at the usual spot?

The answer came less than a minute later. I loved how she always seemed to be waiting for my messages. It was flattering to know a woman was sitting around hoping to hear from me. Particularly since Lucy always had her own thing going on. Lucy didn't wait around for anyone, especially her fiancé.

Jenn: I was hoping to hear from you! Pick me up?
Me: I plan to go for a run, so I'll meet you there.

This time there was a pause, and I wondered about it. I felt the stirrings of annoyance at her delay. What was the problem? I started to tap out a testy response when she finally replied.

Jenn: Okay. Meet you there.:-*

She had been adding kissy faces to all her messages recently. I knew we were dancing closer and closer to the line we would inevitably cross.

Jenn was attracted to me.

I was attracted to her.

But there was Lucy. And our wedding. And the life we were supposed to be building together.

In a fit of uncontrollable rage, I clenched my hand into a fist and hit the wall beside the mirror, which gave me nothing but bloodied knuckles. Screw Lucy and the stupid wedding. I was sick and tired of worrying about her feelings all the time.

I put a Band-Aid on my hand and headed back to my room and changed for my run. My frustrated anger needed an outlet. I jogged down the stairs, called out a goodbye to my mom and closed the door behind me before she could try and talk to me.

Lately even my mother was pissing me off.

As I was leaving, my phone vibrated again. Thinking it was from Jenn, I looked at the screen.

Bailey: Hey Rhett! Wanna go see the new Marvel movie this weekend? We haven't hung out in a while!:-(

This time I did feel a little guilty. Lucy wasn't the only person I had been blowing off lately. But I didn't want to feel bad about all the ways I was letting the Herbaugh girls down. So I ignored the text and shoved my phone back in my pocket.

I didn't bother to give my muscles time to warm up before I began running, heading for Jagged Point.

The streets and houses grew farther apart, and then the landscape turned green and lush. Trees and bushes took the place of houses and storefronts. A small, curved bridge finally took me over a burbling creek before I joined the mostly paved path and felt the steady incline of the earth beneath me as I headed into the mountains.

About halfway up, the path turned to gravel. From there it was a fairly straightforward hike, with a windy elevation to the cliffs. Once I reached my usual turnaround spot—an old, gnarled oak tree—I headed back for the overlook.

The isolation of this place never bothered me the way it bothered other people. Lucy hated Jagged Point and refused to come with me when I hiked or ran. The place's creepy history had always put her off.

Suddenly a sharp cramp shot through my calf. I cried out and stumbled before tripping over my own feet and landing with a loud grunt. I rolled onto my back, lying there for a while, breathing heavily.

Pain throbbed through my limbs, but I was pretty sure nothing was broken, and I breathed a small sigh of relief. Lucy would *not* be happy if I had to wear a cast for the next six to twelve weeks. My broken limbs—and pride—would heal, but bad wedding photos would haunt us for a lifetime.

"Sorry I'm late," a familiar voice called out.

I struggled to get to my feet, wincing as the broken skin stretched, blood oozing down my leg. I almost fell back down when Jenn caught my elbow and held me upright.

"Well, this is embarrassing," I snapped, pulling away from her. If my face hadn't already been red from exertion, it would definitely be red with humiliation. "You can let go, I am capable of getting to my feet myself, you know."

Her pretty face fell, and I felt awful for talking to her like that. It had been happening more and more—my impatience growing, my temper spiking for no reason. I held out my hand, which she immediately took. "Actually, thanks. I appreciate the help." Jenn wrapped her arm around my waist and pressed her soft body against mine, but I didn't let myself lean on her for support.

No, I could never do that. To her, I would be a man that could stand literally on his own feet.

The immediate warmth that flooded my insides at her presence outweighed the angry mortification. She leaned down to look closer at my leg. "Looks like it hurts. Come on, let's get you cleaned up."

She helped me sit down on the grass at the side of the road, her bracelets tinkling like windchimes.

"I think I have a tissue in here somewhere." She rummaged through her large backpack. Despite the pain, I couldn't help but grin at her. She looked up at me with a questioning look. "What?"

"I'm really glad to see you."

She caught my eye and we both fell silent for a long moment. She was beautiful in a way that wasn't obvious. I loved that she was understated, not needing a face full of makeup like Lucy.

"Being with you is always the best part of my day," she murmured.

The thread that connected us tightened and loosened with every breath we took. We were at the point of no return. She felt it. I felt it.

Jenn pulled out a pack of tissues and began dabbing at my knees carefully.

I felt flattered by her attention. I reached out and touched her hand.

"It's nice to spend time together without being interrupted," I said, thinking of our run-in at the bowling alley and how terrified I'd been that Mrs. Young had seen us together. It's why I had insisted on spending time with her away from the prying eyes of Fern River.

I knew I was betraying Lucy on almost every level. Shame consumed me and yet, here I was, alone with Jenn once more, finding myself purposefully breathing in the floral scent of her hair and imagining my lips tasting the soft skin at the base of her throat.

"Hey, so while I love our hikes, I was thinking," she gnawed on her bottom lip in a way that I had learned meant she was anxious, "maybe we could go bowling this week."

I thought about Tanya Young and her group of gossipy friends and knew there was no way in hell I'd put myself on their radar again. It was too risky. I'd been lucky she hadn't mentioned anything to Lucy—or Mr. Herbaugh—and I wasn't risking it a second time.

"I like it up here, though. There's no cell service except out at the overlook. That's why I wanted to share it with you; there's no one around for miles, no way for people to get in contact with you." I didn't answer her question, yet she didn't push it.

"Yeah, that's not creepy at all. Good thing I know you're not a killer." Jenn laughed a little nervously.

I held up my bloody palms in defense. "I'm innocent, I swear." We both laughed, lightening the mood. "But seriously, being up here, I feel like I can finally breathe."

Jenn nodded. "I get it. Sometimes you need to get away from everything." She pressed a tissue against my knee, and I put my hand over it to keep it in place. "I don't have any water to flush it out, but I do have some Band-Aids." She pulled the box out of her book bag and placed them over the worst of the cuts before helping me stand up.

"You have everything in that bag of yours," I commented as she zipped up the knapsack.

"I've learned to be prepared for anything," she replied. "I've had to look after myself for a while now."

Jenn seemed so young and vulnerable. "Maybe you need someone to look after you, then."

She gave me a shaky smile. “Maybe.”

I wanted to know what had happened to her. I could tell someone had hurt her badly. I could tell she was running, but I didn’t know from what or from whom.

“That feels a lot better, thanks,” I said as we began walking back down the hill.

Jenn grabbed my hand. “Good. I’m so glad to be here with you, Rhett.”

It felt natural and comfortable between us, not awkward or forced. We continued to hold hands, like a couple. We probably looked like one too. I realized I liked the idea of that.

“So,” I began, “we’ve been hanging out for weeks now and I’ve been wanting to ask you, what *are* you doing in town? Fern River isn’t exactly known for being a go-to spot.”

She appeared torn, as if she wanted to tell me something but was scared to. I placed my hand on her arm and pulled us to a stop.

“You know you can tell me anything. I care about you, Jenn. I want us to be honest with each other.” The irony of my statement wasn’t lost on me. I wasn’t being honest with her at all, yet I was urging her to share everything with me.

“I know I can, Rhett.” She took a deep breath. “I ran away from home. I couldn’t stay there any longer. I wasn’t safe. I had to get away from someone.”

She sounded sad and defeated, and I sensed her past had battered and bruised her.

“Are you okay now?” I asked, wanting to know more.

She nodded, but I could see the pain in her eyes. “I will be. Spending time with you is definitely helping.”

“I want you to feel safe with me, Jenn.”

Jenn brought out a protective instinct in me. Lucy didn’t need my protection. Her dad had that covered. But with Jenn I felt like, for once, I could be the one someone turned to. The one to fix things.

I felt like I was a man in control.

The power of that was intoxicating.

"I do feel safe with you. We've only known each other for a short time, but you're important to me." She leaned into me. "I want to be with you." She seemed embarrassed by the admission.

I reached down and tilted her chin up so she looked at me. I took a deep breath. Then I jumped over the cliff head first. "I feel the same way, Jenn. I really do."

There was a thick tension in the air between us. I found myself looking at her full mouth . . . and then I kissed her.

It started off sweet and simple, our mouths pressed together. I could tell she didn't have a lot of experience and it was this, paired with the thought of being the one in charge, that had me wrapping my arms around her, pinning her body to mine. I groaned in the back of my throat and pushed my tongue between her lips. She startled, but obediently opened her mouth, allowing me access, which drove me wild. I wanted to taste every inch of her. I wanted to own her completely.

After a few minutes, she pulled away, breaking the kiss. We were both breathless, and I had to resist the urge to pull her back to me.

"Jenn." I said her name like I was drowning. I wanted to kiss her again. I felt starved for her affection.

"I know," was all she said. Her eyes were wide as she looked up at me, her chest heaving.

My phone vibrated in my hand, startling me out of my reverie. I looked at the time and blanched. "I uh, I have to go." I didn't want to see the hurt on her face, so I looked away.

"I'll text you later," I told her before I left.

"Promise?" she called after me.

And like the last time she asked this of me, I kept quiet.

* * *

"I've been calling and texting you for over an hour! Where have you been?" Lucy asked worriedly as soon as I arrived at her house. "I thought something had happened to you!"

I was a horrible liar, but I needed to learn how to do it better—and fast. "I was running at Jagged Point. You know there's no cell reception there."

She frowned. "You're always up there lately." I wasn't sure she entirely believed me. "Maybe I need to take up running and join you. That way we can actually spend some time together."

My heart thudded erratically as I gave, what I hoped, was a dismissive chuckle. "Come on, Lucy, running will only mess up all that pricey makeup."

Lucy pursed her lips. "You think I'm only interested in my looks? How little you think of me, Rhett." She turned away, but I could see the hurt on her face.

"It's true, though, isn't it?" I laughed, more at her than with her. "Besides, you hate it there. I wouldn't want to put you out or anything." I knew I sounded aloof, but I needed to shut down the idea of her coming to Jagged Point hard and fast.

Lucy narrowed her eyes. "What's with you? Why are you being such a jerk?"

"I'm not," I said defensively, my frustration rising. "Maybe you're just overly sensitive. I think this wedding stuff has gone to your head." I pointed to my temple. "It's making you crazy."

She looked like she wanted to say something else, but then she noticed the Band-Aids on my leg and the dried blood crusting my skin. "Good God, Rhett, what have you done to yourself?" Lucy's hurt faded with her genuine concern for my well-being.

"It's no big deal. Just a little road rash."

She looked at my wounds with a troubled expression. "Where'd you get the Band-Aids? You came straight here from your run, right?"

"I had a couple in my pocket," I lied quickly.

Lucy raised an eyebrow, as if sensing my dishonesty, but surprisingly didn't say anything else. "Maybe you should spend less time running up there and more time doing the things you're supposed to," she remarked flatly.

The image of Jenn and the kiss we shared earlier flooded my brain, and I had to move away from Lucy for fear she'd sense the other woman on me somehow. "I'm okay, honestly. It's only a scrape."

I finally forced myself to kiss her; a quick peck on the lips.

"Well, now that you're here, you can look at the seating plan." Lucy led me toward her parents' large dining table, where the seating plan had been laid out, and I held in my groan of annoyance. There was a large sketch of the banquet room at Blue Hound Vineyard, where Mabel had insisted we have the reception. Names had been written on small flags and stuck at each table indicating where everyone was to be seated.

"My Great-Aunt Emily asked to be put somewhere near the front because her eyesight is bad and she wants to be able to see us. I know we said this table was for your friends and your mom, but I think you'll agree that great-aunts are more important than friends any day of the week, and your mom will have a great spot next to the window."

"I don't have a lot of people coming as it is, Lucy. And it doesn't feel right to put my mom all the way back there," I said, pointing at the table near the back of the room where my family and friends had been moved.

"I'm sorry, I didn't even think of it that way." She winced. "Of course you're right. Okay, so maybe your mom could sit at this table near the front with my cousins who are flying in from Louisiana." She began shuffling some of the seats around again.

I didn't care about any of this, but Lucy mistook my silence for something else entirely. "You seem out of it. Let me get you something to drink. I think the fall really banged you up. Stay here, I'll be back in a sec." Lucy was out the door before I could say anything.

"She's gone completely nuts over this wedding stuff, hasn't she?"

I looked up as Bailey came into the room. She was only fifteen but was a breath of fresh air. She possessed that breezy, carefree attitude most teenagers had. She still expected life to go exactly as she wanted and believed nothing could go wrong. And if things did go wrong, then her daddy would fix it for her.

But I noticed how badly she wanted her parents' attention—and how rarely she got it. Because of that I had taken to spending time with her. Bailey laughed at my jokes and thought I was cool, which felt good. I worked hard to make her feel special because it was nice to have the adoration of *someone* in the Herbaugh family.

"Yeah, I'd say she's completely lost it," I agreed with a lopsided smile, enjoying the pointed joke we shared at Lucy's expense.

"I tried messaging you a few times earlier. You never replied." The younger girl pouted.

"Sorry, just been busy." I put my arm around her shoulders, giving her a squeeze. "I'll make it up to you."

Bailey leaned into me, giving me a cute smile. "You'd better."

Appeased, she looked down at the seating plan, rolling her eyes when she saw that she had been put at the kid's table.

"You don't approve?" I asked, giving her a nudge.

She side-eyed me. "I'm fifteen, not five," she grumbled. "I swear, when I turn eighteen, I'm outta here."

Lucy came back into the room carrying a pitcher of lemonade and snorted at Bailey's dramatic words. She rolled her eyes in an exact copy of her younger sister. "Yeah right, Bai."

"I am!" Bailey pouted indignantly, glaring with all the fury of a misunderstood teenager.

"You have no idea how lucky you are. Mom and Dad do everything for you—*way more* than they ever did for me." Lucy didn't have much patience for her little sister, who obviously looked up to her.

"Give me a break. You're the princess of the family and always have been," Bailey snapped, her frustration with her sister growing.

Lucy laughed, unaware how she pushed Bailey's buttons—how she pushed everyone's buttons.

"Poor little Bailey. Always the victim," Lucy spat out.

"Lucy, stop being so nasty—" I began to interject.

"Stay out of it, Rhett," Lucy warned, glaring at me. I closed my mouth instead of telling her to watch her tone like I wanted to. I thought about how, in that moment, what I really wanted to do was smack that prissy expression off her pretty face.

Bailey's eyes flashed and in a sweeping motion she pushed the seating chart off the table and onto the floor.

"Bailey!" Lucy screamed.

Then Lucy picked up the pitcher full of lemonade and heaved it in her sister's direction. Bailey ducked as the glass shattered against the wall.

We all stood there in a moment of shock at how quickly things had escalated. Bailey and Lucy stared at each other, their faces a mirror of barely suppressed rage.

But it was Bailey's anger that dissipated first. She glanced at the mess of paper on the floor then at her sister, and I could see her regret.

Bailey chewed on her bottom lip, looking worried and apologetic. "I'm really sorry, Lucy." She glanced at her watch. "Shoot, I'm late for volleyball practice."

Lucy looked up sharply. "Sure you're sorry, Bai. You're *always* sorry," Lucy snarled. "And weren't you kicked off the team?"

Bailey had started backing away toward the door, probably realizing that the best thing to do was to retreat. "Dad spoke to Coach, so everything's fine now."

"Of course Dad fixed it for you," Lucy muttered tiredly.

"Like you're one to talk," Bailey shot back with one final burst of indignant irritation.

"Just go, Bailey." Lucy wouldn't even look at her.

Her sister hesitated for a few seconds longer. She looked at me, and all I could do was shrug. "See you later, Bailey," I said, wanting for all the world to follow her out the door.

Instead, I watched as Lucy started picking up the mess of papers on the floor. "I don't know why you're taking your bad mood out on Bailey," I said. "You're the one that wanted all this." I waved a hand at the ruined seating plan.

Lucy looked at me in shock, her lower lip trembling. "I'm doing all this for *you*, Rhett."

I wanted to laugh, because it was definitely *not* for me. "Still, you need to chill out and leave Bailey alone."

Her eyes darkened. "Are you taking up for Bailey? She wrecked the seating plan with her temper tantrum!"

"And you threw a pitcher of lemonade at her. I think you're even."

"I guess I should expect this from you, given how checked out you've been lately."

My phone vibrated in my pocket. I pulled it out to see a message from Marty.

Marty: You busy or are your balls still in your woman's purse?

I felt a flush of shame.

"I've got to go," I told her hastily.

Lucy looked up at me, her brow furrowed. "You're leaving me to clean this up by myself? Are you serious?"

"Wedding stuff is your department, remember?"

I quickly typed out a message to Marty.

Me: Pick up some beer, I'll come get you.

Marty: Sure the Mrs. won't mind? We both know she's the one calling the shots.

Lucy frowned in confusion. "What's wrong with you? You're never here when I need you anymore."

I was thinking how to respond when my phone chimed again.

Marty: Maybe I need to come over there and show that chick of yours what a real man is like.

"I told Marty I'd pick him up. I'm late," I explained, knowing it was no excuse.

"Marty? The guy who works for Sal? Since when do you hang out with him? He's a total sleazeball, Rhett." Lucy looked aghast.

Me: I'm on my way.

"I've got to go, Lucy. Stop being such a bitch about it," I snarled. I didn't have the patience to listen to her talk about wedding flowers or the reception menu. I didn't care about any of it.

She gasped. I had never called her that before, and I didn't know how to take it back. Or whether I wanted to.

"What did you call me?" Her voice wobbled slightly, but I knew she wouldn't let herself cry in front of me.

I wouldn't apologize. Not to Lucy. "I'll text you later."

"Promise?" Lucy asked, and I was hit by a wave of déjà vu. But this time, I knew I had to give her the word she craved. The one I had so easily withheld from Jenn.

Because I needed to placate her in order to keep her off my back.

So, I looked at the woman I was supposed to marry and gave her an insincere smile. I felt a sense of satisfaction in lying to her.

"Promise."

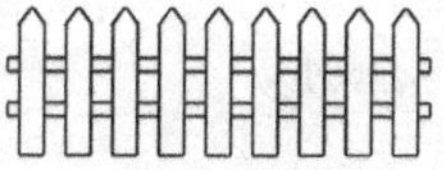

Message

I can't stop thinking about you. I need to see you again. I wish we could run away together and never look back.
-Rhett

Options **Back**

CHAPTER

13

Lucy

The Past

Early August—Fifteen Years Ago

CHUCK YOUNG HANDED me a glass of iced tea. "Take your time, Lucinda. There's no rush. I want you to get your statement right." My father's best friend patted my shoulder.

We were sitting in the sun-room at the back of the house. My mother's plants crawled up the glass, making me feel like I was in the middle of the jungle.

My dad told me Chuck needed my statement about the whereabouts of Rhett and me the night of the . . . murder? Unexplained death? I wasn't sure what to call it, but Dad said the police believed it was a homicide. And I knew they were looking at Rhett—and me, by association.

I took a drink and put the glass down, tracing the mosaic pattern of the table top with the tip of my finger. "There's not much to tell, Uncle Chuck."

Chuck cleared his throat and clicked a button on the recorder he was holding. “Lucinda, you need to call me Chief Young for the record.” He grimaced as if embarrassed that he had to say it at all. He rewound the recorder then looked at me for confirmation that I was ready.

“I’m sorry, of course, Chief Young.” I glanced back at my father, who was sitting against the wall. He had insisted on being present for the interview. He nodded with encouragement.

Things had been strained with my father since Jenn’s body had been found. He was a lot more cagey. A lot more secretive. He was on the phone constantly or whispering to Mom in dark corners. When I came into a room, they’d instantly stop talking. My father was normally unflappable. It was clear this pillar of the community who sat on his bench handing out judgments with firm resolve was floundering.

There was a distance between us now that had never been there before. He wouldn’t quite look me in the eye, and his demeanor toward me had become frosty. My father was my rock. I thought, at one time, Rhett was as well. That he made up the other bricks in my foundation. I thought he was reliable. That he would look out for me. It’s why I had chosen him out of all the boys I could have been with.

It’s why I had gone against my parents’ wishes and stood by him.

But he had let me down.

And now I was trapped by my own bad decision. To admit to my parents that I had been wrong about Rhett now would make me even more of a disappointment in their eyes. And I had been striving my whole life to make them proud of me.

I stared at my father’s oldest friend, and he looked back at me sheepishly. We both knew this was only a formality, and he seemed in a hurry to scratch it off his list.

I was pretty sure if I just said, “Blah, blah, blah” to every question, he wouldn’t even bat an eye.

Chuck pressed the record button again. "It's August third, and I am speaking with Lucinda Herbaugh. Her father, the Honorable Clifford Herbaugh, is in attendance." He took a drink of his own iced tea before giving me his full attention. "I need you, for the record, to tell me where you were on the night of July twelfth."

I held up my hands in mock surrender. "It wasn't me, Officer," I retorted. My joke fell flat, even to me.

"This isn't a laughing matter, Lucinda," my father barked behind me, and I felt the weight of his disapproval like an anchor around my ankles.

Chief Young smiled wryly. "Please, Lucinda, I need you, for the record, to say where you were on that night."

I couldn't give him my truth, so I gave him my lies.

I told Chuck that Rhett and I had been together. That I hadn't seen Jenn that night. That Rhett would corroborate everything I said.

The dishonesty poured out so easily, it should have worried me.

And while Rhett struggled with everything that had happened, I embraced the deception with a fanatical tenacity because I had to. I had twisted the story around in my head so much that I could almost believe the things I was saying were true.

Or maybe I just wished they were.

* * *

A few minutes later, Chuck turned off the recorder and got to his feet. "That's all I need. Thank you, Lucinda." He tucked the device into his pocket. "And I can't wait for the wedding. Tanya may have gone a little crazy with that registry of yours." He laughed, and I laughed with him.

My dad joined him at the door and clasped the chief's shoulder. "Let me walk you out, Chuck. We still need to finalize our plans for the cabin. Mabel hired cleaners to get it ready for our annual fishing trip."

The chief of police and my father, the circuit court judge, chatted together about normal, everyday things and definitely not the murder I had just been questioned about.

I checked my phone and was relieved to see a message from Rhett. He had finished meeting with his academic adviser and was heading back to town. I was surprised that after everything, he still wanted to change his major. Given I knew what—or more importantly *who*—was the catalyst for that.

"I owe it to myself to do this. I need to do it for Jenn," he had told me when I brought it up last week. He said her name with the reverence of a priest in church. I had asked him not to say it. I thought he'd at least *try* to act contrite. But I knew that the days of him protecting my feelings were over.

We had entered a war and neither of us, for our own reasons, were able to call a ceasefire.

I hated that I still loved him. Even worse was that I couldn't be sure he had ever really loved me.

How could I have been so wrong about him? It was starting to look like the elaborate wedding I had planned may have to be scrapped in place of a smaller, more intimate ceremony to get it done quickly.

It was ironic how in death, Jenn pushed us together as surely as she had pulled apart while she was alive.

Dad mentioned that as spouses, we couldn't be compelled to testify against each other. And that might be important depending on how long, and how serious, this investigation became—and how guilty Rhett and I looked.

We had spun lies that required us to remain a united front. And I wouldn't let his betrayal pull me down with him. So, no, I couldn't walk away from him, or that night, even if I wanted to.

I headed down the hall toward the stairs and stopped as I heard my father talking to the chief in a harsh whisper. I strained to hear what he was saying.

"This has to go away, Chuck."

The chief of police cast a careful look around, and I ducked back behind the corner. "I'm doing what I can, Cliff, but you know I have to follow protocol. I think Lucinda's statement should be enough to strike her and Rhett's name off the list, though."

"If it didn't make my daughter look bad, I'd tell you to hold that little shit's feet to the fire," my dad seethed.

I wasn't surprised to hear him speak about Rhett that way. After everything, Rhett would have to work damn hard to redeem himself in my father's eyes. If he ever could.

"Well, it's not only Rhett and Lucinda that I need to steer the investigation away from," Chuck said knowingly.

I heard my father clear his throat. "Chuck, I should probably tell you—"

"Don't say anything, Clifford. Just don't. Keep whatever you have to say to yourself. That particular eyewitness that heard you threatening Jennifer Moore the day before her death has been told, in no uncertain terms, that what she heard was wrong. The respectable Judge Herbaugh would never lower himself to intimidating a young girl all because she was sleeping with his son-in-law."

"He's not my son-in-law *yet*. And he wouldn't be at all if I had anything to say about it," Dad growled.

I could hear Chuck laugh. "Well, we both know you have *nothing* to say about it."

"Unfortunately." Dad sighed.

"But I'm saying this, as your friend, it's a damn good thing I spoke to Cora Stanley at the guesthouse before anyone else in the department did. Because it didn't sound good. How could you be so stupid, Cliff? Going there and shouting at her in earshot of that busybody? That woman would share gossip with the devil himself." Chuck sounded annoyed with my father.

"How was I to know Cora had her hearing aids on for once? And yes, I acknowledge it wasn't my finest hour, but after what I'd been hearing about Rhett parading that damn woman in front of half the town, I needed to do something. Lucinda loves him for some reason, and I didn't want her heart broken," he said darkly, and I shivered at his words.

"That's enough, Cliff. I don't need to hear anything else. I don't have to tell you to speak of this to no one. You and Mabel need to keep yourselves far away from all this until I can get it to die down.

And it *will* die down. She was an-out-of-towner. A nobody. She had no connections to anyone here as far as I can tell, and it could have easily been a hit and run, looking at the injuries." I heard my dad make a noise of agreement. "That's what will make the most sense to everyone," Uncle Chuck continued, "it's bad timing that James retired from the medical examiner's office last year. Hopefully this new guy will see things the same way we do. I don't need an unsolved homicide dangling over my head in an election year." I heard the chief's phone ring. "I've got to take this. I'll call you later."

I hurried back to the sun-room and away from my father's secrets that I wished like hell I hadn't overheard.

* * *

"Oh my God, Bailey, stop taking my stuff!" I yelled, stomping into my sister's room and scooping the pile of hair clips from her desk.

"Those are mine," she protested without much conviction.

I glared at her. "What is with you? Why do you have to take my stuff all the time?" I snatched a shirt from the back of her chair that still had the tags on it. "Did you even buy this, or did you steal this too? You're such a weirdo!"

Bailey snatched the shirt back from me and shoved into her drawer, which was all the answer I needed. "What's your problem? Why are you in here yelling at me?" Bailey's lower lip trembled, and I struggled to hold onto my anger. Yes, my kid sister had sticky fingers, but my rage wasn't focused on her. She was simply an easy target.

I gripped the pilfered hair clips in my hand and pointed at her. "Stay out of my room, and stay away from my things."

"I'm sorry, Lucy," she blubbered, tears dripping down her cheeks. "I don't know why I do it. I can't help it!"

The anxious frustration I had aimed squarely at my little sister dissipated. I sat down heavily on her bed, the hair clips gripped in my hand, digging into my flesh. I let out a sigh heavy with a burden I couldn't share.

Bailey tentatively sat down next to me, careful to keep some distance. "You seem upset. Both you and Rhett do. He never messages me anymore. I haven't seen him in weeks. I hate it." Her voice quivered. "And Mom and Dad keep arguing—I can hear them at night. I wish there was something I could do." She sounded so small. More like a ten-year-old than the almost sixteen years old she was.

Guilt blossomed in my chest. Sometimes it was easy to forget she was still a kid. My parents and I tended to treat her as if she were already grown up. Maybe it was because she often strutted around like she knew everything already. She engaged in behavior way beyond her years: smoking and drinking with friends out at Perry Dunlop's field every weekend and hooking up with football players after the games. She was doing stuff I never even thought of doing at her age. Mom and Dad spent so much time cleaning up her messes, we often overlooked the fact that she was still, in many ways, a little girl. And seeing her like this, I realized she had no idea how precarious things were right now.

The tension in our house was thick, and I knew she felt it too. It must be terrifying to have her stability on such shaky ground.

Plus, I wasn't the only one Rhett had flaked on. Bailey adored him, and he had discarded her as easily as he tried to discard me.

"How did it all go so wrong?" I moaned, closing my eyes.

I sighed again and looked down at the hair clips. I didn't even care about them. I hadn't worn them in years, yet seeing them in Bailey's possession made me see red.

Was it the same with Jenn and Rhett?

I had never felt jealousy before. Never had a reason to; Rhett had always been loyal to a fault. Yet now, I knew how stupid I had been. The idea of him smiling at someone else, laughing with someone else, had unleashed a violent frenzy inside me that desperately needed an outlet.

And now, afterward, it still swirled around, looking to strike out.

Rhett was *mine.*

Just like these stupid hair clips.

One thing was for certain. I wouldn't go through all this again.

I'd make sure of it.

* * *

I knew where he went. And I knew who he was with.

Our fight had been horrible. The worst we'd ever had. My body thrummed with the violence of it.

My hands shook as I picked up my keys.

I knew what I needed to do.

I wouldn't let her get away with this.

I knew where he was.

I knew where she was.

At Jagged Point.

"Where are you going?" My mother's voice trembled as she called out to me. I turned to find her watching me from the shadows.

I didn't answer her. I didn't have time. Instead, I went to leave.

Mom reached out and roughly grabbed my arm, holding me in place. "Don't go after him. Have some pride, Lucinda," she hissed.

I couldn't think clearly. I was acting on instinct. Like a cornered animal, I struck out indiscriminately and shoved my mother. The viciousness of the action horrified us both. Mom stumbled backward, catching herself on a table so she wouldn't fall. I wanted to apologize immediately, but I was too far gone—lost in a haze of agony and heartache.

"How dare you—" she started to say, but I interrupted her.

"I won't let them treat me like a piece of trash. She has to pay for trying to take what belongs to me!" Tears dripped down my face, and I didn't bother wiping them away.

"Lucinda, he's not worth it," my mother said, her voice now a ragged whisper. But she didn't comfort me. I couldn't remember a time she had ever told me things would be okay. That I was enough. That I was worthy. Her words were always a toxic mix of condemnation and displeasure.

"How can you say he's not worth it?" I asked, my voice hoarse. "You've been planning my future for me since I was old enough to walk."

My mother reared back as if I had slapped her and honestly, I felt like doing just that. "Because he wasn't supposed to be part of that future. And honestly, how can you plan to be with a man that sleeps with another woman?"

I shoved her again. Hard. What was wrong with me? If I wasn't so angry, I'd be horrified by my actions.

She pressed a hand to her chest, her eyes wide in saddened shock. I knew she was seeing something in me that scared her and she didn't know what to do about it.

"Don't you dare say that. Don't. You. Dare." I picked up my keys that I had dropped in our scuffle. "I'm going to fix this. That's what us Herbaughs do, right?"

I stormed out of the house like the devil was on my tail, leaving my shaken mother behind. I raced along the familiar streets, barely stopping for red lights. I made my way to the hills.

I parked my car, noting that Rhett's car wasn't there.

Was I too late?

Or maybe I was wrong. Maybe he hadn't meant all the awful things he'd said and had come to his senses. The hope was there, flickering beneath the weight of doubt and indecision.

I had to be sure.

I ran up the graveled path toward my destination, convinced of what I'd find there.

So I was surprised when I arrived at the overlook and found Jenn there alone.

She looked up at the sound of my footsteps on the gravel.

The air was heavy with the weight of an impending storm. Thunder rolled in the distance. Sheets of heat lightning flickered like strobe lights. The dark, inky valley was like a black hole below us.

Each flash lit up her ashen face streaked with dirt and tears. Blood trickled from the corner of her mouth.

Where was Rhett?

I looked around and could tell she was alone out here.

Why would he leave her when she was clearly injured?

"Where is he?" I demanded, my voice shaking with a fury I could barely contain.

Jennifer's mouth quivered and she let out a sob. "I don't know. I left him here. But then—" She covered her face with her hands, her shoulders shaking as she cried.

I advanced toward her, my hands curled into fists. What was I going to do? Punch her? Pull her hair? I wanted to destroy her. To tear her limb from limb for trying to take what was mine.

I wasn't above debasing myself by starting a cat fight.

Her eyes widened. "What do you want?" she asked, her voice thick with tears.

There was another flash of lightning, and this time I noticed something shimmering around her neck.

"What is that?" I reached out and ripped the gold chain from her neck.

"What are you doing?" She put a hand to the hollow of her throat, her skin lined with an angry red welt from the chain being pulled against her flesh.

"Did he give this to you?" I shouted, holding up the class ring that, at one time, I had worn around my *neck.*

Sensing danger, Jennifer took a step backward. "I . . . he . . . it was just . . ."

"This is mine!" I screamed, losing what little control I had. I shoved Rhett's ring in her face. "None of this belongs to you, do you hear me? None of it!"

She was crying again. Silent tears dripped down her cheeks. "I know," she said and even I could hear the defeat in her tone. "I'm sorry. I'm so sorry for everything. I never meant—"

Her tears mingled with her blood, and I almost felt sympathy for her, but then I looked at Rhett's class ring in my hand. My anger grew.

"What do you want?" she asked again. Her voice was low and husky, the words cracked and broken on her lips.

Lightning flashed like it was pushing me on. Encouraging me.

What did I want?

I looked at this woman who I felt was responsible for every horrible thing that had happened recently.

My humiliation.

My heartache.

I blamed her so completely that I had lost all sense of reason.

I grabbed hold of her wrist, squeezing it, my nails digging into her skin.

"What do I want?" I growled, our eyes clashing in a savage battle of wills. A battle I knew I would win.

"I want you gone."

CHAPTER

14

Jenn

The Past

July 1—Fifteen Years Ago

"I CAN'T BELIEVE YOU'RE able to keep up with me," Rhett exclaimed, a little out of breath.

"As a kid, I spent as much time as I could outdoors," I told him.

What I didn't tell him was that I stayed outside because it was a lot better than what waited for me *inside*. But Rhett didn't need to hear all that awful stuff. I didn't want to burden him with my problems. They were my issues to deal with.

Rhett, however, must have noticed the way my grin faltered. "What's wrong?" I had come to realize he was incredibly observant. He picked up on all the things I thought I hid so well.

I liked the way he watched me closely and how protective he seemed. Even though I thought I was being Miss Independent by striking out on my own, I had underestimated how much I'd miss someone looking out for me, even if it had been stifling.

This was the first time I had made decisions for myself, and old habits had me turning to this sweet, level-headed man I had only just met. I craved his regard and his attention in a way that should have made me scared, but instead made me feel safe.

I wiped the sweat from my brow and took the bottle of water he held out for me.

"It's okay, you can tell me, Jenn. You can trust me, remember?"

"My family." I stopped, took a deep breath, then continued with the ugly truth. "My home was practically a prison. I wasn't allowed to do anything they didn't monitor. That bowling league I told you about?" Rhett nodded. "That was the highlight of my childhood. But I was only allowed to go as long as one of them was with me. And then I met someone. And when they found out, they stopped me from going there too. I wasn't safe there."

"God, that's awful." He put his hand on my arm and squeezed. "It sounds like you've been through a lot." His eyes were warm.

I turned to face him. We were so close I could smell the mint of his gum. "Tell me about your family," I urged.

Rhett gazed off into the distance, his expression clouding over slightly. "Not much to say, really. Growing up, my mom tried her best, I suppose. But she wasn't really around. I practically raised myself. The good thing was she was always too busy working to be a strict parent." He was trying to sound blasé, yet I could hear the slight tremor as he spoke about his mother.

"What about your dad?" I asked, my voice gentle.

"He left when I was little—just upped and walked out on us. It's been me and my mom ever since. She always made sure I knew I was loved, but it was hard without a dad." His face became tender as he spoke, even if there seemed to be anger below the surface.

My eyes welled up, and I hastily wiped away my tears. "Your mom sounds nice. And for the record, I think dads are overrated." I gave him a weak smile that fell away quickly. "Mine is a hard man—all the men in my family are the same. I'm not even sure he loves me."

Rhett reached out and took my hand, giving it a squeeze. "Jenn, I'm so sorry." And he didn't let go. His thumb traced slow, even circles on my palm, making me shiver in the hot sun. I appreciated that he didn't ask for more details.

"It's okay. I got out, because here I am," I said, forcing the smile back.

"Here you are," he repeated softly, his eyes staring into mine and not letting go.

Together we turned to look out over the valley. It was breathtaking. "Wow," I let out with a sigh. "It's so beautiful."

"Yeah," Rhett agreed, but I felt his eyes on the side of my face and knew he wasn't looking at the view anymore. He was looking at me.

I had been thinking about our kiss constantly. I'd replayed it over and over in my head as I fell asleep. Even now, I could remember the feel of his lips and the way his tongue had invaded my mouth. Rhett wasn't my first kiss. Even with my strict upbringing, I was able to sneak a make-out session or two. But my family had always found out, and it never ended well for me.

The kiss with Rhett was different because it was the first since I had broken free. Because of that, it was a thousand times better than any kiss I'd ever had before. And I wanted to do it again.

I wanted to do a lot more, too, which shocked me. I was a good girl. A chaste girl. But Rhett had me thinking not so chaste thoughts.

Feeling my face flush, I took another drink of water and sat down on the rock, stretching my legs out in front of me. He sank down beside me, sitting close. We had established an intimate rapport in such a short time.

"These hikes have become the highlight of my week," he said, pulling some protein bars out of his backpack and handing one to me. "Well, that and the late-night texts." He bumped me playfully with his shoulder.

"Me too. Though you are having an effect on my sleep," I teased.

His lips quirked mischievously. "I hope it's worth it."

I swallowed, suddenly feeling nervous. "More than you know," I whispered. The tension between us practically sizzled. I wasn't sure how much longer I could live with the anticipation that seemed to be building. We had crossed one line. How much longer until we crossed another?

I had planned to have moved on by now, but I was finding it hard to say goodbye to Fern River. And I knew it had everything to do with Rhett.

I needed to start thinking seriously about my next steps. Money was getting tight, and I would have to find work soon. My stolen savings had gotten me pretty far, but they wouldn't last forever. If I stayed, that would mean putting down some roots, and remaining in one place had never really been an option. It couldn't be.

I knew I had to keep running because the feeling of being followed never left me. I was looking over my shoulder constantly.

Yet, here I was considering the impossible—I was thinking about staying.

The foolishness of the impulse was warring against my better sense. Because on more than one occasion, I thought I had seen *him* on the street, in a parked car, in a crowd at the grocery store. Watching me . . . He was always watching me. Yet I dismissed it as paranoia. There was no way he was here. I was being ridiculous.

But the fear was still there, thrumming below my skin. Spending time with Rhett was the only time I didn't feel hyper-alert. I relished not having to check every shadow and watch my every move. I knew whatever happened, if Rhett was there, he would take care of me.

"Do you want to go bowling with me this Friday? Jeremy told me it's ladies' night. Women bowl for free," I said.

I held my breath and waited for his answer. I had posed this question several times before, and he always turned me down. Because as much time as we were spending together, as much as we messaged and talked on the phone, I felt like he still kept me at a distance.

"Oh, um, I'm not sure." Rhett looked away, shoving the rest of the protein bar into his mouth.

My shoulders sagged. "If you don't want to go bowling, maybe we could do something else. Jeremy said he's throwing a field party on Saturday for the fourth; maybe we could go together. I'd like to meet some new people," I suggested a little desperately.

He still wouldn't look at me. "I don't know. Jeremy's parties can get pretty wild. Plus, I don't think you'd like those people."

"Oh. Okay, if you say so," I replied hurriedly, feeling silly and hurt.

Finally Rhett turned toward me and must have seen my disappointment. "How about we pack a picnic and come up here instead? Just the two of us. There's meant to be a meteor shower this weekend. It'll be a lot more fun than getting drunk in a field."

"Yeah, that sounds nice." I couldn't help but sound a little defeated. It felt like it wasn't simply the party he was avoiding, but going to the party with *me*. I didn't bother to ask why. I had learned that pushing for answers to some questions caused Rhett to close up on me entirely.

He could be cold and withholding when he got mad. His silence was worse than a raised voice. Though, I saw how hard it was for him to maintain control of his emotions. Part of me was scared of what would happen should he ever lose it. At least his anger never lasted long and he was always apologetic—eventually. He was different from my father, who never said "sorry" for anything he did. Yet, there was a similarity, too, that I didn't want to focus on either.

Rhett scooted closer and put his arm around my waist, pulling me into his side. "I love spending time with you, Jenn. I don't have to think about the exams I probably failed or the degree I hate."

I laid my head on his shoulder. "If you hate pre-law so much, maybe you should drop it."

I felt his whole body tense. "I've told you, you can't just tell me to change my major when you have no clue what that would mean for me." He pulled away. I felt the ice form between us immediately. "I have enough people telling me what to do without you adding your voice to the damn choir."

"I'm not trying to tell you what to do—"

"That's *exactly* what you're doing," he spat out. I flinched at his reaction.

With trembling fingers, I reached up and turned his face toward me. "I'm not trying to upset you, Rhett, but take it from me, life is too short to be doing something you hate."

Rhett frowned, his expression conflicted, but then he smiled, revealing that dimple I was coming to love so much. He cradled my face between his palms. "I'm sorry I shouted at you. I know you're only trying to help." He kissed my temple. Then my lips. "How did you get so smart at only eighteen?"

I shrugged. "What can I say? I'm a genius." We both laughed, the tension beginning to ease. "I remember you saying you wanted to be a teacher." I took his hands in mine, holding them tight. "So, why can't you do that instead?"

He seemed to consider my words. "I wish it was that easy." He didn't sound convinced.

I shrugged. "Nothing worth doing is ever easy, Rhett," I said. I knew I should shut up and stop pushing him. I had been conditioned to do as I was told my whole life. But for once, I wanted to speak up.

"Maybe I *could* be a teacher," he said. "No, I'm *going* to be a teacher." He grinned, his face bright.

"You'll be a wonderful one," I stated emphatically. I believed it too. He'd be amazing at whatever he wanted to do.

Something flickered in his eyes, and then he kissed me again.

And like before, it was one of those movie kisses where the whole world seemed to stop. The sun came out and the birds began to sing all together.

Our arms wrapped around each other as the kiss deepened. I climbed onto his lap, straddling him, and he began to kiss a trail from my mouth to my collarbone.

I felt his hands drift up my shirt. I shuddered and thought briefly about stopping him. I had never let a man touch me like this. I had been raised that you saved this sort of thing for marriage. But I didn't want to stop Rhett.

So I didn't.

His mouth became insistent. His hands roamed over my body like it was his to claim. He unzipped my pants and his fingers slipped inside. My body was on fire, but my brain was shouting at me that this was wrong. That I needed to stop and think about what I was doing.

The next thing I knew, Rhett had me on my back and was on top of me, prying my legs apart so he could position himself between them, pebbles digging painfully into my skin. My shirt had somehow ended up on the ground beside me and I felt the warm air brush my bare skin as he made quick work of removing the rest of my clothes.

I loved kissing him. I really did. But I couldn't silence the voice of my father in my head berating me. Calling me a slut. An embarrassment.

Just as Rhett started to take off his own shorts, I slithered out from underneath him and gathered my discarded clothes to my naked chest.

"I'm sorry, Rhett, I can't do this."

"What? Why?" he demanded roughly.

Was he angry?

I peeked at him through my hair to find him struggling to get his breathing under control. He grabbed his shirt and yanked it back over his head before turning to me with narrowed eyes. "I thought you wanted to. You sure acted like you did." He looked away from me, as if he couldn't stand the sight of me. "Should've known you were a tease," he muttered under his breath but loud enough for me to hear.

"I'm not!" I exclaimed, feeling a fresh wave of mortification. "But I've never done this before. And I'm scared."

Rhett's expression changed instantly. Then he gathered me to his chest and kissed the top of my head. "You don't have to be scared with me, Jenn. Not ever." He ran his hands through my hair. "I'll be gentle. I promise."

Long moments passed between us with him stroking my hair and kissing me. In between kisses he whispered that he would look after me. That it wouldn't hurt. That it would be special. I was lost in his words, and the feel of his lips on mine.

I didn't want to disappoint him.

I was starting to love him and I wanted, more than anything, to be with him. The quiet was finally broken by an alert on his phone. He moved away from me and pulled it out of his pocket. His face darkened, and he jumped to his feet with a near frantic energy.

"I didn't realize it was so late. I have to get back."

Then, as if only just remembering I was there, he held out a hand and pulled me to my feet.

I quickly put my shirt and shorts back on with shaky hands. "You're always in a rush," I teased, though there was a hint of reproach too. How could he leave me so quickly after what we had almost done? Maybe he *was* angry, after all.

Rhett looked annoyed. "I told you, Jenn, I have a lot on my plate right now. I thought you understood that." He began to head toward the gravel path that led to his car, leaving me behind.

"I do!" I jogged to catch up with him and reached for his arm. "I just hate that we keep having to cut our time together short."

Rhett relaxed marginally and pulled me into his arms again. He buried his nose in my hair. "I know, Jenn. I'm sorry." I melted into him and lifted my face so he could kiss me once more. But all too soon he moved away from me again. "Come on."

He led me back to the car, where we would go our separate ways, without saying anything else.

He held my hand the entire time, though, and I let myself be happy about that. A thousand thoughts went through my mind, but the most prominent one was how glad I was that I came to Fern River.

Because this town was going to change my life forever.

CHAPTER 15

Rhett

The Present

ALL I WANTED to do was push McKenzie on the swings at the park like I used to. I liked how we had so many things that were just for us. Sometimes it felt like we didn't even need Lucinda.

Every Saturday we would get up, eat pancakes piled high with butter and syrup, then head off to play for a few hours, leaving Lucinda at home.

However, this Saturday, I woke up to find McKenzie already downstairs eating oatmeal with Mabel, their day planned around going to feed the ducks.

I was livid.

I was McKenzie's father. *I* was the one who fed her breakfast. *I* was the one she looked at with adoration.

I imagined pulling Mabel away from my daughter by her hair and flinging her across the room.

It was strange how the things that hurt the most were the ones we least expected.

It wasn't the way Lucinda watched me warily with distrust written on her face. Or the way Cliff practically snarled at me every time he walked into a room and found me there. It wasn't not being able to be in my own home or go to the job I loved so much.

It was that McKenzie had become so quickly accustomed to her mornings being spent with her grandmother and not me. That I had been so easily replaced.

Is this what it would be like if I went to prison?

Would she forget about me completely?

The thought made me want to hit things, starting with my intrusive mother-in-law.

My phone dinged with an incoming message. I had been ignoring most of my calls and texts for days, but I knew I'd have to answer them eventually.

Some were from so-called friends who seemed to only want to tell me they always thought I was guilty.

Jeremy: You should have stayed far away from that girl. Now you're going to pay for being a selfish dick.

Jeremy and I hadn't spoken in a long time, but I'd had no idea he harbored such animosity toward me. Though I remembered how weird he was about Jenn. But did that mean he was actually waiting to celebrate my downfall?

"Do you need to take a minute to answer that?" Lucinda asked, her voice decidedly neutral as she looked pointedly at my phone. I promptly put it in my pocket as she poured herself some coffee.

She was more tense than usual, and I forced myself to listen to what she was saying. It was hard to focus on anything right now, though. My every thought was consumed with the realization that I might be going to prison. That I could lose everything.

My daughter.

My job.

My life.

"I'm sorry. I didn't sleep well," I said, the lie slipping out easily.

Mabel glanced up at us. She looked between Lucinda and me before her gaze fell back to McKenzie. "I'll get her cleaned up and leave you two to chat."

"I can do that," I exclaimed, reaching for my daughter, giving her my biggest smile. "How about Daddy take you to the park?"

McKenzie frowned in a way that was so reminiscent of Lucinda. "No. Nanna take me."

Her casual, childlike dismissal broke what was left of my heart.

Mabel waved me off as I tried to pick my daughter up anyway. "No, no, you'll get oatmeal on your shirt. You and Lucinda talk. McKenzie and I will get out of your hair. Besides, you're on house arrest, Rhett." The reminder was a cruel blow. One that Mabel seemed all too happy to deliver.

She scooped my little girl up in one quick motion and headed out of the room before I could even say goodbye.

"My God, Rhett, can you focus? My dad says Judge Balfour won't talk to him, not that he was surprised. But a judge that plays it straight is the worst thing for you, in case you didn't know." Lucinda barely looked at me.

"Apparently the judge loves every opportunity to stick it to anyone and everyone associated with my father," she continued. "It's really bad luck that he was assigned to your case. Everything seems stacked against you."

I scrambled to think of anything or anyone that could help. Cliff *always* had connections. He always knew someone that could get him what he wanted. Why now, when I needed him the most, did he suddenly have no one to turn to?

"It's not that hard to understand, Rhett." Lucinda sounded slightly patronizing, as if she'd read my mind. "No one will help you this time. It seems like you're on your own." She slammed her mug down on the counter and it cracked, its contents spilling out.

She put a hand to her mouth and attempted to put her anger back inside its carefully contained box.

The kitchen filled with an empty silence as the coffee dripped onto the tile.

I let the truth of her words sink in.

No one will help you.

I had been thinking the same thing, but to hear it out loud made it all too real.

I was screwed, and we both knew it.

I thought of Mackenzie's little face as Mabel took her from the kitchen and how she hadn't even reached for me.

How long would it be before she forgot about me altogether? Because if I went to prison for murder, I would likely never see her again. Cliff and Mabel would make sure of it.

I curled my hand into a fist and punched the wall. The impact caused paint and drywall to crumble to the floor.

"I'll let you explain that one to my parents," Lucinda remarked, displeasure and maybe a little fear in her tone.

I was used to the disapproving looks she gave me, which was standard these days, but recently, there was something else in her expression. A rage tinged with terror I hadn't seen in years. She was trying to cover it, but I could see it. Lucinda and I knew each other better than most couples did.

"You have no idea what I'm going through. What this is doing to me. Who cares about your parents' wall? I might go to *prison,* Lucinda." I ran my hand down my face. "And like I said, I'm not really sleeping. Every time I close my eyes, all I can think of is—"

"Her," Lucinda finished for me, that one word icy cold.

I didn't refute it because lies were what got us here in the first place.

I forced myself to take my wife's hand, even though touching her made me shudder. I needed her on my side. I needed her to work on her father so I wasn't hung out to dry. As much as I had always resented the Herbaugh name, I needed it now. I had been able to sway her many times over the years, and I had to try again, for my freedom's sake. "I'd like to spend some time with you and McKenzie this weekend. Maybe we could have a picnic in the backyard since I can't go anywhere—"

Lucinda made a noise in the back of her throat and pulled her hand from my grip. Clearly my charm didn't have the same effect it once did. I should have known better. Her resentment was stronger than my ability to influence her. "Are you serious? Sure, let's have some peanut butter and jelly sandwiches and pretend you didn't blow this family apart."

My temper, once again, slithered out between the cracks. "You think I don't know I'm to blame? You've spent the last fifteen years reminding me," I snapped back.

It always came back to this. Every argument we had wound its way back to my betrayal.

To that night and the things I said and did.

I could never forget because Lucinda made sure I never would.

I forced my anger aside and pulled on her arm, making her face me again. "But we both know this wasn't all my fault. That it goes deeper than the things I did."

Lucinda wrenched out of my grip, loathing written on her face. I knew how quickly I could change her hate to fear.

"I need to spend time with our daughter," I said, desperation and frustration sticking to my words like mud. "Do you despise me so much that you would deny me that?"

Lucinda stared at me silently, her eyes dark and tumultuous.

"If I go down for this, I might never see her again, Lucy." Her old nickname slipped from my lips. I hadn't called her that in years. I knew why I used it now. It was the same reason I had tried to charm her. I knew her weaknesses. I knew how much she still, deep down, wanted what we used to have. I could use that now to get what I wanted.

I swallowed my rising hysteria. A small part of me wished she would put her arms around me and tell me it would all be okay like she used to. But over the years, Lucinda had become cold and distant, just as I had, like we both had already said goodbye to our life together.

It hadn't always been easy, and it certainly hadn't always been good, but we had gotten through it. Though our differences were stark, we had always held it together. Because we had to. The shadow of Jenn's murder hovered over us, and we knew we had to rely on each other, in sickness and in health, if we were going to weather the storm of suspicion and accusation.

Secrets bound us together tighter than our rings ever could.

"Haven't I paid for my mistakes already?" I demanded.

We stared at each other, neither of us giving an inch. Both of us were too distrustful and bitter to bridge the gap that had opened between us after years of pretending we were fine.

"I have to go out," Lucinda announced, her features pinched. "I need some fresh air."

I watched her go, barely giving me a backward glance. Moments later I heard her car start and the crunch of tires on gravel, and then I was alone in the quiet of the house I despised.

I cleaned up the mess she and I had made, as was our way, then stared out the window, wondering what my life would have been like if the events of fifteen years ago had never happened.

Would I be in business with Cliff? Successful and rich, but miserable doing a job I hated?

Would I finally have come to my senses even without Jenn's input, and gone on to teach high school math anyway?

Or would I have left town with Jenn, and Lucinda would be the distant memory?

Just then, my cell phone rang in my pocket. I didn't recognize the number and was reluctant to answer it. I'd had several anonymous calls since I was arrested. They were mostly crank calls from people telling me I was a murderer and deserved to rot in jail. I could tell from their young voices that they were probably kids from my school. I answered anyway. Maybe I was a glutton for punishment. "Hello?"

"Hey there, Rhett."

The lazy drawl on the other end was one I knew all too well. A voice I would recognize in an instant, despite not hearing it in years. The person it belonged to made me both angry and very, very worried.

"Marty."

He laughed low and deep. "Wondered if you'd know who it was. It's been a long time, buddy. Though maybe not long enough for you, huh?"

The last time we had seen each other, he had threatened to kill me. He had threatened Jenn too. I hadn't known the man I befriended was a psychopath. That night had been a blur of blood and savagery.

He knew more than anyone else about what happened the night Jenn died. He was the one holding the rope that could hang me.

"How could I forget you?"

For a short while it had felt like he was the only one who knew the real me. He had made me ashamed of myself, of how weak I was, and then he had changed my way of thinking completely. Now I was only ashamed of the thoughts that had been planted so easily and nurtured into something horrible.

But those thoughts and ideas were still there bubbling below the surface. I simply had learned to keep them quiet. Most of the time.

Marty had been the one to change me. He had turned my innocent thoughts into seeds. Seeds that had eventually grown into something dark and wicked. And once the tree had matured, there was no uprooting it.

"It *was* a long time ago." I could hear him exhale as he smoked. "I'm back in town for the big event," he continued, "wondered if you wanted to meet up to talk. Reminisce about old times. Maybe we could grab a beer or two and head up to the cliffs."

I knew his suggestion wasn't as innocent as he made it out to be. Marty *always* had an ulterior motive. It was because of him that this whole sorry mess had been dragged back up again and I was about to lose everything.

It was partly because of him that I had lost her.

Yet, there were so many questions I wanted to ask him. How'd he end up with my bloody shirt, anyway? I hadn't given myself any time to really think about that in the chaos of being charged with murder.

The truth was, Marty had never been my friend and he'd been lying in wait to destroy me all these years.

But why?

Why did he hate me so much that he'd resurface now to torpedo my life? What had I ever done to him to deserve this?

Even as I thought it, I knew the answer.

Jenn.

The woman that we had both loved.

The woman we had both hurt.

"You have some nerve," I growled through clenched teeth.

He let out a low whistle. "*I* have some nerve? My friend, you're the one accused of murder."

"Because of you!" My hands were shaking, and I gripped the countertop to steady myself.

Marty had always known how to get under my skin. He could get under anyone's skin if he wanted to. It was something he seemed to enjoy.

"Now Rhett, we both know what happened that night. We were both there—ain't no point lyin' to me, even if you're still lyin' to yourself."

"I'm not lying about anything, and you know it." I felt hot and sweaty. "You were there, goddamn it. *You saw her alive.*"

"What I remember is you got really angry after she told you she was leavin' town. You got violent too." His voice turned to a growl. "I saw what you did to her."

"I didn't mean to." I sounded whiny and heartbroken.

"Sure looked like you meant it. She wanted to get away from you, buddy. And who could blame her? After you embarrassed her at that party and turned her into the town slut." He tutted in my ear.

I slumped into a chair, fearing I might fall over if I didn't sit down. I had never meant to do that to her. To do any of it. Things just got out of control. The lies . . . the truths, it all got mixed up in the end.

But I had never meant to hurt her. At the party or at Jagged Point.

The man I had been reduced to because she wouldn't hear me out was not someone I was proud of.

If she had only shut up and let me explain myself, none of this would have happened. *I loved her!*

That mattered more than the awful things I did to her.

"It should never have happened, and it wouldn't have if you hadn't egged me on," I said finally, at least partially admitting that he might be right, but putting some of the blame at his feet as well.

He whistled low in my ear. "Wow, you really believe that too. I wasn't the one who spilled her blood, Rhett. I wasn't the one who scared her that night."

The weight of his words settled between us both.

"Why are you doing this to me?" I said, my words a whisper as my too-tight throat tried to keep them inside.

"If you can't see why, then you're even more of an idiot than I always thought."

"Marty, please, leave me alone."

There was a beat of silence where I wondered if he'd actually agree to go. I should have known better.

"Listen, I'm in town to testify at that preliminary hearing of yours. Let's meet. We can talk about this like men," Marty suggested, but I knew I had no choice. "It time we finally hashed out everything that happened, don't you think?"

"Where?"

"Usual place. Around five. I'll bring the beer, just like old times."

And with that, the line went dead. It had always been like this. He spoke, I listened, and then I made stupid mistakes.

I had a lot of regrets in my life, but getting mixed up with Marty Richards was one of the biggest.

Regardless, I had no choice but to meet him. My life depended on it.

I stared down at my blinking ankle monitor. I needed to remove it without setting off the alarm, which would be tough since I wasn't particularly good with tools. Another way Marty would say I was completely inadequate.

But I needed to figure out a way. And fast.

I looked at my watch and saw I only had an hour before I was supposed to meet him. I covered my face with my hands and wished, not for the first time, that I could wipe away the years and go back to that night and change everything.

But when I pulled my hands away, I was still here.

Alone in a house that I hated, with my life being held together by threads.

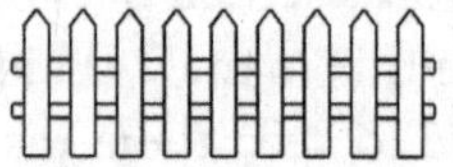

Today 13:39

Hey Gail, have you heard anything from Rhett? Everyone is really worried about him.

I spoke with him a little last week. He's just so upset and worried! I can't believe this is happening to him! I can only try to keep his mind off of it.

I heard Sherry put him on administrative leave, which was a shock. People are saying some crazy stuff. I know you two talk all the time so I thought you might have some news.

I wish I did! I'm hoping to see him soon though and I'll pass on your well wishes.

CHAPTER

16

Lucinda

The Present

I FELT TENSE FROM the argument with Rhett. I was tired of dancing around the things we really wanted to say. We liked to pretend we were completely honest with each other, but our entire marriage was based on lies and deception.

I had thought that after everything that happened with Jenn, he would remember that he wanted to be with me. He would see that I was committed to him no matter what.

Rhett had made a joke of our marriage from day one, embarrassing me with his infidelity and lies. Though maybe I was responsible for my humiliation by staying with him.

A wandering eye never stayed home and I knew, deep in my heart, that Rhett could never really be trusted.

I had been so stupidly in love with a man that only loved himself.

Yet, I continued to pray that my faith in him wasn't misguided. And every day it became harder and harder to breathe.

I sat on a park bench, watching families spending time together in the spring sunshine. Fathers and mothers and their broods of happy, contented children. It's all I had ever wanted. I had worked so hard to craft the kind of life others would be envious of. A well-kept house, a pretty little girl in pretty little dresses, a seemingly doting husband who bent over backward to make me happy. I had protected that image with claws and teeth. That Rhett could so cavalierly destroy what I had worked, and paid for, with my pride, had me seeing a violent shade of red.

"Hey there, little rabbit." I felt his warm breath on the back of my neck but made sure not to react to his proximity.

Marty sat down on the bench beside me. Luckily, the park was almost empty. It was the middle of the day, so most kids were in their classrooms and parents were at work or enjoying their few hours of freedom.

Marty stretched out his long legs, crossing them at the ankles. He pulled out a pack of Lucky Strikes and held it out for me to take one. I didn't bother pretending I didn't smoke with a guy like Marty Richards. He knew better.

He lit my cigarette with his Zippo and watched as I took a long drag, his eyes heating as he drank me in.

We hadn't seen each other in fifteen years, even though we had stayed on each other's radar the entire time.

"What are you doing here?" I demanded.

"I've been called to testify, remember?"

"The preliminary hearing isn't until next week."

"Thought I'd catch up with some old friends in the meantime," Marty said, lighting his own cigarette.

"You called Rhett." I should have known Marty wouldn't be able to help himself.

His jaw tensed at the mention of my husband. "We have things to talk about. But don't worry your silly head about it. It's man stuff."

I turned to look at my own dirty little secret. I flicked the lit cigarette onto the ground. "You may talk like that to every other woman you know, but you know damn well you won't talk to me like that."

We stared at each other for a long minute. Marty clenched his teeth and flared his nostrils. He was a man used to treating women like they were beneath him, but he never dared treat me that way. I had set a precedent early on and, surprisingly, he had listened.

Predictably, Marty settled down, keeping whatever vile comments he was thinking to himself. He sat back, staring out across the field. "Maybe Rhett shouldn't be the only one worryin'."

"What's that supposed to mean?"

Marty's grin was full of malicious joy. "Because with my testimony everyone will know your alibi was bullshit."

My body tensed.

Marty still wouldn't look at me. "You and I both know Rhett wasn't with you that night, and now the police know it too. Because I was there. I saw what he did."

I didn't bother to argue because he was the one person still alive that would know that.

"I thought I was doing the right thing." That was the only excuse I could give.

I knew it looked bad that I had lied.

Because Rhett wasn't the only one police should have been looking at. Everyone in town knew that I had been angry enough at Jenn to kill.

"Sure, sure." Marty pulled out another cigarette and lit it.

"Is that why you want to talk to him? To discuss our bullshit alibis? Because that has nothing to do with you."

"Among other things," he murmured, flicking ash on the ground.

"What other things?"

This time Marty did look at me, and I couldn't help but stare at the ugly scar that was so prominent on his face. I often wondered how he got it.

"Stay away from Rhett. It will accomplish nothing talking to him now."

Marty frowned. "Maybe this isn't about Rhett."

It was a shame that such a handsome face hid such a black heart. "Who is it about, then?"

Marty met my eyes, and I felt the earth tilt underneath me. I, of course, already knew the answer.

He hesitated and took a deep breath, looking oddly vulnerable.

"It's about Jenn."

* * *

The Past

July 4th Weekend—

Fifteen Years Ago

The field was packed with practically everyone I had graduated with. That was why I didn't want to go to Jeremy Major's field party. I loved my small town, but that didn't mean I wanted to socialize with them all the time.

I told Rhett I didn't plan to come, which he accepted a little too easily. Normally, he'd at least try to talk me into it.

But not this time.

I knew something was off, but it was further proven as soon as I arrived at the party. I kept my eyes peeled for Rhett, who should have been there by now. "Lucy, I didn't know you were coming!" Bethany Strummond, a girl I played field hockey with in high school, gave me a too-wide smile. She turned to MaryBeth Rutz, who I had known since preschool. "What a surprise, right, MaryBeth?"

MaryBeth smirked, drinking from her can of Smirnoff Ice. "Such a surprise." There was something in her tone I didn't like. I also didn't like the way they seemed to be laughing at a joke I didn't understand.

"I'm looking for Rhett. Have you seen him?" I asked, losing patience. MaryBeth had never liked me. I had won every pageant and

every school contest, including Homecoming Queen, and she was always the runner-up. She had even tried to start a fight with me after our first Young Miss Fern River Fair pageant. She ended up with a black eye for her efforts, while I went home with the crown.

MaryBeth and Bethany were openly laughing now. "Oh, he's here somewhere," Bethany said. She looked around and then pointed to the bonfire. "Wait a minute. There he is."

I followed the direction of her finger and finally saw my fiancé. "Thanks—" I started to say but then realized why they were so amused.

Rhett wasn't alone.

A pretty redhead stood beside him, her hand on his arm, his on the small of her back. Rhett was talking to Jeremy, Caleb, and Alison, but I noticed how close he was standing to the girl. They looked like a couple.

I felt the world stop spinning. Because I recognized her. It was the girl from that day at the ice cream stand. My gut had told me then that I needed to take note of her. That there was something in the way Rhett looked at her.

I had known for months something was going on with him. He had become harder to get a hold of. He was always busy or blew me off entirely. And he was constantly looking at his phone. He never had much interest in wedding planning, but lately, he didn't bother to help at all.

And he had become angry and cruel at times. He had called me a bitch and never apologized for it. He made a habit of hurting my feelings with his callous disregard, and I didn't know if I should forgive him or hold him accountable. At some point I lost my ability to navigate our relationship. It felt like I was walking on eggshells, not knowing what he was thinking or what he planned to do.

He was always up at Jagged Point, and I convinced myself he simply needed the space and time to think. I knew he was under a lot of pressure. He even brought up changing majors, claiming the law wasn't for him.

And I supported him. I went to my dad and told him that Rhett didn't want to be a lawyer, but a damn math teacher. Dad was understandably angry given the financial outlay he had already invested in Rhett pursuing the law and going into practice with him. But in the end, Dad respected that I wanted my husband-to-be to be happy, so he backed off.

I bent over backward to accommodate his wishes for the wedding as well. I tried so hard to be a kind and considerate partner, the opposite of how my mother was, and this was what I got?

I could hear Bethany and MaryBeth snickering behind me as I watched Rhett lean toward the girl and whisper something in her ear. She looked up at him, her face flushed, and I could tell, even from that distance, that she loved him. It was written all over her stupid, pretty face.

I wanted to run both of them over with my car.

"How nice of Rhett to show our new friend around. He said he'd be bringing her tonight," I said hoarsely, the lies slicing my tongue.

"Your new friend?" MaryBeth asked skeptically.

"Of course. You know Rhett, he's such a sweetheart. Didn't want the new girl in town to be all on her own. The three of us hang out all the time." I breezily waved my hand, never taking my eyes off the two people lost in each other.

"Well, you better go let them know you're here, then," Bethany remarked sweetly. Too sweetly.

"I think you're right. Bye, ladies." I wiggled my fingers at them and sashayed over to the bonfire, with barely suppressed rage in every step.

Rhett noticed me first. He glanced up and blinked. Then blinked again as if his eyes were playing tricks on him. His hand was still on the girl's back. She was still plastered to his side like a barnacle.

"Hi, Rhett."

Rhett's friends looked from me to Rhett and then to the girl at his side. Their eyes widened collectively. Alison already had a furious expression on her face and when she saw me her mouth popped open, but I could see her delight at being front row for the drama. Caleb grabbed her arm and dragged her away.

"Lucy," Rhett croaked out my name.

The girl, finally sensing something was wrong with him, turned my way questioningly. "Uh, hi?"

I didn't look at her. Not yet. I only had eyes for my two-timing piece of shit fiancé. "Are you going to introduce us, honey?"

Rhett opened his mouth. Then closed it.

The girl frowned. "I'm Jenn. Jenn Moore." She didn't put out her hand for me to shake, which was a good thing, because I'd probably break her fingers.

Rhett still hadn't said anything, so I turned to the girl and gave her a smile that could kill. "Hi, Jenn. Nice to meet you. I'm Lucy." I paused for dramatic effect. "Rhett's fiancée."

I saw the moment it sunk in. Jenn looked from me to Rhett, who had turned to her, his expression pleading. He wasn't even looking at me—he didn't seem to care about my feelings at all. His focus was entirely on Jenn.

I wanted to scratch her eyes out—then go somewhere and sob.

"Rhett?" His name came out as a broken whisper on her lips.

"Jenn, I can explain—"

I stood there, watching them, like I *was the one intruding and not the other way around. I moved closer to Rhett, pushing Jenn out of the way. "I'm sure Rhett has told you all about our wedding next month, though I hope he explained that the invitations have already gone out. Otherwise, I'd tell him to invite you."*

Jenn appeared in shock. "Your wedding?"

I nodded with a grin, looping my arm through Rhett's. Rhett, who was still staring at Jenn like I wasn't even there. Like she was the only woman that mattered.

"Yes, our wedding." I playfully swatted Rhett as if my heart wasn't breaking. "My Rhett sure is modest. It's going to be the event of the summer, isn't it, babe?" I turned back to Jenn, whose face had gone alarmingly white. If she wasn't a homewrecker, I might have been worried about her.

I heard Rhett audibly swallow, and he finally had the wherewithal to look at me. "Um, Lucy, I think we should talk—"

"Yes, I agree, we have so much to talk about," I said between clenched teeth. I looked at Jenn, wanting her to feel my anger and my hate directed solely at her. But her eyes were locked on something on the other side of the bonfire. Her face drained of its remaining color. She suddenly let out a whimper and turned and ran toward the tree line.

"Bye, then," I called after her with as much venom as I could summon. I turned back to Rhett, expecting him to look apologetic, but his eyes were on the girl that had just taken off. And his eyes weren't the only ones following her.

I noticed how Jeremy stared after here, a strange look on his face. One that was almost hungry.

And Alison looked as if she were still filled with a rage I wasn't sure she had the right to feel. Why was she so angry? I was the one who had been publicly humiliated.

"Jenn!" Rhett hollered. Then, without a word, he snatched his arm away from me and ran after her. I was left standing there like the jilted idiot I was.

I glanced around, horrified that everyone was watching me. No one came to check on me. No one offered me any support.

I had never felt so alone.

And just when I thought it couldn't get any worse, the whispering started, growing louder and louder. Eventually, people weren't even trying to hide what they were saying.

"Oh my God, did Rhett just ditch Lucy for that girl?"

"I heard he's been sleeping with her for weeks."

"Caleb told me he heard Rhett was planning to call off the wedding."

"If you ask me, Lucy deserves it."

I straightened my back, lifted my chin, and oh-so nonchalantly headed back toward my car, my head held as high as possible. I wouldn't let these people see me crumble.

Even if I wanted to fall onto the dirt and wail.

One thing was for sure: I was now the laughing stock of Fern River. There were enough people in this town who had been waiting for an opportunity to see me brought low, and my fiancé had served me up to them on a damn platter.

I fumbled with shaking hands to get my keys out of my purse and dropped them on the ground. When I leaned down to get them, someone picked them up and held them out in his palm for me to take.

I stood back up, snatching the keys from him. "Thanks," I muttered, not bothering to see who it was.

"You look like someone ran over your cat." He laughed. "Maybe you should run them *over."*

Now I looked up, recognizing his voice.

Marty Richards leaned against my car, thumbs hooked through his belt loops, a cigarette dangling from his lips like a freaking Marlboro ad. His dark hair fell into his eyes. He looked messy. And dangerous.

"Move," I commanded, crossing my arms over my chest.

He didn't.

"I saw what happened back there." Marty inclined his head in the direction of the bonfire. "Looks like my buddy Rhett has been dipping his wick elsewhere."

His words were clipped and hard, and I could hear a trace of anger beneath his blasé exterior. Marty was pissed off, but it was nothing compared to what I was feeling.

"He is not dipping his—" I shook my head.

My disgust at the crudeness of his words, and the actuality that it was probably true, stopped me from finishing my sentence. Rhett had been cheating on me with that woman. Had he really been planning to call off the wedding? How long had it been going on?

The questions pummeled me.

The devastation fed my rage.

Marty snorted. "I didn't take you for one of those chicks who rolls over and takes somethin' like that lyin' down. But I guess a woman should know her place when it comes to her man." He shrugged as if he hadn't just said the most sexist thing I had ever heard.

I let out a peal of shocked laughter. "Are you for real?"

Marty frowned. "What'd ya mean?"

"'A woman should know her place'?" I rolled my eyes. "What kind of 1950s bullshit is that?" I shoved him hard in the side. "Now get out of my way. I need to get out of here before I commit murder."

Marty wrapped his calloused hand around my wrist and squeezed. "Who the fuck do you think you're talkin' to?"

Something twisted inside me. I had taken enough crap for one evening. I whipped around and shoved him again. This time firmly in the chest. He looked surprised when he stumbled backward.

"Don't touch me." I pointed my finger at him. We stared at each other for a long time. Marty was good-looking, despite the scar across his face, but he was also a jerk. He was a man who looked down on almost everyone, especially women, despite him having nothing to offer.

Marty's eyes started at my feet and slowly worked their way up my body. "I've never met a woman quite like you, Lucy." I couldn't tell if that was a compliment or not.

"It's Lucinda."

Marty looked over his shoulder then back at me. "So, you gonna let him get away with making you look like a fool?"

"I am not *a fool."*

Marty shrugged again. "From where I'm standing, you don't look too smart either. That man of yours just flaunted his side piece for the whole town to see." He leaned in close, his breath fanning across my face. "So what are you gonna do about it, Lucy?"

"Why do you care? Aren't you Rhett's friend? Shouldn't you be looking out for him?" I posed the questions as a challenge.

Marty's eyes became dark and ominous like an impending storm. "Rhett ain't no friend of mine."

He continued to stare at me with a note of challenge. He was disgusting, and I hated the way he looked at me like I was a piece of meat. But he wasn't Rhett. And right then, that made him incredibly appealing in the worst possible way.

"I'm getting out of here," I told him.

We stared at one another, weighing each other up, and it was clear we were both thinking the same thing.

"I'm coming with you," Marty stated, heading to the passenger side and getting in. He didn't ask. A man like Marty never asked for anything. He took what he wanted, and it was obvious that he wanted me.

If I got in that car, I knew exactly what would happen between us.

I could still hear people laughing and saying my name. The humiliation of Rhett's betrayal burned me from the inside out.

Right then, I thought this was what I needed to take back control of my life.

So I got in the car and drove us to the same remote spot where Rhett and I used to go to be alone.

Then we climbed in the backseat and I tried to forget about Rhett. And Jenn. But it wasn't that easy.

Being with Marty felt like the perfect payback, but I also felt like the worst kind of hypocrite. I hated myself for letting my jealous rage dictate my actions.

My needs were simple. All I wanted was to be loved.

I wanted Rhett *to love me.*

And Marty was no substitute. Giving him my body felt like a betrayal of myself more than of my relationship.

Because the whole time I was with Marty, I could only think about how I tried to be the perfect fiancée. Pretty, smart, well-mannered. I knew what was expected of me as a partner, and I made every effort to be everything for Rhett.

But it wasn't enough.

I *wasn't enough.*

Sleeping with Marty made that crystal clear. All it left me feeling was alone and ashamed.

And afterward I hid my tears as my heart turned to stone.

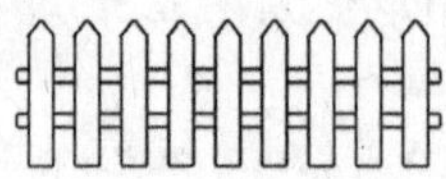

09:41
MaryBeth
Today 11:55
I always thought Rhett got away with murder.
You and me both! Do you remember him that night of the field party? Rhett was screaming and after her like a crazy person!
How could I forget? And Lucinda too! She looked like she was going to m*rder that poor girl! Think they did it together? LOL
Um, I've been saying that for years. I bet he killed her to get back in Lucinda's good graces. We all know what a controlling BITCH she is! She's not above making that poor guy kill someone to make her happy.

CHAPTER

17

Rhett

The Past

Weekend of July 4th—Fifteen Years Ago

"I'M NOT GOING to Jeremy's party. I don't feel like taking care of you while you get wasted and end up vomiting in a field," Lucy said. She was sitting in front of her vanity applying lip gloss. "I don't know why you still go to those things. You always get sick and have a hangover for two days afterward. Doesn't seem worth it."

I was irritated that, once again, she was judging how I chose to spend my time. She never seemed able to relax or want to be around my friends. I used to never want her to be the kind of girlfriend Alison Schaffer was, someone who liked to hang out and drink with the guys. Because that wasn't Lucy and she never tried to change, which now bothered me.

I began to notice the things I once found endearing about Lucy were now obnoxious. The way she always seemed to think she knew what was best for me. The way only she could initiate anything intimate between us. The way she was so singularly focused on the wedding and nothing else. It was annoying.

Lucy's interests were her own, which was a startling contrast to Jenn, who was more interested in what *I* liked.

"Fine. Well, I'm going," I bit out.

She stared at me in the mirror, examining me like I was on the witness stand in her father's courtroom.

Lately I found it harder and harder to have a conversation with her. As my heart drifted away from her, I became less interested in anything she had to say, anyway.

She shrugged, but I could see the hurt that was always in her eyes these days. "Go, then. I don't care."

I knew she wanted me to say I'd stay.

But she wasn't the one I wanted to spend my evening with.

I felt my phone vibrate against my leg. I knew it would be Jenn without even looking. She was always there when I needed her, as if she could somehow sense when I was upset, or angry, or anxious. Marty said that's how a woman should be—wanting and waiting. He was right.

I hated that Lucy made me feel less than a man. I didn't want a woman who didn't need me. I knew that if I wasn't in the picture, Lucy Herbaugh would be just fine.

That bothered me—a lot.

"I've got to go," I said, turning from Lucy. Her disappointed anger irritated me.

She stood up and walked toward me. "I don't know what's gotten into you lately, but I hope you get it out of your system before the wedding." She brushed past me, storming from the room, leaving me annoyed and tired.

My phone vibrated in my pocket again and I pulled it out, smiling automatically.

Jenn: Hey, are we still on for the meteor shower? I'm missing you.:-*

I looked to the bedroom door and knew I needed to make a choice. Follow my fiancée or follow my heart? When did those become different things?

Me: Absolutely. I'm missing you too.

Lucy's words echoed in my head. *"I hope you get it out of your system before the wedding."*

I was getting married soon.

Jesus, what was wrong with me?

Lucy held my life in her hand.

"And your balls in the other," Marty would say.

I knew now that I didn't want to get married.

I didn't even want to stay in Fern River.

Yet I wasn't ready to entirely give up on the idea of a future with Lucy, even if I was getting closer and closer to going razed earth on the entire plan.

And if we didn't work out . . . I would still have Jenn. I knew she'd always wait for me.

Jenn: I can head up now if you're not doing anything. I know you're probably busy. No pressure. I can wait until later.

How did Jenn get it so easily when Lucy didn't? She understood that I had a life. That I had commitments.

I wondered what it would be like if Jenn was my commitment and not Lucy.

Me: I can make time for you.:-D
Jenn: <3
Me: I'm on my way.
Jenn: Heading there now!

I looked at Lucy's jewelry box on her vanity, knowing that my class ring was inside. I had given it to her when we were juniors, and all she had done was put it away in a box.

Glancing over my shoulder, I opened the box and rummaged around until I found the ring I had saved up four whole paychecks from my part-time job at the movie theater to pay for. And here it was, discarded underneath Lucy's pageant costume jewelry.

It pissed me off.

I snatched it up, shoved it in my pocket, and then in a burst of rage, I emptied the contents on the floor. Let her pick it up. Then I hurried out of Lucy's room before she saw me.

I drove to Jagged Point, eager to see Jenn. I felt things for Jenn, more than I should for a woman who wasn't my fiancée.

My mom would be ashamed of me if she knew. She'd say I was just like my dad.

And maybe I was.

But then, what did my mom's opinion really matter? Ever since Marty had suggested I think about what she had done to drive my dad away, it had lingered in the back of my mind like a bad taste.

I looked at her differently and the more I thought about it, the more I realized it wasn't only Lucy holding me back. My plans for my future were as much about my mother as they were about Lucy and her father. Why couldn't Mom be the adult for once and provide for herself? Why did she need me to have a better life? It didn't seem fair when all I wanted was to simply worry about myself.

Maybe it was in my DNA to not want to be tied down. To not have my life dictated by a woman. That was what Marty had said so many times now. That men were the gods of their own universe.

I turned the corner, the gravel crunching underfoot, and saw that Jenn was already there waiting for me. She was always waiting for me. Always ready when I needed her. I smiled my first genuine smile of the day.

"Hey, you," she said as I drew closer. I reached for her and pulled her close, breathing her in.

"I brought some snacks. And I found a pair of binoculars at the B&B. I've never seen a meteor shower before." She sounded excited. But I didn't care about the meteor shower. I knew what I needed, and it wasn't to look at the sky.

I held her face between my hands and pressed my mouth to hers, kissing her, softly at first, then roughly as the urgency and desire took over.

"I've needed to see you all day," I said between kisses, my hands running up and down her back.

She laughed, trying to pull away. "Come on, let's get ready. I don't want to miss it—"

I grabbed her and wrapped my arms around her, covering her mouth with mine so she couldn't say anything else. She made a noise in the back of her throat that sounded like a gasp. I felt starved for affection. Starved for Jenn. I needed her now more than I had ever needed anyone in my life.

I pulled her down to the ground with me, feeling her hesitance but knowing that with me, Jenn would be okay.

I would look after her.

I would take care of her.

I would provide for her.

God, that was a rush.

I lay Jenn down, my hands fumbling with the buttons of her shirt. She gasped as I palmed her breast a little too roughly. I felt her stiffen and vaguely noticed she wasn't kissing me back.

"Rhett, can we please wait?" There was a hitch in her voice, but I was too far gone.

I grabbed my shirt and pulled it over my head, wanting to feel my skin against hers. Her hands were by her sides as I kissed her stomach, undoing her jeans and sliding them down her legs.

"Rhett, I'm not sure about this," she said, but when I looked into her eyes, I could tell she didn't mean it.

She wanted this as much as I did. It's why she had been meeting me up here for weeks, all alone, and wearing those tiny little shorts that drove me wild. She knew what she was doing.

She wanted to, even if she was too scared to admit it.

"Shh, you'll enjoy it. I promise," I murmured as I positioned myself on top of her, unbuttoning my shorts and kicking them away as I stared down into her beautiful face.

She was biting her lip and wouldn't quite meet my eyes. I grabbed her chin and held her in place. I wouldn't let her look away from me. Not now. "Do you trust me?" She nodded, her mouth quivering slightly. I knew she was as eager for this as I was. "I'll look after you, Jenn."

I kissed her again, pushing her legs apart with my knee, not caring about the rocks scraping her skin as I pressed her into the ground. Heat rolled off me, desire thrumming through my veins like I'd never felt before.

"Rhett," she said my name again, her eyes fluttering closed. A tear slid out from beneath her lashes and I kissed it away.

"Please," she let out in a ragged whisper, and I smiled with satisfaction.

"You belong to me, Jenn. Always," I said, knowing that this moment would define my life.

* * *

Jenn had been quiet since we got back to the car. I wondered shamefully if we should have waited. I had thought she wanted it as much as I did, but looking at her now, I was second-guessing myself, which ignited my guilty anger.

"Are you okay?" I asked, sounding short. She nodded.

Her shirt was torn from the rough gravel. I stroked her shoulder and she shivered, almost as if she didn't want me to touch her.

I didn't like that. And I didn't like that she wouldn't look me in the eye. What the hell was wrong with her?

I forced myself to calm down. It wasn't really her I was annoyed with.

"I have something for you." I was glad when she finally turned her face toward mine.

Her cheeks were still flushed, her long hair full of twigs. I pulled them out, chuckling as they snagged. She winced and pulled away to take care of it herself.

Before I pulled out onto the road, I fished my class ring from my pocket and held it out to her.

"Jennifer Moore, will you wear my class ring?"

Her eyes lit up, the spark returning to them. "Oh my God, really?" Her mood changed entirely.

I nodded and slid it onto her finger. We both laughed at how big it was on her.

"Wait, let me . . ." She reached around her neck and unhooked her necklace. She slipped my ring on the slim gold chain. She pulled down the visor to admire the ring nestled in the hollow of her throat in the mirror.

"I thought you'd like it," I said, my confidence returning.

"I do, thank you. This means so much to me."

She looked like she wanted to cry. I didn't want her to cry; tonight had been perfect.

"I think I love you," I blurted out, shocking myself as much as her. I hadn't even realized I was going to say it until I had. Her eyes widened in shock.

"I love you too," she said with only the slightest hesitation. Jenn reached for me and I pulled her into my arms, and we kissed each other like our lives depended on it.

This was it. The decision had been made.

I couldn't go back to my old life. The thought of moving forward with Lucy instead of Jenn felt wrong on every level. But how could I look my mom in the eye and tell her what I had done? How I had betrayed Lucy by falling in love with someone else behind her back. Would she see my father when she looked at me now? I was pretty sure I didn't even care. What did that say about me?

"I feel like we should celebrate or something." She laughed, both of us high on the moment.

Now that I knew I wanted to be with Jenn, and only Jenn, I felt an almost self-destructive need to tell everyone. I was awash with a wave of impulsivity that under normal circumstances, I would have tamped down.

"How about we go to Jeremy's party? I can introduce you to my friends," I suggested, throwing caution to the wind. There was no going back now.

"That sounds like a plan." She grinned.

"All right then, let's go." I laughed and started up the car, driving toward the field party and exposing my betrayal to everyone.

Lucy was going to kill me.

That was, if Cliff Herbaugh didn't get to me first.

A few minutes later, doubt crept back in and I felt myself start to sweat with anxiety. "You sure you want to go to this thing?" It had seemed right in the hazy glow of post-sex euphoria. Now, I wasn't so sure. Was I letting yet another woman push me into doing something I didn't want to do?

"I want to meet your friends," she said emphatically. "The people that are important to you will be important to me." Her words erased my misgivings. She lifted my hand, kissing the knuckles. "I love you, Rhett."

"I love you too," I told her.

My heart was pounding as I parked in the ditch down from the Majors' cow pasture where he held his parties. It was pretty tame so far because it was still early. The sun had only just started to set, and music blasted from some speakers in the beds of a few pickup trucks parked around the field. There were a couple of kegs, and someone had lit a bonfire.

Jenn looked around, taking it all in like she'd never been to a party before. And maybe she hadn't. From what she had said about her homelife, it sounded like she wasn't allowed to do anything fun. I took her hand, confidence flowing through me.

We headed toward Jeremy and Caleb, my two best friends, and their mouths opened in surprise when they saw Jenn and me together.

Caleb seemed curious, but Jeremy's expression was more than curious.

He seemed mad.

"Hey, guys," I called out.

"Hey," Jeremy said, and his eyes were dark as they clung to Jenn in a way that felt like ownership. "I guess you found some better company, huh?"

I glanced at Jenn questioningly. She appeared uncomfortable and seemed to hide behind me.

Jeremy took a step toward us. Was he trying to be threatening? What was up with him? I put an arm around Jenn, staking my claim. "I wanted to introduce Jenn to everyone, but it seems you guys know each other."

Jeremy lit a joint and handed it to Caleb, his eyes still glued to my girl. "Didn't realize she was taken already."

I frowned. "What's it to you?"

Jenn still hadn't said anything, but I felt her tremble against me.

Jeremy shrugged, his face still hard. "It's nothing now." But I got the sense his pride had been hurt in some way. Jeremy had a short fuse. I had seen him beat the shit out of a guy for taking his parking space before, so I wondered if I had to brace myself now. Because he seemed pissed that Jenn and I were together.

Though I noticed his anger was focused squarely on her.

Soon, Alison, Lucy's friend and coworker at the daycare, sidled up next to Caleb. They'd been dating almost as long as Lucy and me. She was nice enough, but she liked to hang out with the guys more than other girls. Lucy used to joke that she was only with Caleb to get closer to me, which I thought was nuts. But seeing how she stared daggers at Jenn, I wondered if Lucy was right. Alison was definitely not my type. There was no chance in hell I'd date her.

"Hey there, Rhett," she said, her tone full of heavy accusations as she eyed Jenn. "You're looking good this evening."

"Uh, thanks," I muttered. We stood awkwardly, Alison and Jeremy watching Jenn like they either wanted to jump her or eat her, and Caleb completely oblivious to the mounting tension.

Good manners dictated I should introduce Jenn, but my tongue felt too big in my mouth, my throat too dry. Things were going south already, and I knew now it was a mistake to bring Jenn, but for reasons I hadn't anticipated.

Agitation began to rise inside me.

"You wanna get a beer?" Alison asked Jenn. It sounded less like an invitation and more an act of aggression. Not waiting for a reply, she dragged Jenn toward the keg.

As soon as they was out of earshot, Caleb shoved me in the shoulder.

"Who is that?" he asked.

"Her name's Jenn. She's new in town," I explained, casting a quick look at Jeremy, who was watching her closely.

Caleb nudged our friend. "You know her or somethin'? You're acting like Rhett took your matchbox car."

Jeremy cracked his knuckles and gave me a lazy grin that I knew hid something more sinister. "She comes into the bowling alley sometimes. Thought she was hot so was gonna shoot my shot, but it seems someone got there first."

Caleb grimaced. "For real dude, what gives? She's hot and all, but man, you've started a shit storm by bringing her here. Everyone will be able to tell you're screwin' her, it's written all over your face, ya dumbfuck. Lucy is gonna have your nuts in a sling once this gets back to her."

I glanced over at Jenn, who looked back at me and smiled. "It doesn't really matter . . . Lucy and I are done."

There. I said it. And to my friends. I had put it out into the universe, and there was no taking it back.

"Does Lucy know this piece of information? Because I just saw her yesterday looking through bridal catalogs at the coffee shop," Jeremy remarked hatefully. "Maybe you should leave some chicks for the rest of us, you selfish prick."

Was he joking? I couldn't tell.

Caleb shook his head. "You'd better hunker down, my friend, because you know she'll sic her daddy on you."

"Shut up, okay? Let me handle it." I gave them both a stern look as Alison and Jenn came back, both of them carrying Solo cups. I took the one Jenn offered and downed it in one go. She looked taken aback. I felt out of control, and that wasn't a side of me she was used to seeing.

Jenn held her beer out to me. "Here, you can have mine. I don't really drink anyway, remember?"

I took it from her, forcing myself to calm down. I was doing the right thing. Because when I thought about Jenn and I together earlier at Jagged Point, I knew there was no going back. I was obsessed with her. I couldn't stomach the thought of being with anyone else.

"So, uh, Jenn, is it?" I noticed the way Caleb smirked and Jeremy glared.

Jenn, in all her innocence, was totally oblivious. "Yeah, it's Jenn. Jenn Moore." I could tell she wanted them to like her, even as she cast nervous glances at Jeremy.

"How long are you planning to stay in Fern River?" Caleb asked.

Jenn gave me the cutest smile. "Oh, I'm not sure. Depends on Rhett, I guess."

I saw Caleb and Jeremy share a look. Jeremy started laughing, and Caleb joined in. They weren't even trying to act like they weren't mocking us. I was getting irritated by how rude they were being.

"I think we should get out of here," I whispered in her ear, needing to get far away from all this judgment. Jenn nodded, clearly feeling as uncomfortable as I was.

"I had no idea you guys were so close," Jeremy stated, drinking from the flask he always kept in his pocket. He could be a mean drunk, and it seemed that was the direction the night was taking. He leaned toward Jenn, who recoiled at his closeness, and plucked some grass from her hair. "Looks like you two had a roll in the hay before you got here."

Jenn's face turned beet-red, and I glared at my friend.

Alison had been silent since coming back with the beers. She was openly scowling at Jenn, her disgust obvious. She glanced between us, clearly not happy with what she was seeing. I also knew it would take her less than a minute to spread the news to everyone. Alison was the first to spread a rumor.

I put my arm around Jenn's waist and pulled her close. I knew what everyone was thinking.

Then I saw Alison's gaze shift to something over my shoulder, her eyes widening. "Uh-oh."

I looked up and felt everything inside me freeze.

"Hi, Rhett."

My heart plummeted and I thought I might be sick.

Fury was etched on Lucy's features with barely controlled violence simmering below the surface. I had seen her like this a couple times, and the outcome was never good.

Jenn, picking up on the shift in vibe immediately, though not understanding it, gave Lucy a tentative smile. "Um, hi?"

Lucy didn't even look at her. Her eyes were glued to my face. "Aren't you going to introduce us, honey?"

Jenn frowned, clearly unnerved. "I'm Jenn. Jenn Moore."

No, no, no, no . . .

I wasn't sure exactly how I expected tonight to go, but it wasn't like this. I had wanted one night for myself before I officially ended things with Lucy. Before I changed the course of my life forever. Jenn and I having sex had solidified the decision that had been lingering in the back of my mind for weeks. I had been on the fence, and now I was ready to jump over it.

I looked between the two women, wanting to drag Jenn away and protect her from Lucy's wrath. Yet I didn't say anything, almost as if I had become paralyzed by my own stupidity. It was too late to do anything, anyway. We were facing down the barrel of Lucy's gun, and I had given her the ammunition.

"Hi, Jenn. Nice to meet you. I'm Lucy." She paused for only a moment before blowing my whole world apart. "Rhett's fiancée."

Jenn looked like she had been slapped. She turned to me for confirmation or denial, her eyes widening with horror when all I could do was stare at her.

"Rhett?"

"I can explain," I started to say, but then stopped. What could I say to make this right? Why should I have to say anything in the first place?

This was my life. *My choice.*

In spite of the situation, I felt the flickers of irritated anger come to life.

I was sick of my decisions being dictated by other people.

But I could see the cogs turning as Jenn began to unravel my lies.

"I'm sure Rhett has told you all about our wedding next month," Lucy continued, but I barely heard her. I was focused entirely on the girl I loved, who looked like she was about to break down.

"Your wedding?" I heard Jenn whisper.

I vaguely felt Lucy loop her arm with mine. My skin instinctively rejected her touch. She was still speaking, but I wasn't listening.

Jenn had gone pale. I wanted to hold her and promise that she was the one for me. That Lucy didn't matter.

Yet, I didn't.

Why couldn't I be a man when it counted?

I finally looked at the woman I was supposed to marry. "Um, Lucy, I think we should talk—"

"Yes, I agree, we have so much to talk about, Rhett," she seethed through a painful smile. I knew she was trying to save face in front of everyone.

Jenn was no longer looking at me. She was staring at the bonfire, her eyes wide, her lips trembling.

I tried to see what—or who—she was staring at, but the light from the fire made it hard to see anyone clearly. She looked like she had seen a ghost. Then she let out a sob as if her whole world were ending and turned and ran toward the trees.

"Bye, then!" Lucy called out hatefully.

I glared at her, the woman I was *supposed* to love, and snatched my arm out of her grip.

"Jenn!" I bellowed, not caring who heard me or what they were saying. I only had one thought on my mind—get to Jenn.

I took off after her, my rising hysteria threatening to drown me. I didn't even know where I was going, only that I had to find her.

"Jenn, please talk to me!" I called out into the darkness. When she didn't answer me, I stopped, pulled out my phone, and began calling her over and over again.

But no matter how many times I called, she didn't answer.

"Jenn, answer me!" Worry was slowly turning to anger.

I understood she was upset, but I loved her. I had given up everything for her—didn't that count for anything?

"Fuck!" I shouted, trying Jenn's phone again. When she still didn't answer, I curled my hand into a fist and lashed out at the trunk of the nearest tree. I stopped myself from hitting it full force but I still left behind a bloody smear.

Why wasn't she answering?

She said she loved me, but maybe she was like every other woman in my life, only out for herself.

Emotions warred against each other inside me. Fear, sadness, guilt.

And anger. So much anger.

For everyone, including Jenn.

Jenn, who was ignoring me. Who had left me all alone to deal with everything. She had run off at the slightest hint of trouble.

Deep down, I knew I wasn't being fair. I had lied to both Jenn and Lucy, and now it was biting me in the ass. But, at that moment, none of it mattered. Because I was all alone, deserted by the woman I had set fire to my life for.

"Jenn, get back here now." I heard the threat in my tone, and I knew she would too. She had to talk to me at some point—it's not like she could run from me forever.

I kept calling and texting her. On some level, I knew I was acting insane. But I didn't care. I just needed her to talk to me so we could figure this out, together.

"Jenn, answer your fucking phone!" I yelled to her voicemail.

"Jenn, where are you? You need to listen to me."

"Goddamn it, don't fucking ignore me."

Each message became angrier and more desperate than the last. I was heartsick and worried, but I was filled with so much fury I could barely see straight. I had hinged my future on Jenn, and she was not going to blow up our plans because of a stupid misunderstanding.

Around midnight, I drove to the Millwood Guesthouse and banged on the front door until Ms. Stanley came out onto the porch, looking troubled.

"Why are you making all that ruckus at this time of night?" She peered at me closely. "Have you been drinking, young man?"

"Where's Jenn? The girl who's staying here? I need to speak to her, *now*," I insisted. I attempted to get inside, but the door was locked.

Ms. Stanley left the screen door closed, creating a barrier between us. "You need to go home and leave that poor girl alone."

I slammed my hand on the doorjamb, making the wood rattle. "Tell her Rhett's here. She'll talk to me," I panted, my breath coming in shallow gasps.

"You're in no position to talk to anyone in your state—"

"Jenn!" I screamed. "Get out here and talk to me, goddammit!"

Ms. Stanley held her robe closed at her neck, her eyes wide with fear. "You need to leave, or I'm calling the police."

That gave me pause. The last thing I wanted was for the cops to show up, particularly after what I had done to Cliff Herbaugh's daughter that evening. "Fine," I grumbled, backing down the stairs, staring up at the darkened windows.

Ms. Stanley watched me until I was on the sidewalk and then closed the door. I stayed for a long time just waiting, hoping Jenn would see me. I kept calling and texting her.

She never answered.

Finally, as the sun began to make its way upward in the sky, I headed home, knowing one thing was for certain: I would make her listen to me, even if she didn't want to.

I had detonated my life to be with her, and I'd be damned if I'd let it all be for nothing.

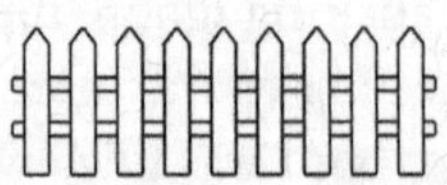

Me	11:07AM
✓	Please talk to me! I know you must hate me, but there's more to the story.

Me	11:43AM
✓	Jenn, answer me! Let's talk this out! I love you so much!

Me	12:23PM
✓	Why aren't you responding to any of my messages? What the hell, Jenn? I need to see you!

Me	1:30PM
✓	DON'T IGNORE ME!

CHAPTER

18

Jenn

The Past

Weekend of July 4th—Fifteen Years Ago

I LEANED MY HEAD back on the headrest, feeling the breeze in my hair as Rhett drove us to the field party. I closed my eyes, enjoying the sensation of being driven to our destination. It was the first time I had ridden in his car, and I wanted to savor the moment. My body was still buzzing from our evening together at Jagged Point.

I replayed Rhett and I finally being together over and over. Yes, I would have liked it to have been more romantic. There were no flowers or candlelight as I always imagined there would be. I touched the torn sleeve of my shirt, tucking it into the hem so it wasn't too noticeable. I wiped the tears that were still drying on my cheeks with the back of my hand. My thighs felt sore, and there were scraps on the back of my arms from the gravel. I throbbed deep inside, making it uncomfortable to sit. I hadn't expected it to hurt so much, but I didn't want to tell Rhett and make him feel bad.

For a moment, I had been afraid. I hadn't been sure I wanted to sleep with Rhett. Not yet, anyway. But he was so insistent, and I knew that I couldn't say no.

I didn't want him to leave me, so I gave him what he wanted.

In the end, my doubts didn't matter because Rhett told me he loved me.

This man was my future. I knew it.

I opened my eyes and glanced at his profile, the love I felt silencing the twinges of uncertainty that had started to grow in the back of mind.

I loved him. He loved me.

I was surprised when he'd suggested we go to Jeremy's party, but I was glad. He finally wanted to introduce me to his friends and it had solidified everything in my mind, especially when he had given me his class ring. He'd had an almost frenetic energy about him, like someone before they dove into the deep end of a pool for the first time. But I had jumped at the chance to go somewhere with him. It felt like this was the first step toward being a real couple.

But the closer we got to the field, the darker his mood turned. I noticed the tense set of his shoulders and the clench of his jaw. I ran my fingers through his hair to try and settle him down. Was he nervous about something?

"You okay?" I asked him.

Rhett looked at me quickly. "Yeah, all good." I didn't push it. I knew he wouldn't appreciate it, and I was learning when to keep quiet.

I sat back in my seat and lifted the heavy gold class ring from the chain around my neck. I still couldn't believe Rhett had given it to me. It was such a sweet gesture. Tangible proof of his feelings for me. So whatever was going on with him now, I convinced myself it had nothing to do with us.

"You sure you want to go to this thing?" Rhett tried to sound nonchalant, but I could hear the tremor in his voice. Was he regretting the offer to take me now? It made sense that he would be nervous, I guess.

"I want to meet your friends," I told him. "The people that are important to you will be important to me." I lifted his hand and brought it to my lips, kissing his knuckles. "I love you, Rhett."

He squeezed my hand before extracting himself from my grip. "I love you too," he said, but a thread of apprehension had taken root, and I had to force myself to believe him.

* * *

I could tell something was wrong as soon as we arrived at the field party.

It began when I saw Jeremy. He was so intense. So *angry*. Had I led him on somehow? I had been around enough men who felt they had a claim on me for one reason or another. I knew the look when I saw it, and I knew I had to be careful.

I was thankful for Rhett by my side, even though I could feel the undercurrent of anxiety that coursed through him.

Then there was Alison. She was just as angry as Jeremy, but it seemed for very different reasons. I got the impression she was dating Rhett's friend Caleb, but she only had eyes for the man by my side, which he was oblivious to. She pulled me over to the keg and handed me a Solo cup. When I fumbled with the nozzle, she took my cup and filled it for me with a sigh of annoyance.

"So you and Rhett—?" She didn't finish the question. She didn't need to. Her question was full of accusations.

"Yeah, I guess so," I told her, my voice small. I kept darting looks over to where Rhett stood with Jeremy and Caleb.

"Who *are* you?" she asked rudely.

I felt jittery with nerves. "I'm Jenn," I squeaked.

"Jenn what?"

I swallowed a mouthful of beer, hating the taste. "Jenn Moore. I'm new in town."

Alison filled up another cup of beer, her eyes never leaving me. "I figured, because I've never seen you before." She took a sip of beer, watching me over the rim of her cup. "It looks like you make friends real quick." She glanced at Rhett, who was watching us closely, his eyes worried.

"Yeah, Rhett's been great. He's so sweet," I gushed, thinking this might be a way to get her to like me if she and Rhett were close. "Are you and Rhett friends?"

Alison glared at me. "I've known him for years. Rhett's special. I thought he was better than this." Her mouth twisted like she tasted something sour. "He's too nice for his own good. Doesn't realize when he's being taken advantage of."

I gaped at her. "I'm not taking advantage of him. That's not what's going on at all."

Alison grabbed my wrist, twisting it slightly, making me gasp. "Watch your step, little girl. We don't take kindly to women who think they can take what—and who—doesn't belong to them."

She dropped my arm and I cradled it against my chest, the skin throbbing. I didn't even have to question if her words were a threat. It was obvious she meant me harm. For reasons that seemed all too clear.

She was jealous, even though she had a boyfriend.

I didn't understand the strange dynamic I had stumbled into.

I touched Rhett's ring around my neck, trying to soothe my fearful anxiety. Alison's eyes darkened as she watched me slip the ring on and off my finger.

"Is that Rhett's class ring?" she demanded.

I looked down at it and couldn't help but smile, despite the situation. "Yeah, it is. He gave it to me this evening."

"I can't *believe* him," Alison fumed.

"This looks like a great party," I commented, trying to sound upbeat and friendly. Wanting to turn this around, if at all possible.

Alison didn't respond. She kept staring at me angrily. Her antagonism put me on edge. "I think we should get back over there." I nodded in Rhett's direction. "I don't want Rhett to wonder where I am."

"Of course. Can't have Rhett worrying over you, can we?" Her voice held a nasty note of sarcasm.

I rushed back to Rhett, wanting him to shield me from everyone. I was starting to understand why he hadn't wanted to bring me tonight. His friends weren't very nice. I couldn't make sense of why the kind, sweet boy I was in love with would hang out with these people.

I handed Rhett one of the beers and was surprised when he drank it quickly. He'd told me he wasn't much of a drinker. That grain of mistruth disturbed me.

I held out my own beer for him to take. "Here, you can have mine. I don't really drink anyway, remember?" He took it without hesitation.

"So, uh, Jenn, is it?" Caleb asked. I couldn't tell if he was trying to be nice or if he was simply filling the awkward silence.

I looked from him to Rhett, who appeared uncomfortable. "Yeah, it's Jenn. Jenn Moore." I gave him a sweet smile. Like with Alison, I really wanted him to like me. These were Rhett's friends, and they were clearly important to him.

"How long are you planning to stay in Fern River?" Caleb asked.

I glanced at Rhett again, and his face was frozen in a stiff smile. "I'm not sure. Depends on Rhett, I guess." It was meant as a flirty joke until I saw Caleb and Jeremy's expressions.

"Oh, really?" Caleb asked, and he and Jeremy started laughing, which seemed to piss Rhett off.

Jeremy smirked hatefully, his eyes hooded and furious. "I had no idea you two were so close." Then he leaned toward me. I felt his invasion of my personal space like a violent act. Jeremy threaded his fingers through my hair and I shuddered at how casually he touched me, as if he had every right to. Then he pulled something out of my hair. It looked like grass. He held it up. "Looks like you two already had a roll in the hay before you got here."

I wanted to die inside.

Was it that obvious that Rhett and I had slept together?

I glanced around the field at all the people who seemed way too interested in us. Could they tell too? The whispering and blatant staring was awful.

Rhett leaned close to me, his lips brushing my ear lobe. "I think we should get out of here." I nodded gratefully. I wasn't having a very good time, anyway.

Not with Jeremy watching me like he owned me and Alison glaring like she wanted to kill me.

I took Rhett's hand again, lacing our fingers together. He didn't pull away, and I took that as proof that I wasn't wrong about us. Then I saw the change of expression come over Rhett's face. He looked like he had seen a ghost.

Alison's eyes widened, and Caleb whistled low under his breath. "Uh-oh."

"Hi, Rhett."

I glanced up to see a gorgeous woman with long blond hair walking toward us. She seemed angry even with her dazzling smile. I wanted to cower behind Rhett and hide from her. She had the aura of someone who would stomp all over me, and I wanted to get as far from her as possible. She was incredibly intimidating. Even Caleb and Alison hurried off, clearly eager to be far from this woman's fury.

I could see Rhett swallow thickly. He pulled his arm back and took a noticeable step away from me.

She stood in front of us, her eyes blazing. I stood as straight as possible and gave her a smile. "Uh, hi?" Then wished I hadn't said anything as she turned all that rage onto me. She looked like she wanted to squash me beneath her shoe. Who was she?

She put her hand on Rhett's arm, moving immediately to his side.

It was a purposeful move.

Them against me.

An alarm was blaring inside me.

"Are you going to introduce us, honey?" she said.

Honey?

A buzzing started in my ears, making it hard to hear. Rhett still hadn't said anything, so I spoke up.

"I'm Jenn. Jenn Moore," I heard myself say as if from a distance. I felt like I had left my body and was watching everything from up above. I looked small and pathetic next to this beautiful woman who practically vibrated with strength and power. She was everything I wished I could be. And she was making it apparent she had a claim to Rhett. That I was nothing and nobody. I had never felt so insignificant in my whole life.

"Hi, Jenn. I'm Lucy." There was a loaded pause while I waited for my world to end. Because I wasn't stupid, and I could see something was going on between them. "Rhett's fiancée."

I wasn't sure what happened next. I looked in horror at Rhett, who seemed to have turned to stone. I think he said my name, but I couldn't hear him. All I could think was I had sex with this man not two hours ago. I had given him something I thought I would only give to the man I would be with forever. I had stupidly thought that was Rhett.

And this whole time, he was engaged.

To Lucy.

This poor woman had no idea that she, too, had been betrayed.

My heart didn't break. It dissolved inside my body.

"Let me explain," Rhett said, but all I could think was, *Run.*

Lucy said something about a wedding next month.

Next month?

"Your wedding?" I croaked, hoping this was all a bad dream.

Then Rhett's attention was on Lucy, his expression shattered and ruined. I felt like I was intruding. I needed to get out of there.

I looked up, my eyes drifting to the other side of the bonfire where a man stood watching me.

I blinked, hoping the smoke was messing with my eyes.

But I knew what I saw wasn't my imagination.

Marty stood there staring at me, a devilish smile on his mangled face.

I *hadn't* been imagining him.

He had been here this whole time, and now he had just witnessed my humiliation.

He lifted his hand and waved, his grin growing wider and twisting his lips. I could see the scar on his cheek, shiny in the flickering light. I felt a momentary malicious joy at the sight of it, remembering I was the one to give it to him. Then my entire body began to shake, and the truth hit home.

He had found me.

Rhett was speaking, but I couldn't understand what he was saying. My entire focus was on getting as far away from here as possible.

Marty walked around the edge of the fire, heading in my direction, his eyes never leaving me.

I let out a sob and ran as fast as I could for the trees, barely seeing where I was going. I heard Rhett scream my name, but I kept going.

I had to get away.

I ran and ran, blindly making my way through the thick woods, hoping it would lead me back to town. My phone pinged in my pocket with an incoming message. Stopping to catch my breath, I pulled it out and stared at the screen with trembling hands.

Marty: Leaving so soon, little rabbit? Don't worry, I'll find you.

I could hear Rhett calling my name in the distance.

"Jenn, please, talk to me." He sounded frantic and out of control, which scared me. "Goddamn it, where are you?" His worry turned to anger. "Jenn!"

I almost stopped. Despite his horrible betrayal, my heart yearned for him. And I knew if I gave him a chance, I'd forgive him. After seeing Marty, I wanted Rhett's love and protection more than ever.

I was such an idiot.

So I kept running, not letting him catch up with me.

I had to hide.

Before it was too late.

I continued running, my phone ringing over and over again as I went. I eventually turned it off. Somehow, I made it back to the Millwood Guesthouse. Out of breath, I let myself inside, trying to be as quiet as possible so as to not wake Ms. Stanley.

Just as I started up the stairs, I heard the older woman come out of her bedroom.

"You're late tonight." She said it with a note of accusation.

I swiftly wiped away my tears and hid my face behind my hair. "Yes, sorry if I woke you, Ms. Stanley. I'm going to my room."

Ms. Stanley peered up at me. "Are you okay?" I detected a note of concern.

"I'm fine." I still wouldn't look at her. "But I . . . I'm going to be heading out soon. I think it's time I left town." Just saying it broke the last pieces of my heart.

"You know you can stay as long as you need to," the older woman said. "And, take it from me, running won't solve your problems. Sometimes you have to stand still and face them."

All this time, I had been avoiding Ms. Stanley. Yet she had somehow seen more than I gave her credit for.

"Thanks," I muttered and hurried to my room and closed the door before I broke down in front of her. She had no idea how her small kindness was almost my undoing.

I threw myself on the bed and sobbed for everything I'd lost. My family. The future I had only just started envisioning for myself.

Rhett.

Because, now thinking about it more clearly, there was no way I could forgive this. He had betrayed me in the worst way possible. He had let me trust him, all the while lying to my face every day.

He wasn't simply dating someone else. *He was getting married.* And tonight, he had taken my virginity. It felt like he had taken the last innocent part of me. A part that still believed there was good in the world. But I could see now that I was wrong.

When I left home, I thought I'd be smarter. That I wouldn't be fooled ever again by those who professed to love me.

And yet, at the first cute smile and smooth words, I had handed over the most sacred parts of myself. I had given everything to a man who didn't deserve any of it.

Would men always ruin me?

I put my book bag on the bed and started packing my things. There wasn't much to pack, anyway. But then I thought about leaving Fern River, and I couldn't finish the task.

I didn't know what to do.

Or where to go.

When I had first run away from home, the thought of the open road in front of me had felt exciting. But now, after my short time in Fern River, a place I was starting to see as a home, the thought of leaving paralyzed me.

Soon there was a commotion at the front door.

I could hear Rhett shouting my name outside and Ms. Stanley trying to get rid of him.

I stayed upstairs, too scared to face him. I loved him so much. Even now I yearned to go to him and let him lie to me all over again. If only I could go back in time to earlier at Jagged Point.

Would I still go to the party and find out the truth? Or would I want to stay oblivious? I wasn't sure.

Ignorance was bliss, or so they said.

It had gone silent outside and I peered carefully from my window, feeling both sad and glad that he had gone.

But then I saw something.

The figure of a man standing across the street.

Marty?

No. I was pretty sure it was Rhett's friend Jeremy.

How did he know where I was staying?

Feeling sufficiently creeped out, I quickly closed the curtains and got out of sight.

Stupidly, I turned my phone back on. I had twenty-two voice messages and dozens of texts. Each one more unhinged than the last.

Rhett was angry. Really, really angry.

That shocked me. I expected his tears and his pleas, but not his rage.

Hearing his fury brought me back to a place I never wanted to be again. A place where I was scared and anxious about what I said and did. That confirmed my need to get out of Fern River as quickly as I could.

I had been living without a plan since leaving home. That needed to change. Because if I was going to survive, I had to be more careful, which meant taking time to decide where I was going and what I was going to do.

Marty had found me, and that meant Rhett would too.

So, for now, I needed to stay hidden from the men who were looking for me.

At least until I could figure out what to do next.

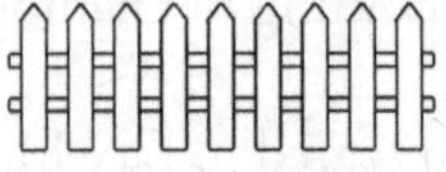

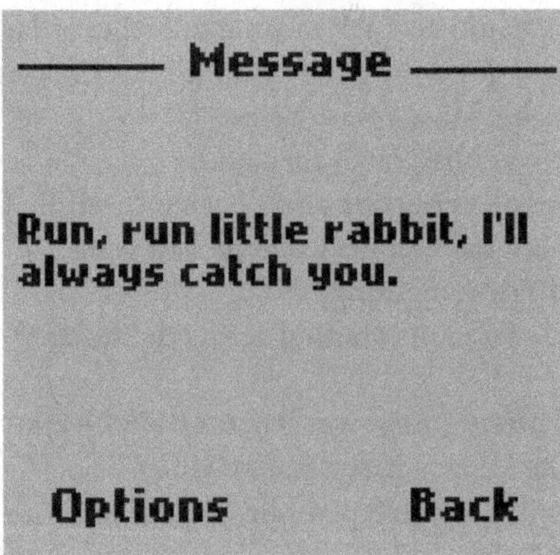

CHAPTER

19

Lucy

The Past

Early Evening of July 12—Fifteen Years Ago

MY PHONE PINGED with an incoming message. I grabbed it eagerly, hoping it was Rhett. I had been calling him all day, but per usual, he was avoiding me.

At least now I knew why. The mystery was solved, and she had red hair and was everything I wasn't.

> **Alison:** Girl, Amy is having a fit. She says you've called out of work three days in a row. Is this about Rhett? Bethany said you two broke up and he's left town with that Jenn girl. Is that true?

I had been fielding questions from every corner in relation to the status of my engagement. Too bad I didn't know how to answer any of them. Rhett and I hadn't really spoken since Jeremy's party. His mom claimed she hadn't seen him in days. Given her lack of concern, I knew she was covering for him.

But I couldn't let the rumors about a breakup fly. I wouldn't let anyone think that homewrecker had won. So I quickly tapped out a reply to my so-called friend.

Me: Rhett and I are fine! See you at work on Wednesday!
Alison: I'm so glad to hear that! I'll make sure Bethany and MaryBeth know what's going on. Those two have been telling everyone that Rhett and that girl were screwing around for weeks behind your back. Though, to be fair, I wasn't so sure myself because of how they seemed together. It really pissed me off, if I'm being honest. That girl was hanging all over him like a slut. I was ready to kick her ass.
Me: Can't believe everything you see, Al.

I slammed my phone down on the table, the screen cracking down the middle. I didn't even care. Everyone in town was talking about me, and not in the way I liked.

They were laughing at me.

Even worse, some of them *felt sorry* for me.

And of course I'd deny Rhett had two-timed me. Then I'd defend him because how dare they speak about my husband-to-be like that? A good bit of gaslighting would ensue, where I would question the validity of any "eyewitness" accounts until everyone believed my version of events.

Then Rhett and I would get married, and maybe then I could hold my head up again.

Because there was no way I was letting it end like this. I had planned our lives out. I had chosen him when I wasn't sure I had a choice about anything. The memory of his wide-eyed awe when I approached him all those years ago made it hard to turn away from him now.

My parents, particularly my father, had always said he wasn't good enough. My God, what would they say? Dad would be furious. This would not only reflect poorly on me, but my family because everyone connected Rhett Clark with the Herbaughs.

This would be a lot easier to deal with if the man in question had the balls to show up and deal with the fallout from his mistakes. Instead he seemed to be hiding away, like a coward.

Maybe I could just walk away. I could cut ties and find a new life with someone who wouldn't cheat on me.

Who was I kidding?

Things weren't that simple for a girl like me, with a mountain of expectations balanced on my shoulders.

"Everything okay, Lucinda?" My dad poked his head around the door of my bedroom as he headed down the hallway.

I thought about lying, but Dad made his living by reading people, and he'd be able to see through me in an instant.

"No," I sighed.

Dad frowned. "Is this about Rhett?" He took a step into my room, never coming all the way in, as if he were allergic to teenage girl.

His question caught me off guard. "Why would you ask that?"

Dad crossed his arms over his chest, his graying hair slightly disheveled, his shirt untucked. Outside the courtroom, he looked like your everyday doddering father. That is, until he opened his mouth and intimidated the hell out of you.

"I ran into Tanya Young at the FoodMart on Monday. She had an interesting story to tell about that man you insist on marrying."

I felt my insides knot up. "Oh yeah?"

Dad's expression darkened. "Seems he's been spending time with some woman from out of town who's staying at the Millwood Guesthouse. Tanya saw them at the bowling alley. Says they were pretty handsy, not like two people who are just friends."

Was there anyone in this town not privy to my humiliation? "So I've heard," I muttered.

"It's true, then?" Dad demanded as if he were the one being cheated on.

"I don't know, Dad. All I know is her name is Jennifer Moore and Rhett seems to have taken it upon himself to make her feel really welcome." I wouldn't admit the worst of it.

"He's making you look like a fool," my father bristled. "You need to end this, now."

"I'll deal with it, Dad." I crossed my arms in an imitation of him. We were mirror images of stubborn pride.

"Don't you think this has gone far enough, Lucinda? Not only do you insist on marrying a boy we don't approve of, but you're so preoccupied with proving your point that you can't admit your mother and I were right," he said with an edge to his voice. "Part of being a grown-up is knowing when to accept defeat."

I swallowed around the angry lump in my throat. "I'll fix it."

He stared at me with a disapproving frown, then turned on his heel and left so suddenly, and with such anger, I was surprised he didn't slam my door behind him. No sympathetic reassurance or hand on my shoulder. My dad didn't do the touchy-feely stuff. He showed his love in other ways. It usually involved taking care of things we couldn't handle ourselves.

His words rang in my head, and I knew I couldn't back down. Rhett was the only time I had ever stood up to my parents, and I would die on this hill before admitting they had been right about him.

So I was trapped by my own poor choices with no way out.

I didn't have time to think about what his sudden departure meant because a few minutes later, Bailey yelled up the stairs.

"Rhett's here!"

I hurried down to the front door, where I found my fiancé looking washed-out and exhausted, like he hadn't slept in days.

Good.

"It's been over a week since I've seen you," I reprimanded him after Bailey scurried from the room, perhaps sensing the dark tension between us. "What the hell, Rhett? What is wrong with you?" I demanded, my voice shaking, though I didn't know if it was from anger or fear.

"Don't talk to me like that. Why do you always treat people like dirt, Lucinda?" Rhett's mouth was pressed into a thin line, and his eyes, while sunken, flashed with fire.

"Excuse me? I don't think you're in any position to talk about treating people like dirt. Not when you made me look like a complete idiot in front of all our friends," I hissed. I grabbed his arm, trying to pull him farther into the house.

He wrenched himself free and backed away, putting space between us. "Well, I'm here now, as you beckoned." He mockingly bowed, and I could only stare at him in shock.

"What has gotten into you?" I put a hand to my chest in indignation. I didn't want to think about how much I probably looked like my mother.

Rhett was breathing heavily as if he were trying to get himself under control. "I don't want to get married, Lucinda."

The earth dropped out from underneath me.

"What?" I wasn't sure I heard him right.

Rhett closed his eyes briefly, and when he opened them again, I saw a resolution there that I had never seen before. "And I'm not studying pre-law anymore. I'm going to be a math teacher—"

"I already said that was fine," I insisted desperately.

"You're not listening. Why do you never listen to me? I'm going to be a math teacher, but not here in Fern River."

"Okay, so maybe we can look at moving to Jessop County. Their schools are always hiring—" My mind scrambled as I tried to find a way out of this mess. A way that meant we would end up together.

"You're. Still. Not. Listening. To. Me!" Rhett shouted, and I snapped my mouth closed.

Rhett paused, took a deep breath, then launched a grenade into the center of our relationship. "I'm leaving town, Lucinda. But not with you."

I blinked, my vision going fuzzy. "You're going with *her*?" I rasped.

Rhett shook his head. "I don't . . . I'm not sure what Jenn's plan is, but I hope so." His shoulders slumped. "I can't stay here anymore."

"You bastard," I whispered.

I noticed a tick in his jaw as he clenched his teeth. "Lucinda, you have to see this isn't working out. We want different things—"

I curled my hand into claws and launched myself at him. "You lying piece of shit!" I screeched. "I loved you! I gave you everything! How can you do this to me?" I was sobbing, I couldn't stop myself. And then I became mean. Words slipping out that I would never say under any other circumstances.

Rhett grabbed a hold of my wrists and shoved me backward. The back of my legs hit a chair and I stumbled, falling against the wall. We were both momentarily shocked before Rhett straightened up.

"You're a controlling bitch," Rhett lobbed at me, his words like homing missiles. "You think because you're beautiful, you can tell everyone what they can and can't do. But here's the thing," he dipped his voice low, a nasty edge tainting his words, "nobody even likes you. You have no real friends. No one but me has ever given a shit about you. You're popular because of your family. It has nothing to do with *you*."

I stared at him, hardly able to believe what he was saying to me. These were things neither of us could ever take back. He knew it. I knew it.

"I love her, Lucy. She's the kind of woman I want to be with. She's everything you're not. So when you're placing blame, look at yourself. You don't have what it takes to keep a man, and you never will. Maybe you should go run to your daddy. He's the only one that can stomach you, and I bet even he wishes you'd go away."

I was stunned. The air left my body, and I felt like I was crumbling from the inside out.

But I wouldn't let him get the best of me. And I wouldn't roll over and let him walk all over me.

"At least I still have both my parents." My lip curled in derision. "My father didn't leave me high and dry and expect me to figure things out on my own. My father wanted me, but you wouldn't know anything about that," I spat out, going for the low blow. The one thing I knew would undo him.

Rhett reared back, his hand connecting with my cheek. The sound reverberated through the open hallway, and I gasped. His anger slipped as he realized what he'd done.

He had never hit me before now. But something had changed in him these past few weeks. Something dark had been growing below the surface that I had willfully turned a blind eye to.

I glared at him, my skin stinging. "You're a pathetic nobody without me, Rhett. I hope you've told your mom how you've ruined everything. Now both the men in her life have let her down."

Rhett felt my verbal attack like a strike to the chest. I saw how it took all the fight out of him. His expression drained of rage and was replaced with something so much worse.

Sadness.

As if it was his heart breaking, and not mine.

He looked at me, his eyes agonized. "This isn't how it should be. If we really loved each other, we wouldn't be trying to tear each other down like this." His tone faltered like he might cry at any moment.

"And I suppose *Jenn* is perfect," I scoffed bitterly.

At the mention of his side piece, Rhett's face hardened again, his eyes turning to flint. "I *love* her, Lucinda."

The truth fell between us, cementing our fate—and hers.

"No, you don't," I growled.

"Yes, I do. And there's nothing you can do about it." He turned and opened the door, stepping out onto the porch.

He paused, as if realizing once he walked out, nothing would ever be the same. We were no longer Rhett and Lucy. We were something so much worse.

But he did leave, and I watched him walk away from me.

And head straight to *her*.

"There's nothing you can do about it."

His words branded themselves on my brain.

"I wouldn't be so sure," I murmured as I closed the door behind him.

Rhett had no idea the lengths I would go to keep what was mine.

CHAPTER

20

Rhett

The Present

IT WAS RIDICULOUSLY easy to find a YouTube video on how to remove an ankle monitor. I watched a few before putting it into practice. I couldn't believe it was that simple, but ten minutes later, my ankle was a lot lighter.

I shoved the monitor in the nearest drawer and hoped I could figure out how to put it back on.

My phone buzzed with an incoming text, and I briefly closed my eyes, already knowing it would be Marty.

Marty: I'm here. Where are you? I hope you're not thinking of standing me up. That wouldn't turn out so great for you.

I had no idea why Marty was doing this, after all this time. What did he hope to gain from ruining my life? We hadn't seen each other since that night. It would almost make sense if he had tried to bribe me at some point for cash, but no, he seemed satisfied with going nuclear on my very existence.

For a brief time, I thought we were friends. Yet, looking back, I could see more clearly, with the benefit of hindsight, that we never had been. But that still didn't explain *why now*. He had been holding on to the video and my damn T-shirt for fifteen years, waiting for the day he could barge back into my life.

Who does stuff like that?

Perhaps I should have headed to this meeting with a bit more hesitance. Who knew what Marty would do, or what other bullshit he'd pull out of his hat like some kind of psychotic magician?

But I wasn't known for my great decision-making.

I grabbed my keys and slipped out the back door then headed through the side gate. I climbed into my car and drove straight to Jagged Point.

The journey felt agonizing.

All these years, I had stayed away from the spot I once escaped to. Since Jenn, I couldn't go there. The memory of her was all tangled up with her death, making the place that was once a respite now a nightmare.

I parked far away from the road so no one would see my car, and began the arduous trek. I walked slowly . . . deliberately. Each step took me farther up the winding hill that cut through the dense forest. Sunlight filtered through the thick canopy above me, casting dappled shadows on the path. It was daytime, yet the atmosphere felt pervaded by an eerie stillness that sent shivers down my spine.

The gnarled trees with their twisted branches seemed to reach out like skeletal fingers toward me. The horrific ghosts of long ago were making themselves known, as dread reverberated through me.

The underbrush was thick, and the air heavy with the scent of decaying leaves and wet earth. The path that used to be well-trodden now felt abandoned. I knew that even the locals had started giving the once popular spot a wide berth. The dirt and trees had seen too much bloodshed.

Some of it was because of me.

It had once been my favorite place to be, but now it was only filled with haunting memories.

As I climbed higher, I couldn't shake the feeling that I was being watched. Every rustle of leaves, every snap of a twig, seemed louder in the silence.

I glanced over my shoulder, half-expecting to see Marty behind me, but there was nothing. It was only the shadows—and my own anxiety—playing tricks on my mind.

And then I saw him—a figure, shrouded in shadow standing at the edge of the overlook. Marty raised a hand and grinned his familiar sadistic smile. I took a deep breath as I headed toward him.

"Hey there, buddy," Marty greeted me with a note of sarcasm. "Long time, no see."

"Cut the crap, Marty. How much do you want?"

Marty held his hands up in defense. "Woah there, Rhett. Thought we'd make some small talk before we got down to business." He laughed, his dark eyes offering me nothing but unfiltered hate.

"Glad to know I was right, at least. I knew it had to be about money. You really have no shame, do you? You're messing with my life, Marty. My *daughter's* life." I tried to contain my anger. My hatred for him grew as I thought about all the things he was trying to take from me.

Marty and Lucinda made a great pair. Both seemed hellbent on obliterating all semblance of happiness in my life. They wanted me broken and destroyed, though at least Marty didn't hide his loathing.

"No shame? Really? Are you really going to stand there and pretend you don't remember exactly what happened, *buddy*?"

"No, you're the one misremembering, *old friend*," I spat out as something flashed in Marty's eyes. Blink and I would have missed it.

"I wasn't the one who hurt Jenn that night."

His words triggered something in me. A flash of red hot anger clouded my vision, and I lunged for him, furious. Marty dodged me at the last second, and I stumbled toward the cliff's edge. Surprisingly, he grabbed me before I could fall over, pulling me back to safe ground. A prickle of fear ran through me at how close I came to going over.

In a moment of maudlin self-pity, I wondered if it would have been better for me to fall to my death. Then McKenzie wouldn't have to grow up with her dad in prison, living with the shame and resentment that would undoubtedly cause. A tragic accident was preferable to a convicted murderer for a dad.

I thought of her sweet face and how she always looked at me like I was the most important person in her life. I was her favorite. I knew it. Lucinda knew it.

Then I remembered how she held onto Mabel this morning. Her small arms wrapped around her neck as she turned away from me.

I had been abandoned by all the women in my life in one way or another.

Jenn and my mom were both gone. Lucinda had emotionally left me a long time ago. And now my own daughter wanted nothing to do with me.

It didn't matter what happened next. In the end, I would always end up alone.

"Get off me!" I yelled, snatching my arm from Marty's grip. He let go with a grim chuckle.

"Easy there." He laughed. "No need to get so feisty."

"Just tell me how much you want to make this all go away. I can get it—whatever it is."

Marty's wiry frame was taut like a coiled spring. His full height towered over me. It made him incredibly intimidating. He jabbed a finger painfully into my chest.

"You can't buy me, asshole! Don't you get that yet?"

"Then why, if it's not for money?" I asked, desperate for answers. "Why *now*?"

"Because of what you did. Why should you get off scot-free because you married the right piece of ass?"

I stared at him, frantic but also annoyed. My future—my *life*—was on the line.

"You have no idea who you're messing with. You do realize who my father-in-law is and what he can do to you, right?" I drew myself upright, trying to make myself as physically intimidating as possible. "I know a guy like you has spent some time in jail. Do you want to go back?"

My palms were sweating as I waited for him to react. Marty's cheeks flushed, his eyes hardening. Then he started laughing. He laughed so hard, he had difficulty catching his breath. He slapped his knee as if I were a stand-up comedian.

"Are you trying to threaten me? Seriously?" He wiped tears from his eyes. "You really are a piece of work, Rhett. As if you could do anything to me. I'm not a weak woman you can throw around because you're pissed off. I'll punch back. You should know that by now." His humor was gone and was now replaced by cold, calculated anger. "And we both know you would never have met up with me if you had any other options. You're fucked, buddy. We both know it."

"Marty," my voice broke on his name, "please don't do this."

I was not opposed to begging at this point. I didn't care. I would do whatever it took to make this go away. If not for me, for McKenzie. I couldn't bear to think of her living without me. Marty grinned, enjoying the power he had over me. He was as arrogant as ever. I found it hard to reconcile the man in front of me with the man I thought had been my friend all those years ago.

I had looked at him as a brother figure. He had seemed worldly. Like he knew how things worked. He opened up my eyes.

I had always thought myself a good man. Until Marty. Until that night. Until everything afterward.

How wrong I had been.

"I didn't do what you think I did, Marty. We both know I couldn't have. I loved her. I still do."

"Don't give me that pussy bullshit. What you did to her didn't look like love." His lip curled in derision in the way I remembered so clearly. He looked at me like I was pathetic. Maybe I was.

"I loved Jenn. I wanted to be with her. I was leaving Lucinda and we were going to be *together*."

Marty shrugged, seeming unconcerned. His almost apathetic demeanor was a mocking contrast to my tension. He had nothing to lose, only things to gain. His dark eyes were filled with an emotion I couldn't place. He pulled out a pack of cigarettes and lit one, exhaling a long plume of smoke while I waited, tortured as the seconds ticked by.

Finally, I spoke again, needing to plead my case as if this were a different kind of courtroom. "We both know who killed her, and it wasn't me."

Marty eyed me, smoking casually, as if he had all the time in the world.

"Marty . . . It was Lucinda, not me."

I said the words I had never dared say out loud.

Words that had been locked up inside me all this time.

Lucinda and I had never spoken about that night. It had been a silent agreement to leave the past behind us and move forward. I thought I was doing it for the woman I decided, in the end, to build my future with, mostly because I was too broken to make any other choice. I was being a good husband. It felt nice to be able to protect my wife in a way I had never been able to before. And it gave me a power that had been lacking in our dynamic. That one, huge secret leveled things between us.

I didn't need her to say it. The truth was always there between us, a darkness that permeated everything. I didn't need her to tell me. Blood spoke louder than words ever could.

It's why we were each other's alibis.

And we never breathed a word of it to anyone. We wouldn't dare.

In truth, the idea that she would kill to keep me was strangely erotic. I had never realized my cool, composed fiancée was capable of such a savage act. I was flattered by the lengths she went to keep me.

After all, I'm a man who liked to be wanted.

The words fell between Marty and me. But instead of the nuclear explosion I had expected, there was barely a ripple in the air. My impatience for a reaction grew until it erupted as anger.

"Did you hear me? Lucinda killed Jenn!"

"I heard you just fine, Rhett. But that's bullshit. Lucy may be a little unbalanced at times, but she couldn't have killed Jenn—not like that. That type of violence was unhinged. No way a woman could do that. That kind of crazy was all man." Why did he sound proud of that?

I was taken aback at his use of Lucinda's old nickname, but before I could dig into that, Marty kept speaking.

"So, tell me this, if you loved Jenn so much, and your wife killed the supposed love of your life, why continue to protect Lucy? It doesn't make sense."

"We have a family. And we have a daughter, which is exactly why you have to stop this. It's not just my life you're ruining. It's hers. And she's innocent in all this."

"I didn't do this, buddy, you did. If your little girl gets caught up in this mess, that's on *you*, no one else." Marty threw his cigarette to the ground and stomped on it. He glowered, all pretense gone. "I saw Jenn that night. After she was already dead." His breathing became shallow, and he had to swallow before continuing. His eyes blazed with hatred that should have incinerated me. "I saw what you did to her—"

"What? How?" I stammered, feeling like I was going to throw up.

"Because I went back."

A cold sweat broke out across my forehead.

I had pictured Jenn lying dead on the side of the road a thousand times. I imagined her body crumpled in a heap, her blood staining the ground around her. My brain loved to torture me with the worst possible version of what had happened. The photos had been enough to haunt me, but Marty had actually seen Jenn, dead and abandoned.

"I saw what you did to her, and you're finally gonna pay for it."

It was over.

I was done for.

He was never going to go away. This wasn't about money. This was about revenge.

This was about Jenn.

The girl we both loved.

"I wanted to look you in the eye and tell you that I *know*. I have waited fifteen long years for this moment. But now you'll get what's coming to you, and I will be there to dance on your fucking grave."

Decades of suspicion and hatred arched between us. The air was thick with foreboding, as if Jenn's ghost lingered among the trees, waiting for justice.

"Marty, I didn't—" I started to say, but then stopped myself. I narrowed my eyes as I stared at the man determined to destroy me.

I had been trying to figure out why, when maybe the reason was a lot more clear-cut than I thought. "How do I know you weren't the one who killed Jenn? You said yourself, a woman could never do that. Maybe you're trying to make me take the fall for *your* crime. You seem to be working really hard to convince everyone I'm guilty. Maybe this anger is all for show."

Marty bared his teeth like a predator about to devour his prey. "We all have blood on our hands, Rhett."

Did he just admit to killing Jenn? "There was another man Jenn was scared of that night. A man who had followed her around for months. She was terrified when she saw you in the back of my car." I felt like I was getting to the truth.

Marty leaned so close I could smell the stink of cigarettes on his breath. "Save it, Rhett, and don't go thinkin' you can turn this around on me. It'll never work. Even if I have to make up some shit to seal the deal, I'll do it. There's only one man going down for this, and it isn't me. I had to keep her away from men like you because I knew you'd only ruin her," he snarled, his hands curling into fists, and I wondered if he was going to hit me. It wouldn't be the first time Jagged Point had tasted my blood.

Marty gave me a smile as twisted as the scar on his face.

"Your life is over, Rhett." His words were bullets fired from a loaded gun.

"Everyone is gonna know that you killed my sister, you son-of-a-bitch."

Today 14:13

Great chat today, buddy.

Not gonna answer?

Guess I've given you a lot to think about.

I'm looking forward to seeing your face when you fry.

CHAPTER

21

Lucinda

The Present

RHETT DIDN'T COME back until late in the evening. He snuck in the kitchen door and tried to be quiet as he made his way toward the stairs.

My parents had taken McKenzie out to dinner, but I had decided to wait for my husband. We had a lot to talk about.

"How was your catch-up with Marty?" I asked, coming into the hallway from the living room.

"Jesus!" Rhett jumped. "What the hell are you doing lurking around like that?" He peered past me into the shadowed corridor. "Where's Kenz? And your parents?"

"Mom and Dad took McKenzie to dinner," I told him, crossing my arms over my chest. "Are you going to answer my question?"

Rhett frowned. "I should have known you'd figure out where I was. Which one of your little spies reported to you this time?" he asked nastily, pushing past me toward the staircase.

Rhett started up the stairs, and I followed him like a dog on his heels. "What did Marty say?" I asked, following him into my room.

"Why don't you ask him yourself?" he challenged.

His entire body was trembling. I needed to know what happened.

"Rhett, talk to me, what did he say?"

Rhett gripped his hair as if he wanted to pull it out. He looked crazed. "He's not backing down. He's going to testify and make sure I fry for it."

"Well, you knew Marty was going to go on the stand. Why are you acting surprised?"

Rhett's face flushed an angry red. "This is all your fault!" he screamed.

I couldn't help but take a step back, unsettled by the savage glint in his eyes. I had worked hard to learn how to handle my husband with varying degrees of success, but this man in front of me was unpredictable.

This was the same man I had encountered that night fifteen years ago. The man that only slipped out when his control was lost.

Despite my burgeoning fear, I couldn't let him place the blame for this at my feet. My indignation wouldn't stand for it.

"How is any of this my fault? You were the one who decided to sleep around with a woman who ended up murdered," I shouted back.

Rhett stared at me, his eyes alarmingly flat. Like a snake's. They were the eyes of someone who was close to losing everything and had no more shits to give.

"I should never have married you." He closed his eyes briefly as if in pain. "I should have run far away from you and your god-awful family."

"But you did marry me, Rhett, and here we are in my parents' home, and my family is the one that has always protected you—"

"I wouldn't need protection if it weren't for you!" he roared, raising his clenched fists as if he wanted to pummel my face.

I swallowed nervously and glanced at the open door, wondering if I could make a run for it.

I felt like a trapped animal in the room with a wolf.

"Rhett, please, just calm down," I whispered, thankful McKenzie and my parents weren't here, but also terrified that I was all alone with him.

"Your parents wanted a good little yes man, and for years I was that. I became what you wanted, but none of you thought of what I wanted." He was seething. He really thought he was the only one that had been cornered with no way out. He was incapable of seeing what anyone else thought or felt about anything.

I always knew he was inherently selfish, but the depth of his self-centeredness was startling.

"You think it's only you that had your voice taken away?" I rasped, trying to speak up over my growing fright. "I've been locked in this life with my humiliation hanging over me for over a decade. I've never been allowed to make any choices for myself—except you—and look where that got me."

We stared at each other, Rhett practically vibrating with fury and me trying not to recoil.

"Poor, poor Lucinda, the little rich girl thinks she has real problems." Rhett's laugh was cruel. Until that moment, I had no idea how much he hated me.

"Oh, because you have it so bad? Poor, poor Rhett, the sad little boy whose daddy didn't want him—" I started to say, knowing it would provoke a reaction.

I just wasn't expecting the one I got—though I probably should have.

In a split second, Rhett grabbed me by the throat. My eyes bulged, and I felt myself quake at the sight of his sadistic smile.

"Rhett." His name came out as a gasp. He pushed me backward until my legs hit the bed and I fell onto my back. Rhett climbed on top of me, his hand still pinning me down by my throat. He leaned over me, his face a terrifying blend of madness and ferocity.

"If I'm going to prison for murder, I should make it worth it, don't you think?" His fingers tightened and I fought against him. I clawed at his arms, trying to get him to release his hold.

"Rhett, let go," I wheezed as black spots swam in front of my eyes.

He squeezed even harder. "I should have left you fifteen years ago. I should never have let you talk me into marrying you. I've thought about you dead every single day since our wedding. It's the only thing that made me feel good in our whole fucking marriage."

I reached up and scratched his face, digging my nails into his flesh. He yelled, releasing me, and I slithered out from underneath him. I scrambled to my feet, my skin throbbing.

"What are you doing?" I whispered, not able to speak any louder.

Rhett prowled toward me, and I found myself backing up until I collided with the wall. There was no escape.

"I don't think I ever loved you."

I thought I had hardened myself against him, but his attack stripped away my defenses. I was naked and vulnerable before him.

"I only wanted us to be a family." I tried to reason with him.

Rhett's face contorted into an ugliness that was devastating to see. "We'll never be a family, Lucinda. In fact, as soon as this whole thing blows over, I'm taking *my* daughter and getting as far from you, and your horrible family, as we can get. Because I'd rather die than let *my* girl grow up to be a hateful bitch like you."

Just when I thought he would end me, he turned and left the room, slamming the door behind him. I sagged to the floor, my legs not able to hold me up any longer.

I waited until I heard him leave the house before I got back to my feet. I went to the window and watched him storm down the road.

I wondered where he was going and if I should go after him.

But then I stopped myself.

It didn't matter.

The important thing was that he was gone.

I couldn't believe he thought all this was my fault when he had shown his hand years earlier.

I let out a long, pent-up sigh. One that was heavy with fifteen years' worth of fear and love all tangled up together.

I had made so many mistakes.

But perhaps the worst was ever loving Rhett Clark.

* * *

"I want you gone."

Jenn was crying. I wanted to tell her to stop. That I should be the one wailing over everything she took from me. It started to rain. Large drops of water pelted my skin.

I advanced toward her, my hands curling into claws. Was I going to scratch her eyes out?

She cowered with fear, and I liked it.

"He says he's leaving town with you. Is that true?" I demanded.

Jenn swallowed, her hand going to her throat, looking for the ring that was now in my pocket. "We've talked about it," she admitted.

I saw red.

"You bitch!" I growled, imagining all the ways I could hurt her. We were alone up here. No one for miles. This place had seen its fair share of bloodshed, what was a little more? It would be easy to get away with it too. Covering my tracks wouldn't be hard.

Then she wouldn't be a problem anymore. She'd be just another story in Jagged Point's horrible history.

"I'm sorry, Lucy."

"Excuse me?"

"I had no idea Rhett was with someone. If I had known, I would never have—I would never have let him—" She covered her face, and her shoulders shook with the force of her sobs.

"You never would have what?" I snarled, unmoved by her grief.

And then it hit me what she was trying to say.

"You slept with him." My voice cracked, the words slipping out before I could snatch them back.

"I . . . I thought we would be together forever. I didn't know that he—I wouldn't have . . . I'd never been with anyone." She began to cry even harder.

Rhett had been her first.

I felt sick.

"You love him," I said. It wasn't a question. I could tell by the devastation on her face. I couldn't help but feel for her. She had given that moment to him thinking what they shared was special.

That she *was special.*

I knew that feeling, because I had been there once myself.

"So do you," she whispered, looking miserable.

"But I'm the only one who has a right to," I told her.

* * *

I waited at least twenty minutes before I felt it was safe to move. I opened my bedroom door and went out into the hallway. My neck throbbed from Rhett's assault.

We had entered no-man's land. There was no coming back from this. How could I get on a witness stand and perjure myself to protect a man who had tried to strangle me then threatened to take my daughter from me?

It was bad enough I had lied for him once before after what he'd done. I didn't have it in me to do it again.

I had known, on some level, this was going to happen. I had felt his disdain for me grow over the years, but I pretended it wasn't there.

Was the white picket fence really worth it?

With shaky legs, I walked past Bailey's childhood bedroom that was, like mine, untouched. Mom kept them as pristine shrines to the young women we used to be.

Remembering how Bailey had kept Rhett's class ring, a terrifying thought suddenly occurred to me: What else had my magpie sister unknowingly gotten her hands on? What evidence lay tucked away in the nooks and crannies of her room that could come back and bite me in the ass?

I darted inside and headed straight to the closet where I knew she used to hide trinkets. Drying my tears, I focused on my search. Pushing aside clothes that hadn't been fashionable in over a decade, I felt around for the shoebox I knew would be there.

It was covered in stickers and glued-on sequins. *Keep Out* was written in my sister's sloping script.

I dropped the lid on the floor and began to rummage through the meaningless junk inside, not surprised to find more than a few items that had once belonged to me.

Bailey really was a pack rat.

But then something caught my eye. Something that nudged at a memory I had buried in the chaos of my mind.

Something that brought with it recollections from *that night.*

* * *

"You're right. I shouldn't love him. But I do," Jenn gasped, her hand clutching her head. I noticed she wore three silver bangles on her right wrist. They sounded like windchimes as they clinked together on her arm. I watched, with some concern, as blood dripped down her face.

"Are you okay?" I found myself asking her.

I noticed the dark stains on the ground near her feet.

Jenn lifted her fingers away, staring at the red stain on her skin. "I don't know."

Then she started to cry. Deep, heaving sobs that racked her body. And despite my anger, I couldn't help but be moved by her devastation.

I found a pack of tissues in my purse and held one out for her to take.

"Th-thanks," she hiccupped, pressing it to her wound.

"Who did that to you?" I asked. "Was it Rhett?" I couldn't believe I was contemplating that my fiancé could hurt someone like that, but there were a lot of things I would never have imagined him capable of.

"He didn't mean to." Jenn wouldn't meet my eyes.

"What?" I asked, thinking about how he had put his hands on me just a few hours earlier. Had he done the same to Jenn?

"I pushed him to it. I told him I couldn't be with him. It's only because he loves me." Jenn was all excuses. I recognized them well. They were the ones I had just been telling myself.

"Rhett Clark doesn't love anyone but himself," I spat out, feeling a fissure of rage on her behalf.

She shook her head. "I had to get away. He wouldn't listen. Then he and Marty—"

"Marty was with you?"

Her eyes widened. "You know him? You know Marty?" She seemed terrified and concerned. "Lucy, you have to be careful. He's not who you think he is. He's dangerous."

Marty? Dangerous? That didn't surprise me. There was something dark and sinister about him, but maybe that was what I liked.

"This isn't about Marty. Tell me what happened with you and Rhett." I took a step closer, annoyed and pissed off that she, too, had a connection to them both. It disturbed me that we were involved with the same two men. What did this girl have that I didn't?

I swallowed my irritation, knowing I was being unreasonable.

Jenn shook her head, her face clouded with uncertainty. "We were fighting, Rhett and me. I told him I was leaving town." She paused then looked at me, the tears drying on her face. "I told him I was leaving by myself."

Thunder rumbled overhead, and rain soaked our clothes. "Not with Rhett?"

Jenn's expression hardened. "He lied to me, Lucy. He lied to both of us. And he hurt me. So, as much as I . . ." She swallowed. "As much as I care about him, I can't be with someone like that. I've spent my whole life loving the wrong people. That stops now."

I regarded my romantic rival with something that felt a lot like respect.

"So you and Rhett—?"

The lightning flashed like a strobe effect. Jenn pressed her lips together, a look of firm resolve on her pretty face. "There is no Rhett and me, Lucy. I can promise you that." Her confession seemed to take a lot out of her. She winced. "I ran away, but when I circled back a while later, Rhett was gone. I have no idea where he went."

I felt something loosen inside me. All my anger faded, washed away by the rainstorm. "I blamed you for all this. You humiliated me," I told her.

I thought about my fight with Rhett earlier. The memory of my stinging cheek. The hateful words he flung at me.

Jenn hadn't made him do, and say, those things. That was all on him.

Jenn flinched. "I understand. But I promise you, I had no idea he was engaged. He never said a word about you. If I had known, I would never . . ." Her voice broke and I saw that she was crying again. This time I let myself feel bad for her.

Because none of this was her fault.

Nor was it mine.

This lay entirely at Rhett's feet. He had created this situation, and I would be damned if I'd get into a cat fight over a man who was playing us both. A man who would use his hands when things weren't going his way.

"I believe you," I said, and I meant it.

Jenn wiped her eyes and nodded. "I'm sorry, Lucy."

We stared at each other for a few moments, not as two women who had been pitted against each other, but as people who understood what the other was feeling on a basic level.

We had both been deceived and betrayed.

"What I told Rhett is true. I am leaving town, so you don't need to worry about me anymore," Jenn assured me. "But maybe, you should think twice before marrying a man like that."

I didn't know what to say. Because she was right. But I had also come too far to back out now. There was more than my pride at stake. It was my freedom too. Because I knew that admitting Rhett and I were over would mean handing back control of my life to my parents. And I couldn't do that.

But was I willing to relinquish one prison for another?

Did I really think my love for Rhett was enough to carry us both?

Was my vision for our future worth the inevitable heartache?

I felt paralyzed by indecision. "I'm not like you," I told her. "I can't just up and leave and see where the wind takes me. I have been working for years toward getting married and building a life with Rhett. People expect the wedding. My parents expect it."

Jenn came toward me and put her hand on my arm, the lightning glinting off her bracelets. "You can be anyone you want to be, Lucy.

Rhett doesn't deserve your loyalty. Your parents wouldn't want you to tie yourself to a man like that."

She didn't understand that the thought of admitting I was wrong to them would be worse than tying myself to someone who didn't want me.

I pulled away from her, knowing she meant well, but also not wanting her judgment—or her sympathy. My life was different from hers. "Thanks, Jenn. And good luck with everything." I started to head toward the path that would lead me back to my car, but then I stopped. "And let's hope we're both smarter next time."

Jenn smiled. "Oh, I think we will be."

So I left behind the girl my fiancé had cheated on me with.

It was the last time I ever saw her.

CHAPTER

22

Rhett

The Past

Evening of July 12—Fifteen Years Ago

"I'M SORRY . . ."

Her voice infuriated me.

"Jenn, I'm sorry it all turned out like this. I only wanted you to hear me out. Let me tell my side of the story—" I started to say. The tension in my shoulders was giving me a headache, and for the first time in days I wished I was sober. It had been easier to drink and smoke and try to forget the wreckage my life had become.

But seeing her while I was in this state was dangerous. My emotions were all over the place, the most dominant being rage. But I had to play this right. I couldn't show my hand right away.

Marty snickered in the back seat, and my lip curled in annoyance.

"Is there really another side that matters?" She sounded angry, which surprised me. She never voiced an opinion contrary to mine.

It's why I loved her. Her bitter reply made our situation crystal-clear.

It was too late.

Things had gone too far.

I had lost control, and I didn't know how to get it back.

I could see that she wasn't looking at or listening to me. I drove faster, my attention not on the speedometer, but on the turmoil brewing between us.

"Of course it matters!" I shouted, startling us both.

Marty continued to laugh, and I glared at him in the rearview mirror. He wasn't helping the situation—I could see she wasn't happy about him being here.

No, she seemed scared.

"Can you shut the fuck up, Marty? Jesus, man! Read the room," I snapped, wishing I could leave his ass on the side of the road. Then I might have half a chance of getting her to hear me out.

"Maybe *you* should shut the fuck up, buddy," Marty retorted, with an edge that was becoming familiar. Jenn flinched when he spoke, and I placed my hand on her knee.

"Hey, it's okay. Don't worry about him. Listen, we'll go to our special place and talk. You'll see this is all a big mistake," I tried to reason with her.

I couldn't stop myself from looking at her, even though my eyes should have been on the road. It had been over a week since I'd held her. I craved her like an addict needing a fix.

"Rhett, I told you, I'm leaving—"

I slammed my hand on the steering wheel, and the car swerved erratically. I overcorrected, the gravel spinning beneath the wheels. "And I told you, we're going to Jagged Point and you're going to listen to me. You owe me that much."

I heard a can crack open in the back of the car and the distinct sound of Marty drinking. He leaned forward and offered me a beer. I knew I should refuse. Getting busted for a DUI was the last thing I needed.

"Should you be drinking and driving?" Jenn asked, her voice small.

"Don't tell me what to do." I was already three sheets to the wind and driving like a maniac. I could tell I was making Jenn nervous. I knew she wanted to get out.

But why was this all about her?

What about me, and my feelings?

I grabbed the can Marty held out and chugged it. She started crying.

No one spoke for the rest of the car ride. The only sound was Jenn's soft sobs, which I found strangely comforting. Because if she was crying, then she still cared, right?

And if she still cared, then there was still a chance.

On some level I knew I wasn't making sense. But the booze and the weed were making me irrational. And the prospect of losing not only Lucinda, but Jenn, too, had me close to losing my sanity completely.

What had been the point of any of this if I didn't end up with either woman? No future, no girlfriend, only the disappointment on my mom's face when she saw how much I'd screwed up. I was sick and tired of everyone's goddamn disappointment.

I pulled off the road at Jagged Point, not caring if my car was in a ditch. All that mattered was getting Jenn to the overlook. Then she would remember how good we were together. And she would remember how amazing it had felt when we'd finally had sex. It had been special, and more intimate than anytime I had been with Lucinda. Maybe because Jenn had been so nervous about it.

I pulled the keys from the ignition and got out, then walked around to the passenger side and opened the door for Jenn. Marty had already gotten out, plastic bag of beers in hand, and was walking up the path that led to the cliffs.

"Jenn, come on." My patience was holding on by a thread.

She stared out the window, refusing to look at me. Her seatbelt was still buckled, and her hands were clasped tightly in her lap, knuckles white.

"Get out of the car, Jenn, please. We need to talk."

"I have nothing to say, Rhett. I'm leaving. Without *you*."

I slammed my hand on the roof of the car. Marty stopped and looked back, a grin on his face.

"Watch it, Rhett, otherwise we might think you've grown a pair," he called out, his insulting humor full of barbs.

I ignored him and crouched down by the side of the car. "Jenn, I won't ask you again. I want you to come with me, and I want you to listen to what I have to say. I've blown up my fucking life for you. The least you can do is hear me out."

When she still didn't move, I reached in and grabbed her arm. "Unbuckle the seatbelt, now."

With shaking hands, she did as I asked, then I dragged her out of the car, my fingers digging into her skin.

I barely registered the look of fear on her face. All I was thinking was that I could fix this.

Then tomorrow we could leave town, together.

I would be a teacher and she could maybe go to school, or get a job.

We'd have kids and a dog and we wouldn't be rich, but we'd be together. And my mom would understand because I was happy. And if she didn't, who cared.

"Jenn, move!" I barked, giving her arm a little shake.

She seemed scared and I wanted to tell her that she had nothing to fear from me, but I knew how crazy I sounded.

Because I *was* crazy.

I was madly, dangerously, obsessively in love, and I was willing to do anything to keep her. To stop her from leaving.

I took her hand and we walked to the overlook together. I held onto her tightly, terrified she'd slip away. Her footsteps were slow in the dwindling heat of the day. We didn't speak, and that was okay, because I would say everything to her once we got there. And then she would forgive me.

Marty was up ahead, and by the time Jenn and I made it to the cliffs, he had opened another beer and was guzzling it while sitting on the trunk of a fallen tree. He watched us closely as we approached. There was something unnerving about the way he followed Jenn's every movement.

Her gaze flitted to him anxiously, and then back to her feet. I wanted to know what was going on between them. Did she know him? Because she seemed like she did. Jealousy engulfed me. There was an awareness between them that I could only imagine coming from romantic intimacy.

I thought she had been a virgin. Was I wrong? The thought of her being with anyone else made me want to kill someone.

A summer storm was coming in. The air felt heavy and charged, damp and clinging.

I was annoyed that Jenn still hadn't looked at me. I grabbed both her hands, holding her in place.

"Jenn, I love you, and I want to be with you," I began.

"Rhett—"

"Just hear me out," I shouted, because I could hear the rejection in her voice and that enraged me. "God, you act like you're so high and mighty, like I'm some bad guy, but I'm not. *You know me.* You know my heart, and you know how much I love you. I showed you right here how much."

I pointed to the ground where I had made love to her, and she began to cry again. Her face crumpled as the tears flowed freely.

This was going all wrong.

"I'm leaving Lucinda. It's you I want. It's *you* I see a future with. You understand me like no other woman ever has. I want us to leave Fern River . . . together."

Jenn finally met my gaze. "Rhett, I'm sorry, but no," she said, her words barely a whisper.

"Yes, we will!" I hollered, grabbing her arm again, ignoring how she winced in pain.

What did she mean, no? She couldn't say that. She loved me, and I loved her. Was she trying to punish me or something? Was this her way of making me pay for lying to her? Or did she just need me to show her how much I loved her again?

I pulled her toward me and pressed my mouth to hers. I tasted her tears, and I swallowed her refusal.

I could hear Marty's horrible laughter and knew he was mocking me. It was humiliating. Jenn pushed against me, trying to free herself.

What did she think I was going to do? Force myself on her or something? All I wanted to do was kiss her. Jenn beat at my chest, whimpering. I pulled back, breaking the kiss. I could hardly think through my rage. I shook her. Her hair flew wildly, covering her tear stained face as I tried to get some sense into her.

"Goddamn it, Jenn, stop it, you're being ridiculous!" I yelled. "What is wrong with you? I know I lied, but I was trying to decide what to do. Can't you see that? But I've chosen you. Why aren't you happy about that? Why aren't you even a little bit grateful?"

What was wrong with the women in my life?

Was I cursed to attract thankless, selfish women?

"Women never are." Marty snickered from the shadows. I had almost forgotten he was there. "They're all the same."

"Shut up, Marty!" Jenn shouted.

Her yell shocked me into letting her go. Her sudden anger seemed to surprise all of us.

Marty skulked toward her. "Don't talk to me like that, Jennifer. You know better." Jenn shrank from him as if bracing for a blow. I stared between the two of them as the pieces began to fall together.

"Why are you even here?" she cried, her fear overshadowing her rage.

"For you, of course," Marty answered, and he wasn't laughing anymore.

"So, you two *do* know each other," I surmised, that ugly jealousy shredding my guts.

I was going to kill him.

Then her.

Where had those awful thoughts come from? I needed to get my head together.

"It wasn't that hard to find you, Jennifer," Marty went on, ignoring me completely. "Your MySpace updates were like following a goddamn treasure map. You're such an idiot. As if changing your last name would make you invisible." Marty stood over Jenn, who cowered before him. "The fact that you thought you could get away from me shows that you can't make it on your own. You don't have the brains to survive."

Marty crumpled his empty beer can and threw it over the cliff's edge less than an inch from Jenn, who jumped as if he had thrown it at her.

"I need to go," Jenn whimpered and tried to walk away, which pushed me to action.

I grabbed her again, my grip rougher than I intended. I wrenched her back. "Don't leave me, Jenn."

"Please, let me go, Rhett, *please*!"

I held on to her tightly, as if she were my anchor, my lifeline.

Didn't she understand that I couldn't let her go?

"Jenn, stop it," I yelled, but she kept fighting against me as if my touch repulsed her.

I vaguely registered that Marty had his phone out and was pointing it in our direction. But my thoughts weren't on what he was doing; they were on keeping Jenn here—with me.

"Jennifer, if you leave, I'll only find you again," Marty warned her, his threat clear.

"Please, Marty, just let me go," Jenn begged.

"You know I can't do that, sweetheart. I made a promise to bring you home alive or dead. And after what you did, I'm not picky about which one," he replied.

"Rhett," she whispered, turning to me. "I have to get away."

The words triggered something dark and awful inside me.

No!

I tugged on her arm so hard she cried out in pain. "Stop fighting me and listen!" I roared, trying to be heard over the commotion both inside and outside my head. "Just listen to me!"

Before I realized what was happening, I had backhanded her across the mouth. Her head flew sideways and she let out a whimper of pain.

Her words were on a loop in my head.

I have to get away.

What I heard was, I have to get away from *you*.

I hit her again, harder this time. Her lip split and blood trickled down her face.

"You will never go anywhere without me." I took her by the shoulders and threw her to the ground, her body crumpling in the dirt at my feet. She smashed her head against the rocks and cried out in agony.

As the night began to fall, and the stars came out above us, Jenn lay on the ground, barely moving. Her blood, that I shed, painted the dirt and leaves around her.

The horror of what I had done suddenly hit me.

I dropped to my knees, pulled my shirt off over my head, and pressed it to the wound to stem the flow.

"Oh my God, Jenn, I'm so sorry. What have I done?"

Her blood seeped through the shirt.

My fingers were sticky with it.

I had hit her. I had tossed her to the ground like garbage.

What the hell was wrong with me?

Then I felt calloused hands grab me, dragging me from her.

Marty loomed over me, his face filled with a rage I had never seen on anyone before.

"What did you do to my sister?"

He didn't yell.

His words were preternaturally calm, which made him all the more terrifying.

I stared up at him in confusion. Everything slotting together.

"Your sister?" I asked, dumbfounded.

Marty snarled down at me, and then his heavy boot careened into my side as he kicked me over and over again.

I howled in pain, and I covered my head and face as I tried to protect myself. Marty dropped down, kneeling over me, his fists finding their way through my meager defenses. My vision faded as he pummeled me.

I turned away, finding Jenn lying only a few feet away.

My once white T-shirt now stained red.

* * *

Hours Later

I lost consciousness at some point.

When I woke up, I wasn't sure how much time had passed—but I was freezing cold, and in pain.

More importantly, I was alone. Jenn and Marty were both gone.

"Jenn?" I called out, but heard only silence.

I tentatively got to my feet, wincing and groaning with every movement. I picked up my shirt and was shocked by the amount of blood it had soaked up.

I was trembling, though whether it was from shock or the cold, I wasn't sure. Either way, I needed to get out of there.

I put my T-shirt back on, the now dry blood making the fabric stiff. I looked around, trying to figure out where Jenn had gone. I refused to believe she would leave me unconscious and injured.

I could have died.

Though, I shouldn't have been surprised given what I had done. How could I expect her to stay when I had hurt her like that?

And she wasn't the only woman I had put my hands on.

I didn't trust myself or my anger.

I stumbled to the gravel path and headed back in the direction of my car. My body ached with every movement. My battered and bruised face throbbing as I called her name over and over again.

If she was still up at Jagged Point, she was clearly hiding from me. The realization that I had, in fact, lost her after all, didn't break my heart. It broke my soul. I was a shell. Losing Jenn felt like something worse than death.

Once back at my car I got in and sat there for a while trying to figure out what I was going to do.

Jenn had left me. And, after our fight tonight, Lucinda would likely do the same. I was left with nothing and no one.

This was all wrong.

I was supposed to be a good guy.

Sure, I had acted badly tonight, but they had driven me to it. None of this was my fault.

Marty had been right, even if he also turned out to be an asshole.

Women *were* the problem.

I stared into the darkness and saw him out there. Or at least I *thought* it was Marty.

But could it have been someone else?

And if it was Marty, was he waiting for me?

Even then, I knew I wasn't who he wanted.

He was waiting for Jenn.

Not wanting to face him again, I started the ignition and drove home. Maybe I should have stayed to make sure she was okay. To make sure Marty wouldn't hurt her, because I didn't put it past him. I had seen the possessive way he looked at her.

But my ego, as well as my body, had taken a beating, and I needed to go home and lick my wounds.

And I was already thinking about how to straighten out the mess I had made of my life now that Jenn had ditched me. Maybe I could salvage what was left of my relationship with Lucinda.

Lucinda wasn't the woman I wanted. But I couldn't lose everything—that wasn't fair.

So if I couldn't have the grand prize, then the consolation would have to do.

CHAPTER

23

Jenn

The Past

July 12, 9:22 PM—Fifteen Years Ago

I COULD SEE MARTY and Rhett fighting.

Marty was kneeling over Rhett and punching him over and over. Rhett swung up, hitting Marty on the side of the head and in his ribs, but never doing enough to shake him off.

Repulsion at the violence rolled through me and I forced myself to stand up. I needed to stop my deranged brother before he murdered Rhett.

I grabbed the back of Marty's shirt and began to pull. "Stop it!" I cried, but Marty kept hitting him.

"Marty, stop it, you're going to kill him!"

"Good. Maybe next time he'll think twice before putting his hands on my sister," he grunted, shoving me away.

"Marty, stop it or I'm calling the police," I yelled, pulling out my phone with shaking, battered hands.

Marty hit Rhett once more, then turned to me. There was a look on his face I had seen only once before. That look was the reason I had left home.

That look said ownership.

It said danger.

It said he would do whatever needed to be done to keep me.

Rhett had stopped moving. His face was bloody and swollen, and his ribs were already turning purple. Rhett had gotten a couple of good hits in—I could see that now. Marty's lip was split, and the skin beneath his left eye was now discolored. But Rhett was worse off. He was unconscious, and he needed help.

"Get your bag, Jennifer," Marty said, standing up. "You're coming home."

I shook my head. I couldn't go back there. I couldn't live like that again.

I thought I had been so careful. I took the last name Moore from a girl I met at church when I was little. She had only been in town for a month or two- not long enough for anyone to really remember her.

I should have known there was no hiding from my brother.

"I'm not asking. Now do as you're told."

His knuckles were scraped and bleeding, reminding me of the night I ran away. The night he had beaten up the boy, Brian, from the bowling alley I had been talking to. It had been innocent. We had flirted a little, and I could tell Brian liked me. That night he had kissed me chastely on the lips, nothing more. But Marty had seen it and had lost his mind. He had already warned Brian to stay away from me, and when he hadn't, Marty had beaten him until he begged him to stop. Brian had wet himself, adding to his humiliation. Marty dragged me home when he was finished.

"You shamed yourself and our family. You're nothing but a whore." Then Marty slapped me.

I was called a whore for simply letting a guy kiss me.

I knew then that everything I had been raised on was wrong. That it was warped and messed up in a way that made my life a living hell.

In a fit of uncharacteristic rage, I cut my brother with the knife I kept hidden underneath my pillow. Subconsciously, I think I had always known the day would come when I'd need to protect myself from the very people who claimed to care for me.

Marty had screamed in pain; the cut was deep. He locked me in my room then went to the hospital, probably to get stitches.

My parents were at church, where they spent most of their time. I knew I was alone. So I took the opportunity to escape. I had been practicing picking the lock on my door for months.

I got out of that room, and then I ran.

I had been running ever since.

Because the rules I had been expected to live by didn't apply to Marty. He, as a man, was given free rein. He could date. He could stay out past curfew. He could drink.

Me? I had to uphold an unrealistic ideal of womanhood that was impossible to live up to.

And my brother was the worst of them all.

All my problems, all my worries, began and ended with Marty and his need to control me. He was fixated on obtaining total dominance.

He hadn't always been like that.

At one time we had been close, unified in our fear of our parents and their traditionalism. But as we grew up, things changed. Marty's thoughts—his opinions—became toxic.

Eventually, he started trying to dictate my every move, which my father approved of. He shared his iron fist with his all too eager son, who took every opportunity to wield the power he thought was his birthright.

My father, formidable and terrifying, took him under his wing, intent on molding him into the image of what he thought a man should be. Marty began to watch YouTube videos about "male pride" and I would stand outside his door, my ear pressed to the wood listening, terrified of the things being said. Because in the world my older brother was fashioning for himself, I had nothing—no voice, no say, no rights.

At some point, I had lost my brother and had gained an owner.

His obsession with me had morphed from protection to control.

I pulled out my phone and began dialing. "I'm calling the police."

Marty's expression became scary. "You wouldn't dare," he said angrily through gritted teeth, and I felt my body tremble. "Give me your phone, now."

I shook my head. "You can't tell me what to do anymore, Marty. I don't know what happened to my brother, but you're not him." I put the phone to my ear. "I'll tell them what you did to that boy back home, and they'll see what you've done to Rhett. They'll put you away, maybe not for long, but by the time you get out, I'll be gone."

Marty looked down at Rhett's prone body and then back to me. He seemed conflicted. I knew his desire to restrain and dominate me was at war with his sense of self-preservation.

But in the end, his need to protect himself, and his freedom, trumped his need to drag me home by my hair—for now.

"I'll be back for you," he warned, jabbing his finger in my direction. "I swear to God, Jennifer, this isn't over."

Marty took off into the trees, and I stared after him, frightened tears blurring my vision. Thunder rumbled in the distance, a storm fast approaching.

I knelt by Rhett's side and checked that he was still alive. I was thankful when I saw his chest rise and fall. Despite what he had done to me, I didn't want his death on my hands.

Rhett had ruined everything with his anger and his lies. I wanted to leave this place and the promises he'd broken. I'd no idea he was friends with Marty—perhaps if I had, I could have saved Rhett from becoming just like him. But it was obvious it was too late now.

"Goodbye, Rhett," I murmured, devastated that he had turned out to be as bad as my brother.

* * *

The pain in my head was almost unbearable. A constant throb beat at my skull. Blood trickled down my neck and I knew I needed to stop the bleeding, but it hurt so much. I fought against the black that encroached my vision.

I ran through the trees, leaving Rhett unconscious on the ground at Jagged Point. I didn't know where my brother went, but I knew I had to get away before he came back.

I eventually made my way to Rhett's car and was thankful to find it unlocked. Beside it was parked a gray Cadillac I recognized. With a new sliver of fear, I quickly grabbed my book bag from the passenger seat and headed for the road.

But then I stopped.

I had left Rhett vulnerable to my brother. That didn't feel right at all. I took out my phone and remembered I didn't have a signal.

The only place to get a signal around here was on the cliffs.

With my heart pounding, I made my way to where I had left Rhett, but I chose to head through the trees in case Marty, or the owner of the Cadillac, was out there somewhere. It was easier to go undetected in the dark forest.

Once I was at the overlook, I saw immediately that Rhett was gone. I thought about calling out to him, but fear took my voice.

I gingerly touched the wound on my head, remembering how Rhett had hit me and then thrown me to the ground.

No. I wouldn't look for Rhett. He was at least alive, and that was good enough. I knew Marty wouldn't come for me until daylight. He'd be too worried about someone calling the cops. My big brother always had an aversion to the police.

I sat on a large boulder, nausea bubbling inside me. Slowly things began to come back into focus.

I knew I was badly hurt. But I also knew I was strong, and I could survive this. I had already survived much worse in my short life.

I thought that once I left home, I could put the ugliness behind me.

I was so wrong.

Because there was ugliness here in Fern River too.

* * *

Earlier That Day

I had done a good job of laying low and staying out of sight. My phone was full of unread messages and voicemails from Rhett mixed with vague threats from Marty.

Marty: Maybe I'll come to that B&B and drag you out by your hair. Dad told me to use any means necessary to get you to come home.

Rhett: ANSWER ME! I'm going out of my mind over here, Jenn! I won't let you throw away everything. I'd rather both of us die first!

I eventually turned off my phone and put it in the bottom of my book bag.

I should have left town already, but I couldn't make myself. I kept hoping things would turn around. That I'd wake up and the last week would be some horrible dream. Marty would be far away, and Rhett and I would still be making plans together.

And there was no Lucy.

But that wasn't how it was. I couldn't pretend Lucy didn't exist. Because she did.

I couldn't stop thinking about the look on her face when she stared at me. A mixture of anger but also grief. Like she was losing everything.

I knew that feeling.

Staying was no longer an option. I just couldn't figure out where to go. I stared at the map of the East Coast I'd bought from a convenience store not long after leaving home and began to randomly circle places close to the ocean. I'd always wanted to be by the water, so why not now?

It's not like anything was keeping me here.

And just like that, I started sobbing again.

The flow of my self-induced misery was interrupted by the sound of voices downstairs. My nervous system was instantly on high-alert.

"Jennifer, there's someone here to see you," Ms. Stanley yelled up the stairs. I knew it wasn't Rhett; she wouldn't let him see me after showing up at midnight last weekend, even though he had tried multiple times.

Marty?

I couldn't imagine the devoutly conservative B&B owner letting a man that looked as if he might strangle you at any minute through the door.

Then who was it?

I slowly walked into the stuffy sitting room decorated in outdated florals and doilies on every surface. An older man stood with his hands behind his back as if he were in a military lineup. He was short in stature, with thin graying hair and piercing blue eyes.

"Jennifer Moore?" His voice had a soft southern cadence that was strangely soothing. I could tell he was charming when he wanted to be. He exuded an aura of confidence and gentility that was disarming.

"Yes?"

"Is that a question? Do you not know your own name?" he barked.

I stood up a little straighter. "Yes, I'm Jennifer Moore. And you are?" I would never normally be rude to someone who was my elder. My father would have tanned my hide to hear me speak that way.

"My name is Clifford Herbaugh." He waited to see if I registered any recognition. Which I didn't. "I'm Lucinda's father."

"Lucinda?" I frowned.

"Rhett's fiancée, Lucinda," Mr. Herbaugh explained, spitting Rhett's name out of his mouth like a bad word.

I froze, too scared to move a muscle. I felt like I was a rabbit in a snare as Mr. Herbaugh watched my every move.

"I'm a man of importance in this community, Miss Moore. My name means something. I love my family and don't like to see them upset—or humiliated," he stated, his voice clipped and hard.

"I never meant to—"

Mr. Herbaugh walked toward me until he was standing close. Too close. He wasn't much taller than I was, but there was something about him that made it feel like he towered over me. "It doesn't really matter what you did or did not mean to do, only that you and Rhett have made my daughter look ridiculous carrying on the way you have. You have disgraced my family."

Mr. Herbaugh picked up an iron poker that was leaning against the wall next to the fireplace. "You're new in town, so I take it you don't know what I'm capable of, but let's just say, this will not end well for you." He weighed the sturdy piece of metal in his hand, then looked at me, his blue eyes ominous.

I swallowed thickly and took a step back. There was something scary about this man. Scary and dangerous. Someone much worse than my brother. Marty simply didn't care about the consequences of his actions, but this man, he was used to getting away with things. And I had a feeling he could make his problems disappear if he wanted them to.

And I knew that for him, I was a very big problem.

"Sir, I didn't know that Rhett . . ."

Mr. Herbaugh tightened his hand around the poker, his knuckles white, and my words became strangled in my throat.

"You need to leave town, immediately, before I decide to take matters into my own hands."

I swallowed again. "Sir, I have nowhere to go—"

"I wasn't asking you—it's an order," he bellowed, his deep voice rattling my bones. "And if you don't, there will be consequences." He lifted the poker, only slightly.

Was he going to hit me with it?

I glanced toward the doorway, wondering if I could make a run for it. Would Ms. Stanley help me?

As if knowing what I was thinking, Mr. Herbaugh gave me a cold smile. "No one in this town will lift a finger to help you against me and mine. You are nothing, Miss Moore. You have no future here. Now get out of Fern River before I do something we all will regret. Forget about Rhett. And forget about any plans you might have made together. I don't want to see your face around here again, because I will not be held accountable for what happens if I do."

He put the poker down and without another look in my direction, walked out of the room.

His words weren't a threat.

They were a promise.

So I quickly went back upstairs and grabbed my packed bag, paid Ms. Stanley, and began my walk out of town. Once again with no clear direction.

As I headed down the street, I thought I saw Mr. Herbaugh watching me from a gray Cadillac. I could feel the heaviness of his gaze as I walked away from the B&B. I tried not to act terrified as the car began to slowly follow me.

Would he make good on his threat? And if he did, would anyone even realize I was gone?

The thought made me cold. Because no one would miss me. No one would even realize anything had happened to me. Rhett would simply think I had left town.

I picked up my pace.

I knew then that I needed to get away as fast as I could.

Yet, I had ended up right in the lion's den.

CHAPTER

24

Lucinda

The Present

I PULLED THE THREE silver bracelets out of the box and held them up. The memory of them glinting wildly in flashes of lightning slammed into me.

Her tear stained face, a mixture of sadness and resolve.

I picked at a rust-colored stain on the metal, flaking it off with my fingernail.

I didn't understand how they came to be in this box hidden away in my little sister's room.

"What are you doing in here?" my father demanded from the doorway, startling me. I hadn't heard him and my mother come home. I had been too lost in the memories of that night and the implications of what I held in my hand.

I looked at him as I held up a dead girl's jewelry.

"Why does Bailey have Jennifer Moore's bracelets?"

My father strode across the room and snatched the silver bangles from my hand.

"What are you doing in here?" he demanded again, his voice thick.

"Um, I think the more important question is why my sister has a murdered girl's jewelry," I threw back at him.

Dad looked down at the bracelets like they might bite him. "I'm sure these are Bailey's. She was always buying things. She never could budget her allowance." He cleared his throat. "I don't know why you thought these were that girl's—"

"There's blood on them," I cut him off, grabbing one of the bracelets and holding it up to his face. I pointed to the flaking dried blood. "That isn't paint, Dad."

"Who knows how she got them. You know your sister." My father seemed ready to dismiss it, but I could sense something else in him. It was fear.

"No, Dad, Jenn was wearing these the night she died. I remember because I saw her."

Dad's eyes widened only slightly. The only indication that I had surprised him. "That doesn't mean—"

"Dad, I'm an adult. Treat me like one, please. I can tell by your face you know something about this." My father wasn't the only one adept at reading people. I had learned the skill well.

Dad looked like he was going to blow me off again, but then our eyes met and something changed. His shoulders drooped and for the first time in my life, my father looked old. And tired.

His face twisted as if in pain. "You're being irrational, Lucinda. Why would she take these?" His voice was a broken, agonized whisper.

"Because that's what she's always done, Dad. She was always taking things that didn't belong to her. How many times did I tell you about her stealing my diary, or my clothes . . ." I thought about Rhett's class ring, a sickening realization setting in.

Where had she taken Jennifer's bangles from?

Who had she taken them from?

"Unless *she* didn't take them." I let the implication hang heavy in the air between us.

I knew my father was capable of horrible things if he—or his family—were threatened.

I felt my palms start to sweat. My insides were a coiled spring. I waited for my father to admit the truth, yet I was terrified of it.

Dad closed his eyes briefly. When he opened them again, his strength seemed to have returned. That momentary weakness was gone, as if I had imagined it. His clear blue eyes blazed with a fierceness that made me want to sink to the floor. This was the man who was both feared and beloved by the entire county. A man who lost both of his parents as a child and had to raise himself. A man who put himself through law school and went on to become one of the most well-respected judges in the state.

This was a man not to be messed with.

This was a man that would burn the world down to protect his family and his good name.

This was a man who, if pushed, could commit murder.

But when he began to speak, the story he told stunned me into silence.

From how he was acting I expected a confession.

What I got was something else entirely.

"Your sister was hysterical when she called me," Dad said. "Your mom and I drove out to Jagged Point. Bailey was already at the overlook. She was in shock. The other girl was on the ground."

"What do you mean she was on the ground?" I asked, trying to make sense of what he was saying.

"There was nothing to be done. She was already dead. Bailey had hit her with a rock." His voice broke and he had to clear his throat. Dad stared at the bracelets like they were grenades about to go off in his hands. I couldn't believe what I was hearing.

"But Jenn was found on the side of the road, not at the cliffs," I said, trying to make sense of everything.

"Your mom and I moved her." He cleared his throat, his brow furrowed. "We wanted it to look like a hit and run. Her injuries were similar to those I've seen on victims of vehicular manslaughter. I knew it would be the cleanest and easiest explanation for the investigators. How was I supposed to know the new medical examiner wouldn't listen to Chuck? Or me? He went behind our backs and ruled it a homicide with death consistent with blunt force trauma. Wouldn't even contemplate the idea that maybe a car had hit her and driven off. Chuck almost lost the election that year because he couldn't solve the case. And for over a decade your mom and I have made sure to keep you girls out of it." I must have looked appalled because Dad became defensive. "It was the right thing to do. For your sister."

I struggled to make sense of what he was saying.

My father's words floated around in my head but I couldn't quite grasp their meaning.

I thought I knew what happened that night.

I was so very wrong.

I had never suspected my sister had been carrying around such a horrific secret all these years. I would never think to look her way at all.

"And what about Jenn?" I heard myself asking. For a moment it felt like I was outside my body. As if I were above the scene, watching it happen, not connected to it.

"She made her bed. Carrying on with someone else's fiancé. Embarrassing you—embarrassing *my family*—it wasn't right." He glowered his disapproval. "We do what we have to do to protect our family, Lucinda. I thought I raised you to understand that."

I stared at my dad, hardly recognizing him. This was the same man who used to preside over a courtroom, adjudicating the fate of people's lives with a strong sense of right and wrong. Had his moral compass become so skewed that he would cover up a murder for Bailey and not feel any guilt about it?

But I already knew the answer. Of course he would. He had been providing his own brand of protection for us our whole lives.

"How did Bailey get all the way up there? It's not like she would ever ride her bike that far," I said, still having a hard time believing what he was saying. I had spent the last fifteen years thinking Rhett was a killer. Now, to find out my sister, of all people, was the murderer, was too much to wrap my mind around.

"She stole the keys to my Cadillac. The old gray one I had. She used to do it all the time. I would have to hide them in a box in my office. I forgot that night."

Another piece fell into place. "You mean the one you sold two weeks after Jenn's body was found? *That* gray Cadillac?"

Dad didn't bother to answer because he didn't need to. He sold that car in case someone could connect it to the murder. In case there was a witness that saw it out driving that night. My father was the only person in Fern River who had such a fancy car. It would have been instantly recognizable.

"Your sister was just a little misguided. She always had a habit of getting her head turned around—"

"She killed someone, Dad. She didn't steal a tube of lip gloss, she bludgeoned Jenn to death with a damn rock!" I exclaimed, my voice rising.

"Lower your voice, young lady," he commanded as if I were still a teenager. "Your sister has always struggled to control her temper, and that husband of yours has been tying her into knots for years. Have you ever wondered why she followed after him like some kind of lovelorn puppy? He had been carefully grooming her for years to feed his narcissistic ego," Dad stated in disgust. "Have you never wondered why she hasn't met someone and gotten married?"

I opened my mouth to argue, but hesitated as my mind went back over two decades' worth of interactions and conversations. I thought of all the times Rhett had shown a special interest in Bailey. I didn't believe there was anything sexual going on, but Dad was right, my bastard of a husband had a pathological need to feel loved and wanted, no matter the cost to anyone else.

And my sister, with her twisted ideas of right and wrong, as well as her fiery temper, had fallen prey to his betrayal as much as I had.

But . . .

"So you cleared Rhett's name to keep Bailey off the police's radar. Because Rhett is connected to our family and if Chuck looked at him, he might look at you, or me, or Bailey. You were covering all bases. You didn't protect Rhett for me, you protected him for Bailey. And yourself," I surmised, putting it all together. "But now that Marty's come forward, you're willing to let Rhett go down to keep Bailey safe. You have no loyalty towards him. You never have. He's only useful as your patsy."

Dad's eyes narrowed. "Don't tell me you care what happens to him. We both know your marriage has been a sham for years."

I drew myself up straight. "But Dad, he didn't kill Jenn."

Dad held out the bracelets and I took them from him, their weight heavy in my hand. "But he did almost ruin your life—and Bailey's. He lied to you. He used you, and that poor girl who lost her life. *That's* the kind of man he is. He's not a good person, no matter how much he likes to think he is. I've seen men like him a thousand times in my courtroom. While he may not have murdered Jenn, he killed her all the same, by being a deceiver and a manipulator. It's *his* actions that led to all this."

The remnants of the love I felt for Rhett still lingered there below the surface even after everything he'd done.

I thought about our argument earlier. I could still feel his hands around my throat squeezing the air from my lungs. There had been no love for me in his eyes, only hate. He would have killed me, of that I was sure. It was pure luck I had gotten away.

He was dangerous.

He had made that clear.

He wanted to take my child from me, and I believed he would if given the opportunity. I couldn't trust him with McKenzie. He had shown what kind of person he really was beneath the likable man he portrayed to the rest of the world.

My life meant nothing to him.

That realization was terrifying.

My resentment—and his discontented bitterness—had made contentious bedfellows, and it was only a matter of time until they turned on each other in the most explosive way.

I had stupidly thought that once McKenzie came along, maybe we'd be okay. We'd been trying for so long to have a child. It was the next expected step for us. But my inability to become a mother added yet another failure to the long list I had accumulated. And as the years went by without a baby, our tenuous bond, forged by our shared deceptions, wasn't going to hold. I knew I wouldn't be able to keep him and he knew he wouldn't stay.

But then, like some kind of miracle, I got pregnant and Rhett was so happy. It felt like we had turned a corner in our frigid, acrimonious union.

But the lies were larger than any love that ever existed between us.

Then the lies had turned rotten, and violent loathing took their place.

"Family is the only thing that matters, Lucinda. We have to protect Bailey. Rhett is not worth destroying our family over. Because when he's no longer around, we're all you have. We're all you need." My father was so certain he was right. That every immoral thing he had done, every breach of his lauded ethics, was in the name of protecting us.

My mind was turning in a million different directions, but only one thing mattered: Rhett didn't kill Jenn Moore.

Bailey did.

CHAPTER

25

Jenn

July 12—Fifteen Years Ago

Later That Night

I THOUGHT I COULD escape.

I was wrong. He had found me. They both did. And now I was bleeding and scared, but with a resolve that hadn't been there before.

I couldn't count on anyone to save me but myself.

Then Lucy showed up, and I felt an odd sense of kinship with this woman everyone would have expected me to hate. I saw the loathing in her eyes and knew she blamed me for everything that had gone wrong in her and Rhett's relationship.

But now, I thought we understood each other on some level. Yes, our backgrounds couldn't have been more different, but at the end of the day, we were both women who had put our trust and love in a man who didn't deserve it.

I hoped she was able to live her life on her terms, not on Rhett's. I wished her well. I really did.

After Lucy left, I was alone again. I knew I needed to leave, but I felt too weak to move. I shivered in my drenched clothes. I picked up my backpack and knew I should start walking, but I felt too woozy to take more than a half- dozen steps before needing to sit down again.

"Why are you doing this to my sister and Rhett?" a voice called out, full of aggressive confidence.

I turned and found a young girl, no more than fourteen or fifteen, wearing a bright yellow raincoat. My muddled brain couldn't put together what was happening. Why was this child, really not much younger than me, at this desolate spot so late at night in the middle of a rainstorm?

"What?" My voice sounded thready and without feeling. Black spots swam in front of my eyes. I was pretty sure I had a concussion.

The girl walked closer until she was standing directly in front of me. "You're trying to take Rhett from me. From Lucy. You can't do that."

She sounded so, so young.

"No, that's not—" I tried to shake my head, but that only made it pound harder. I felt bile rise up in the back of my throat and thought I was going to throw up.

The girl's face darkened in a way that if she were a man, would have petrified me. "You are!" she shouted.

I was losing all sense of reality. My head was foggy and I thought, for a moment, I was back home out in the woods behind my house.

"Take it from me, you can't trust anyone," I mumbled, the world around me fading in and out. "Family will only hurt you."

"You don't know what you're talking about. Family is the only thing that matters." Her voice was high-pitched and vicious. I tried to turn my head to look at her but the action made my vision swim, so I closed my eyes.

"I wish that were true." I let out a heavy sigh. "But Rhett's the worst of them all. He will only use you to get what he wants. So watch out for him." My voice sounded muffled. "He's a predator."

I was so sleepy. My head felt like it weighed a ton. I knew I needed medical attention, but I didn't think I could make it back to town on my own.

"You don't know Rhett at all." The girl was still talking, but I could barely register the words. "Rhett loves my sister. He loves *me*. You've tricked him, that's all."

"He's the worst kind of man there is. He said he loved me. He's a liar," I whispered, not sure if I was talking to her or myself.

"He never said that to you. *You're* the liar." The girl was getting worked up. I forced myself to look at her, even if it sent waves of agony through my skull. She was crying, but there was an odd glint in her eyes that should have given me pause.

"What's your name?" I asked.

"I'm Bailey. Bailey Herbaugh."

Fear coursed through me. She was obviously Lucy's kid sister. And Mr. Herbaugh's other daughter. Did that mean he was here too? I was terrified that he'd find me and make good on his threat.

That man would kill me, I knew it. My life was worth nothing to him. He and my father were way too alike.

"I like your sister. She's a good person. You seem like a good person too. Don't let men like Rhett change that."

Her mouth twisted into a strange semblance of a smile. "You don't look so good, maybe I should have a look at that wound. That's a lot of blood."

"Yeah." My voice faded away as I tilted my head back to look at the night sky.

The storm had passed and the stars were starting to shine again. I lifted my hand as if to touch them, reaching out . . .

My silver bracelets jangled together, sounding like windchimes. My heart ached at the memory of my mother giving them to me for my thirteenth birthday.

I missed her. I wondered if she missed me too.

There were times in a girl's life where she longed for her mom, or at least the ideal of the mother she wished she had.

I had been on my own for so long that the horrible memories of my parents were starting to be whitewashed by a desperation for that connection you only feel at home.

I stared at the heavens, wishing I was looking at them somewhere else. Somewhere far away from the sadness that lived here.

I took a deep breath.

There was a blinding flash and the feel of my skull caving in.

Pain radiated throughout my head and into my extremities.

"Momma," I murmured, and then it all went black.

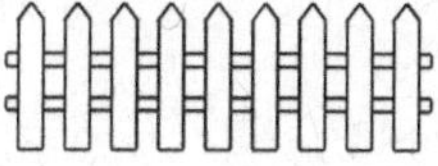

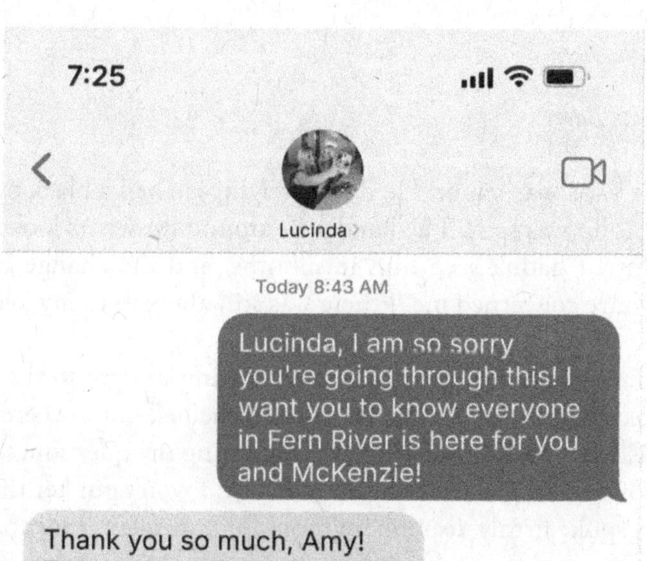

Epilogue

Lucinda

One Year Later

His face was gaunt. He'd lost weight. He had a black eye and his lip was split. The handcuffs around his wrists looked like they hurt. I hadn't seen him in months, and the change in him would have concerned me if there was still any love in my heart for him.

"Have you signed them?" I asked, getting straight to the point. I wanted to get what I came for and get the hell out of there.

"Where's McKenzie?" he asked, ignoring my question.

"This isn't a place for children, Rhett. I won't put her through that." I spoke firmly, leaving no room for argument. I meant what I said. I would never bring my young daughter to this godforsaken place. And especially not to see a man that didn't deserve her love.

Rhett said nothing. He watched me with a guarded expression.

After a few minutes, I pulled a sheet of paper out of my purse and put it on the table with a pen.

"I brought another copy." I pushed the signature page toward him. "I know you want this as much as I do. Neither of us want to be tied to each other for a moment longer. Sign it and you'll never have to see me again," I said, my voice pitched low enough so only he could hear me.

He looked down at the divorce papers. I had already served him—twice—yet he refused to sign. I didn't know why. He had spent the last sixteen years letting me know, in many different ways, that he would never love me.

I had fought so hard to hold onto something that was never mine.

It was way past time to let it go. To let him go.

He looked up at me, his expression cold. "You can't keep my daughter from me, Lucinda."

I sat back in my chair, putting as much distance between us as possible. "I'm not keeping her from you. When she's old enough to make her own choices, she can decide to come and see you for herself. And I'll support her in that. But I won't traumatize her by bringing her here now, not when she's too young to understand. If you cared about what was best for her and not you, you'd agree with me."

On this, I wouldn't budge. It had taken me a long time to find my footing as a mother. It seemed I only needed my treacherous husband to go to prison to find it. I had let myself be sidelined in my own family for far too long.

"I'm her fucking father!" His voice rose sharply and Phil, the prison guard, gave him a look of reproach. Rhett took a deep breath. "I'll get a lawyer. I'll fight you—"

"Or you'll sign those papers and let us get on with our lives," I interrupted. "If you ever loved me, even a little bit, you'll set me free."

His smile was chilling. "Set you free? I'm the one who's in prison, yet you act like you're the one in a cage."

I tapped the divorce papers impatiently, and Rhett shook his head. "I'll never sign them."

"Then you'll never see McKenzie again," I snapped coldly. I hated this place. The smell of it. The sounds. I wanted to leave and never come back. I wanted to put Rhett behind me and never think about him ever again, but without a divorce that was almost impossible. "Have you run into Marty in there? I heard he got picked up for an assault charge a few months ago."

"No, I haven't. I'm sure he'll be kept far away from me. Wouldn't want us comparing notes or anything." Rhett narrowed his eyes. "Funny how the men in your life end up in prison." He regarded me coldly. "Odd how a smart guy like Marty, who spent his life dodging the police, somehow ended up going to jail. Sort of like how strange it was that out of all the judges in the county, I ended up with the only one that hated your dad more than anything," Rhett muttered.

I waved away his comments like flies. "Life is full of weird coincidences, Rhett."

Rhett's eyes flashed with loathing. He leaned toward me only to receive a grunt of warning from Phil, so he sat back in his seat. "Look, Lucinda, I know why I'm in here. I get it, okay? That's why I won't bother with an appeal, even though I probably have a pretty good chance of getting another trial. I've thrown myself on the proverbial sword for you—but please don't take my daughter too. I've given you enough."

I couldn't stop myself from glaring at him, the mask slipping slightly. He didn't get it—how could he when all he cared about was himself? Even after everything, he still saw himself as the victim.

"I know this is my penance for the affairs—"

The word slipped out easily, the small mistake blatant, yet he was so cocky and confident that he didn't think I would notice it.

Affairs with an *s*.

There had been many of them.

He hadn't learned his lesson with Jenn and had instead spent the next fifteen years cheating on me over and over. Making a mockery of our vows and our marriage—mocking *me*. But this went deeper than me being a woman scorned. This was about the person Rhett hid away in the deep, dark recess of his heart. He was a man who hurt the women around him. A man who used their affection to bolster his ego until he moved on and found someone else. He was a cancer infecting everyone that had the bad luck to love him.

"But I'm not the only one who should be in here—am I? No matter what the evidence says," he continued.

The man was stupid.

He still thought he was paying the price for *my* crime.

Phil gave me the signal that my time was up. I got to my feet. "I'd better go," I told my husband. I slung my purse over my shoulder and straightened my skirt. "Please sign the papers, Rhett. This has gone on long enough. For both of us."

"Might as well, it's not like I'm going anywhere," Rhett said, picking up the pen I had offered and finally putting his signature on the paper. He shoved them across the table with a look of distaste. "There, now you can make another man's life miserable."

He had no idea how long and how hard I had loved him. How I had been willing to burn the world to the ground to hold onto our life together.

How I would have killed someone simply for trying to take him from me.

He had never appreciated everything I offered him.

Phil came over and pulled Rhett to his feet to lead him back to his cell. Before Rhett could leave, he leaned toward me, his voice pitched low. "You and I both know your dad rigged my trial. I also know, even if I were to be granted an appeal, he'd find some other way to ruin me. I'd never be free of any of you. Because that's what Herbaughs do. They destroy lives. So, perhaps I'm actually better off in here. At least behind bars I can relax and be myself." His voice cracked.

How had I ever convinced myself that this man would ever love me or be a good husband?

My mind wandered, as it often did, to that last horrific fight. The things he had said. The steadiness in his hands as they wrapped around my neck. I knew he wanted me dead. And he wanted to be the one to do it.

I also remembered Jenn that night so many years ago. The blood on her face. The bruises on her arms.

My husband thought he was a good guy. He believed his own press. He had fooled so many people into thinking I was controlling. That *I* was the problem. They couldn't see the darkness that lingered there in the depths of his hateful heart.

That his love was the killing kind.

"What was so wrong with wanting a life together?" I asked him before he was taken away. "Why was I the bad guy in your story and Jenn the heroine? You had promised me a future, so I held you to it. Why do you hate me for that?" As soon as the words left my mouth, I wanted to snatch them back. The last thing I wanted was for this man to have any power over me ever again.

Rhett stared at me, and I knew he'd never understand what motivated me. How I had been willing to protect him and love him for the rest of my life, no matter his supposed crimes. And all I wanted in return was the promise that he would be loyal. And that he would never hurt me again.

But Rhett had never been able to promise anything unless it benefited him.

"And that's why you did it, isn't it—that's why you killed Jenn. Because I wouldn't marry you otherwise." Rhett extolled his venom as if it were facts. "You were just a jealous bitch and took it out on an innocent girl, and now you're making me pay for it."

He was so sure of my guilt, just as I, at one time, had been so sure of his.

I couldn't let him live with moral superiority. I would be damned if I'd allow him a martyr complex. He had to know his reasons were wrong and that he would never, *ever* see the light of day because of it.

Before Phil could corral him out of the visiting room, I leaned in close, dropping my voice to the barest hint of a whisper.

"It's not my crime you're paying for, Rhett."

I could see his confusion. "What?"

"*I didn't kill Jenn*. I would never harm someone that hated you as much as I do." I let my words sink in.

The thing about marriage is you knew each other's weaknesses—the pressure points. Rhett and I had spent decades honing the art of knowing exactly where to stick the knife.

His eyes widened. "Then who did? Lucinda, please, tell me," he begged, but I ignored him. I'd never tell him what he wanted to know.

The days of me trying to make this man love me were over.

I waved goodbye to my shocked husband as he was escorted back to his cell.

* * *

"I'm on my way home. I'll pick up something for dinner," I said to my sister, who was watching McKenzie. Mom and Dad had gone on an extended vacation. Dad needed to get out of Fern River. The tide had turned against my once indomitable father. The Kentucky Bar Association had investigated him on allegations of corruption after receiving several reports involving his undue influence on criminal investigations.

He was disbarred six months ago, his once sterling reputation tarnished forever. He and my mother were actually talking about selling their house and moving out of state.

It seemed everyone was looking for a fresh start, even if it wasn't the one any of us had planned for.

Perhaps I should feel sorry for my father. He had lost his career. His reputation. His connections. But it was just as well, given what he had done. A person can only circumvent the law so much before karma came to bite you in the ass.

Once I found out Bailey was the one that had killed Jenn, and why, I had been given a choice on how to proceed. But I knew that at the end of the day, my dad, for all his failings, was right. You protected your family at all costs.

That didn't change the fact that at a young age, she had committed a heinous crime. An innocent woman had lost her life.

Because of Rhett.

Looking back, I realized how he had manipulated and emotionally groomed my sister for years. He saw in her the same fragile vulnerability that he found so appealing in Jenn. He made Bailey feel special. He used her need for attention and validation against her to stroke his own ego. And Bailey, feeling that slip away from her once Jenn came into the picture, acted out in the worst way possible.

What Bailey had done was an awful act born from misguided affection and family loyalty. She had been twisted, not only by Rhett's insidiousness, but by my father's mantra of "family first." She was young and impressionable with no outlet for an anger that was too often glossed over. Thankfully now, with years of therapy behind her, she was a healthier person. But she still held onto her childhood infatuation toward my husband. I hated that for her. I hoped it would fade eventually.

Loving a man like my husband confined her to a different kind of prison.

Sometimes I wondered if I had made the right decision in letting Rhett take the fall. Maybe Bailey *should* face the consequences for Jenn's murder even if she never intended to commit it.

But then I remembered why all this had happened.

Why I had set this thing into motion.

I knew it was the only kind of justice for a man who would never learn his lesson otherwise.

* * *

Two Years Ago

The day he came home talking about the new geography teacher at the high school, I knew it was happening again.

"She's incredibly smart for being so young. You know, she only graduated last year and she's already enrolled in a master's program. She wants to be a principal eventually," Rhett had gushed about Gail Travers.

Then came the extra hours spent at the school supposedly co-chairing the debate club with Gail. Then chaperoning the overnight field trip to Washington, DC. With Gail.

The messages coming through late at night.

I had seen the signs before, so I recognized them.

He invited her to our home for cookouts, let her push our daughter on the swings. He insisted she come along on family outings to the park because she was "new in town and didn't know anyone."

God, where had I heard that one before?

Rhett was forever chasing the high only a brand-new love affair could provide. He was a junkie needing his fix, and an adulterous secret kept from his wife was the best drug there was.

And Gail—pretty, naive, butter-wouldn't-melt-in-her-mouth Gail—thought my ridiculous husband was the most amazing guy ever. After all, he had taken this poor, lonely girl under his wing and made sure she felt accepted and welcome in Fern River. He made her feel special and important and she ate it up, not realizing she wasn't the first he made feel that way.

My husband was a sucker for a pretty face with a sad backstory. Gail was simply a new and slightly curvier version of Jennifer Moore. How long would the honeymoon phase last? Would she eventually show some backbone, and would she pay the price for it?

It was only a matter of time until the bloom fell off the rose, and then Gail would see the monster she had given herself to. Then it would be too late. The trap was set. She would be locked in. Just like I had been. Like Jenn too.

Of course, Rhett could sense my unease. He could see the questioning looks, and he batted off my questions like a tennis pro. A kiss on the forehead to hush his silly wife. A bunch of flowers after a weekend away. A bottle of wine after working late at school. He thought he was so clever.

But it was a text exchange late one night that confirmed my suspicions.

I had been checking his phone for months, but he was either deleting his messages before I saw them, or I was being paranoid.

I should have known better than to doubt my intuition.

Rhett: *God, I miss you.*

Gail: *I miss you too. When can you get away again?*

Rhett: *I'm rock hard thinking about last weekend. Lucinda is taking McKenzie to her parents' tomorrow night. I'll come over then.*

Gail: *I can't wait! I bought something special to wear for you.*

Rhett: *I hope it wasn't expensive because I'll be ripping it off with my teeth.*

Gail: *I bought two.* ☺

Decades ago, I would have gone nuclear. I would have blamed Gail for Rhett's infidelity. But I had learned she wasn't the problem. The other women were never the problem—Rhett was. After all, he was the one that was married.

Jenn had understood this as well. We had come to a mutual understanding that our issue wasn't with each other, but with the man in the middle.

Now was the time for careful calculation.

So, I had called the other man that had hurt Jenn. Because he was the only one that could help me now. It was time to use the key to my cell.

I slipped out onto the patio. Rhett was giving McKenzie a bath and then would be reading her a story. It was their daily routine—when he wasn't fucking Gail, that is.

I found the contact "Rabbit" in my phone and called it.

He answered on the first ring.

"It's been awhile, Lucy."

"Marty, do you still have the T-shirt?" I asked.

Marty was silent for a moment. "Of course. And the video. You've been paying me handsomely all these years to make sure that I do. Getting that cash is the only reason I didn't take them to the police myself. Because who can give up such an easy payday?" He laughed, but I didn't join him.

My insides quivered at what I was about to do.

"It's time," was all I said.

"You're finally ready to put that dog down?" Marty chuckled in disbelief. "I thought this day would never come."

"I'm tired of him making me look like an idiot. There's only so much a woman can take, Marty. He needs to face the consequences of his actions. Besides, it's not like he's innocent. I'd be doing the world a favor getting a monster like him off the streets." I needed to remember this wasn't about revenge. Well not entirely.

After Jenn's murder, I thought my problems were over. Jenn's death had devastated me in many ways. Particularly since I believed my husband was responsible for the crime. My guilt at letting him get away with it had kept me awake at night.

But I had kept my mouth shut in the name of the promises and vows I had stupidly taken. I was terrified that by admitting what Rhett had done, I would be implicated as well. I had lied for him. I had crafted an alibi and fed it to the police. I had perjured myself to keep him free. But the threat of getting in trouble wasn't enough to stop me.

Because I had been a coward. Even worse, I was an accomplice.

Yet, in the back of my mind, I was able to justify my silence because the evidence was still out there. Evidence I paid Marty handsomely to hold onto for me. I didn't plan to keep it hidden forever. I told myself, one day, I'd do right by Jenn and hand it over to the police. She would get her justice. But the more years that went by, the more stuck I became in a marriage I had fought so hard for. The truth got lost in the need to create the life I wanted. I knew it was selfish. And morally reprehensible. But anyone could make questionable choices when they were holding their entire world together with lies and misguided hope.

I shouldn't have waited until he humiliated me once more to take action. I should have pulled the figurative trigger years ago.

But, better late than never.

So, with Marty's help, I made sure I always had an insurance plan. He held the keys to my gilded cage.

"He should've faced the consequences when he murdered my sister," Marty barked.

"Marty, we both know why Jenn left home and who she was running from." I could hear Marty's heavy breathing in my ear. I had pissed him off by calling him out. But I also knew he'd never dare

contradict me. For a man who talked a lot about controlling women, he quickly handed over the reins when nudged.

"That's not the point," Marty said. "Rhett is the reason she's gone. He hurt her. I saw him! He threw her on the ground. He fucking backhanded her like the bastard he is."

I had always wondered what happened between Jenn and Rhett that night. I remembered her injuries and her admission that Rhett was responsible.

I wasn't surprised he had hurt her. He wasn't a stranger to lifting his hand against a woman.

"I've trusted you all these years because you said you had a plan for him," Marty continued, "so I bit my tongue and did as you asked and kept the evidence—and my silence, all the while you played happy family with that asshole. The money helped my patience, of course."

"He would have gotten off back then, and you know it. I wasn't ready to admit how horrible he was. I was blinded by love and covered for him. Then my father moved heaven and earth to give me what I wanted. He used his influence to make sure no one ever looked at my husband because I asked him to. Because I loved him. And stupidly, I thought that keeping him free would allow me to have some semblance of control in my own life. It's a shitty excuse, but it's the only one I have."

I could hear my husband laughing through the open window as he spoke to our daughter.

God, I wanted the man to burn.

"Years have shown me what a fool I was to think he was worth any of it." I paused as I thought about how this would work. "There's a judge who hates my father and by extension everyone tied to him. If he thinks Rhett used his connection to my dad to get away with murder, he'll throw the book at him."

"And how will you make sure Rhett is charged, let alone this judge will be the one handling his case? And how do you make sure a jury will convict him? That's a lot of unknowns, Lucy." Marty sounded skeptical.

Domestic Violence/Sexual Assault Resources

United States:
Domestic Violence Support Network:
https://www.hotline.org/
Top Rated Domestic Violence Shelters:
http://www.domesticshelters.org/data-center/state-reports-and-rankings/best-domestic-violence-programs
RAINN (Rape, Abuse & Incest National Network:
https://rainn.org
National Sexual Violence Resource Center:
https://www.nsvrc.org/
United Kingdom:
Refuge:
https://refuge.org.uk/
SARSAS:
https://www.sarsas.org.uk/
International:
NO MORE Global Directory:
https://nomoredirectory.org/

ACKNOWLEDGMENTS

As always, I have to thank my co-writer in crime, Claire, for going on this journey with me. We make one hell of a team and long may it continue.

To Ian and Gwyn (and Otto) because you're awesome and I love you.

To my dear friend, Kristy, for once again being the best beta reader ever. You always help us polish our stories to become the best they can be. We couldn't do it without you.

To our editor, Tara, and the amazing crew at Crooked Lane:The fact that you still want to publish our books never ceases to amaze me. Thank you for opening a door for us that others kept closing.

To our amazing readers: You are why we keep getting to write and publish these twisty tales. Your enthusiasm and support are the best part of this job. THANK YOU!

And finally, this story is very much inspired by a dark, painful chapter in my family's history. One that, frankly, was never talked about as it should have been. This horrible tragedy was treated like a dirty secret and was only let out in whispers. I hope one day, the woman who lost her life in such a brutal way gets justice.

It's our goal that while this book is wrapped in fiction, it can shine a light on the plight of far too many women and girls affected by violence.

Something has to change and it starts with each and every one of us.

Be willing to shout at the top of your lungs for those without a voice and never, ever forget your worth.

You matter. You are important. You are powerful.

—Abbi

For my mum, the strongest woman I know.

You taught me how to be the strong and independent woman I am. You showed me how to raise fierce, independent daughters of my own. And you taught me that standing up for others matters just as much as standing up for myself. The fire in me is the fire I got from you and because of you, I learned that even in the ashes, women like us will rise.

To my amazing daughters who continue to inspire me with your wit and charm. With your wonderful souls and hearts of gold, with the fire in your bellies and your no- nonsense attitudes. You are all going to live such amazing lives and do incredible things and I'm so glad I get to be there for it all.

Becca—I'm so excited to hear you gasp at the ending again!

Thank you also to my husband who puts up with all my nonsense . . . oh, there is so much nonsense isn't there haha! Thanks for your unwavering support in all I do.

Thanks, as always, to the amazing team at Crooked Lane Books for your continued support and your belief in 'Katherine Greene' and everything she stands for. We're thrilled to continue to work with you on these projects.

And finally, thank you to Abbi. I love that we 'battle it out' for our ideas because we're both so passionate about each new story. But more, I love that we always find a way through the madness of so many different plot threads and give a voice to these women. You yourself are truly inspiring and I'm so grateful to work with you (even if we do drive each other to distraction at times when our ideas clash!)

—Claire